# THE IMPOSTOR QUEEN

# THE IMPOSTOR QUEEN

Sarah Fine

MARGARET K. McELDERRY BOOKS

New York   London   Toronto   Sydney   New Delhi

MARGARET K. McELDERRY BOOKS
An imprint of Simon & Schuster Children's Publishing Division
1230 Avenue of the Americas, New York, New York 10020
MARGARET K. MCELDERRY BOOKS is a trademark of Simon & Schuster, Inc.
For information about special discounts for bulk purchases, please contact Simon & Schuster Special Sales at 1-866-506-1949 or business@simonandschuster.com.
The Simon & Schuster Speakers Bureau can bring authors to your live event. For more information or to book an event, contact the Simon & Schuster Speakers Bureau at 1-866-248-3049 or visit our website at www.simonspeakers.com.
Book design by Debra Sfetsios-Conover.
The text for this book is set in Goudy Oldstyle Std.
Manufactured in the United States of America
10 9 8 7 6 5 4 3 2
CIP data is available from the Library of Congress.
ISBN 978-1-4814-4190-2 (hardcover)
ISBN 978-1-4814-4192-6 (eBook)

IN MEMORY OF
MY GRANDMOTHERS,
JUNE AND VIRGINIA.
THANK YOU
FOR BEING SUCH
BRILLIANT EXAMPLES
OF ALL THE WAYS WOMEN
CAN BE POWERFUL.

# PROLOGUE

She didn't know which hurt more—the ice or the fire. At this point, she couldn't even tell the difference between them; both burned in her veins and chest and limbs, each moment more agonizing than the last.

Elder Kauko hunched over her splayed arm, trying to bleed the excess. The *pat-pat-pat* of her blood in the bowl was the only sound in the room apart from her barely stifled moans. If she'd had the strength, she would have told the elder all his efforts were wasted. The darkness was a shadow in the corner of her chamber, creeping closer no matter how fiercely she willed it away.

The magic was killing her.

And yet she still loved it, as much as she loved any other part of herself. It had been her constant companion for nearly ten years, and each day she had tried to use the gift wisely, in service of the Kupari people. Always for them. Only for them. She had wished for infinite time, so she could be their queen forever and protect them always.

But in the end, she had become just like all the Valtias before her, bright-burning, quickly snuffed out. She was too weak to contain a power this great, or perhaps too selfish to use it perfectly, as the magic required. She had thought she was doing right, though. All she had wanted was to reach out to her people beyond the walls, to protect them from the raiders who had so recently come to their shores, to show the outlanders that her grace extended beyond the city. Surely they weren't all thieves and murderers. Surely some of them could be redeemed, even though the elders and priests had scoffed at that foolish notion.

Just as they had scoffed at her idea to travel through the outlands, to be seen by her subjects and win their confidence. But when she insisted, the elders had acquiesced—she was, after all, the queen. They had even tried to help her keep the balance between the two elements nestled within her, afraid that such strain would disrupt the precise equality of ice and fire. Even now, Kauko was still trying, despite their past arguments, despite her defiance.

She turned her head, the movement sending shocks of blazing heat up her backbone while her fingers stiffened with cold. Elder Kauko was watching her blood flow with unwavering focus. Then he slid his fingertip along the flat of the tiny blade he had used to make the cut, capturing a drop, and turned away for a moment. When he looked back, his dark eyes seemed brighter, but his smile was tinged with sadness. "Rest, my Valtia," he said softly. "Close your eyes and rest."

*I don't want to close my eyes. I don't want to go.* Even as the thought came, a wave of darkness rolled over her, the kind of swell that heralded a storm.

Elder Kauko took her chilled fingers in his. "You have served well, my Valtia."

*Kaarin. I was Kaarin once.* That was before she became the Valtia. But she could still remember the way that name had sounded as her mother had shouted it over the cheers of the crowd, as the elders escorted Kaarin to the Temple on the Rock, a six-year-old girl carrying the hopes of an entire people. *Kaarin, don't forget me. Kaarin, I love you.*

That had been the last time she'd ever seen her mother. *Perhaps I'll see her again soon.*

It should have been comforting, but all she could think was, *No. Not yet.*

"Is she asleep?" The voice was Elder Aleksi's. She could hear the swish of black robes nearby.

"Hard to say," murmured Kauko.

"Should you bleed her again?"

"More would be dangerous."

*To whom?* she wanted to ask. *I'm already dying.* Aleksi, though, seemed to know. He remained silent.

Kauko sighed. "It won't be long now. Tell Leevi to take the Saadella to the catacombs and prepare her."

*No, I'm not ready.* But she couldn't move. Her limbs

were locked as ice and fire churned inside her, impatient and ready to break free. *Please don't leave. I have so many things left to do.*

It was a selfish thought. Sofia would probably be a better Valtia than Kaarin had ever been. She was gentle and always thought of others. Purer, perhaps. Certainly more patient. *We won't have another harvest ceremony together, my darling. How I would love to see your face one more time.* Soon the girl would be kneeling on the flat stone of the circular chamber in the catacombs, waiting. They were all waiting now. But Kaarin couldn't make herself let go.

"Sofia," she whispered through parched lips.

No one answered. Or maybe her hearing had abandoned her, all her senses dropping off one by one, touch and sight, scent and sound. A roaring filled her mind, like an autumn gale on the Motherlake, mighty and relentless. The pain welled up, engulfing her. *No, please. Not yet. One more—*

When the power tore itself loose, it took everything with it except for one image: a little girl with coppery hair and pale-blue eyes. She was too blurry to make out—even as Kaarin tried to focus, her vision doubled, creating two wavering, overlapping faces in the fog. Still, she knew exactly who the little girl was, and what was about to happen to her.

Then the last shreds of ice and fire slipped free without a fight, for Kaarin had no strength left to hold on to them. The darkness was complete. The magic was gone. And so was she.

# CHAPTER 1

The heart lies before me, still, colorful, and more mysterious than I want it to be. I lean over the diagram etched onto the scroll, trying to memorize it all at once. The main vessel that carries the blood to the rest of the body is marked in red ink, and I slide my fingertip across the label. *Valtimo*. I like the word. It's vital and meaty. "Elder Kauko, are the vessels in a loop, somehow? How does the blood know when it is time to return to the heart?"

Elder Kauko, seated next to me at this sturdy table laden with scrolls depicting livers, brains, all the bones of the hand and fingers, and so many other fascinating things, adjusts his robe over his round belly. "You are so clever, Elli. Yes, it is like a loop. The blood never leaves the vessels, merely travels through the tunnels until it passes through the heart again."

I frown. "Why, though? Why is it so important, if all it does is flow through our veins? What does it *do*?"

He smiles. When I was little, his lips used to fascinate me; they stick out like two grubs pasted to his pale face. "The blood is life itself. It carries warmth to the limbs and strength to the muscles."

My fingers trace the path of the blood into the lungs. "And what about magic? Does the blood carry magic throughout the body too?"

The elder lets out a breath as if I've elbowed him, then starts to chuckle. "Magic is more complicated than that."

I blow a strand of my hair off my forehead, frustration warming my skin. "I know it's not simple, but if the blood is life . . ." I glance at the elder, who waits patiently for my thought to form. "When magic leaves a Valtia, she dies. So it seems as if magic is life too. And if that's true, then—"

He puts up his hands, as if in surrender. "My dear Saadella, magic infuses the wielder. It is everywhere within her."

I tap the diagram. "Including the blood?"

"Yes, yes. Including the blood. But—"

"Can you distill the magic from the blood, then? Will it separate like oil from water if it sits out overnight? Have you ever—"

The elder starts to laugh, his belly wobbling. "Darling child, do you ever stop? Some things simply *are*, and it is best to be at peace with that."

"And magic is one of them," I say slowly. How many times have I heard that from my tutors? "But where does it come from, Elder? I know the Valtia's magic passes to the Saadella, but what about the other wielders?"

Elder Kauko nudges my hand, which has now curled around the edge of the scroll, and in my eagerness, crumpled the paper. "We never know how it chooses a wielder." He taps the tip of my nose with his index finger. "We only know it chooses wisely."

I smooth my fingers over the wrinkled paper. "But when I had my geography lesson with priest Eljas the other day, he told me the Kupari are the only people in the world with magic. So *why* did it choose us?"

"Why did it choose us?" He gestures toward the corridor that leads to the grand domed chamber of our temple. "Because we serve it and keep it well, and . . ." He bows his head and lets out a huff of quiet laughter. "It just did, my Saadella. But I, for one, am not surprised. There is no better people than the Kupari, none stronger or purer of heart."

Like I so often do in my lessons, I feel as if I am banging against a closed door, begging entrance. "But if that's true, and we should all be at peace that the magic chose us, then why do all the priests spend their days studying it? What are they trying to figure out?" I point to the deep shelves of scrolls in Kauko's personal library. He is the physician, but he is also an elder, one of the more powerful magic wielders in this temple. "I know these texts aren't only about anatomy. When will you teach me about the actual magic?"

He sweeps his hand over the open scroll. "We teach you things every day, child!"

I bite my lip. "I thought when I turned sixteen, my lessons might include more than teachings on the natural world. I hoped I could spend more time with the Valtia and learn how she rules."

Kauko begins to roll up the scroll, and that mysterious heart disappears into a spiral of brown paper. "The Valtia must keep her focus on her magic, and using it to serve the people. I know you mean well, but she cannot be distracted from that." His thick lips quirk up in a sheepish smile. "And I know a horde of old priests are not equal to her company, but please believe we are dedicated to preparing you for the throne."

I look away from him, feeling ashamed of my selfishness. "I do," I murmur. But I can't help the way my heart yearns for my Valtia—nor my desire to learn from her.

Elder Kauko gathers the scrolls into a pile. "You will have all the knowledge you need when the time comes, Elli," he says, his voice gentle.

"You don't know when the time will come," I say as urgency coils in my gut.

His smile becomes wistful as he gives my arm a tender pat. "The other elders and I will guide you in the magic once it is inside you." His dark eyes twinkle with a teasing mischief. "Besides, you cannot possibly know what you most want to ask until you have experienced the magic for yourself, hmm? Then you can bombard us with your questions!"

He takes me by the elbow. "Come. I think it is time for your afternoon rest."

*The only person in this temple who doesn't treat me like a child is Mim.* I almost say it, but my words clog in my throat as he turns me to face him.

"We all know how devoted you are to your duty." His expression is full of pride, and it makes me stand a little straighter. "We prize that in you. My dearest hope is that you come to understand how devoted *we* are to *you*."

My throat is tight, but not with questions now. With emotion. "I know, Elder Kauko. I am so fortunate to have you. All of you."

An echoing shout for Elder Kauko from down the corridor has us both turning toward the door again. "Coming!" he calls.

I follow him into the stone hallway that connects this rear wing to the grand chamber of the Temple on the Rock. The shouting is coming from there. Elder Kauko runs his hand over the dusky shadow on his bald head, his fingers steady and smooth. It's a habit of his. "Elder Aleksi, is that you?"

Elder Aleksi rushes into the hallway, carrying the limp body of a boy who is bleeding from his head, his hands, his knees. My red skirt swishes around my ankles as I stop dead and stare. Aleksi, his heavy chin jiggling, gives the boy a concerned look. "He was hit by a horse cart," Aleksi says as Kauko reaches him. Then he sees me hovering a few steps behind. "He was so eager to reach the temple that he wasn't watching where he was going."

He mutters something else that I don't hear as he lays the boy, who can't be more than ten and is skinny as a pole, on the tiles. "I fear we're losing him."

"No, he'll be fine. I'll do it right here," says Kauko, leaning over the boy, his hands hovering over the child's crimson-streaked sandy hair. He looks over his shoulder and gives me a faint smile. "Our Saadella can watch."

My heart speeds as I take a step closer. Aleksi's brows are low with warning, an expression I see every time I ask to watch the apprentices practice their wielding skills in the catacombs. "My Saadella, this is an ugly business, and—"

"But it will be something I can do when I have the magic inside me, correct?" I ask, edging along the marble floor. Only a few wielders can heal. To do it, they must have both ice and fire magic—a great deal, as I understand it—and the two opposing forces must be balanced. The Valtia's magic is the most powerful, and it is also perfectly balanced, so this means—

"Of course, Saadella, should you ever wish to," says Kauko briskly. "And it is sometimes an excellent gesture of goodwill toward the citizens, to do healings on ceremony days."

"Then show me!" I say eagerly, and then gasp. As Kauko's palms hover a few inches from the boy's scalp, I can actually *see* the skin knitting together over a ragged wound. I open my mouth to ask how exactly Kauko manages it, but Aleksi puts his hand up.

"My Saadella," he says quietly. "Healing takes complete concentration."

Elder Kauko leans back after a few minutes, smiling and rubbing his hands together. I want to grasp them in my own—would they be burning to the touch? Icy cold? Both at once? "There. He is out of danger." He meets Aleksi's eyes. "Take him down to the catacombs and get him settled, and I will attend to the rest of his wounds after I have escorted the Saadella back to her chambers."

"The catacombs?" I ask, peering at the boy more closely now. "Does that mean he's a wielder?"

Aleksi nods. "His name is Niklas. He was apprenticed to a cobbler, who was kind enough to let us know he'd seen Niklas leave scorch marks on a piece of leather he was working. I thought it might be a false lead, but this boy clearly has fire. I knew it as soon as I was in the same room with him."

Kauko shakes his head. "I've always admired your ability to sense such things."

Aleksi grins at the compliment. "I don't know how much magic is inside him yet, or whether he has any ice magic too, but we'll test him once he's well."

I smile down at the boy, whose fingernails are black with grime, whose cheeks are hollow with deprivation. "Then he already knows how fortunate he is to have been found—it's a shame that excitement got him hurt." On impulse, I kneel next to him as his eyelids flutter. My fingers brush over his sharp cheekbone. "We'll take good care of you, Niklas," I murmur. "You have a wonderful life ahead of you."

The boys eyes pop open, and they are dark blue, like the waters of the Motherlake in spring. He blinks up at me, then his eyes trace the white marble walls around him and go round as saucers. Just as his mouth drops open, Aleksi gathers the child in his arms, his plump fingers curling over lanky limbs and holding tight. "I'll take him now," Aleksi says as the boy starts to squirm and whimper, probably still dazed from his injury.

He stands up and strides down the corridor toward the entrance to the catacombs, the maze of tunnels and chambers beneath our temple where all the acolytes and apprentices train and live. Kauko turns to me. "Well, that's enough excitement for the afternoon, eh?"

I look down at his hands, which are firm and strong-looking, unlike Aleksi's. "But I would love to hear more about how—"

Kauko chuckles. "Perhaps another time, my Saadella. Our lesson is over for today, and I am sure Mim would be disappointed if you did not partake of the lemon scones she has acquired for your tea."

My cheeks warm. Mim knows all my favorite things, and the sight of her smile as she gives them to me is loveliness itself. "Well then. I would never want to disappoint my handmaiden!"

Kauko grins and walks with me into the circular grand chamber, toward the eastern wing of the temple—the Saadella's wing. My wing. As we reach it, heavy boot steps sound on the marble and the Valtia's sedan chair is carried into the grand chamber from the white plaza outside. My heart squeezes with longing—I am only allowed to see my Valtia two days a year, at the planting ceremony and the harvest ceremony. She rarely leaves the temple, though, so I am frozen where I stand, gaping rudely. I narrow my eyes, trying to catch a glimpse of her face behind the gauzy material that covers the windows of the small wooden chamber where she sits. All I can see is the coppery glint of her hair, plaited and twisted and pinned into an exquisite coil atop her head.

Elder Leevi, lanky and stooped, walks next to the Valtia's chair. "I was simply saying another trip beyond the city walls does not seem like a good—"

"You saw that homestead, Elder," the Valtia replies. "I cannot in good conscience sit within this temple while our farmers live in fear. The raids are worse than ever, and the people might lose confidence if I did."

"You are wise, my Valtia, but there is danger in the outlands. We could bring . . ." His voice fades from my hearing as the Valtia and her procession disappear down her corridor toward her chambers.

"What kind of danger is there in the outlands, that it could put the Valtia at risk?" I ask Kauko as he tugs on my sleeve, leading me to my own rooms. "I know the outlands are full of thieves and bandits, but the Valtia can defend herself against any threat, can't she?"

"Of course, my Saadella," says Kauko, quickening his

pace. He is probably eager to get back to the boy, the newest magic wielder in our temple, but once again, my questions burn inside me. I place my hand on his arm.

"Is it the Soturi? Is it so bad that they have become stronger than us?" The raiders from the north have struck hard this year—or so Mim tells me. She sneaks information to me from the city whenever she can, even though the elders have admonished her for it twice already.

"The Soturi are no threat to the Valtia," Kauko says slowly, as if he is thinking about every word. "But the strain and stress of the travel is wearying for any queen, and especially one who is a vessel for such powerful magic. Elder Leevi's chief concern is our Valtia's health." He looks back at the doorway to my room, where Mim probably waits for me, laying out a blanket for my legs near my favorite chair by the fire. "A Valtia is all at once a magnificently strong and exquisitely fragile thing. For her to do her duty, she must be careful of what she demands of her body and mind. She must save her energy for when and where it is needed most."

And trips to the outlands must be exhausting, riding for hours over the hilly, rough terrain, having to constantly be on guard for bandits or, stars forbid, the vicious and brutal northern warriors who stab at our shores, seeking plunder.

"She wants to help the farmers, though," I say, my brow furrowing. How terrible she must feel, having to choose between her people and her health. Then I smile as an idea hits me. "Are we compensating the farmers for their losses?" I ask. "We have plenty of copper—I've seen the acolytes wheel it in. Surely we have enough, and it is more valuable than the bronze coins in the town. If she is concerned about the confidence of the people, maybe we could—"

Kauko makes a quiet sound of disapproval that silences me. "My dear, when you are on the throne, we will discuss all of this, but forgive me when I say that right now you are talking of things you do not understand."

I flush with the reprimand, and Kauko's frown softens. "I realize that all your ideas and questions sprout from the best intentions," he says. "And I will speak with the Valtia about ways she can reduce the raids and bolster the confidence of the people while maintaining her health. I will also tell her you are concerned for her." He winks. "And in a few days, you can tell her yourself!"

I nearly bounce on my heels as I think of the upcoming harvest ceremony. I haven't spoken to my Valtia in months. "I certainly will. I want her to be with us for years to come." Everyone knows that Valtias fade young, but Kauko makes it sound like it is possible to live longer if care is taken. And I want my Valtia to take care—not just because I love her, though I do, with every shred of my soul—because I fear I will never meet the standard she has set as our queen. "I—I feel as if I won't be ready for a very long time," I add quietly. "If I ever disappointed our people . . ." Even the thought puts a lump in my throat.

Kauko gives me the most kindly smile. "I am going to tell you something very important," he says. "I was going to wait, but it seems like you need to hear it now."

I stare at him, his smooth face and silly-looking lips, his merry eyes. "What is it?"

"All Valtias are powerful, but not all equally so. Some burn bright and fade quickly, while others are more steady, strong but muted. We never know what kind of Valtia we will have until the magic enters a Saadella. Except with you."

I have the strange urge to claw at my stockings to peek at the red flame mark that paints my left calf with its numb scarlet tendrils, the one that appeared at the moment of the last Valtia's death—when I was only four years old. "What do you mean?"

"There is a prophecy," he says, glancing up and down the hall. "One made hundreds of years ago."

"Yes?" I whisper.

His bald scalp is beaded with sparkles of sweat in the light of the torches that line the walls. "When we found you in that shabby little cottage by the city wall, too skinny for your own good, we made sure to check the town register for the day and season of your birth, and the exact position of the stars in the sky on that very day. It matches what was foretold precisely." He grasps both my arms, giving me a little shake, as if to force this knowledge into me, to make sure I believe. "When the magic leaves our current queen and enters you, Elli, you will become the most powerful Valtia who has ever existed."

# CHAPTER 2

From my balcony, the Motherlake appears infinite. She stretches vast and powerful to the horizon, where she kisses the sky. Trout and razorfin teem beneath her blue skin, all shimmering power and motion, but from here, she looks serene and perfect. She keeps her secrets well.

I lean forward, letting the cool breeze toss my long, coppery hair around my face. In a few hours, I must be flawless and composed, but I'm not on display quite yet. Right now I'm just Elli, and for the moment, it's enough. I spread my arms and pretend I'm flying.

From behind me comes a startled laugh. "You're making my job much harder," says Mim, but her tone is fond. I whirl around and grin at her. Her blue eyes, just a shade darker than mine, sparkle with excitement. She's already dressed in her finest gown and pulled her brown hair into a braided coil. I love the tiny curls that swirl at the nape of her neck. At twenty, she could have found a handsome man to marry by now, but she's been serving me since she was a little girl, chosen by the elders for her sweet and patient temperament.

I know she feels honored to serve me. Sometimes, though, I wish—

"The Valtia and her handmaiden will be here any minute," she says, gesturing inside. "Can we start the preparations now, or are you determined to let the wind knot your hair some more?"

I slap my hand over the top of my head. "Oh no—is it a tangled mess?"

She arches an eyebrow and nods. "But I can fix it. Let me work *my* kind of magic."

A gust of wind chases me inside the ceremonial dressing chamber, making the drapes flap. Mim tsks and pulls the wooden doors to the balcony shut. When I'm the Valtia, I'll be able to do the same thing with a mere thought. *The most powerful Valtia who ever existed*, Kauko whispers in my memory.

I shiver as Mim guides me to the cushioned stool in front of the wide copper plate that serves as our mirror. "Do you need a blanket for your legs?" she asks.

I shake my head, warmer already because of her attention. She places a cup of water in my hands. "I know you get so thirsty on these ceremony days."

THE IMPOSTOR QUEEN

I lift the hammered copper mug to my lips and moan softly at the relief of cold water in my mouth. "You're a jewel."

She chuckles. "I'm a stone. *You're* a jewel. The people will be in awe when they see you." She gives my shoulders a little squeeze and begins to work on my hair. "Lovely. Like burnished copper," she says, drawing the brush through my straight, thick locks.

I close my eyes, enjoying the feel of the bristles against my scalp, inhaling Mim's warm cinnamon scent. Before long, though, my thoughts drift back to where they've been since my conversation with Elder Kauko. Has he really known this thing about me all these years? I became the Saadella so young that I have almost no memory of what came before, but I know it was not special or remarkable, not until the red flame mark on my left leg erupted.

"Your thoughts are far away," says Mim.

"I was thinking of the day I was chosen."

"I was only eight, but it's as clear in my mind as if it were yesterday," she says as she starts to braid my hair. "I would have been screaming for my mother, but you looked as serious as an elder as you were placed on the paarit. Your little fingers clutched the chair so tightly as the acolytes lifted you into the air! A four-year-old with filthy feet and a torn tunic, but my father said he could tell you were the true future queen."

This part, I remember. I wasn't screaming because I was numb. I've long since forgotten my mother's face, but I remember being paralyzed with the knowledge that she had given me to these strange men and allowed them to carry me away. I had no idea yet what I'd gained. "It's amazing how much one day can change everything," I murmur.

Mim pins a coil of my hair into position and stares at my reflection in the copper plate. "More change is coming," she says quietly.

My eyes meet hers. "It won't happen for many years."

"The Valtia is finishing her third decade of life. The apprentices whisper about it in the kitchens. They say she's looking pale these days. Some of them wonder how many years she has left."

"You shouldn't speak of our queen's death in such a casual way, Mim." Knowing that one day another handmaiden will be telling my young Saadella that I will die soon makes my tone sharper than it should be.

Mim bows her head. "You're so right, my Saadella." There's a pang in my chest—she rarely calls me by my title unless we're in public, and her doing so now, with her hands in my hair and her body close enough to feel her warmth, makes loneliness bubble up inside me.

I clear my throat and try to think of a safe place to steer our conversation, but voices in the corridor bring it to a complete halt. Mim's fingers go still, mid-plait.

"—that it's time to intervene," Elder Aleksi is saying, his hard-edged voice sending a chill up my back. "The miners need access immediately."

"Immediately? I don't see the harm in taking the time

to negotiate," comes my Valtia's reply as she's carried into the chamber in her veiled sedan chair. Tiny beads of sweat glisten on the bald heads of the four black-robed male aco-lytes who bear the poles. My toes curl and my hands fist in my skirt as they set the chair down in the center of the chamber. I want to throw myself into the Valtia's arms, but I stay where I am, because I don't want to embarrass her in any way.

Aleksi, clad in his black priest's robe, stands beside the copper-inlaid sedan. "Negotiate? My queen, remember who we're dealing with."

"Human beings, I assume," says the Valtia.

Aleksi looks as if he's harboring a thousand angry words in that swell of flesh beneath his chin. Judging by the way his thin lips are pressed tight together, he's fighting to hold them inside. He gives me a cursory bow.

"My Saadella," he says as he straightens. "Forgive me for intruding on your preparations." He turns to the Valtia's chair and addresses one of the veiled windows. "The raids have made the farmers restless, and now the miners—"

"Tell them to mine somewhere else for the time being."

Though his jowls quiver, his mouth barely moves as he speaks. "My Valtia, they claim there *is* nowhere else."

"What?" My queen's voice has sharpened.

Aleksi looks over at me and Mim. "We can speak more tonight," he says as he turns back to her. "We must make a decision after the harvest ceremony—"

"After the harvest ceremony, I will be dining with my

Saadella, as I do every year," she replies, her voice gentle but firm. "I'll meet with the elders in the morning and no sooner."

Aleksi clenches his fist, then gives Mim and me a side-long glance and tucks his hand into the folds of his robe. He chuckles, a sound as dank as the catacombs. "Of course, my Valtia." With a swish of his flabby hand, he dismisses the acolytes, who bow their way out the door to join the others in the grand domed chamber of our temple, where today's procession will begin. "We'll await your arrival with eagerness."

As soon as Aleksi exits, the Valtia's handmaiden steps around the other side of the sedan chair. Helka, a stout woman with a deep dimple in her chin, shakes her head as she pushes aside the veil at the front of the chair. "You were patient with him," she mutters, opening the half door to allow the Valtia to step out.

As our queen's slippered foot touches the sanctified ground of our chamber, Mim and I sink to our knees. I lower my forehead to the floor, the marble cool against my skin.

"Enough. You're not an acolyte," the Valtia says with a musical laugh. "I haven't seen you in months, Elli. Get up off the floor and let me look at you."

I grin as I rise, but my happiness turns to ice when I see her face. The apprentices were correct—she is pale. Her cheeks are hollow, and there are dark circles beneath her blue eyes. She looks as if she's been carved out with a dull blade, all pointy elbows and sharp collarbones.

I force my uneasiness down and look at her with all the admiration she deserves.

Her full lips curve into a loving smile as she beckons to me. "Come here, darling. Stars, you're so lovely. Can you really be sixteen already? You've become a woman in the last year!" She holds out her arms, and I eagerly rush into her embrace, leaning my cheek against the soft wool of her cream-colored gown. She strokes my face, her fingertips pulsing with warm affection. "I've missed you," she whispers.

"I've missed you, too, my Valtia," I mumble, squeezing her tight, trying to ignore the hard outline of her ribs against my arms. It doesn't matter that I see her so rarely—she is my true mother. I've been told that the connection between the Valtia and the Saadella is as deep and fundamental as the veins of copper in the earth, but that doesn't begin to describe it. From the moment she took me in her arms, I knew I belonged to her.

We pull apart, and she takes my face in her hands. I'm as tall as she is now. Her hair is a perfect copper coil on the top of her head, ready to hold her crown in place. "Shall we prepare to be seen by our people?" she asks.

"I'm ready." My voice shakes with excitement, but also nerves.

Our handmaidens arrange our chairs in front of the wide copper mirror, and Mim sets back to work on my hair as Helka prepares the Valtia's ceremonial makeup.

"Aleksi seemed frustrated," I venture. "More trouble in the outlands?"

Mim clears her throat, and my mouth snaps shut. I'm not supposed to know about any of that.

Helka, her graying blond hair twisted in a bun like Mim's, blows a loose strand off her forehead. "Such questions," she says, clucking her tongue. "Can we not leave our Valtia in peace for a few minutes at least?"

The Valtia pats her maid's hand. "When I'm gone, she'll be queen, Helka. She can ask me anything she wants." Her gaze meets mine in the mirror as Mim begins to plait another section of my hair. "From all reports, it's been a plentiful year for our farmers."

"Thanks to you." She kept the heat from scorching the crops and held back a cold snap that could have killed vulnerable shoots. Our bounty comes to us because of her magic.

Her pale eyes glitter, the same icy blue as mine. "But there have been Soturi raids on some of the farmsteads and cottages, more this year than last, all along the northern coastline. The farmers were already dealing with the criminals who have been banished from the city. They want more protection."

I grit my teeth. "The Soturi are getting bold." We don't know much about them, but perhaps fifteen years ago, they began to cross the Motherlake in their longships, wielding their iron swords, raiding for goods to trade and food to get them through the brutal winter.

Mim pins my final braid into place. "It's scaring the people, my Valtia," she says quietly.

The Valtia nods, even as Helka glares at Mim for her impertinence. "And now apparently the miners are worried that they've run out of places to mine!"

Helka rubs her palms on her skirt. "Forgive me for saying so, but it had to happen sometime."

My Valtia sighs. "I suppose so. But apparently there's a very large cave system in the south that has been left untouched, and now a horde of bandits has decided it would be an ideal place to squat for the winter." She gives me an uneasy sidelong glance. "A group of miners confronted them this morning. It turned into a fight."

"And now the miners want you to take action," I guess.

She nods. "The elders are concerned that if I don't, the miners will petition the city council to raise a militia."

"Without giving you the time to consider the best way to handle it?" After all the magic wielders of the temple have done for the Kupari, it strikes me as ungrateful.

The Valtia's soft hand covers mine, sending warmth radiating up my arm. "They are frightened, Elli. And between the bandits in the caves and the Soturi who are now to our southeast, I can understand why they feel that way."

I scowl. Mim told me how the Soturi crushed the city-state of Vasterut a few months ago, how it's now part of their barbaric empire. "Vasterut is not Kupari. Its people are not blessed, and they had a king." My voice rises with every word. "They did *not* have a Valtia."

She squeezes my hand. "Exactly." She lifts my fingers and lays them against her cool, hollow cheek. "Now let's allow our handmaidens to do their work, so we can calm all our people's fears today."

I nod. This is my responsibility too, and I'm eager to do my part. As our maids mix the vinegar and white lead powder, I breathe slowly, willing myself to be calm. Mim moves her hands to my waist, and I lift my arms so she can draw my simple red gown off. This is a dance we do every day, as she cares for my body as if it were her own. Next to us, the Valtia and her handmaiden are doing the same waltz, their movements perfectly synchronized after years of practice. As the creamy material slides off the Valtia's slender frame, I spot the bandages in the crooks of her arms, each dotted with blood.

My throat tightens. "Valtia, are you ill?" I manage to whisper.

She folds her arms across her chest. "I'm fine. But Elder Kauko's been helping me maintain the balance I need in preparation for the winter to come."

The elder downplayed the presence of magic in the blood, but it sounds like the opposite is true. "How exactly does bleeding help you maintain the balance?"

The air around us cools enough to raise goose bumps. "It siphons some of the fire magic that's lain dormant during the hotter months."

I silently resolve to be a lot more persistent in my questioning during my next lesson with Elder Kauko. The Valtia's eyes narrow as she takes in the hard set of my mouth, and then she looks down at her bandaged arms. "I trust in the wisdom of our elders, Elli. When your time comes, you'll need to do the same."

I lower my eyes, my cheeks hot despite the cold room. "Of course, my Valtia."

A warm breeze tickles the back of my neck, the Valtia's tender caress, and it draws a relieved smile back to my face. "Look at me, darling," she says quietly. When I do, she adds, "We rely on the elders. But always remember—you're still the queen." Then she winks, and my spirits rise like the sun.

I close my eyes and listen to Mim cracking eggs and mixing the yolks with the vinegar and white lead paste, her brush scraping the bottom of the stone bowl in rhythmic swishes. When the people look at me today, I want them to see their future queen, the one who will keep their crops growing and their bellies full, the one who will keep the enemy from our shores. The most powerful Valtia who ever existed. I want to look like I could become that person. I stay perfectly still as Mim brushes the snow-white liquid onto my face. Its astringent fumes burn my nose, but I don't even flinch. From this moment until Mim bathes me late tonight so I can dine privately with the Valtia, I cannot move my face, cannot smile or frown.

Helka finishes with the Valtia and takes her behind the screen to be dressed. The Valtia is silent now, like me, unwilling to damage her perfect exterior. When Mim's covered my face, neck, and chest with the pure white paint, she uses her tiny brush to slick the bloodred stain over my lips. Next she dusts copper powder over my eyelids and temples, holding the thick paper pattern against my skin to get the dots and swirls just right. While she does, I think of copper, and how it defines us, and how I always assumed it was as infinite as the Valtia's magic . . . until today.

27

"You are a living treasure," Mim says, interrupting my thoughts. "Are you ready to be dressed?"

I blink twice so I don't crack my shell. Mim pats my arm, and for a moment I see sadness in her eyes, or maybe pity.

Wishing I could ask her what's wrong, I rise carefully and step behind a screen on the other side of the room. Mim strips off my underskirt and stockings, then rubs my body with rose oil. Like always, she carefully avoids touching my red flame mark, as if she's afraid it will burn her. But though it might look like a flame, in all the years I've borne it on my skin, it's been nothing but a swirling patch of nothingness. I wonder if that will change when the magic is awakened inside me. Perhaps then my mark will burn with the thundering power of the ice and fire magic in my body. I'll have to ask the Valtia about it tonight.

Mim gently rolls new bloodred stockings onto my feet, pulling them all the way up to my thighs. I suppress another shiver as her fingertips slide over my skin, and I cannot help my twinge of disappointment when her touch disappears. She wraps the flowing, gauzy underdress around my waist and lets it fall in waves to my ankles. Her deft fingers lace and tie the corset so tightly that I can barely breathe, but I would never tell her of my discomfort. She'll be judged by the priests if I'm not flawless.

While the Valtia is led to her awaiting ceremonial paarit, much larger than the sedan chair in which she travels around the temple, Mim ushers my other maidservants inside. The Saadella's gown is made from loom-woven wool dyed a deep red with madder root and calf's blood. Copper threads make it sparkle. Mim holds my waist as I step into it, and the attendants pull the sleeves up to my arms and fasten the gown to the corset. This dress weighs a stone at least and is so stiff that if I fainted dead away, it would probably still hold me up.

A little maid who can't be older than twelve comes forward with my slippers on a special cushion. Her hands tremble as she lays them at my feet. I glance at my reflection in a metal plate on the wall, to see what she sees. I am snow white, bloodred, and copper glory. When I stand by the Valtia, everyone will know I belong there.

Mim presses the copper circlet onto my head. Studded with polished agates pulled from the shores of the Motherlake, it's a solid weight on my skull. With that done, I'm led to the corridor, where my own paarit awaits. Impassive and expressionless, I walk slowly to it and take my seat on the chair that's bolted to the platform. It's adorned with intricate carvings of wolves descending from the stars to lay waste to the enemies of the Kupari, meant to symbolize the Valtia's magic.

As soon as I'm settled, the bearers are called. They stride from the side hallways, looking fine in their scarlet tunics and hats. Each year, the priests choose eight of the strongest young men in the city to have the honor of carrying the Valtia and the Saadella on harvest day. The four chosen for my paarit bow to me one by one, then take up their positions at each corner. Their muscles strain beneath their uniforms as they lift me from the ground and set the ends of the horizontal poles on their shoulders. One of them, a boy with warm brown eyes and golden hair, gives me a curious sidelong glance. His cheeks turn red when he realizes I've caught him looking.

For a moment, I recall Mim's pity and think perhaps I understand it perfectly. I'll never know what it feels like to be loved by one, because I must be loved by all. I'll never feel the touch of a lover, because my body is a vessel for magic. It only bothers me sometimes, like when I glance at Mim sitting by the fire on winter evenings. Her secret smile, meant just for me, leaves a pit in my stomach every time. And as I watch the handsome bearer's strong hands wrap around the pole, I feel the same stab of longing.

I tear my gaze from him and look down the corridor. Already the priests are milling about under the dome that marks the main chamber of the temple. Their shapeless, hooded garments are belted with rope to signify their life as servants of the Valtia, their round heads shaved bald, their skin pale from lack of sunlight, their shoulders stooped from hours spent hunched over their sacred star charts or peering through their telescopes. They remind me a bit of the waddling turkeys in the temple menagerie.

Mim scoots ahead of the bearers and looks up at me. "You are blessed, Saadella," she says in a loud, clear voice.

In unison, the bearers and maidservants repeat the phrase, and then we're moving. I focus on being still and regal as I float down the corridor. The priests stride to the outer edges of the domed chamber and stand in a circle, their backs against stone walls inlaid with veins of copper, the treasure hidden within the flesh of our beautiful land.

Next to Elder Aleksi, on the east side of the chamber, is Elder Leevi, his thick red eyebrows slashing across his prominent, smooth brow, his deep-set blue eyes darting. And beside him is Elder Kauko, potbellied and square-jawed.

The elders are so different and yet similar. It's difficult to tell how old they are—though they have a few gray hairs, their skin is smooth and youthful. In fact, all the priests share those qualities, as if they age more slowly once they ascend from apprenticeship.

The acolytes—both female and male—and the apprentices, all male, kneel at the back of the round chamber, their hoods over their heads, their faces concealed, their pale hands clasped in front of them. Some of them are small, no older than ten—and I wonder if one of them is Niklas, the little fire wielder Aleksi brought to us a few days ago. I hope he is well enough to join us today.

My paarit bearers stride to the center of the chamber and take up their position over the symbol of the Saadella, three circles entwined, one for fire, one for ice, and one for the balance between the two. It is pure potential, as I'm supposed to be. My heart kicks within my chest as Kauko raises his arm, signaling that we're ready for the Valtia's entrance.

Her bearers' steps are synchronized as they carry her from an alcove on the west side of the domed chamber, and all the acolytes and apprentices bow until their foreheads touch stone. She's now wearing her magnificent crown, which is polished and shining with the single agate that adorns its apex, a perfect eye of carnelian and amethyst. Her gown is a grand confection of woven copper thread, with a high, round collar that fans around her head. The bearers lower her to the ground, positioning her over her own seal, the symbol of infinity, two loops of pristine, snowy marble within a solid circle of copper, symmetrical and simple.

Kauko steps forward with a carved wooden box in his hands. He bows to the Valtia and opens it, revealing the cuff of Astia, copper emblazoned with red runes, the sacred object she uses to project her power. She holds out her arm, and he reverently fastens it to her wrist.

As soon as it clicks into place, she raises her finger, and the candles in the room burst to life at once, vibrant pricks of light in the dim chamber. The acolytes and apprentices rise to their feet and throw back their hoods, revealing their shaved heads and somber expressions. The trumpeters just outside the temple see the signal and blow their horns. A massive cheer floats in from the city. The Valtia and I are carried out of the Temple on the Rock and into the sunlight, our bearers slowly walking down the long set of marble steps until we reach the white plaza. Our procession, the priests, apprentices, and acolytes trailing behind, strides between the two stone fountains from which jut majestic statues of the first Valtia, one gazing out on the city, the other facing the Motherlake.

At the southern end of the white plaza, the ceremonial

gates are wide open, and our citizens line the road outside the temple grounds. They toss coneflowers and dahlias and amaranth blossoms into the mud at the bearers' booted feet as we pass. A regal tune from the pipes and drums fills the air, as does the scent of roasting venison and bear meat. My stomach growls, and I'm happy no one can hear it. My skin pricks with sweat under the midafternoon sun, but then a cool wind blows across my face, a gift from the queen by my side.

We enter the town square to a roar of adoration. The people keep up the steady stream of blessings and prayers and shouted words of love as we are carried up the steps of the high platform at the northern end of the square. The apprentices and acolytes stand in rows around the platform, keeping the citizens at a distance. As soon as the bearers set us down and descend the steps, the Valtia rises and the crowd falls silent. She offers me her hand.

I rise to a soft, collective intake of breath. They see how I'm like her. My lips tighten to rein in my smile, and I lay my palm on hers. Together, we face our subjects, and my chest nearly bursts with pride. There are thousands of people in this square, filling every inch of space. At the southern side, which leads to our farmlands along the coast, the men and women who till the earth raise their pitchforks and scythes in salute. If they're angry about the bandits and Soturi raiders, you wouldn't know it today. At the eastern side of the square, which leads to the main gates of the city, the mines and the outlands, the trappers and hunters have hung gorgeous pelts from the wooden arch that overhangs the road, and the miners lift their hammers high. I can't tell from this distance if there is desperation in their movements, if they truly fear that there is only one source of copper left on our sprawling peninsula.

At the western side of the square, which leads to the docks where our fleet of fishing boats is moored, the men and women who sail our Motherlake wave their caps in the air. Their wind-chapped, rosy-cheeked faces are a sight to see, and—

Several of them stumble forward as they're hit from behind. Four men, their faces sweaty and red with exertion, push their way through the crowd as whispers roll through the square. "Valtia!" one of them shouts, his voice cracking. "Valtia, you must come!"

The Valtia raises her arm, and the crowd parts to allow the men through. They stumble up the steps and throw themselves at her feet, their chests heaving. "Please, Valtia," the oldest one says between ragged breaths, sweat dripping from his iron-gray hair. "We were bringing in our catch about ten miles off the tip of the peninsula, and we saw . . . we saw . . ."

He succumbs to a fit of coughing, and a younger fisherman pushes himself up to kneel in front of us. His blond, curly hair sticks out in crazy hunks around his head, and his eyes are glazed with horror. "The Soturi. We rowed back to shore as quickly as we could," he says between panting breaths.

A violent twist of heat and cold shoots up my arm, and I cannot suppress my gasp. The Valtia holds my hand tightly as Elder Aleksi steps forward, his jowls trembling. "How dare you interrupt the harvest ceremony to tell us of a petty raid," he hisses at the man.

The older fisherman groans and shakes his head. "Not a raid! Two hundred longships at least. We were only a few miles ahead of them. They'll be here before the sun sets."

*Two hundred longships.* Raw fear blooms inside me. The barbarians from the north aren't raiding this time—they're *invading.* I stare at my Valtia. We all do. Waiting for our queen to save us from destruction and death.

Her skin is ice cold as she releases my hand. And when she speaks, her voice is quiet but startling in its steadiness. "Take me to the docks. I'm going to need a ship."

# CHAPTER 3

The square erupts into worried muttering. A few people race for their homes, but most of the crowd seems riveted in place, still gaping at us. I stand stiffly on my paarit as the Valtia touches the cuff of Astia and turns to me. "You must go back to the Temple on the Rock," she says. Her perfect white makeup is chipped and cracking around her mouth, and the hair at her temples is damp with sweat. "Aleksi, take her."

For a moment I allow myself to be pulled backward by the elder, but then a wave of pure urgency crashes over me. "What are you going to do?"

She gives me a small smile, but her pale-blue eyes glint with ice. "I'm going to bury their ships at the bottom of the Motherlake."

The fishermen look up at her in awe. "Valtia," says the old one, his voice hushed, "there are so many. It will take more than a cold wind to throw them off their chosen course."

She gazes down at him. "I know." Her eyes meet mine again. "Go. You belong in the temple."

Something about the way she says it makes my entire body clench. "Take me with you," I blurt out. For some insane reason, I feel like I should go. Like I *must* go.

Her brow furrows, further cracking her formerly perfect shell. "Darling, there's nothing you can do. Someday this will be your duty. Today, it's mine."

Because today I'm a powerless, ordinary girl. An empty vessel, waiting for the magic to fill it. Aleksi's fingers close around my upper arm and guide me to my chair. "My Saadella, you'll be safe in the temple."

"Safe?" I blink at him. There is worry in his eyes, and it makes me want to slap his smooth, round face.

His cheeks turn red as if I already have, and he bows to me. "The Valtia will keep us all safe, but her mind will be more focused if she knows you're well protected," he says in a tight voice.

My Valtia regards the elder coolly, then steps forward and takes my hand. "Tonight we'll dine together, just like we planned." She squeezes my clammy fingers and sends warmth flowing along my skin. "Elli," she says quietly. "I'll see you very soon."

Even though I don't want her to go, fierce pride beats

within my breast as I look at her. "I can't wait for that moment, my Valtia." I will my voice into steadiness, just like hers. "And I'll keep watch from my balcony so I can see you return in victory."

Her smile brightens. "Until then." She lifts my palm to her lips, laying a tender kiss there. It leaves a smear of red on my skin. Then she lets me go and takes her seat. "Quickly now," she says to the bearers.

They carry her away from me. A moment later, my own bearers lift my paarit from the platform and whisk me down the steps. The acolytes and apprentices press the citizens back to give us a path. The jubilant mood has been siphoned away, replaced with brittle fear. Their faith is weak. Their doubt so easily overwhelms them. It's pathetic. The Valtia can raise infernos with her fingertips. She can wield icebergs with her thoughts. She creates a dome of warmth over our city that lasts from the end of fall to the beginning of spring. What other people in this cold climate can grow fruits and vegetables in the frigid winter months? What city can build any time of year because the ground never freezes? Only us! All because of her power, which she uses only to serve them.

And yet, they seem cowed and uneasy as they look up at me. Suddenly this paint on my face feels like a prison. I want to scrape it from my skin and burst forth, vengeful and shouting. Instead I sit placidly as my bearers jog up the road to the temple, which sits at the northernmost tip of the peninsula that juts like a giant, curving thumb deep into the waters of the Motherlake.

I hold my head high as we move. I want everyone to see that I, for one, am not scared. I'm not. I'm *not*. Yes, my heart is beating like a dragonfly's wings. Yes, my palms are sweating over the armrests of my grand chair. But that's only because I'm hot and frustrated. Not because I'm scared for my Valtia. She'll crush those Soturi. I saw the promise in her eyes.

She doesn't break her promises.

The bearers mount the steps leading up to the temple. The blond young man at the right front side, the one who tried to steal an extra peek at my face, stumbles halfway up. My paarit lurches forward, and I grit my teeth to hold in the scream. But before I topple off the chair, the corner jerks upward. Kauko—who always remains behind to guard the temple on ceremony days—stands in the pillared entrance to the domed chamber, his fist raised as he commands the swirling icy-hot air around my paarit. The elder releases his grip only when an apprentice rushes forward and grabs the pole. As the blond bearer stammers his frantic apologies, more apprentices and acolytes crowd around, helping the bearers heft the weight of my paarit and my dress and my useless, as-yet-unmagical body. We move up the steps again.

A few minutes later they've put me down and disappeared, leaving me alone in my own corridor, waiting for my maids. More than anything, I need Mim, and it's all I can do not to call her name. But before I reach my breaking point, she's at my side, taking my arm and guiding me off my paarit and into my chamber.

"Do you want the others to come help?" she asks me.

"No. Please. Can you just do it?" Right now I couldn't stand to have all the maids quivering with anxiety and whispering gossip as they work on me.

She gives me a quick nod and undresses me with practiced fingers. She huffs with strain as she lifts my dress from the floor and strides to the door with it. I close my eyes as I listen to her giving the other maids orders to put it back in its special case in the catacombs below the temple. She's gone but a moment and then I feel a cool, dripping cloth on my chest, wiping the lead paint from my skin. "Please hurry," I say, my fists clenching and unclenching.

"I am, Elli," she replies in a strained voice. "I know this is hard. I know you're scared."

"I'm *not* scared!" I shriek, so abruptly that she stumbles back. "How dare you suggest that? Your doubt is probably weighing heavy on her, right when she most needs her strength!" My voice breaks over the rocks of my rage. I can't get the sight of the Valtia's bandaged arms out of my head.

Mim's eyes are round as dinner plates. "S-s-aadella," she stammers, "I'm so sorry."

The shock on her face brings me so much shame that it burns. Tears start in my eyes and overflow in a mere second. "Apologies," I whisper. "Please continue."

She approaches me as if I'm a wounded bear, and I feel like I'm going to be sick. But I hold everything inside as she finishes cleaning my chest and neck and face. She gingerly removes my copper circlet, then draws my arms through my nightgown and pulls it down over my head. "Would you like something to eat?"

"I'll be eating with the Valtia when she returns." I take a step backward. "Until then, I'll be on my balcony." I whirl around, and she races ahead of me to pull the heavy wooden doors open. I stride through them. "Please don't disturb me."

Her only reply is the sound of the doors closing behind me. Reeling with the loss of the cheers, the thrill of the day, and my precious, rare time at the queen's side, I move to the railing. In the distance, the tiny silhouettes of three sailing vessels float away from our peninsula and into the open water of the Motherlake. The sun draws its yellow tongue along the surface of the waves, rendering them golden and sparkling. It's slowly sinking into the west, casting the boats' shadows long as they cut through the lake, moving north. The oars move steadily and in perfect synchrony. The sailors know they carry the queen, and they know what's at stake.

I stare at the northern horizon. Somewhere beyond it lies the seat of the Soturi empire. They're coming for us, planning to take us over right at the harvest, just before the winter descends. No other people has dared to test us before, but these barbarians are different, descending from the far north and spreading southward like a plague. Until now, they have been satisfied with small-scale raids, killing and looting, burning what they can't steal. It happens at least a dozen times each year at various spots along the coast, and each year there are a few more than the last. But this summer they took the entire city-state of Vasterut, and now they've set their sights on Kupari. What has changed?

At the point where lake meets sky, the water has turned dark and spiny. My breath catches in my throat—it's the masts of the Soturi longships. There are so many of them that they seem to take up half the Motherlake.

I grip the stone railing and lean forward. "Your boots will never touch our shores," I say, my voice dripping with menace.

Because I can see it now, the swirl of clouds over the Motherlake. And I know what my Valtia is going to do.

*"Would you like me to make you a storm?" she asked as we ate roasted sweet potatoes and parsnips in her chambers, lounging and relaxed after a long harvest ceremony.*

*"Inside?" I asked. "How is that possible?"*

*Her eyes flashed with mischief. She rose from her pillows, her cream-colored gown flowing around her body as she moved to the carved stone bathing pool in the corner of her chamber. I followed, fascinated by the flex of her fingers, by the power I could already feel in the air. She gazed down upon the smooth surface of the water. "It's not that hard. Watch."*

*She flattened her left palm high over the water and moved it in a slow circle. "Cold air up here," she told me. Then she scooped her right hand into the water and raised it slowly, turning it to steam before it could drip from her fingers. "And lots of warm, wet air down here."*

*I stared in awe as she kept moving both her hands in those unhurried rotations, as the air began to swirl and crackle. And* then, clouds of vapor burst from nothing. She grinned when my mouth dropped open.

As the first droplets of rain hit the surface of the bathing pool, I started to giggle. "Amazing!"

She winked at me as she contained the tiny storm, as she made it hail and rain. And then she made all of it vanish in an instant. I laughed with delight. "Did one of the elders teach you that? I wish they'd teach me about magic. I'm so tired of reading about agriculture and constellations and the life cycle of a cow and—"

"They want you to understand our world before you wield magic that can change it." She looked down at the water dripping from her fingers. "And as for your first question, no. They didn't teach me that trick. My Valtia did," she said quietly, drying her hands on a cloth. "And someday, maybe you'll show it to your Saadella."

"Assuming I'm ever that good," I said, unable to contain my awe of her—and my own uncertainty.

She nudged my chin up. "When you are the Valtia, you'll be better than good, Elli. You may doubt anything in this world, but never doubt yourself."

My eyes fix on the churning clouds as they roll chaotically in the sky, spreading outward. A distant crack of thunder splits the quiet. "Never doubt," I whisper.

As the storm takes shape, the three boats disappear into the darkness like they're passing through a veil. The sky roils, turning purplish green as lightning flashes down in jagged, bright blades. I picture the bolts stabbing the Soturi longships, breaking them in half, sending barbarians tumbling into the waiting mouth of the Motherlake.

May she grind their bones in her watery jaws.

I cheer when I feel drops of rain on my face. The storm is so massive that its edges lick at our city, spitting pellets of ice. I can only imagine what it's doing to the barbarians. I wish I could see what's happening, especially when the first waterspout erupts, rising so high that it kisses the raging, swirling thunderclouds. It goes on and on, the wind becoming an animal roar in my ears.

There's a crash behind me, and Mim grabs my shoulders. "Come inside!" she shouts over the gale.

I tear myself away from her. "Not a chance." My voice is full of laughter. "Look, Mim! How could anyone be scared when their queen can do that?"

She wraps her arms around my waist like she's afraid I'll be blown away. Tendrils of my hair, torn loose from my braids by the fierce wind, tangle with her brown curls. Her cheek presses to mine. "No one should ever doubt the power of the Valtia," she says in my ear. "I'm sorry that my fear got the best of me. Forgive me?"

"Always," I say, turning my head and kissing her rain-speckled cheek. I've never been this happy, this full of ferocious, throbbing certainty. "Someday, Mim, that will be me."

She squeezes me tightly. "Someday it will be you. And I'll be so proud to be your handmaiden."

My hands fold over hers, holding them against my body.

I wish I had fire magic to warm her, but even as I think it, I feel my temperature rising, along with a delicious tingling along my skin. She starts to pull away, but I tighten my grip. "No," I whisper. "Stay right here."

"But Elli—"

"Please. Don't move." It feels so good. My blood is pounding in my ears, and Mim's arms are perfect right where they are.

She obeys me. She must, because she is my handmaiden, and suddenly a tiny part of me feels guilty, because I'm not sure if she likes it quite as much as I do. I stare at the storm, wanting things I cannot have. That I should not have. I clear my throat and let go of her hands. She squeezes me and pulls away, but stays next to me, watching the massive swells, the blinding flashes of light, the billowing clouds.

After an hour or so, the storm quiets abruptly, folding in on itself like a scroll. I squint into the distance, but all that lies in front of me is foggy darkness.

"The Soturi must be at the bottom of our Motherlake," says Mim. "Now will you come inside?" When I shake my head, she gives me an exasperated smile and puts her hands on her round hips, and I am relieved that she seems to have forgiven me for wanting to be too close to her. "Don't you want to wash up before she comes back—or do you prefer to greet her looking like a drowned ferret?"

"In no way do I resemble a ferret." I giggle as I swipe my hands across my wet cheeks. As much as I'd like to stand here and wait for the Valtia's boat to come sailing into port, I spend the next hour inside, reliving the storm, my chest buzzing and thrumming while Mim dries my skin and changes my clothes, draping me in a flowing gown of soft red wool. She undoes all my braids, brushes my hair, and plaits it once more. She lays her palms on my cheeks when she's finished. "*Now* you look like a princess."

Fresh and clean, I go back out to the balcony. Sure enough, guttering torches moving across the water mark three ships returning to our docks. I bounce on my toes. "Mim, are they preparing our meal? I want it to be ready when she reaches us. She'll probably be starving."

"I'll go check," she says, and leaves me alone to watch the sailing vessels glide into the harbor.

I pace my balcony. I can't wait to ask my Valtia what it was like, if she actually saw the Soturi being tossed by her storm, if the sailors around her were frightened or steadfast as she made the gale rage around them. Those are but a few of the questions I have for her.

Somewhere out in the city, a horn sounds. Its eerie call steadily grows louder as the minutes pass. Finally, just as I'm wondering when Mim will return, she bursts through the doorway.

Her face is pasty pale, like she's painted her own skin with white lead. "Your sedan chair is being brought now," she says, her voice quavering.

I frown as I step forward. "What's wrong?" Alarm clangs in my head, louder than that stupid horn, which is still blaring. "Did some of the Soturi ships make it through?"

She shakes her head. Her mouth twists into the saddest smile I've ever seen. "No, Saadella. By all accounts, the Valtia dealt them a devastating defeat."

I sag with relief. "Then why the long face? Were some of the sailors hurt?"

She comes forward and takes me by the arms. "Elli," she whispers. "You have to come now. You've been summoned."

"Of course," I say.

"By the elders," she adds.

I pause, the oddest feeling stirring inside me, like a beast awakening from its winter sleep. "Mim." It comes out in a snap, and my handmaiden flinches. "Where's the Valtia?"

"She's being brought to her quarters now." Mim pulls me into an embrace, close enough to feel her shudder. "But they're saying she won't live out the night."

# CHAPTER 4

I push Mim away. The ringing in my ears is so loud that I can't hear her voice anymore. I blunder toward the door of my chamber, my only thought to reach my Valtia, begging the stars that when I do, this will all turn out to be a mistake. She'll greet me with affection and we'll have our meal and she'll tell me how she sent the Soturi to their graves in the deep.

Mim loops her arm around my waist as I reach the corridor. "Slow down, Elli. Your chair's coming."

A waste of time. "No."

"Please. Prepare yourself for what's about to happen."

With her hanging on to me, I stride down my corridor toward the domed chamber. It's like wading through deep water as Mim tries to hold me back. *Prepare yourself.*

But I can't bear the thought of losing my Valtia, so I can't bear to think of preparing for it.

When I'm about halfway, Elder Leevi comes toward us from the domed chamber, his apprentice trailing behind him carrying a lantern that throws distorted shadows against the stone walls. "She's in her quarters," he says to us. "You will be taken to the catacombs, the Stone Chamber, to wait for—"

"No." I slap at Mim's clutching hands and quicken my pace as soon as she lets me go. "I will see her now."

Leevi blinks at Mim and then at me. "My Saadella, that is not how we do this."

"I need to see her." My voice echoes off the walls. "I'm not going anywhere else."

Leevi scowls at Mim, as if she's responsible for my behavior. "Very well," he finally says. "Handmaiden, pack her things."

Mim's eyes are red-rimmed and her face is pinched. "Yes, Elder," she says hoarsely. "I'll have them ready to be moved in a few hours."

I gape at him. He's already planning for me to move into the Valtia's chambers, and she's still alive. Disgust burns in my throat as he takes my arm and leads me forward.

"Who's with her now?" I ask when we reach the main chamber, its copper dome arching above us, dark and ominous as the candles gutter around the edge of the room.

"Elder Kauko is attending to her body, but—"

"Her body." It comes out as a squeak.

He purses his lips. "He's trying to make her comfortable. If you insist on being there, it's best if you wait in the antechamber."

It feels like there's a stone on my chest. Each breath is an effort. "I won't wait outside, Elder. I *need* to see her." This time, my voice is loud and sure. I'm not a little girl. And though I've been taught the value of obedience, my Valtia's voice in my head also reminds me that I'm the someday queen. And if Kauko's right, I'll be more powerful than any before me. I'd best start owning it now.

Elder Leevi bows his head. "As you wish."

I enter the corridor where her quarters are located. A few acolytes and maidservants are milling about, their faces ashen. Some of them are crying. Helka's down the hall, weeping loudly. I grit my teeth. They're grieving for a queen who still lives. I walk past them without acknowledging them, striding into her antechamber, which is paneled with carved wood. The hammered copper ceiling looks like it's on fire as we pass beneath with the lantern. Leevi tells his apprentice to wait while we enter, and I'm grateful. The Valtia doesn't need prying eyes right now. She needs me, her Saadella.

Leevi gently grips my shoulder. "Elli, please prepare yourself—"

"Why does everyone keep saying that to me?" I lurch away from him and barrel into her bedchamber.

The room is lit with a few candles. Aleksi stands at the foot of her bed, still as a statue. The door to the balcony is wide open, the drapes fluttering with the breeze from the Motherlake. Goose bumps ride across my skin, but a moment later a gust of heat washes over me, raising beads of sweat. I walk slowly toward the Valtia's bed as Elder Leevi strides ahead of me to alert Elder Kauko, who is hunched over it, his back to me.

Elder Kauko looks over his shoulder and frowns. "You should be in the Stone Chamber. You don't want to see this, my Saadella."

"Don't tell me what I want."

His brows rise in surprise at my defiant tone, but then he gives me a sorrowful, apologetic smile. "I shouldn't have presumed." He bows and moves aside.

My stomach clenches. The Valtia writhes on her bed, her naked body covered in a thin, gauzy sheet. All her adornments have been removed—her crown, her dress, the cuff of Astia—probably taken back to the catacombs. Blood-dotted bandages cling to the crook of each arm. Her white face paint has washed or chipped away, revealing only horror beneath. My heart crumbles as I hear the pained hiss of her breaths. Her beautiful face is marred by black and red patches of blistered skin, but as I move closer, mounting the steps up to the platform where her mattress sits, I see that other parts of her are gray-blue and fissured. Bloodless and frozen. Two of the fingers of her left hand have cracked and fallen away. They lie like chipped stones in the folds of the sheets, ice crystals melting and leaving a wet pink stain. Her eyes are squeezed shut, her head thrown back as agony consumes her.

Sarah Fine

"My Valtia," I whisper, my bottom lip trembling.

As soon as she hears my voice, her eyes open. Once a majestic icy blue, now they're crimson. "Elli," she wheezes. "I'm sorry." A blood-tinged tear slides down her cheek.

As I reach for her right hand, Kauko strokes my arm. "You must be careful, Saadella. Her touch could burn or freeze you in a moment. She can't control it now."

"I'll take my chances," I say, a sob choking off my words. She needs to be touched and to know she isn't alone. I kneel at her bedside and caress her fingers. They're stiff, covered in a layer of ice, but when she feels my palm on hers, the cold melts away. "You did it, didn't you?" I say. "You sent them to the bottom of the Motherlake."

"I did it too well." She moans from between gritted teeth. "All it took was a moment of distraction to lose the balance."

Something Kauko had been trying to prevent. Ice and fire are unpredictable, especially when they collide. A little too much of one or the other and things must have spiraled. "And yet you contained the storm. If you hadn't, all our ships wouldn't have returned."

She looks up at me. "A Valtia protects her people. That is your first duty. Remember."

I will my tears away, but they're stubborn. "Please stay, Valtia. Don't go."

It is the prayer of a child, not a woman. My head is full of memories, of the first time I was carried into her presence, of the kindness in her eyes as she took me into her arms. I was so scared, but as soon as I felt her warmth, the fear melted. *You are precious,* she said. *Your home is with me now.* Her eyes had been filled with tender sadness, but also with love.

"I belong with you," I whisper. "You told me that, my Valtia."

"Sofia," she says as ice crystals prick my palm. For a moment it's so cold around us that I can see our breaths, but it fades quickly. "That's the name I had before."

A name she shed the day she became the Valtia. That she's reclaiming it now is a knife in my heart. But her eyes are pleading, and I cannot deny her. "Sofia."

"You're ready, darling," she rasps. "You're going to be the strongest Valtia there ever was. The stars have foretold all of it. The world has never seen such power."

My mouth goes dry. "You knew about the prophecy?"

She cries out as blistered patches rise on both her legs. Her injuries are coming from the inside out. So much magic, out of balance, tearing its vessel apart. "Can't you do something?" I ask Kauko, forcing myself not to scream. "Help her restore the balance!"

He shakes his head, his fleshy lips pressed together. "It's too late, my Saadella. And too much for a humble priest. Only a Valtia could do such a thing."

What I need to be to save her, she must die for me to become.

"This isn't fair." I lower my head to kiss the frozen skin of her wrist. "If I had the magic now, I would use all of it to make you well."

She squeezes my hand, but her fingers are so hot that they're burning me. I clench my teeth and smile at her, tears streaking down my face. Her hair is haloed around her head, sections of it singed to a blackened crisp, others covered over with ice. It crunches softly as she moves. "I know the bind of it," she says in a halting voice. "I remember the day my own Valtia died. But you will go on, Elli. I'll always be with you, and so will all the Valtias before me. You'll carry our magic inside you. You will never be alone."

I bow my head. I don't want this. Not yet. But to deny my duty would be to fail her—and all of Kupari. "I will honor you."

She looks at me, her ruby eyes full of pain and love. "You already have," she says, her voice fading to nothing.

Her body convulses. Elder Kauko cries out and yanks me away from the bed as flames burst from her chest, spiraling high enough to reach the ceiling. I scream, unable to look away as icicles stab their way out of her belly, her back, her neck. She makes no noise, but I am made of sound. I'm a frenzied animal, lost to reason as I try to get to her. I am so certain. So certain:

If I touch her, I can make her better.

Kauko is crushing me, his shoulder pressed over my face, his hand cupping the back of my head. He smells of sweat and blood and failure as he holds me to the floor. I stare at the hammered copper ceiling, which reflects the inferno below, the Valtia's arched back, arms and legs flung wide, bleeding and burning and freezing.

Dying.

There's a loud hissing sound. "Let it burn out," I hear Elder Aleksi say. "We need to take the Saadella to the Stone Chamber. We shouldn't have waited this long."

Kauko's weight lifts from me, but before I can lunge for the bed again, he and Aleksi drag me away. Sofia's still burning, thrashing weakly. Her blood is smeared across the sheet and dripping onto the floor. The sight of her red eyes, wide open and begging for release, follows me into the ante-chamber. My thoughts are spinning. My body humming and buzzing. It feels like a chasm has opened inside my chest, ripping asunder what was once tightly knit. I shudder as my stomach revolts, emptying me out. Two acolytes dive for the marble floor and absorb the mess with their own robes.

Leevi shouts orders to the apprentices and acolytes as Aleksi and Kauko carry me through the domed chamber, all the way to the back, where a stone staircase leads below. Their hands are gentle but relentless. No matter which way I twist, they won't let me escape. My Valtia. My *Valtia*. I scream for her over and over again until my voice is shredded. I hear mourners calling out, but I can't make out their words. The growing void inside draws me inward, commanding all my attention while it crashes and roars like an avalanche, carving me hollow.

My feet skim the floor as the elders reach the bottom of the stairs. We're in the catacombs now, the walls oozing with the essence of the Motherlake, blades of rock jutting from the floor and ceiling of the caverns and tunnels. The way is lit with torches, but it's still a tomb, full of inky shadows that swim with secrets and age-old ritual. The elders finally pull me into a small, round chamber and set me down on a slab of smooth stone that takes up most of the room, leaving only a narrow aisle around the edge. The slab is neither cold nor hot. It feels like hard, unforgiving nothing beneath me.

"When the magic rises within you, don't fight it," Kauko says, his breath sawing from his lungs, his brow sheened with sweat. "It's seeking its new home. It won't hurt you."

I kneel and look down at my hands. There's still a faint smear of red where the Valtia's lips touched my palm. "It killed her. It tore her apart."

"You cannot fear the magic!" Kauko urges. "Sofia was destroyed because she made a mistake."

I think of the bandages in the crook of her arms and how drawn she looked this afternoon. "Why did you bleed her? Are you sure that didn't make her weaker instead of stronger?"

"I had been trying to help her maintain the balance of magic in her body by draining off some of the excess," says Kauko. "She was not the strongest Valtia we have known, and she overestimated her power today. You will be stronger. Wiser. Better." He hesitates when I glare at him. "She was right, Saadella, when she said the stars had foretold your power. I'm not criticizing Sofia, I'm simply—"

"Call her *Valtia*," I snap. Her name on his fleshy lips is a blasphemy.

His dark eyes are full of patience and pity, which makes me want to scream. And when he starts to talk about the prophecy again, the one that foretold my birth, the power I will control, I can't take it.

"*Stop.*" My palms slap against the stone and my head hangs. Is this how it's supposed to feel? The red flame mark on my leg is sending waves of numbness along my limbs, all the way to my fingertips and toes.

"It's happening," Aleksi whispers eagerly.

The void inside me grows, clawing at the walls of my chest, at the soft flesh of my belly. I let out a sob. "I just want her back." I lay my forehead on the stone as the grief eats me up.

"You must welcome the magic," says Kauko. "Open your arms to it. Stop fighting."

"I'm not fighting." How can I? I'm just lying here as the emptiness devours me. I'm too desolate to fight.

"You're focused on *her*, and not on accepting the magic!" shouts Aleksi.

The sudden frustration in his voice chastens me. If I am to honor her, Sofia, my Valtia, then I need to accept what she's given me. I suck in a shaky breath. My legs are folded beneath me. My face is pressed to the stone. I spread my arms, palms up. Though I never wanted to say good-bye to her, I've been waiting for this day for as long as I can remember. With fear—and with eagerness. Finally I will know. Finally I will be complete, what I was always meant to be. A new Elli—no. A new *person*. One who is powerful. And useful. And vital. I'll gladly take what's left of my Valtia inside me. I'll become someone who would make her proud. "I'm ready," I say, my whole body trembling.

Aleksi and Kauko murmur their approval.

From above us comes a deep *boom*, and my ears pop. Aleksi and Kauko gasp. A wave of nothingness crushes me to the stone slab, so heavy that I can't move. It forces the air from my chest. I can't feel my legs or arms. Terror pulses in my veins as my vision goes black. My head becomes a roaring blank space. I squeeze my eyes shut. More than anything, I wish my Valtia would appear and take my hand. I wish she would tell me I'm hers, and that everything will be all right soon.

I push the thought away. Magic. I must focus on the magic.

I lose my grip on time.

Tears drip from my cheeks, from the tip of my nose. But gradually, my breaths come a little easier. The noise in my mind fades, moment by moment. My limbs tingle and my lips buzz with numbness. When I've finally gathered the strength, I push myself up, my arms shaking. Kauko and I stare at each other. His eyes are shining.

"It's done," he says, his voice tremulous. "Aleksi, call the others."

Aleksi disappears into the corridor, and Kauko kneels at my side. "You did well," he says. "How do you feel?"

I look down at my body, now in possession of a magic that can sink ships. Raise crops. Heal wounds. My heart beats in my chest, and I swear I hear it echo. *Hollow*, I almost say. "I—I don't know. I feel . . . all right?"

His brows tent upward in puzzlement, and then a smile

splits his round face as he laughs. "'All right.' You feel 'all right.'" He stands up slowly, shaking his head. "Only the most powerful Valtia in all the ages would say that."

Seeing his mirth draws a weak smile to my lips. I rise to my knees but have to catch myself as dizziness overwhelms me. My legs feel like wooden blocks dangling from my torso. "Maybe not so all right," I murmur.

"You'll need to rest for a few days. Your dreams . . . be prepared for the dreams. The ice and fire work their will while you slumber. It is a burden the most powerful wielders must bear, but as your magic finds its balance within you, they will subside."

"Of course. Dreams." I rub at my temple. My head feels like it's been stuffed with wool.

The sound of thumping footsteps precedes a group of priests, apprentices, and acolytes. They crowd into the Stone Chamber and hover in the tunnel outside, trying to get a good look at me, offering kind smiles and bows. They're depending on me. I sit up straighter, ignoring my echoing heartbeat, my numb legs, my tingling lips. I need to look like the queen I am.

Aleksi pushes his way through the onlookers and kneels before me. "Are you ready to accept your fate?"

I nod.

He takes a carved wooden box from his apprentice. I recognize it immediately. He sets it on my stone slab and opens it, revealing the cuff of Astia. "This is your ally, your sword and shield."

He looks down at my right hand, and I lift my arm. It feels like a hunk of rock, but I hold it steady as Aleski fastens the cuff to my wrist. It glints in the torchlight, the same shade as my hair, deep and burnished and swirling with the bloodred runes that give it power. As soon as the clasp is in place, Aleksi releases my arm, which falls to my side.

"From this day until you take your final breath, you are no longer Elli," he says, getting to his feet and gesturing for me to do the same. "That name belonged to a girl, and now you are a queen."

It takes all my focus to get my legs to push me from the ground. I feel like a fawn taking its first steps. My arms rise from my sides to aid my balance. I draw in a breath. I *am* balance. Perfect balance.

Everyone smiles as I stand steady before them. Aleksi holds out his arms, presenting me. "From this day until you take your final breath," he continues, louder this time, "you are the Valtia!"

I incline my head, and they clap. Kauko is grinning as one of the acolytes hands him a stout candle on a copper plate. It's a perfect column of beeswax, never lit.

Kauko gives me a sheepish smile. "I know it's a small thing to ask of such profound magic, but it is our tradition. If you will, my Valtia . . . light this candle with your magic. Illuminate our way as we ascend into the temple and greet this wonderful new era."

I take a moment to thank Sofia for this gift of her magic, and I promise her I'll use it well, just as she did. Then I stare at the wick, yellow and waxy. I imagine it bursting into a perfect tongue of flame.

Nothing happens.

I close my eyes and wait for the fire to rise within me, a jewel of golden heat to adorn the candle, to melt the wax, to . . . I open my eyes.

"Ah," I say in a shaky voice. "How am I supposed to do it?"

Aleksi's brow furrows. "It shouldn't be difficult for you, Valtia. Unless you're worried you'll set us all aflame with your power?"

There's nervous laughter around the chamber—if the magic were out of control, that's exactly what could happen. But my magic, the Valtia's magic, is completely balanced, and therefore easy to control.

*Until it isn't,* whisper my thoughts. The memory of Sofia's body being torn apart appears before my eyes. Kauko touches my arm and snaps me back to the present. "There's no need to fear, my Valtia," he says. "You can stop holding back. The barest passing thought will light the candle. Simply wish for flame, and it will appear."

I thought I'd already tried that. But I do it again, focusing hard on the torch guttering at the back of the chamber. I capture the image of fire in my mind and then stare once more at the virgin wick. My heart thuds in my hollow chest. I reach out and lift the candle from its plate, wrapping my fingers around its base and holding it up in front of me. The cuff of Astia lies heavy and comforting on my wrist. Only a few hours ago, it helped raise waterspouts from the lake and draw lightning from the sky. Lighting a candle is child's play. I chuckle, pushing down the uncertainty rising within me. "Never doubt," I whisper.

Kauko smiles and returns his gaze to the wick. So do I. My stare consumes it. I call for heat to blaze at its tip, to blacken the wick, to burst into flame. I imagine the waft of warmth against my cheeks and the cheers of my new subjects. My arms begin to tremble with the strain. I clench my teeth.

*Please.*

*Please catch fire.*

*Please burn.*

It doesn't.

# CHAPTER 5

I don't know how long I stand there before Kauko takes pity on me. He takes the candle from my stiff fingers. "My deepest apologies, Valtia," he says, bowing his head. "You have been through so much tonight. It was selfish of us to ask you for anything before you've had a chance to rest."

His hands shake a little as he removes the cuff of Astia from my wrist and places it in the wooden box. While he gives it to his apprentice, I blink down at my empty hands, at the tiny, faint smear of lip paint on my palm. Hesitantly, I raise my head. No one speaks, no one smiles, but all of them stare.

Aleksi's eyes meet mine. "Clear the room!" he barks, his jowls quivering. "Our Valtia must have quiet and rest."

Leevi, his slender shoulders tense beneath his robe,

ushers out all the apprentices and acolytes. As the last apprentice steps into the rocky corridor, I hear him whisper to a female acolyte next to him, "I can light a candle without even thinking about it."

The words hit like stones in a pool, sending ripples of misgiving along my limbs. "Elder," I say in a hoarse voice. "What's wrong with me?"

Kauko takes my arm and helps me step off the stone slab. My stockinged feet are soaked and aching, no longer numb. In fact, my whole self hurts. I feel like I've been trampled by a horse. My red gown is damp and stained with sweat. Surely I'm the most bedraggled Valtia that ever was.

"I'm sure nothing is wrong with you, my queen," Kauko says quietly as he guides me out of the chamber and toward the steps. Aleksi mounts them ahead of us, and I wonder if he's going up to make sure I don't have an audience as I'm led to my bedchamber. "I think the strain of witnessing Sofia's final moments has jarred you. It was a mistake to allow you to see her that way." His grip on my elbow is steady and comforting as he takes me up the stairs.

"I insisted," I say, rubbing at my throat, raw from my cries of grief. "It wasn't Leevi's fault."

"You are generous, Valtia." His frown is so deep that it looks like someone's carved a divot from the corner of his nose to the edge of his jaw.

I pull my gaze away from it, because it stirs up uneasiness within me. "I'll rest," I tell him. "I'm sure that in the morning, I'll have recovered."

"I have no doubt." He puts his arm around my back as we stride through the domed chamber and into the Saadella's wing. "You'll stay in your old bedchamber tonight while we ready the Valtia's quarters for you."

While they scrub scorch marks from the ceiling and floor, while they scour her blood from the stones, while they mop up the icy water and toss the burned mattress in the refuse pile. Bile rises from my stomach. I'm not sure I could ever sleep in that room. "Will we have a funeral?"

One of the few memories I have outside this temple is of the last Valtia's funeral, her white body covered over with coppery gauze and bedecked with spring blooms. It was the day before I was found. My mother took me to the docks, where she lifted me in her arms so I could see between the shoulders of the other citizens who'd come to bid the queen farewell. The dead Valtia had looked perfect and unmarred. I remember thinking she would sit up and wave as they slid her boat into the waters of the Motherlake, as it silently carried her from our shore. I remember being horrified when tongues of fire raced up the sides of the pyre to devour her.

I remember screaming.

I also remember the new Valtia, *my* Valtia, standing on her paarit at the end of the main dock, her arms raised. At the time I didn't know that she was the one who moved the boat into the deep waters, that she was responsible for the fire. I only knew it scared me.

"The elders will meet to discuss it," says Kauko as we reach my wing. "There are complications."

My stomach convulses again. Complications. Like the fact that she was torn and burned to pieces. She could not be a pretty, peaceful corpse. For all I know, she's nothing but a soggy pile of ash. "Oh, stars," I moan, doubling over to retch.

"Elli!" Mim calls down the hall. Her hands are on my waist a moment later, and she presses a dry cloth to my mouth.

Kauko clears his throat. "You are not to call her by that name ever again, handmaiden," he says sternly. "She's the Valtia now. Show respect."

Mim steps back and bows low. "My Valtia." Her voice reeks of tears. "Let me take you to your chamber."

Kauko releases me. "We'll come for you tomorrow." He rubs his hand over his bald head and looks me over. "You'll be better then."

Mim raises her eyebrows as he turns his back and stalks toward the domed chamber. She leads me into my quarters. "Why did he say that?"

"I can't, Mim. Just clean me off, please?" I whisper. It's bad enough that I couldn't light the flame. If I have to tell her about it, I'll shatter into a million shards of sorrow and shame. *My Valtia.* I put my hand on my chest. *Please don't be disappointed.*

While Mim bathes me, handling me like a living doll, I concentrate on finding the magic inside me. Is it in my gut? My heart? Deep inside my bones? Just behind my eyes? Why can't I feel it? Why is it hiding from me? I expected it to come bubbling forth like a spring of icy water, to evaporate on my fingertips in a cloud of steam. I expected it to fill me to the brim, to make me what I always should have been, to be so thick and shimmering that I would feel nothing but confidence. But all I feel is . . . emptiness.

Mim tucks me into my bed and spreads extra blankets over me. "Tonight I'll sleep at the foot of your bed instead of going to my room," she says. "If you need a single thing, water, a cool cloth, a hot stone for your feet, just say my name. A mere whisper will draw me to your side." She smooths my hair from my brow. "I know you weren't eager for this day to come, my Valtia, but you were born for this. I'm proud to serve you."

I am so lost and desperate for comfort that I almost ask her to lie next to me, to allow me to press my face to her neck and coil my arms around her. But I remember that moment on the balcony earlier, when I realized she only remained close because I commanded it. So I shut my eyes as she withdraws, readying myself for what comes next. Kauko warned me of the dreams, and with the way Mim is coddling me—even more than she *usually* coddles me—I suspect he warned her as well.

The breeze from the Motherlake slips through the open balcony door and cools my face. I dwell in the darkness, relaxing into it. In my silent sleep, I wait for the dreams that come with powerful magic.

They never arrive.

A warm hand caresses my cheek. "Valtia, the priests have summoned you."

*Valtia?* My eyes flutter open. Sunbeams filter through the balcony doorway, filling my chamber with warm light. For a moment, I'm all confusion. What time is it? Is it harvest day? But as I sit up, the truth winds around me like a rope. My Valtia is gone, and I'm the queen now.

Mim gives me a half smile. "You slept like a stone. From what Kauko described, I thought you'd be thrashing all night!" She takes my hand and pulls back the blankets before helping me to stand up. "Though I suppose the strongest Valtia in all of history would weather such things with grace." She grins. "As she always has."

I force myself to smile back. I had no dreams. All I had was darkness as deep as the Motherlake, as empty as a cavern. "I am eager to learn the extent of my powers today." I am ashamed at the quaver in my voice, but Mim merely nods.

"I have some information before you go, if you want it," she says.

I step forward to allow her to pull my nightgown over my head. "About the Soturi?"

"No. They are not the only problem in the outlands, and now that their invasion has been repulsed, the city council and the elders will turn their attention back to the bandits. Especially after what happened yesterday."

"What?" I ask, my heart beginning to pound.

"That fight the Valtia mentioned as we prepared you for

the harvest ceremony. A group of miners took it upon themselves to clear the cave system they plan to mine."

"The one where the bandits are squatting." And the one Aleksi said might hold the last unmined copper on the peninsula.

She nods. "I got more details early this morning. Two miners died of their injuries."

I want to bury my head in my hands, but I stay completely still. This is my responsibility now, and I will deal with it as a queen should. "When I meet with the elders, we will discuss it, and I will decide how we will proceed."

She bites her lip. "There's more. The miners who died . . . they were burned."

My brow furrows. "Burned with what?"

She leans forward, nearly bursting with her news. "The rumor is that it was magic."

I sit down on the bed like my legs have been swept from under me. "A fire wielder in the outlands?" The priests scour the city and the homesteads for magical children every month, and it is considered a great privilege to live in the Temple on the Rock, so their families give them up readily. And the only people in the outlands are criminals who have been banished from the city. "That seems unlikely, Mim. Besides, a torch could do the job just as handily."

"I said the same thing to Irina, the scullery maid who told me, but she said there have been whispers about rogue wielders for years, Ell—" Mim presses her lips shut and gives me a sheepish smile. "My Valtia." Then she claps her hands and pulls me to my feet again, like she is about to give me a special treat. "Now that you are the queen, you can find out for sure instead of relying on me for gossip! And then you can deal with any rogues who threaten our miners. Or anyone else, for that matter." She's almost glowing now, and it makes my stomach hurt.

While Mim clothes me in a simple red gown and plaits my hair down my back, the feeling only intensifies until I finally recognize it as hunger. "Can you get my breakfast for me, Mim?"

Her smile falters. "The priests said I am to give you nothing. But . . . I'm sure that after you meet with them, we can order you a fine spread from the kitchens."

"Water?"

She bites her lip. "They forbade it, Valtia," she mumbles, her glow dimming quickly.

"Since when do the priests overrule the Valtia's wishes," I snap. When I see her blanch, I realize I've put her in a terrible position. "Never mind," I say, squeezing her hand. "I'm not thirsty anyway."

I'm parched, but I care about her too much to say so. I walk to the door with my head held high. Today will be the day I show the elder priests the magic inside me. I'll make them quake with the certainty of it, and then I'll deal with the bandits and any rogues hiding among them. Today I begin my reign. "Where to?"

"The catacombs," Aleksi says as he enters my chamber. "Good morning, Valtia." He bows. As he raises his head, his dark eyes sweep up my body, as if he expects me to have transformed overnight. "I hope you were able to rest despite the dreams."

I bite the inside of my cheek. "Thank you for your concern, Elder Aleksi. I'm quite well rested." A splinter of doubt pierces my determination. Too well rested, perhaps.

I keep my back straight and my head high as we descend into the catacombs. I wish I could face all this in the daylight instead of in this cold, dank tomb. This is the realm of the cloistered acolytes, the ones who are not chosen as apprentices and live in seclusion after they reach the middle of their third decade. They live together, one united community, completely hidden from the distractions of the world above, devoting themselves to the Valtia's magic. I have always wondered how pale they must be after years without sunlight, but whenever I asked, Elder Kauko merely chuckled and reminded me that some of them wield fire—they do not want for light or heat. *And I will be able to wield fire now too. Starting today. Starting now.*

Veins of green and orange copper glint in the torchlight as I follow Aleksi past the Stone Chamber to another circular room. This one is larger, with four tiers of wide, steep steps leading down to a small arena that looks more like a pit from where I stand. Sitting on the steps are the priests, thirty of them in all. No acolytes or apprentices today. Elder Aleksi takes me to a set of shallow steps that lead to the bottom. "Take your place in the arena, Valtia, and we'll begin."

My heart thuds, and again I feel it reverberate within me. When I reach the flat, slippery stone floor, I turn in place. Aleksi is sitting down with Kauko and Leevi, our three elders, on the lowest tier of this arena. If their robes weren't so long, from this vantage point I'd be able to see what hides beneath.

"After the events of last night," says Leevi, his voice filling the chamber, "we wanted to make sure you are ready before we proceed with the coronation." He smiles at me, but between his gaunt face and his jutting brow, it looks more like a grimace. "We know you have always been an obedient and loyal Saadella, if a bit too inquisitive." He pauses, as if to make sure everyone notes that fault, before continuing. "But you have always respected the role of Valtia. Therefore we expect you to understand the crucial nature of what we ask."

I clasp my hands in front of me. The feel of my own clammy fingers sends a chill down my back. "Of course, Elder. At a time like this, having lost their beloved queen, the people need to know they're secure and protected."

Kauko nods his approval. "Well said, my Valtia. This could not be a more critical time for that. Now, all we ask is that you practice your ability to wield ice and fire. As soon as you complete these simple manipulations, we'll proceed with your coronation. It shouldn't take more than a few minutes."

I swallow, but my mouth is so dry that it hurts my throat. "What would you like me to do?" I say, my voice pitifully soft in this roomful of staring priests. I wonder if Sofia had to go through this. I wonder how she felt.

"Three basic tasks is all," says Aleksi, smiling as if it

is nothing. "The same that we ask of all our apprentices and acolytes when they first come into our care, so that we may evaluate which element—ice or fire—is more powerful within them." He chuckles. "Of course, you will easily complete each."

He gestures to my left, where a shallow copper bowl full of water sits on a stone pedestal. "Turn the water to ice." He points to my right, at a sheet of parchment on another pedestal. "Burn it to ash." Then he slides his plump finger over to the third pedestal, directly in front of me. On it sits a pebble, the kind that litters the shore of the Motherlake. "Make that rise into the air and float."

All things they expect from apprentices and acolytes. Simple.

I hitch what I hope is a serene smile onto my face. "As you wish." I move to the basin of water first, because I remember trying to awaken the fire inside me last night, and I don't feel ready to burn the parchment just yet. My heart drumming in my hollow chest, I close my eyes and reach for the magic that I know must be there.

*Help me, Sofia, my Valtia. I know you would never abandon me.*

I hold out my hand, palm down, a few inches above the surface of the water. There is complete silence in this arena, but I can feel the priests' rapt attention like fingers clutching at the hem of my dress. I blow a slow breath from between my tingling lips and summon the cold. I picture the thick ice that forms in rough plates over the Motherlake in winter, the chunks of it that bob and collide in the spring. When I feel the shiver, my soul cheers. Here it comes.

But when I open my eyes, the water is . . . as watery as ever. What I felt was the chill of the chamber, nothing more. For the first time, a blade of fear slices straight down my backbone. I try again, gritting my teeth and drawing the cool air around me like a cloak, willing it to coalesce in a frigid blast of air.

Behind me, I hear a soft grumble, one priest whispering his doubt to another. I whirl around—it's Eljas, his flattish nose and wide-set blue eyes giving him the appearance of a toad. He was one of my tutors, assigned to teach me the geography of the known world, and I remember his musty, dank smell better than any of my lessons. "How am I supposed to concentrate if you're gossiping, Priest Eljas?"

Eljas crosses his arms over his chest. "You shouldn't have to concentrate," he says in an even voice. "Freezing the water in that bowl should be as easy as breathing."

I scowl up at him. "It's not as if I've ever been taught a thing about how to wield the magic."

"You need to be *taught* how to do something this paltry?" He waves his hand, and the water in the bowl turns to cloudy ice. The priest next to him mirrors the movement, and the ice instantly melts—and then the water begins to boil.

It turns to steam that bathes my face, leaving it slick and warm. It's a mercy, because perhaps it conceals the tear that slips from my eye. My Valtia said she'd never leave me, and now I can't find her. She promised. She *promised*.

THE IMPOSTOR QUEEN

But her promises weren't unbreakable, as it turns out.

Kauko stands up. "Try the stone, my Valtia," he says softly. "Use the heat and cold to raise it from the pedestal." He gives me an encouraging smile, but it's the only one in the room. All the others wear frowns of doubt, and Aleksi's is particularly vile, his black brows so low that I can barely see his eyes.

I compose myself and stride over to the stone pedestal that stands between me and the elders. I recall all my lessons with Aleksi about the weather and wind, about what happens when hot and cold air collide. Straining every fiber of my muscles and heart and brain, I focus on changing the temperature of the pedestal, on heating it up while I cool the air above it. But instead of feeling the swell of power inside me, all I have is the echo of my pulse thrumming inside my head.

Aleksi shoots to his feet and points at me. "You denied the magic," he growls, his thin lips pulled back from his bright-white teeth. "You were so wrapped up in your affection for Sofia that you chased away the power!" He looks around the room. "I can't sense magic in her at all. She doesn't want to be the Valtia!"

Kauko grasps Aleksi's arm. His square jaw is tense as he says, "I was there. She submitted to the magic. I heard her words with my own ears. And you know very well that the Valtia's magic is harder to detect because the elements balance each other out."

Aleksi tears his sleeve from Kauko's grip. "She said the words, but she didn't mean them. How else can you explain

75

this?" he hisses, gesturing at the tiny pebble that still sits, unmoving, on its pedestal. He clenches his fist and raises it in the air, and the stone glides upward. As it rises, my stomach sinks. With a flick of his wrist, he sends it flying across the room, so violently that when it hits the wall, it shatters above the heads of several priests in the top row. "She couldn't even make it wobble! She couldn't alter the water, and I would bet my *life* that she can't burn the parchment."

His dark eyes meet mine, full of challenge. "Prove me wrong, *Valtia*." He says the royal term like a curse.

"How dare you," I whisper, but I can already see that I've lost the faith of my priests. My doubt floods in, peeling off my fragile confidence and leaving only raw pink skin, so easily bruised and torn. "I loved my Valtia. I was loyal to her. And her magic is inside me."

"But you've corrupted yourself," he says. "Gorging yourself on petty gossip from your handmaiden, on childish sentiment—" He bites back more accusations and turns away, as if he cannot stand to look at me. All his quiet resentment of my questions throughout the years seems to have risen now, at the most terrible time, right when I need the guidance and support of my elders.

The priests are murmuring among themselves, their puzzlement and anger rippling through the chamber, buffeting me from all sides. Leevi stands before me, and for a moment he looks as hollow as I feel. "The shock," he says. "She had such a shock last night."

"A shock? No thanks to you, Leevi." Aleksi's double chin

wobbles as he speaks. "If you were so concerned, you should have brought her straight to the Stone Chamber instead of indulging her selfish whims." He jabs his finger at Leevi. "And Sofia was shocked too, when her Valtia wilted and faded over the course of a fortnight. But the power roiled within her as soon as Kaarin took that final breath. That is how it's always been. Don't tell me about shock."

"The copper, then," Leevi whispers, tossing the priests a nervous look.

Aleksi shakes his head. "We'd all be affected. And here of all places, that would not be a problem."

"What about the copper?" I ask, loudly enough for several priests to stop their grumbling and turn to us.

"I said it is not a problem," Aleksi replies in a low voice, every word drenched in contempt.

Kauko gives me a sidelong glance. "You read the prophecy, Aleksi."

Aleksi's nostrils flare. "The part of it we have, yes."

"You only have *part* of it?" I whisper, but doubt mutes my voice, and they don't seem to hear me.

Kauko sighs. "We read the star signs together, Aleksi, and they confirmed it. You've seen the clarity and size of her blood-flame mark—you were the one who found her! But perhaps the magic is buried deep. Maybe this is the part of the prophecy that was lost. Perhaps we're witnessing something completely new. And perhaps the current"—he, too, glances at the priests, many of whom are still staring—"*shortage* merely heralds the start of a new age."

Leevi, fidgeting on Aleksi's other side, nods his agreement with Kauko, and upon seeing it, Aleksi's eyes narrow. "Then we must try to dig this magic up from wherever it is buried, because that would mean we need it now more than ever."

The way he says it, little flecks of spittle flying from his mouth, fills me with dread. "Perhaps," I say, "if I had a little more time—"

"We have no time," shouts Aleksi, his face turning red. "The Soturi will regroup, or they could use their forces in Vasterut to strike again. The thieves' caverns are brimming with criminals who are raiding the farmsteads and attacking our miners! We need to get that copper. And the winter is coming—the people depend on that dome of warmth. We have no time!" His shrieking tone makes me wince, and when he leans forward, I nearly stagger back. "But what we do have is an obstinate girl too absorbed in her own feelings and desires to wield the magic *we* need to survive!"

I bow my head, afraid he might be right. "Wh-whatever you ask of me, I will do, Elders," I stammer.

Kauko clasps his hands in front of his belly. "What about the trials?"

Leevi's jaw drops. "No Valtia in our history has ever been put through—"

"But perhaps we are witnessing something completely new." Aleksi throws Kauko a resentful look and puts his hands on his wide hips, his fingers bunching in the rough black fabric of his robe. "I think Elder Kauko's suggestion is wise, as always."

The other priests, who have all been whispering to themselves while the elders argue, fall silent. Kauko kneels on the step, and I look up at him. There is a dark shadow of stubble on his jaw and apology in his eyes. "Sometimes magic wielders are unable to summon the power at will," he explains. "But in a stressful situation, it never fails them." He winks. "It usually bursts forth with such strength that the wielder herself is surprised at the force of it."

"Let us proceed, then," I practically shout. At this point, I don't care what they do to me, as long as it brings the magic out. I know I can't do it on my own. I feel nothing inside me but empty numbness. Is that my grief, suppressing the ice and fire? If so, then why didn't Sofia experience the same thing after the death of her Valtia? I remember how sad she looked when she greeted me for the first time. She was still in mourning. Yet she'd already been crowned Valtia. She was already able to wield her power with ease and grace. But if my inability to do the same thing isn't because of grief, then what's wrong with me? Am I corrupted by my hungry curiosity, as Aleksi says? Are my desires, which I barely understand myself, causing this? Whatever it is, I'd give anything to fix it.

I straighten my shoulders and slowly turn in place, letting my icy-blue eyes take in every face. I feel the buzzing waves of numbness radiating from my blood-flame birthmark. I am not a mistake, not a commoner. I was chosen to be Valtia, and the stars were aligned on the day of my birth, and though I don't know exactly what that means, I know what Sofia said to me.

*Never doubt.*

"Elders," I say in a high, steady voice. "I will face the trials with eagerness."

Kauko nods his approval. "We will begin at midnight, then."

The priests get up and begin to file out, but Leevi comes down the stairs and takes me by the arm. "Are you taking me back to my quarters?" I ask. I can't tell Mim of all my fears—I couldn't bear to disappoint her—but more than anything right now, I need to feel the warmth of her touch.

Leevi's blue eyes are as dark as a grave. "No, my Valtia. We have another place for you to wait." His grip on me tightens as he marches me up the steps.

# CHAPTER 6

It is all I can do not to scream. With every breath, I will myself into silence. I tell myself to be still, to focus. I ignore the pain in my knees, my hips, my shoulders, my head. A bit of discomfort is nothing compared to what is at stake.

When I first saw the copper trunk, I came to a lurching halt, and Leevi dragged me the rest of the way. A single torch lit the tiny chamber, with dripping ceilings and a metallic scent hanging heavy in the air. Leevi had to stoop to avoid hitting his head. He leaned forward and opened the heavy lid, sickly green in the flickering light. Then he gestured toward the hallway, and two female acolytes entered, their eyes downcast. "Remove her clothes and help her inside," Leevi instructed as I gaped in horror.

"Elder, why—," I began.

He let out a sigh. "We are doing everything we can for you, my Valtia," he said, an impatient edge sharpening his voice. "Must you question us now? Perhaps your time is best spent focused on the magic and how to use it to serve your people, who so desperately need this gift only you can give them."

My cheeks burned with shame. "Yes, Elder," I whispered.

He left, and the acolytes stripped me of my clothing, leaving me shivering and naked. They had to help me climb into the cold, unforgiving box because I could not control my trembling. I curled my knees to my chest and lay on my side, the metal walls cold against my shins, my spine, the back of my neck. My nose burned with the scent of sweat and terror.

"I know you have the magic, my Valtia," one of the acolytes whispered as she looked down at me. "I hope this helps you."

She shut the lid, and I gulped back the first of a thousand stifled screams. I don't know how long ago they left me here. Long enough for me to see things. Sofia, arching back in pain, her eyes bloodred. Mim, letting down her hair when she thought no one was looking, stroking her hand along her throat as firelight made her skin glow. I hold on to that one for as long as I can, because I swear, I can feel the darkness eating me, first my toes, then my fingertips. I can sense its breath, chilling my skin, reeking of secret horrors.

I am not the first person to lie in this box. I am not the

first person to stain it with the weakness of my body. And I wonder how many others have curled in here before me, and how many of them lost their minds as a result.

"Stop," I whisper. "If the elders put you in here, it is because they believe it will help."

I saw the need in their eyes, and I know their anger at me comes from that need. They love and serve the people, who depend on the wielders in the temple to protect them. So they have encased me in a copper sarcophagus. . . . Several bits of knowledge interlock at once, pulling my thoughts from my own plight. The Kupari people produce magic wielders, when no one else does. We live on a peninsula rich with copper—it decorates our homes, our bodies. We eat off copper plates and drink from copper pitchers. And to stimulate the magic within their new queen, they have encased her in a copper coffin.

Copper has something to do with our fire and ice magic—the source of our greatness and our shield against the world—but it seems we are running out of it. And here I lie, prophesied to be more powerful than any Valtia before. Maybe it's because the Kupari need their queen more than ever.

*Please*, I pray. To the magic, the stars, Sofia, and all the Valtias past. *Please do not abandon me.* I lose myself in those pleas until the coffin squeaks open and the acolytes pull me out. My hair hangs around my face in damp, greasy tendrils, and my fingernails are grimy. I stink—the acolyte wrinkles her nose as she pulls my dress over my head and down my legs, covering my nakedness. If Mim were here, she would never stand for this. Stars, how I wish she were here. I swallow back my sorrow as I think of her face. If she ever looks at me with disappointment, I'll break.

Maybe I should be grateful she's not here now. I want to return to her victorious, so together we can move to the Valtia's wing as queen and handmaiden. She's given up so much for me—a regular life, a family, the chance to have children of her own—she deserves honor and ease, and I'm determined to give it to her.

"We're taking you back to the testing chamber now, my Valtia," one of the acolytes says as she takes my elbow and leads me to the corridor.

I smooth back my hair and try to wet my sticky tongue. I remember Kauko's assurance, how the trials always work, how under stress, even suppressed magic bursts forth to protect its wielder. I wipe my clammy palms on my dress and follow the other acolyte, who carries a torch to light our way. The three elders are waiting inside the room, the same place we were early this morning, along with one other young female acolyte and a lean male apprentice.

In his hand is a whip.

A cold, tingling sensation descends from the top of my head all the way down to my feet. The whip is multi-tailed, several braided strips of leather hanging from the stiff handle. I've heard Mim tell of how disobedient servants sometimes get lashes, up to ten at a time, and can't lie on their backs for days. My stomach goes tight. Very well. The whip. If the prickling, icy feeling in my gut is any sign, the copper grave I've just escaped has awakened my sleeping magic, and this will be more than enough to bring it out.

When I reach the base of the stairs, the apprentice looks me in the eye. But when I smile at him, he looks away, his jaw clenched. The three female acolytes, shaved bald like their apprentice counterparts, push back their hoods and regard me somberly. The elders take their seats, and Aleksi spreads his chubby fingers over his robed knees. "The trials will begin with thirty lashes," he says loudly. "Acolytes, strip her to the waist."

*Thirty* lashes? I turn my back to the elders so they can't see my fear. I don't want the apprentice or the acolytes to see it either. Cool hands touch my shoulders. "Pardon, Valtia," one of the young women says. She has pale-blue eyes like mine and gentle hands like Mim's. She unbuttons the back of my dress and bares my skin to men and women alike. My eyes sting with the humiliation as they pull my arms from my sleeves and leave the bodice to hang down over my skirt. I cross my arms over my breasts.

"This way," says another of the acolytes, this one with spots all over her face. She was the one who closed the lid of the trunk, whose words of faith were the only spark of light before it all went dark. Her hands are hot as she guides me to the opposite wall; she must have an affinity for fire magic. She and the third acolyte, who has a lovely, wide face and well-defined cheekbones, each take one of my wrists and raise them over my head, placing my palms flat against the stone wall of the arena. They reach up to the first tier and pull down two bronze cuffs attached to the floor of the tier with a thick chain.

I let out an involuntary whimper as they close the heavy shackles over my wrists. How different these feel from the cuff of Astia I wore last night. That copper cuff was my ally. I *felt* it. But these chains—they're the enemy, heartless and cold. My bare chest touches the damp stone wall, and I shiver violently. After so many hours spent naked in a metal box, with no water and no food since yesterday afternoon, I have no strength to steady myself. The spotty acolyte squeezes my shoulder before releasing me, as if she forgives me for all of it. I want to kiss her cheek in gratitude. I'll remember that small kindness.

"Ice magic could shatter those chains," Kauko says from behind me, his voice echoing off the walls in this near-empty arena. "And fire magic could melt them, allowing you to pull your arms free. Ice and fire together could fling the shards or melted metal away from your skin. Those are but a few of the ways you could show us that the magic is awakened within you."

I press my forehead to the stone. "Proceed."

When nothing happens, I look at the apprentice out of the corner of my eye. He has hollow cheeks and a soft chin, caught halfway between man and boy. "Go ahead, apprentice," I say gently. "Do your duty." I turn my face back to the wall.

For a moment, there is silence. I wonder if the apprentice will refuse to hit me. But then I hear the quick slide of boots against stone and the whistle of leather in the air, and after that I am made of pain. It explodes across my back like a lightning strike, and no sooner has the agony dulled than it happens again. And again. And again. The inferno of hurt rips a scream from my throat. My back is on fire. The searing flames wrap themselves around my body, licking at my ribs and breasts and stomach. No part of me is safe. The apprentice strikes me again, grunting with the effort.

"Shatter the chains, Valtia!" cries one of the acolytes.

Her plea jolts me back to the purpose of this torture. Magic. I am no longer an ordinary girl. I felt something last night as I lay prostrate on that stone slab—the Valtia's power finding its new home. And I just spent hours encased in copper, which has to be the source of our strength. I have the magic inside me somewhere, and now I need it. Badly.

*Ice, come to me.*

The whip bites at the flesh from my neck to my waist. My body moves without my permission, my wrists yanking against the cuffs as the leather claims its prize once again. My backbone arches and bows, desperate to save itself from the molten agony. My mind is burning to ash. Finally, numbness splashes over me, filling every space. My legs give out, and I hang, my cheek pressed to cool stone, my hair plastered to my forehead.

"Please, Elder," says the apprentice, his words coming between heavy breaths. "Enough." His tone is pleading.

"That's only been twelve," says Aleksi. "Continue, Armo."

Armo the apprentice lets out a shaky breath.

I squeeze my eyes shut. "Continue," I say in a broken whisper. I want him to cut me open with that whip. I want him to unearth my dormant magic. I'm not whole without it, and I'm depending on him to bring it out. "Armo, please."

Armo makes a choked noise, but a moment later the whip strikes, so hard that I cannot help the shriek that comes from my throat. On and on it goes, until I lose count, until I'm beyond reason, until I'm on fire—but I have no ice to save me. I hang from my cuffs, blood from my wrists trickling down my forearms and dripping onto my shoulders and chest. Smearing on the rock.

Blood. Copper. Fire. Ice. I am Kupari, and these things make me what I am.

*"Show me your mark," my Valtia said as we sat on her balcony. "Where is it? They never told me."*

*I tugged up my gown with my skinny ten-year-old fingers and showed it to her. She smiled. "Lovely," she said. "So vivid." She stroked it with the backs of her fingers. "Would you like to see mine?"*

*I nodded, my cheeks warming. She turned her back and swept her thick, coppery locks to one side, then pushed her gown off her left shoulder. And there, on the wing of her shoulder blade, was the flame. "It's so small," I blurted out, itching to trace my fingers over it.*

*She chuckled. "Tiny," she said, winking at me. "Only half the size of yours. And yet still I made the firebreak that saved us from the inferno at the edge of the Loputon forest last summer.*

*And I was strong enough to summon cold so complete that it choked that same mighty fire out of existence."*

*I began to stammer my apologies, embarrassed at my clumsy words, but she shook her head and pulled her gown back onto her shoulder. She put her arm around me. "Darling, you have nothing to be sorry about." She touched my burning cheek with her cool fingertip. "Only remember what I can do, though my mark is tiny, though it took the elders months to find me, though it was only by chance that they found me at all. And imagine what you will someday be able to do."*

I fall backward into the arms of one of the acolytes, my arms splayed, my wrists free. *I did it. Thank the stars above.*

The young woman looks down at me with tears on her lovely face. "Please use your magic, Valtia," she begs, holding me tight as we sink to the floor.

I stare at the ceiling, too weak and agonized to move. "I didn't?" I whisper. But my whole body is on fire! "Didn't I just melt the chains?"

She shakes her head and gestures up at the shackles, hanging open, still dripping with my blood. Behind me, I hear a terrible noise. Armo, sobbing. The girl with the spots is cooing to him, telling him he only did his duty, reminding him that I asked him to. But it doesn't console him. His grating cries only stop when Elder Aleksi's voice strikes as surely as that whip. "Clean her up," he barks. "And then bring her to the temple dock for the next trial. We'll prepare the boat."

"Elder," says the spotty acolyte, her voice breathy. "She's too weak. Maybe—maybe Elder Kauko could heal her wounds first?"

"She is the Valtia!" Aleksi roars. "If she's not strong enough to heal herself, she's not fit to rule. And if you question me again, I'll order your immediate cloistering." His stomping footsteps fade from hearing, followed by the slower, less violent footfalls of Kauko and Leevi.

The spotty acolyte's hand shakes as she rubs it over her bald head. "I'm not due to be cloistered for another five years at least," she says in a squeaky voice.

Next to me, Armo vomits all over the floor. "I can't," he moans. "I can't witness this."

The spotty acolyte frowns. "If he doesn't pull himself together, priest Bernold might call for *him* to be cloistered and find another apprentice to take his place."

"Then let him stay here," says the acolyte with blue eyes and soothing hands. She has a mole on her cheek, small and round. "We can take her to the dock."

I float in a fog of hurt as the three female acolytes press cloths to my back, then pull my sleeves over my arms and button my dress. "Those bandages won't hold, Kaisa," says the spotty one.

"I know, Meri," says Kaisa, the girl with the mole. "But if we take too long, the elders will be furious."

"I'll stay with Armo," says the girl with the wide, pretty face. She pats his back. He's staring down at the bloody whip. "I'm due to be cloistered soon," she adds with a sigh,

"so it won't matter if they make me start it a few days early."
She offers all of us a smile. "Besides, Salli was cloistered
a few months ago, and I'm looking forward to seeing her
again."

Meri and Kaisa lift me from the floor and drape my arms
over their shoulders. Slowly, they half carry me up the stone
stairs and into the maze of the catacombs. My head hangs
forward, and it's all I can do to move my feet.

"They've already started the search for the new Saadella,"
Meri says quietly.

"I hope they find her soon," murmurs Kaisa. "People are
scared. They need something to buoy their spirits."

A tear falls from my eye. I'm supposed to buoy their spirits. I would do anything to give my people that confidence.
But these two acolytes are speaking as if I'm a hunk of bear
meat and nothing more. As kind as they are, I know they're
full of doubt, and it echoes in the hollow place inside of me,
filling my chest with painful pressure as it joins with my own
fear that I am failing everyone.

Meri pulls me to the left, guiding us down a dark corridor with a single lit torch at the end of it. "Did you hear
about the fight at the thieves' caverns? Armo was telling me
earlier."

"I heard the same rumor—that two miners were burned."

"Wielders?" I whisper. *Do the elders know there might be
wielders in the outlands?* I want to ask, but the one word I've
already said has drained all my energy.

"More likely, one of those sons of weasels tossed a

shovelful of flaming pitch at the miners," Kaisa scoffs. She squeezes my arm as we reach the end of the corridor, and her voice softens. "But even if there was a fire wielder in the outlands, he will be no match for you once you find your magic, my Valtia."

Kaisa and Meri escort me into a chamber with a long wooden table along one side. Stars, it smells of blood in here. But then again, that might be coming from me.

"Whether it's a wielder or not," says Meri, "the people need reassurance now." There's a pause, and though I don't raise my head, I know both of them are looking down at me. I'm what the people need. As soon as I find my magic, I'll settle the issue in the caverns and rid that place of squatters so our miners can do their work. Determination flutters beneath all the doubt. I will not give up yet.

We leave the chamber and proceed down the long, wide tunnel that leads to the dock. Kaisa lets Meri hold me up while she pushes open a rusty metal door, bathing us in the chilly night air. The sound of the Motherlake lapping at the dock is like coming home. It finds me within my shell of pain, my core of numb, and I take a deep, shuddering breath.

Meri strokes a hand over my hair. "Valtia, we're almost there," she says softly. "You've been so brave, but you will need more than that now. Please."

She and Kaisa carry me to the waiting boat. "Do you want us to accompany you, Elder?" Meri asks when we reach it.

"No," snaps Aleksi. "We'll manage this by ourselves. Wait for us here."

I hiss as Kaisa accidentally touches my back, and she jerks her hands away. "Apologies, *Valtia*," she says, her blue eyes full of regret. She steps back as I sink onto the floor of the boat. It's of middling size, with two sets of oars and a large, heavy object sitting at the prow. In the shadowy night, the moon covered over by clouds, I can't quite make it out.

The elders are grim and quiet as they push off into the lake. They don't bother with the oars—Aleksi raises his arms and the boat slices through the water as if blown by a steady wind. Leevi sits next to me. "I'm sorry the last trial didn't help you," he says. "But this one . . . It has more urgency to it. We think it will work."

"Good," I mumble. Because I need my magic. I need to heal myself. I'm certain that my back is a mess of welts and gashes, and my whole body is racked with pain. I'm too hurt to cry now, too tired to fight. Magic is the *only* thing that can save me now.

We reach a spot where the water is inky and smooth. Leevi drops an anchor, and the three elders take me by the arms and lead me to the front of the boat. Metal clanks softly, and Kauko raises a lantern.

In front of me is a bronze cage attached by a thick chain to a boom and winch that's bolted to the deck. Aleksi pulls the door open and gestures inside. "When you're ready, *Valtia*."

It's as if he believes I'm doing this on purpose, and he wants me to suffer for it.

As I remember Meri's small kindnesses, I will also remember Aleksi's cruelty. Forever.

I try to stoop to get into the cage, but the pull of fabric against the wounds on my back sends me to my knees with a shrill whimper. Leevi and Kauko pick me up and help me into the tiny prison, so cramped that I have to draw my knees to my chest and bow my head over my legs. My back is screaming. Leevi turns the crank on the winch, and my cage is lifted into the air. Aleksi slams the door and latches it.

"You could freeze the surface of the lake before you fall in," Aleksi says as my teeth begin to chatter. "Or you could grow an ice platform from the lake's floor to lift you out of the water. Conversely, you could use fire to evaporate the water around you and hold it back. There are so many ways to use the magic, Valtia."

Kauko grips the bars. "Trust your instincts. Don't force it. Just let it come to you." He reaches into the cage as far as his arm will allow, and his fingertips brush my knee. I know I should grasp his hand, but I'm shaking too much to control my fingers. "We need your magic to survive. Please. We've been waiting so long for this. Remember who you are," he says, his voice harsh with desperation.

I almost laugh. I used to think I knew exactly who I was. Now? *I have no idea.*

My breaths are ragged and fast as they swing my cage out over the Motherlake, dangling me like bait over her frigid waters. Leevi releases the chain, and my cage plunges into the water. The blast of cold shocks my vision white. I'm no longer on fire—now it's the cold's turn. Frozen blades of pain stab into every inch of my skin. An icy noose pulls tight around my neck.

*Fire, come to me.*

But this time, when it doesn't come, I'm not even surprised. I claw for air, my arms extending through the top bars of my cage and waving just above the surface of the water. It's so close. I jerk my face upward, colliding with bronze. I can see the dark shadows of the elders above me, their upheld torch, the moon that's now visible through a hole in the clouds. The pain in my chest sparks and burns like smoldering charcoal, the hurt moving upward, consuming me. And yet the water stays cold, and so do I.

*I'm going to die.*

As soon as the thought comes, the rest of me rejects it with the force of a mighty storm. My body convulses, and I fight. Oh, stars, I fight so hard. I claw and kick and grasp and push and shake those bars with all my strength. I suck in a mouthful of water and my chest squeezes tight, my body twisting and writhing against the waters of the fearsome, relentless Motherlake.

This was what it was like for the Soturi invaders. This is how they perished.

*"Have you ever killed someone?" I asked my Valtia. We were eating delicate sweet potato pastries, lying on her massive bed after a long day at the planting ceremony, watching our reflections in the hammered copper ceiling.*

*"Not yet," she said. "But I probably will, someday."*

*"You sound awfully sure." And awfully calm. I'd just turned thirteen and was amazed by her serene beauty, her smooth surface. Envy filled me.*

*She took my hand, sending a pulse of ice along my palm. "I do what I need to, in service of the Kupari. Sometimes you are chosen, and sometimes you must choose. If I take a life, I won't regret that choice. I'll know it was to protect our people." She turned her head and looked into my eyes. "And so will you, Elli, when the time comes. You'll do what you need to do. Never doubt."*

Never doubt.

I rise from the water like a firebird from ash.

But not by magic.

As the elders swing me back over the deck, I vomit a bucketful of water onto their bald heads. Aleksi grunts with disgust. "That was hardly magical."

I hear him like I'm still underwater. I'm made of ice. I'm bleeding. All they need to do is set me on fire, and I'd be complete: Blood. Copper. Ice. Fire. It is life.

And now I've learned it's death, too.

With contempt etched onto his fleshy face, Aleksi unlocks the clasp on my cage and swings the door open. Kauko and Leevi pull me out. I'm still convulsing and coughing, shivering so violently that they can barely hold on to me. They set me heavily on the deck. I barely feel it. I sink deep inside the empty, gaping space inside me, drowning again, this time in defeat.

The elders talk quietly among themselves as they use

their magic to propel the boat back to shore, but their words are carried away by the breeze and the splash of water against the hull. They help the acolytes carry me to the Saadella's wing. I know I'm home when I hear Mim cry out. They set me on my bed, soaking my sheets with pink and red. Kauko sits down next to me and touches my shoulder.

"Did you read the stars wrong, Elder?" I whisper.

"No, child. You were the one it referred to. I am certain."

"The prophecy, then—you said part of it was missing."

"That is true." For the first time, I hear anger in his voice. "We have priests scouring all our texts, trying to find hints of what it could have said. In the meantime . . ." His shoulders slump as he looks me over.

"I . . . I will go back in the copper trunk if you think it would help." Even though the mere thought makes me shudder.

He shakes his head. "It's not necessary now."

I nearly choke as the tears come. "I'm sorry for disappointing you."

His thick lips tremble. "There is one more trial," he says, sorrow in his eyes. "One more trial, and we're hoping this one will work."

"Do it, then," I croak. "I'm eager to face it."

He squeezes my arm. "You'll have to be very brave. But you are, aren't you? We can all see that. Even Aleksi."

What they can also see: my bravery is not enough. Not nearly enough.

"I'm courageous enough for one more trial."

"I wish we didn't have to ask these things of you, but I'm grateful you understand their necessity." He bows his head. "Rest tonight. Look at the moon. The clouds are clearing." His voice falters, and he clamps his lips shut for a few moments before continuing. "It is a sight to behold. Lovely, like you are. Then sleep, and may your dreams be peaceful. I will see you tomorrow."

After he leaves, I squint at a small piece of sky through my open balcony doors. I can't see the moon, but its reflection shines in the Motherlake. I drift outside myself, out of the temple, over the lake, and float toward that gorgeous orb. How heavenly. The weight of responsibility falls away. No one needs me anymore. No one even knows I'm gone. The sweetest sense of freedom envelops me, welcoming me into its embrace. It's so nice, so peaceful. . . .

"Elli," whispers Mim. "Wake up."

She shakes me, and I groan. It's hard to draw breath. I slip my hand under the loose collar of my gown. A length of gauzy fabric has been wrapped around my chest and back, binding my wounds. My hair is braided. My sheets are clean. I'm wearing a simple dress of brown wool, like the kind Mim wears every day. But it is still dark out, with no sign of the day to come.

"Is it time for the final trial?" I whisper. Stars, I'm so, so tired.

"Sit up, my Valtia. Sit up now." She pulls my arms and then apologizes when I let out a strangled moan. Once I'm up, she slides a pair of plain leather slippers onto my feet and takes my face in her hands. "You must be very brave."

"Kauko said the same," I mumble. "I'm doing my best. Mim, I'm so sorry for letting you down."

Her blue eyes shine with tears. "Oh, my love, you could never do that. Get up now."

"Where are we going?"

Her brow creases with fear and sorrow. "Away, Elli. We're going away."

"But the trial—" My words are cut off when she presses her fingers over my lips.

"I overheard the elders speaking in the domed chamber, making preparations."

I cringe. "I don't think I want to know."

"Yes, you do." She carefully helps me to my feet. "Because in a few hours, they're going to come get you, and they're going to take you deep into the catacombs." Her eyes meet mine. "And then they're going to cut your throat."

# CHAPTER 7

They're going to kill me. Kauko must have consented to it. Even he gave up on me in the end. I should be shocked. I should be enraged and hurt. But right now, all I can summon is weary resignation.

"Have they found the new Saadella?" I ask as Mim leads me to the door and peeks into the corridor.

"I don't think so. But she's out in the city somewhere, and they're determined to find her. They think that if they drain your blood, it'll strip the magic from you and free it to be awakened in the Saadella. They're desperate to appease the people, and the Kupari cannot be without a Valtia, even if she's still a child. I think it's ludicrous, but I bet Aleksi and Leevi are pleased at the chance to mold an impressionable young queen. The last Valtia was too headstrong for their tastes." She guides me to lean against the wall.

"Sofia," I whisper, remembering Aleksi's clenched fists as she refused to bow to his wishes. "Aleksi was trying to get her to act quickly."

Mim rushes over to a chair and pulls a brown cloak from the cushion. "The acolytes and apprentices are full of information. The elders wanted to get the Valtia to cleanse the thieves' caverns, but she had refused until she knew more about the situation. The elders were offended that she didn't trust them. They're supposed to be her eyes and ears—but she wanted to see for herself."

"So they're going to make a little girl the Valtia so they can have their way?" I ask in a choked voice.

Mim doesn't seem to hear me as she shakes out the cloak and returns to my side. "I don't agree with the elders' methods, but imagine what would happen if the other city-states knew we had no Valtia. Or even those bandits in the caverns. Our Valtia is what keeps them from raiding the town and taking what they want. We must have a queen." She probably doesn't realize how every word stabs failure a little deeper into my heart.

"Even with all of that, my first priority is *you*," she adds. "Elli. You will always be my queen."

*But not your Valtia*, my mind whispers as she wraps the cloak around my shoulders, tying it loosely so as not to aggravate my wounds. I look like a maid now, a common, ordinary girl. And maybe that's what I've been all along. Maybe all this time, I've been a pretender, and now I'm wearing the garments that were always meant for me. "Mim, why do you think this is happening to me?"

Her eyes are shadowed with sorrow. "I don't know, Elli. And it's not my place to know." As I watch, her sadness seems to crystallize, glittering in the darkness. "But there is one thing of which I'm certain—you've done nothing wrong. Let the elders use *their* magic to give us winter warmth and save us from our enemies. It's about time they did some of the work."

Mim leads me into the corridor, to the right, away from the domed chamber. Not a single torch lights our way, but Mim appears to know exactly where she's going, and her confidence seems to grow with every step. "Where are the acolytes who stand guard at night?" I whisper.

"Some are helping clean the Valtia's chamber. It was nearly destroyed when she died, and they're working at all hours to fix it. And then I bribed another." She smiles when she sees my wide eyes. "Elli, if you think for a moment I would hand you over to be slaughtered by the elders, you don't know me at all."

I lean on her gratefully as she takes me to the servants' stairs and helps me descend. "I love you, Mim," I mumble against her ear. "I always have."

She giggles. "You're delirious."

I think about that for a second. Every part of me hurts, but my mind is clear. And the more I think about what's happening, the more frightened I am. "Where are we going?"

"I'm taking you to my family. But first I have to report in

to the temple matron to keep her from raising the alarm, so you'll be on your own for an hour or two. I'll join you as the sun rises, before the elders even know we're gone."

"You're really coming with me?"

Her grip on me tightens. "I would never leave you." She chuckles. "Who would dress you in the morning? Who would brush your pretty hair? And we could go anywhere from here. It's an adventure, if you think about it."

I *am* thinking about it—the possibility of living with her, however humbly, is like a bright torch in all this darkness. And so is her love for me. I know it's the love of a servant for her mistress, perhaps a big sister for a little one, not the same as mine for her. Still, it's real and warm and I need it, especially now that I've lost everything else.

We reach the bottom of the steps and Mim pushes open a thick wooden door, wincing as it grates against the stone frame. The inky wash of night greets us, though I know dawn must be approaching. "If you walk this path here—" She moves her finger along a trail of white stones shielded by a high wall so that the views from the temple and the white plaza aren't marred by servants going back and forth. "You can go around the gates this way—it'll get you to the northern road. Follow it until you reach the square, then wait for me next to the blacksmith's. It's a warm place to sit and rest. I'll bring more food with me when I come." She presses a hunk of bread into my hand. It's been ripped open and a thick slice of hard cheese has been wedged into its center. My mouth fills with saliva.

"Go," she whispers. "I'll see you soon."

Her brown curls are a chaotic tangle around her face, and the brightness has returned to her blue eyes. Her cheeks are flushed. She's so beautiful and cheerful as she saves me from certain death, and it makes salvation seem possible.

"I'm not delirious," I tell her. "I meant what I said."

Her face crumples, and for an instant I see the fear she's been working so hard to hide. "Elli, go. Please. If they catch you, I won't be able to protect you."

"But what about you?" Aleksi might blame me, but what if he blames Mim, too, for giving me information? "Come with me now. We can—"

Mim shakes her head. "We'll have more time to get you hidden if I check in with the matron first. But I'll be with you before you start to miss me. I promise." She tugs my hood up until it covers my half my face, then gives me a gentle nudge toward the world outside the temple. My slipper hovers over the dirt and grass and stone. I haven't set foot on the bare ground since I was four years old. In all the years since then, I've been carried on a paarit or in a sedan chair. But if I don't take these steps, I'll die.

It makes it surprisingly easy to move forward.

My feet are silent as I tread the white stones that lead me away from the only home I remember, the fortress from which I was supposed to rule. I should be weeping or falling to my knees in despair, but like the magic, I can't find those feelings inside me. I am sad, though. Desperately so.

I let everyone down. I failed my people. I failed my Valtia. And when they find the child Saadella, who will love her and watch over her? I've failed her, too.

Maybe I deserve to be cast out. Perhaps I even deserve to be killed. I reach the edge of the grounds and look back at the domed silhouette of the Temple on the Rock towering above me, majestic and mighty, pale-green copper and snowy marble ice. Am I being selfish? Should I go back and offer myself up?

Or would that doom a little Saadella to an early death after spending her youth serving the will of the priests?

I shiver and keep moving, walking along the road that leads south to the main square. Far off to my right, over by the docks, I can hear the distant rumbling voices of the sailors, our earliest risers, preparing for a day of pulling nets full of shimmering trout from the great Motherlake. My stomach grumbles at the thought of a steaming dish of glazed trout, cooked crisp and dripping. I take a bite of my bread and cheese and moan at the salty taste. Before I know it, I've shoved the entire hunk in my mouth. My cheeks bulge and I chew fiercely. I'm alive. I feel the chill of autumn on my face and hard cobblestones beneath my feet. I breathe. My back aches and itches and burns. My heart beats. Surely I'm not meant to die? Not yet. I'm not ready for that.

I gather my cloak around me as I enter the square, wishing for invisibility. When the elders realize I'm missing, what will they do? Sound the alarm? Reward the first citizen who turns me over to them? I hunch my shoulders and quicken my steps. The blacksmith's forge is a three-sided building with a metal roof and stone walls. The front is fenced and gated. The blacksmith is already at work, his hairy, muscular arms flexing as he shovels charcoal into his forge. He doesn't notice me hovering beyond his fence, a gray-cloaked ghost alone in the square.

I pad to a spot against the stone wall of his shop, right at the front. As he lights the fire, I feel the heat radiating outward. This is where Mim wanted me to wait. I peer at the eastern sky, which is slowly transforming from black to purple. It's so strange to be standing here, huddled in plain clothes, my tender soles aching from the journey I've made. The pain in my feet draws me to the ground, where I lower one of my stockings and peel back my slipper to see a line of blisters below my bony ankle. Have I ever had a blister before? Not in my memory. I don't know how to care for it—but Mim will. She's the only thing that makes any of this bearable.

My fingers trail up under my dress to brush my blood-flame mark. It pulses a numb greeting, sending a buzzing sensation up my leg. Why do I have this mark, if I'm not the Valtia? What else could I possibly be if not the true queen? I grip my leg and look back toward the temple.

I won't give myself up. I'll find a way to wield the magic inside me, and then I'll return to the temple victorious. Kauko said I would be the most powerful Valtia who ever lived. He said I was the one.

"Never doubt," I murmur.

Stars, who am I kidding? I am *made* of doubt right now.

106

I lean against the rough stone wall and have to bite back an agonized cry as my flayed back touches the unforgiving surface. Mim did a good job with my bandages, and she must have smeared a numbing cream on them, because the pain has been manageable. But she'll need to dress them again tonight. I'm not sure I want to know what my skin looks like. It used to be smooth, and now . . . now it is probably forever scarred. Perhaps when I find my magic, I'll be able to heal myself. It's a comforting thought.

The sky gets lighter, and my stomach burbles, first happily, and then hungrily. That bread and cheese was the only thing I'd eaten since before the ruined harvest ceremony. I pray for the sun to rise a little faster, because it will signal Mim's arrival with breakfast. She never fails me. I bet she'll bring something special, just to make me feel better.

Finally, the sun tears itself loose from the horizon and begins its arcing ascent. Orange and pink fingers of light stretch across the sky, and the city wakes. The plodding of horses' hooves and shouts of peddlers hawking their wares begin to fill the air, first only a few, and then dozens. Bells clang as the fishermen enter the harbor. The blacksmith's strikes on his forge are shrill stabs of sound. The breeze brings me the scent of meat pies and baking bread and garlicky, spicy sausages. I think I could eat one as big as my own arm.

I watch the space between two stout buildings at the northern end of the square, the road leading north to the gates of the temple grounds. The sun has risen above the city council's meeting hall now, and my heart beats faster. She said she'd be with me before I started to miss her, so she needs to come soon.

And then there she is. Her hooded figure strides down the road, a covered basket in her hands. I push myself to my feet but remain against the wall. I don't want to be seen. Mim emerges from between the two buildings, and I stare greedily at her basket, wondering what she's packed. I also wonder what her family will think of me when we arrive. Will they understand what's happening and sympathize? Surely she wouldn't take me to them if she thought they'd alert the elders.

Instead of coming toward me, Mim turns left and walks across the square. She must not have seen me—even though I'm waiting right where she told me to. Pulling my hood low to make sure it covers my face, I step onto the road and cross the square, weaving my way around peddlers' carts and maids and houseboys out to make morning purchases for their households. Mim disappears into the bakery, and I chuckle. If there was nothing special in the temple kitchens, then she's probably getting something for me there. I'm almost skipping as I near the bakery. The scent of lard and yeast is making me dizzy.

She comes out of the bakery, her basket now laden with buns, her hood thrown back.

Which is when I realize: she's not Mim. That's Irina, one of the scullery maids who mops the corridors and minds the fireplaces. I turn away quickly as she strides down the main road to the east, probably going home to her family for a few days off.

My hand covers my stomach as that hollow feeling inside me grows. It's midmorning now. She said she'd come for me at sunrise. Where is she?

I return to my little spot next to the blacksmith's shop. To keep myself from squinting endlessly down the road to the temple, I watch the people in the square. They're wearing their light fall cloaks, which is the heaviest garb they ever have to don within the city walls, because the Valtia keeps us warm even in the depths of winter. Their cheeks are full and their limbs are strong, because the Valtia ensures the gardens and farmland are protected from too much heat in the summer. They wear adornments, bangles and tunics of all colors, because the Kupari are wealthy and can trade our bountiful food for goods from the southern city-states of Korkea, Ylpeys, and, until a few months ago, Vasterut. All these people going about their lives, trusting that the Valtia and her magic wielders within the Temple on the Rock are protecting them. It is an intimate and precious trust, as some of the citizens have brothers and nieces and sons and cousins who were discovered to be wielders as children and welcomed within the temple's white walls. It is a great honor for any family to have produced a magical child.

What will happen to these well-dressed, straight-backed citizens if they don't have a Valtia to keep them warm and protect them from raiders and bandits? Do they know the girl who failed them is in their midst? Some of them look my way, and each time, I tense up, expecting their eyes to widen with recognition.

But their gazes slide away. I don't hold their attention. They don't know me, not without my bloodred gown and my makeup—the white face, the crimson lips, the copper swirls.

As the sun reaches its peak, sweat slides in drops down the back of my dress, stinging my wounds like a hundred angry hornets. But if I pull my hood away and reveal my hair, will the people know me then?

Again, no. When I really pay attention, I realize that one in every five or so has hair that glints with reddish gold, that shines beneath the sun. Many of our citizens also have pale-blue eyes.

I'm not such a rarity after all.

I ponder that as I wait. As I wait and wait and wait. Finally, I'm drenched from the combined heat of the forge and the sun and my frustration, and I move across the square to sit closer to the northern road.

I'm still there as the fishing boats return in the afternoon, as the sky clouds over and the day turns gray.

And as the twilight comes, chasing away the heat of the surprisingly warm autumn afternoon, I am *still* there. Hollow with hunger and shock and worry. Mim hasn't come.

"—already searched the Lantinen," comes an unmistakable, reedy voice—it's Leevi. "So we'll search along Etela Road next. I sent my apprentice ahead to give them notice."

My whole body jolts. As a distant rumble of thunder rolls across the Motherlake, I yank my hood up and scramble away from the northern road, ending up by the bakery again, just in time to watch Elder Aleksi and Elder Leevi stride into the square. People back away from them as they pass, bowing with reverence when they notice the elders' belts, shot through with the copper that marks their status. A few women coming out of the bakery whisper to one another, and I hear the one word that tells me exactly what Leevi and Aleksi are doing.

*Saadella.*

They're searching for the little girl with the copper hair, the ice-blue eyes, and the blood-flame mark. My replacement. The one who would be Valtia, if only I were dead. Or, at least, that's what they think. I cross the square to walk slowly behind the two elders. I want to know if they're looking for me, too. As we leave the square and start down Etela Road, which leads directly south until it meets the timber wall that rings the city, people gather in the street even though it's starting to rain. Mothers and fathers wipe drops from their faces and push their daughters to the center of the road. All the girls have copper hair. Pale-blue eyes.

There must be at least ten of them on this street alone.

I step into an alley between a cooperage and a brewery as Aleksi and Leevi reach the first girl. She's perhaps three or four, and her damp red hair falls in tangled waves to her shoulders. Her mother grasps her by the rib cage and lifts her into the air. "She's got an eerie, calm temperament, Elders. She has since she was a babe. Wise beyond her years. I've always wondered."

My breath comes faster. Was that what it was like when I was found?

Aleksi leans forward and sniffs at the girl's curls. "What is the true color of her hair?" When the woman's eyes go wide, he grins. "I know the smell of henna, my dear woman." He swipes his hand along the girl's wet hair and then waves it in front of her mother, his palm stained orange-red. "Better go inside and wash it out before it stains all your linens."

Leevi scowls. "And before we call for your banishment for attempting to deceive an elder."

Aleksi and Leevi move on, and the now ashen-faced woman drags her little girl back into their shabby cottage. I am frozen where I am as the rain begins to fall in earnest, watching from the alley as the elders discard one girl because her mark is brown, not red, and another because her blood-flame mark turns out to be rose-madder paint. Every little girl is a pretender, every parent a desperately hopeful fraud. Leevi comments that perhaps they should stop offering such a rich bounty for the Saadella, since it inspires so much trickery among the Kupari people. Aleksi says they've been way too lenient over the years and wonders aloud if they should call the constables to immediately banish the would-be deceivers to the outlands. A few other parents who had been waiting their turn hustle their daughters back inside when they hear the threat.

The doubt squirms inside me. Is that all I was, a source of wealth for my parents? Did they take the bounty and flee the peninsula to start a new life someplace far away, where no one would know they'd fooled the entire Kupari people? Have I been an impostor from the start? I touch the hair beneath my hood. I blink my eyes. Could there have been another, one just like me, who was never found?

If there were anything in my stomach, I'd be retching it onto the mud at my feet. Did my parents find a way to fool the priests? Or was it an innocent mistake? My head aches with horror and exhaustion. My ears throb dully. My back is a hard shell of agony. When I blunder out of the alley, Leevi and Aleksi have moved on, thank the stars. I stumble down the street, rain drenching my cloak, mud pulling at my heels. I have no idea where I'm going. I wish Mim had told me where her parents live—I'm willing to go there right now and beg them to take me in.

I need to find a place to bed for the night. In the morning I'll wait for Mim again. I want to be right there when she comes, so we don't miss each other. She must have thought it wasn't safe to leave just yet. Maybe someone else discovered I was missing, and she had to pretend she was shocked. Maybe she's having to help look for me. But it's only a matter of time until she slips away. I keep saying that to myself, even as my worry for her grows like a vine, strangling my hope.

The people on the streets cast long shadows in the fire-light shining from cottages along the lane. I stagger along, barely avoiding the clomping horses and rattling carts that go by, their drivers slumped and hooded against the down-pour. Then the loveliest scent reaches me, powerful and gut-clenching. Just ahead, there's a market, the attendants pulling in their goods for the night. Beneath the overhang, at a table in the corner, is a wooden plate that hasn't been cleared yet, and on it is a small stack of meat pies.

My body scrambles forward before I can form a thought. My hands reach out, shaking with need. In half a moment I'm stuffing a pie into my mouth. As the salty, earthy taste explodes on my tongue, I close my eyes and sink weakly onto one of the chairs next to the table.

"Here, what're you doing?" says a coarse, rasping voice.

I shoot to my feet as a stout woman in an apron marches out from the storeroom. I step back, my gaze darting between her—mouth squinched over missing teeth, brown-gray hair hanging in sweaty tendrils from her cap—and the plate, on which there are still two uneaten pies. Probably a day old, probably headed for the refuse pile.

I lunge for the table, grab the pies, and run.

"Thief!" screeches the woman. "Thief!"

My breath saws from my throat as I sprint along the road, my feet splashing through deep puddles, each stride sending a bolt of pain up my legs.

"Stop, thief!" roars a male voice. Heavy footsteps stomp behind me. Getting closer. But ahead is an alley. If I can get there, if I can lose them in the darkness—

He hits my back like a millstone, and I scream as we fall to the ground. The meat pies fly from my grip and land in a puddle at the edge of the road. Agony blasts along my spine as the man crushes the breath from my chest. "Got her!" he shouts as boots and slippered feet gather around me. One of them kicks muddy water onto my face.

The man gets off my back and grabs a handful of my hair. He yanks me to my feet. Someone holds a lantern in front of my face. "You know we don't tolerate thieves, girl. Where's your family? Do you have a husband?"

I am a jumble of terror. If they figure out who I am, I'll be taken back to the temple to have my throat cut. But if I'm not myself, who am I?

"They're—I don't—don't know," I cry as the man shakes me, making me whimper with pain.

He wrenches my head back. He has a thick blond beard and a scar across the bridge of his nose. His cap marks him as a miner—his hands are hard as granite. His dark-blue eyes roam my face, and I can't breathe for the fear. Will he recognize me? Will he hand me over to the elders?

He glowers at me. "You stole from decent, hardworking people." He looks at the market woman. "Probably a runaway, living on the streets."

The market woman spits at my feet and wipes her gummy mouth. "Call the constable."

The bearded miner grunts. "No need." He drags me down the road, and when I peer through the pelting rain, I see lights up ahead, hanging from the archway of our city gate.

I had no idea I had walked so close to the edge of the city. Panic strikes like lightning, and I twist in the man's grasp. He clamps a hard hand over my flayed shoulder, and I shriek with the pain. Fighting and clawing helplessly, I'm hauled through the mud with a small crowd following me, shouting insults. When we reach the gates, I'm held up before a man with black hair and black eyes and black teeth. He's wearing a scarlet tunic and a brown cap. There's a club hooked to his belt.

"Thief, Constable."

The black-toothed constable looks at me with puzzlement. "Here now, you look familiar."

The only sound that comes from me is a ragged squeak. His brows draw together. "Where have I seen you before, girl? Speak up, now. I could help you."

My mouth opens and closes, but I have no words.

"Obviously has something to hide," says the market woman. "Nasty little thief. I'm sure she's done it a hundred times. That's probably why you recognize her—she's escaped your clutches before!"

Several people laugh, and the constable's mouth crimps with the insult. He stares at my face for a moment longer, then turns his attention to the crowd around me. "You were witnesses to her crime?"

They all begin talking at once, how they saw my brazen theft, how I have no family, how I'm a boil on the arse of society, a lamprey that sucks away their hard-earned wealth. I'm hurting too much to defend myself—and what would I say? The truth, even if they believed me, would only result in certain death. But when the miner's knuckles press between my shoulder blades, I arch back, made of agony, and wonder if death wouldn't be easier.

The constable finally holds his hands up. "I've heard enough. She's banished."

"Banished?" I shriek, but before I can say anything else, the constable calls for the gates to open, and I'm shoved and chased through them. When I fall on my face and inhale a mouthful of mud, the bearded miner grabs the back of my cloak and dress. His iron fingers scour along my back. He tosses me forward as I cough and gag.

I land on the grass at the side of the road. Behind me, the heavy wooden gates slam shut.

My breath shudders from me as I stare at the city I love, the city I was supposed to rule. Dim lights wink within. Warmth pours from it. And now it's lost to me.

Mim is lost to me too. What will she think, when she emerges from the temple and I'm not there? How can I let her know I'm here, that I need her?

*And what if she needs* you? If the priests realized she helped me escape, would they whip her? No. She's too clever to be caught. Even now, she's probably leading anyone looking for me down the wrong path, buying time. Even she would never think I'd be where I am, though. I can hardly believe it myself as I clumsily rise from the grass. Shock buzzes inside my head, making it difficult to hear my own thoughts. But I know I need help. Perhaps one of the farmers will have mercy on me. Perhaps someone will have mercy.

I limp down the sodden road, the long, thick grass of the marshes lit by occasional, distant flickers of lightning. The rain is tapering off, and the clouds are slowly clearing, revealing the moon and stars, needle pricks of light that once foretold the birth of the most powerful Valtia the world had ever known. I can't fathom how I ever believed I could be her.

Beyond the marsh, to my right, is a patch of trees, the northernmost tip of the woods that divide the east and west of our peninsula. The mud sucks at my ankles as I pause to stare at it. Now that the rain has stopped, a cold wind has taken its place. I'll die of chill if I stay out here like this. I need shelter. But no one lives in the outlands, not really. The city takes up the entire northern quarter of the peninsula. The farmers have their homesteads along the shores. The miners descend into the craggy hills to the southeast. But the area in the center, all the way down to the border of the Loputon Forest, belongs to the thieves and beggars, the ones who've been banished.

I need to get off this road.

When I reach a hill that slopes over the marshland, I climb it with hands and feet and then trudge along its crest toward the woods. By the time I reach the shelter of the trees, I am staggering and senseless, yet stupidly defiant. I refuse to give Elder Aleksi the satisfaction of my death, especially since it would do no good—I'm a fraud. I've never been the real Saadella, and I could never be the Valtia. I should have been left with my parents to live a normal life.

I didn't choose to be chosen, and I will not choose to die.

Brambles tear at my cloak and hands and cheeks. My skin is hot enough to singe. My feet are bricks of pain fastened to my ankles. My mouth is an ash pit. I press the edge of my hood between my lips and try to suck the rainwater from it, but it's not nearly enough to satisfy. I manage to keep walking until I reach a small clearing with a little pond at its edge. Whimpering with thirst, I throw myself down and scoop the bitter water into my mouth. By the time I sit up, I feel sloshy and dizzy, but vaguely triumphant. I can take care of myself. Mim will be proud of me when I tell her about this, and her smile will make it all worthwhile. When I see the starlit shimmer of red at the base of a tree nearby, I can scarcely withhold my joy.

A pile of berries. I crawl forward. I have no idea why a pile of ripe berries would be sitting out in the open, but I barely care. There's no one around to see me take them. I reach out to scoop them up.

Too late do I see the glint of something else—metal ridges, poking from the pine needles. I yank my hand back as the berries fly into the air and wicked bronze teeth slam shut with a shrieking clash. I land on my side, my whole body buzzing with alarm. Almost caught in a hunter's trap. I let out a gasping chuckle and reach up to wipe pine needles from my cheek.

My palm is covered with blood.

My ears ring as sticky crimson streams down my wrist and into the sleeve of my dress. I stare at my hand. The shape is not right. My fingers . . .

A strangled cry falls from my lips, and the darkness claims me.

# CHAPTER 8

ain has taken me in its monstrous arms, laid me on
its table, and now it's eating me alive.

     I feel the movements of its mouth. Every time
its teeth close around me, the hot agony pulses from my
shoulders to my toes. It's rhythmic and steady and endless.

     It grunts. "Stars, you're heavy."

     My eyes snap open, but I'm surrounded by darkness. I'm
curled into a ball, imprisoned in a cocoon of scratchy material that reeks of blood and animal musk. I squirm feebly
against its stiff walls. My damp gown is bunched about my
legs. My cloak is gone. My hair is tangled around my neck
and face. My left side is mashed against something hard and
cool and unyielding, and I'm held in place by a tight binding that presses against my hips and shoulders. I try to raise

my head, but I'm completely enclosed. I try to tear at the fabric, but a grinding wave of searing heat scorches its way down my arm. I scream.

Pain stops chewing. And then he curses.

The binding around my hips loosens, followed by the release of the tension at my shoulders. The world spins and I'm falling, but my collision with the ground is surprisingly gentle. Something pokes at my head, and then the scratchy material is pulled away from my face. I wince as daylight jabs at my eyeballs. The blurry green-orange-yellow blobs around me slowly become trees. The wind gusts, and a few colorful leaves spiral down. The air is filled with a scent I can only describe as *green*. In the temple gardens, there were a few trees, but nothing like this.

Someone leans over me. I blink, trying to bring him into focus. A young man, perhaps a few years older than I am. Granite-gray eyes and dark-brown hair pulled back into a tail at the base of his neck. A few strands have worked their way loose and hang around his face. He has deeply tanned skin and some of the broadest shoulders I've ever seen.

"Thirsty?" he asks, his voice deep but hushed.

*What?* My lips move, but no sound comes out. My captor loosens the top of my cocoon and pulls it wide. Horror wells up as my gaze rakes from his leather boots to the knives at his belt, one a straight blade, one curved with a sharp barb at its end.

When he reaches for me, I slap at his face with all my strength. But since I have almost none, he easily catches my flapping arms and holds me by the wrists. "Cut it out," he snaps. "You'll start bleeding again."

"What—what—what—," I stammer, my voice so dry and hoarse that it sounds more like the squawks of a crow.

"Relax," he says, looking down at my right hand and frowning. "I'll get you some water."

I glance down at my hand as it throbs with hot, fresh pain. It's tightly wrapped in crimson-stained wool. "No," I moan. Because I remember.

"Two fingers. Clean off at the knuckles," the young man says, pulling a water skin from his satchel, along with several strips of dried . . . something. "You were lucky you didn't lose the whole hand." He scoots back over to me. "Either you were stupid with hunger, or you're just stupid. Elk stick?"

"Elk . . . stick?"

He holds up a shriveled stick of brownish-red meat. When I hesitate, he pokes my lips with it. "Come on. It's pretty tasty. And obviously you make terrible decisions when you're hungry." He grins as I open my mouth and tear off a piece of the dried meat with my teeth. It's salty and chewy and greasy, and stars, I could eat a mountain of it. He feeds me half the stick, bit by bit, and then tugs the last section away as I try to snap my jaws over it. "Slow down. I don't want to make you sicker than you already are. Especially not while you're in my game bag."

*Game bag?* Fear prickles across my skin, cold and sharp.

He cups his hand behind the back of my head and lifts

me a few inches, pouring a tiny splash of water between my parted lips. I swallow, and he lets out a low chuckle as he gives me a little more. "Was it your trap?" I ask in a gargly voice.

He scratches at the dark stubble along his jaw. "No. I never use that kind. More?" He holds up the water skin.

I shake my head. "Why am I in a game bag?"

"Because you're too weak to escape it, I imagine," he says, then takes a few long pulls from the water skin. He lowers it from his lips and wipes his mouth with the back of his worn woolen sleeve. I look again at the material around my destroyed hand and then back at him. There's a large swath missing from the side of his tunic. I can see the hard ridges of his ribs and stomach through the hole. Three slashing, silver-pink scars mar his side. He sees me looking and tugs at the fraying fabric as if he's embarrassed. "I had to stop the bleeding somehow."

"Thank you," I murmur, closing my eyes.

"Don't thank me yet," he replies. "We've got a few miles to go."

"Where are we going?" I whisper. I barely care if he cooks me over a fire and eats me for supper. The longer I'm awake, the more it hurts.

A rough fingertip nudges my cheek. "Hey. *Hey.* Don't go anywhere."

"Hmm?"

"Don't die. If I have to stop to bury you, I won't make it home by sundown, and it gets cold out here at night."

He tugs the scratchy material over my shoulders, but when he tries to pull it over my head, I begin to thrash, and he pauses. "Your head was lolling around back there and I started to get scared I was going to break your neck on the uneven terrain. If you promise to stay awake, we can leave your head out of the bag."

"I promise." I'll do anything not to be encased in that smelly material.

His smile softens the hard edge of his jaw and makes the corners of his eyes crinkle. "Good girl."

"Who are you?"

His dark, slashing eyebrows rise. "Me? I'm nobody. But you can call me Oskar. You?"

I let out a wheezy, bitter laugh and tell the truth. "I'm nobody too. But you can call me Elli."

His gray eyes roam my face. "Done. And now that we know each other well, it's time to get going." He takes me by the shoulders and pulls me up so I'm sitting with my arms wrapped around my knees. I must look ridiculous, a lumpy burlap bag with a head sticking out of the top. Oskar picks up a length of thick rope lying on the ground next to me. "This is going to hurt."

"Everything hurts."

He stares at the ground for a moment, then gazes into my eyes. "The wounds on your back bled through the bandages. And your dress. Also, your wrists . . ."

My cheeks blaze and I look away. My wrists are scabby and stinging from the wounds left by the shackles.

"It's all right," he says quietly. "No one out here's had an easy time of it."

Oskar sits with his back to me and slides the thick straps of the hunting bag over his muscular shoulders, snugging me up against his body. Then he grabs either end of the rope and pulls it tight against my hips. He loops it around his waist and ties it across his middle. He winds the second section of rope around my shoulders and knots it over his chest.

"Up we go." He leans forward, and I grit my teeth as he rises to his feet with his satchel in his hand. He slings it over one shoulder. I breathe slowly, trying to wish the pain away, but it's still there, doing its work. As he begins to walk, I notice how high off the ground I am and realize Oskar must be well over six feet tall. The motion of his body as he moves over the rough ground makes me feel dizzy again. I lean my head against his shoulder blade and close my eyes. His hair, pulled to the side so the straps don't tug at it, tickles my cheek. He smells like wood smoke, thankfully, and not like the inside of his game bag, which counts as a definite improvement.

As he hikes, I listen to the sounds of the forest, the crunch of his boots over twigs and newly fallen leaves, the twittering of birds above our heads, the rustle and dash of small creatures bolting up trees or into burrows. It reminds me a little of the hours I used to spend in the enclosed garden that contained the temple menagerie and aviary. I loved to run my hands over the silken fur of the gray rabbits and to watch the ferrets and badgers running in circles around their pens. I would sit so still, my hand held out to offer seeds and crumbs, and some of the blue jays and black-capped chickadees would come down and peck at my palm. We also had a grumpy crow and one majestic, silent eagle that had a cage all to itself. So did old Nectarhand, the grizzly bear, who used to loll, lazy and fat, in the beams of sun that came at midday. I used to toss him berries dipped in honey and watch his thick pink tongue slide out to capture them. His massive claws were so long that he could barely walk.

Something tells me the bears in this forest move a lot faster.

My eyes pop open. "Is it safe out here?" I whisper.

"Mmm?"

"The animals? Bears? Wolves?"

Oskar laughs. "Well, I've already claimed you, so the other predators are out of luck."

The humor in his voice pushes fear out of reach. Or maybe the raging fever that's eating my bones makes it impossible to care either way. "And are you planning to feed your family with my carcass?"

My cheek vibrates with his silent amusement. "Nah. Truth be told, you're a bit too skinny."

"I am not!"

He laughs again, and it's a sound so free and happy that I actually smile. "Well, all right," he says, "you've a nice heft to you, and I'm sure you'd be very tender with a delicate yet satisfying taste, but . . ." He trails off. "No, I'm not going to eat you. I'm taking you to a medicine man, because I'm fairly sure you're going to die if I don't get you some help in the very near future."

*Someone had mercy.* It's an island of relief in a vast lake of horror. I clear my throat, and it makes me wince. "Why are you helping me?"

Oskar's steps are rock steady as he negotiates a steep downhill and then picks up a trail at the bottom. "No one else was there to do it," he says, as if it should be obvious.

The trail leads out of the woods and across a stretch of grassland, strands of gold waving in the cool breeze. I've never seen such a wide-open space. It's like looking out over the Motherlake, only instead of water, there's land. No walls, no buildings. Oskar hikes like he carries people on his back all the time, frequently turning his face to the bright sun. He doesn't offer any information about himself, and neither do I. Even though we're not in the city, I would never tell anyone who I am.

Or really: who I *was.*

I'm so ashamed that I wish there was a way to remove my blood-flame mark, to scrub it from my skin. It's been a point of pride for so long, but now even the thought of it makes me cringe. Have I deprived the people of their true Valtia? Will the Kupari fall because of me? It doesn't matter that I didn't have a part in this fraud; I still feel responsible.

Something else I feel responsible for: Mim. Did she make it to our meeting spot and find me gone? Is she looking for me, worried out of her mind? Or worse . . . was she caught somehow?

The farther we go, the more the grass gives way to craggy stone capped with wigs of scraggly weeds. Soon our path is bounded on either side with walls of rock, and we seem to be descending deeper into the earth. Even through the haze of pain, I feel a twinge of anxiety. "Where is this medicine man?" I finally ask.

"Where no one can threaten or harass him," Oskar says in a hard voice. "Same as the rest of us."

His tone, so different from his casual, joking words before, shuts me up. After several more minutes on an increasingly narrow trail, he stops, his feet skidding in loose rock. "I think this'll go more smoothly if we pull the sack over your head. It's not a great time to bring a stranger here. Sorry."

Without waiting for my approval, he reaches back and pulls the edges of the sack up, then ties it over the top of my head. I tense as darkness engulfs me.

Oskar begins walking again, and only a few minutes later, I hear someone shout his name. "Oy, Jouni," Oskar calls out in response. "Any trouble?"

"None," says a deep buzz of a voice from somewhere above us. "We've been on watch all day. I expected the new Valtia to be at our doorstep by now." He chuckles. "Or at least a horde of constables."

My anxiety grows into a stab of fear.

Oskar lets out a growl of displeasure and begins to walk

again. "Don't let down your guard. Sig's actions will bear consequences."

There's a grunt as boots impact stone, and then footsteps shuffle right next to Oskar's. "I'm thinking the elders and city council are dealing with other troubles now," Jouni says. "Between the Soturi threat and the fall of the Valtia, the death of a few miners seems a petty concern."

"Now a human life is a petty concern?" Oskar mutters something about hypocrisy, and his pace quickens.

My arm throbs with pain, but my head throbs with knowledge: Oskar has brought me to the thieves' caverns. And he's talking to this other man like he belongs here.

I must squirm, because Jouni makes a sound of surprise. "What did you bag today? Beaver?"

Oskar snorts. "Wolverine."

Jouni laughs. "And you're carrying it on your back while it's still alive? I'm all in favor of fresh meat, but . . ." I hear the hum of metal being freed from a sheath. "Do you want me to put it out of its mis—"

Oskar pivots suddenly, swinging me away from the sound of Jouni and his knife. "No," he says sharply. "It's not necessary," he adds, gently this time. "The creature is mostly dead anyway."

"Let me know if you need help skinning it," says Jouni. "I'll check in later."

His voice is already fading as Oskar continues on his way. "Hey," he says in a hushed voice. "Keep still until I tell you to move."

"These are the thieves' caverns," I hiss, out of patience and plagued by hurt.

"I'm terribly sorry," he says evenly. "You would have preferred to bleed to death honorably in the woods?"

I have nothing to say to that, so I huddle within his bag. Wherever he's brought me, it's getting colder. Oskar shivers, and his footsteps falter for a moment—but only for a moment. The needle pricks of daylight that reach me through the bag grow dim and gray, then disappear, replaced by the dull glow of several small fires. All around me, I hear people, laughing, arguing, discussing how best to season the stew, who's next up for guard duty, who would like to join a game of Ristikontra, who's stolen the only complete deck of playing cards . . . so many conversations . . . and the laughter of children. Children—in the thieves' caverns! And their mothers, who scold them for straying too far!

Several people greet Oskar by name as he passes them by. A few joke with him about what's in his bag. He gives a different answer every time—a wild pig, a few dozen squirrels, a coyote, a nice fat goose—and I stay very still and play dead so no one else offers to turn my pretend into a reality. One high-pitched voice, that of a child, asks him when he'll be home, and Oskar says he's not sure yet. A woman asks him where he's going, and he says he's taking his kill to Raimo because the man's too skinny for his own good. I hear so many things, but I don't learn much. Especially because my head is pounding, and my eyeballs are so hot that it feels like they're going to burst like cherry tomatoes held over an open fire.

The voices fade after a while, and Oskar is hiking a dark, slippery path. Water plinks and thunks into puddles. Oskar shivers and curses and splashes and growls. He sounds a bit like old Nectarhand the bear in a bad mood. It makes sense—Oskar's nearly the size of a grizzly too.

"Please tell me you're still alive back there," he finally says, breathing hard. "You haven't moved in far too long."

"You told me not to," I say, my voice cracking.

"Stars, you sound awful."

"So many compliments," I whisper. I'm not sure he hears me. He clumsily makes his way along, and then comes to an abrupt halt.

"Raimo!" he calls out. His gruff voice echoes off cavern walls. "I'm coming in. Don't try anything."

From perhaps twenty feet away, there comes a reedy cackle. "Why, boy, would you actually defend yourself?" The voice is clearly that of an elderly man, but his tone is full of challenge.

Oskar lets out an irritable sigh and moves forward again. "I've brought you a patient."

"I'm busy."

"You're playing solitaire."

"I'm at a very tricky point."

Oskar is silent. After a few moments, Raimo lets out that creepy cackle again. "Such a fierce glare. One would think you're actually dangerous. Well, where is this patient—is he here? I'm not hiking all the way to the front cave."

"She's right here," Oskar says, and by his movements

I know he's untying the ropes around his waist and chest. They fall away one after the other, and then he lowers himself to his knees. My world cants crazily as he slides the straps of the game bag down his arms, and then I'm on my side on a cold, rocky floor. It feels good. I'm burning from the inside out. Oskar opens the bag and pulls it away from my face. I can't focus my eyes. All I can see is the dim glow of a fire and shadows dancing on wet rock walls.

"Try a waltz," I murmur. Mim taught me once, and we spent all evening giggling and twirling, and the world is spinning like that right now. Thinking of her makes my throat so tight that it's hard to breathe, and I let out a choked sob.

Oskar places the backs of his fingers against my cheek and curses. "She's got such a fever."

"I haven't seen this one before," Raimo says.

Oskar is staring at someone just out of my line of sight. "Found her in the north woods, maybe an hour's hike from the city."

Raimo makes an annoyed sound in his throat. "And what will you give me in return for my help?"

"Full beaver pelt," says Oskar.

Raimo scoffs, "You insult me."

"Two, then."

"Take her away, boy. My cards await."

"The next bear I take down," Oskar snaps. "Meat and pelt."

"You know that's not what I want."

"The answer is no."

"Then take. Her. *Away*."

"She'll die!" Oskar shouts, his voice ringing through the cave.

"People die every day, boy, especially here. You have to stop collecting strays."

"I recall you saying the same thing about Sig at first."

"That kind of lightning doesn't strike twice, as has been proven every time you've brought some other lost, sickly soul here to foist upon me. It's been at least one each year, and you used up your allotment this past spring when you dragged Josefina in from the marshes. That mad old bat was a handful—and not an experience I'm eager to repeat, at any price." He's quiet for a moment before adding, "Except one."

Oskar crosses his arms over his chest. "I'll do it," he says from between clenched teeth. "Just me, though. Not Freya. And you'll stay quiet about it, or . . . I'll kill you."

Raimo's laugh echoes loudly, making me wish I had the strength to cover my ears. "I have no interest in your sister, and you have no idea how silly you sound. But you have my word. It stays between us until you decide otherwise—or necessity dictates."

"Oskar," I whisper. "It's all right." I have no idea what he's offering in exchange for Raimo's help, but it sounds like it's killing him.

"Where do you want her?" he asks, ignoring me.

"Over there. What's wrong with her?"

Oskar lugs me across the cavern. He sets me down on

something soft, making sure to place me on my side instead of on my back. "Lost two fingers in a bear trap. But she wasn't in good shape before then. She'd been whipped, I think."

"You think?" Raimo's voice is much closer now, and it makes me shudder.

"I didn't strip her naked and check," Oskar says drily. "But she'd bled through, and I know what lash marks look like. I assume she was a servant in the town. Her dress is plain but well-made, and she's got some meat on her bones."

"A runaway maid. How romantic," says Raimo. "Well, take your bag and go. I should have her fixed up by morning."

*By morning?* As nice as that would be, I think it's going to take longer than that.

But Oskar doesn't seem surprised—he tugs the bag loose and carefully folds my ruined hand over my chest, then straightens my aching legs. His strong fingers close right over my blood-flame mark, and it pulses another wave of numb through my body.

"So you'll help her," he says, sounding hesitant. "You'll do your best for her."

"No, boy, I'll butcher her and make myself a nice stew. Get back to your mother. Oh, and tell her thank you for the rye loaf, by the way. It was delicious."

Oskar leans over me. His face is smeared with grime and sweat. "Raimo's going to fix you up, Elli," he says softly. "I'll check on you later." He touches the back of my left hand, his fingers cool, his voice kind.

I doubt I'll see him again. My mouth is filled with the copper-iron taste of blood, and I think that means I'm going to die. I want to tell him thanks for trying, but I'm too tired to speak. He gets up and walks out. His footsteps fade soon after.

Another face leans over mine. Bald except for two tufts of white hair above his ears. Sunken cheeks. A prominent chin, from which hangs a stringy white beard. A long, hooked nose. Clever, calculating ice-blue eyes. "Name?" he asks.

"Elli," I whisper.

"All right, Elli the runaway maid." He clucks his tongue. "Let's see the hand."

I drift while he unravels the brown wool, then cry out as he peels it from my wound. I try to pull away, but his grip on my wrist is relentless. "Pity," he says as he looks at my grotesquely swollen hand and the empty space where my pinkie and ring finger used to be. "What made you desperate enough to reach into a bear trap?"

I don't answer, and I don't think he expects me to. He disappears for a few moments and returns with a wet cloth. I roil with bubbling pain as he cleans the raw, bloody meat of my hand. His pale eyes meet mine. "I'm going to heal this, and then I'll do your back." He says it with confidence, as if I weren't hovering on the precipice of death.

He takes my hand between both of his and stares intently at it. I feel faint flashes of heat, then cool.

*Magic.* This medicine man is a wielder. Here, in the outlands. In the thieves' caverns.

And he is a *healer*. No one with that much magic could have escaped the elders' notice—they would have found him as a child and brought him to the temple to serve like all the rest. They'd never have left him in the outlands to molder in a cave! For a moment, all my questions about who Raimo is and how he came to be here sharpen my mind and drag me back from the shore of oblivion. But then the old man moves my hand and another bolt of pain scatters all of them.

A deep wrinkle appears between Raimo's bushy white eyebrows. He peers with even more intensity at my wound. More flashes of cold, then hot, then cold again, but I feel them only vaguely, like the idea of temperature instead of the reality.

And now Raimo is scowling.

He mutters to himself, then matter-of-factly unbuttons the back of my dress and pulls it down my arms. The action tugs at the bandages over my flayed back, and I writhe help-lessly. Once again, I feel wisps of hot and cold, this time across my backbone. I have no idea how long it goes on, but when I'm jerked into solid awareness again, Raimo is leaning over me.

"You're keeping secrets, my dear." He uses the pads of his thumbs to lift my eyelids wide. "Ice-blue," he says. He coils a lock of my hair around his finger. "And burnished copper."

My heart skips unsteadily.

He moves closer, until his hooked nose is only a few

inches from mine. He smells of fish and wet fur. "I am going to ask you a question, and it is very important that you answer me truthfully. Your life depends on this truth. Understand?"

I nod, though my heart is thumping madly.

"Do you have a mark?"

"Wh-what?" I whisper. "Why are you asking me that?" Panic swirls inside me. How could he know?

He smirks as he reads the fear in my eyes. "You're not strong enough to stop me if I want to search for it, but it will be easier if you'd just tell me where it is. I'm not going to hurt you."

I search for malice in his eyes, but I see nothing except ice. Cold, but not evil. I hope. "On my leg."

He wrenches the hem of my skirt up. I know the moment he sees it, because he curses. "It's certainly hard to miss. Oskar—has he seen this?"

"No."

"Does anyone outside the temple know who you are?"

I think of Mim, but I refuse to expose her to more danger. "No."

"Good. No one can know. Stars, I've been waiting so long for this." He moves back up to my head and takes my face in his gnarled hands. "You were born the day Karhu and Susi aligned, yes? Do you know?"

"No . . ." But Kauko said the stars predicted my birth— was this what he was talking about?

Raimo's chin trembles as he smiles. "You might have

secrets, but you're terrible at keeping them. You've been a princess all these years, haven't you?"

My skin burns with shame, and I close my eyes.

"You're the one who was found," he says. "They thought you were *her*. But you're not."

A low sob escapes from my throat as he flays me with the truth. "How can you possibly know this?"

He lets out a bark of laugher. "Because I am *very* good at keeping secrets. So—what happened when you didn't inherit the magic? Did you run away, or did they cast you out?"

"I ran. They . . . were going to kill me."

He grins as if I've given him wonderful news. "Ah, they never figured it out!" He claps his hands over his thighs, which are covered in a black robe very much like the ones the priests wear. "Well, you've complicated my evening. Try to keep breathing while I prepare a few poultices."

I frown. "But you were healing me with magic."

The shadows nest in the hollows under his eyes and make his face look like a skull. "I was trying. But as it turns out, that won't work."

"Why not?"

Something akin to delight deepens the rows of wrinkles on his gaunt cheeks. "Because you, my dear, are completely immune to magic. It won't help you." He raises his eyebrows. "But it can't hurt you either."

I blink at him in confusion. "What are you saying?"

"There are more magic wielders in this land than you

could possibly know." His gaze strays down to my leg, where my blood-flame mark lies stark and red on my exposed calf. "And to every one of them, you could be either their most powerful asset—or their worst enemy."

# CHAPTER 9

I draw my dry tongue across my chapped lips. "You're saying I definitely have no magic?"

"Not an ounce. Not a jot. Not a drop." Raimo has moved from my side and is hunched over a wooden board, chopping herbs that fill the room with a fresh, astringent scent. "Not even a tiny little splinter of it. Not even a—"

"I get it," I snap, then cough with the effort. "Then why would anyone think I was dangerous?"

"All people have some amount of fire and ice inside them. Even if it's just enough to make them hot-tempered or easygoing. Even if it only makes them fit for ice-fishing or blacksmithing. Even in people not from Kupari, where the copper flows through our veins and enhances those elements in a few, causing it to manifest as magic."

"Copper . . . they locked me up in a box of copper. . . ."

He rolls his eyes. "Of course they did. But you understand—copper is the source. It's the reason the Kupari have magic when no one else does." He snorts. "And the Kupari people love their magic—so long as the wielders are shut away tight within the temple walls. But never before has one such as you walked among us, completely devoid of fire and ice."

Shame fills me again. "Was I always like this?"

He shrugs. "Before the Valtia died, you had no ice or fire, but you probably weren't immune to its effects. You weren't the vessel you are now, just like the Valtia is an ordinary girl until the magic awakens inside of her."

Perhaps his words explain the vast, shapeless void that's opened inside me, the hollow thump of my heart. The numbness that radiates from my blood-flame mark. "How does that make me anything but useless? I'm a mistake."

"You shouldn't even exist," he comments as he picks up a wooden-handled pitcher from near the fire and waddles over to me again.

I close my eyes. "Then let me die."

"Not a chance." Warm water pours over my back, and he begins to peel away the bandages Mim wrapped tightly around me. "Nothing like you has *ever* existed, Elli. I was starting to believe I'd been wrong all along. But your arrival marks the beginning of a new era for the Kupari. You're going to change everything, for better or worse." He makes a sound of disgust as he tosses a bloody strip of cloth away. "Assuming you live out the night, that is."

"How could it be anything but worse?" I croak. "The Kupari need a Valtia."

"Oh, she's out there." He pulls away the final strip of gauze. The cool air of the cave bites at my broken skin, but then he spreads something sticky over the lash wounds. It smells like sage and onion, honey and slippery elm. "In fact," he says as he works, "she'll be immeasurably powerful."

Like the stars foretold. "How do you know?"

"Because if she wasn't, the cosmos wouldn't have created you to keep the balance."

"But the Valtia *is* balance." This is a truth embedded in my bones.

His eyes meet mine. "Not this time."

"How do you know so much?" The elders and priests guard their knowledge closely, which has always been incredibly frustrating. And Sofia once told me that most citizens have only the barest understanding of the magic, which makes sense, since the children who reveal themselves as able to wield it are taken to the temple as soon as they're discovered. Except for this man, apparently. Which could mean only one thing.

"Were you a priest?"

His smile glistens in the flickering firelight. "Not during your lifetime."

It's not a denial. "Why did you leave?"

One of his bushy eyebrows twitches like a living thing. "Let's just say I found my fellow priests to be a bit bloodthirsty." He takes my ruined hand and lays it on a clean scrap of brown wool. "This is still oozing. I'm going to have to cauterize it."

I shiver. "You said fire wouldn't affect me."

"I said magic wouldn't affect you. Ordinary flames made from ordinary fuel are a different matter entirely." He moves close to the fire. I hear the clang of metal. My stomach clenches.

"What will happen if it's not cauterized?"

"You'll bleed to death. Or possibly die of blood poisoning."

Neither of those sounds terrible at the moment. Perhaps Raimo senses my thoughts, because he looks over his shoulder at me. "You were raised as the Saadella, were you not?"

"I was," I whisper.

"So you were brought up with the understanding that you exist to serve the Kupari."

I look away from his gaze.

"*Nothing* has changed," he says, his voice right next to my ear. His hand clamps over my wrist. I feel a flash of heat and then a pain so bright that it lights me up, arches me back, fills the cave with the scent of my burning flesh and the sound of my hoarse screams. White flames burst before my eyes, and I pray to the stars for release that doesn't come. By the time he's finished, I'm wishing for death, but he reminds me over and over of my purpose, of my duty, awakening all my memories of my lessons from the elders. My life is not my own. My body belongs to the people. My magic is for them, not for me. Magic. *Magic.*

If I could laugh, I would. Raimo is so wrong. *Everything* has changed.

I wake with a jolt, tightly encased up to my neck, warm and unable to move. My body feels like it weighs a hundred stone. My eyelids are too heavy to lift. But my ears work perfectly, and now I hear what wrenched me from the void: arguing.

"Why didn't you just do it while she was asleep then?" It's Oskar, his deep voice as sharp as the blades that hang from his belt.

"You would have me violate the wishes of a young woman simply because she's vulnerable enough for me to force my will upon her?" Raimo asks. *His* voice is full of teasing amusement. "My dear boy, I never thought I'd hear such a suggestion from you."

Oskar makes a growling sound of pure frustration. "If her wishes were the product of a bigoted, fever-addled brain, then—"

"Oh, she was quite lucid. Her desires were perfectly clear. No magic. Only the ordinary means of healing."

I never said that, did I?

"Did you explain that she could have been well by now? Did she understand that those 'ordinary means' would amount to days of pain and—"

"Give me some credit. She's stubborn as a stump." Raimo's voice rises in quavering, high-pitched imitation. "'Don't come near me with that sorcery! I won't have it!'" He cackles.

Oskar sighs. "If I'd known she felt that way . . ."

"You'd still have brought her here. And you did the right thing. She's already better. The fever has broken. She's going to live, and we should all be thankful for that."

"And her hand?"

"No more bleeding and no signs of rot or blood poisoning so far. She probably won't lose it. But she'll be in pain."

The scrape of boots against stone tells me Oskar has moved closer to my resting place. If I had the strength to move or speak, I would greet him. I have the oddest desire to see his face again.

"Will she be able to fend for herself?" he asks.

"Eventually. Until then, you'll fend for her."

"What?" Oskar's voice bleeds with shock. "The weather is colder every day, old man. I have to—"

"You have to do what I say. She'll need protection until the spring if she is to survive. I can heal her wounds, but I can't keep her belly full or look after her safety."

"But *winter*. Thus far, there's no warmth from the temple, and for all we know, it's not coming. Right now I'm the absolute worst person to help her."

Raimo chuckles. "Oh, son, I couldn't disagree more. And if you do it, I'll release you from your promise until the spring thaw. As it turns out, we can't wait longer than that."

Oskar is silent for a long moment. "I'll have to talk to Mother. And Freya." He sounds like he dreads the idea.

"Then do so. Come back for Elli in . . . let's make it eight days. I'll look after her until then, but any longer than that isn't possible. I'm pushing it already." He pauses for a moment before adding, "And if we happen to be visited by constables again, do us all a favor and don't mention you brought her here, hmm?"

"Did she tell you something about where she came from, or why she was banished?" Oskar asks.

"No," Raimo replies quickly. "But you were right—she'd been whipped. Whoever did it might be searching for her, and the last thing we need is to be accused of kidnapping servants from wealthy families."

"They're much more likely to come here because of what Sig did to the miners than because I came to the aid of a banished servant." Oskar's voice has gone low and bitter.

Raimo grunts. "Perhaps, but we don't need to give them any more reason to bring temple-dwelling wielders to our doorstep, do we? Now leave me alone, and I'll see you in eight days."

Grumbling, Oskar thumps out of the cavern, and Raimo's gnarled fingers close over my shoulder. "Necessary lies," he says, but I'm already drifting again, and if more words fall from his lips, I don't hear them.

Raimo is an excellent medicine man, even deprived of magic. Over the next several days, he comes to know my body as well as I do, perhaps better, and though it's awkward and embarrassing to allow him to attend to my every need, I have no choice. Besides, I'm accustomed to having people take care of me. It's just that they've always been women. I have no energy to waste on modesty or protest, though, and I doubt Raimo would do anything but cackle at me if I did.

Within the cave, I have no sense of day or night, only sleeping and waking. Raimo feeds me stew and constantly presses a cup to my lips, urging me to drink some concoction that coats my tongue and makes me gag. He is the most persistent and attentive of physicians, caring for every wound, applying new poultices every few hours. My right hand throbs and aches as if my fingers were still attached and badly mangled. The sensation invades my dreams, where I relive the trap slamming shut over and over again. But when I wake up whimpering, Raimo is always at my side. He never offers words of comfort, but his touch is gentle as he sponges my sweating brow with a warm cloth.

A few times, in the hopeful moments before I remember where I am, I mistake him for Mim, and I strain to move closer, to catch her scent. *You're a jewel,* she whispers, her bright smile making my stomach swoop. I long to twist my finger into the curls at the nape of her neck. I am desperate to hear her say my name. But when I reach with my good hand, when my fingertips brush over skin, it is dry and veiny instead of soft and warm, and I jerk back with the wrongness of it.

*Please be safe, Mim. And please don't forget me.*

That is my prayer to the stars, mouthed over and over in the darkness.

I shed more tears during these days than I have in the first sixteen years of my life. I mourn what I thought I was.

I worry about what I really am. I drift in and out of restless sleep, my dreams full of blood and ice and fire. I surface again, full of questions that Raimo assures me we'll discuss when I am lucid enough to remember his answers.

"Oskar is coming for you today," he tells me after one such waking. "Remember what I told you about guarding your secret. We can't afford for word of your true nature to spread."

"But I still don't understand my true nature!" And I'm horrified to discover I've run out of time to learn from him. I push myself into a sitting position with my left hand, keeping my right folded against my chest. "If you're sending me away today, I think you'd better tell me."

Raimo's eyes narrow. "You must have seen the adornment the Valtia wears around her forearm, yes?"

Only every time I saw her. "The cuff of Astia."

He nods. "And you know what it does?"

I bite back impatience. I may not know much about magic, but I'm not an idiot. "It helps her amplify and project her power. She told me she didn't need it most of the time. Only when she performed large-scale magic, like creating the dome of warmth in the winter months." *And when she created the storm that killed her.*

"Exactly. It is a tool. Like the copper lightning rods that jut from the roofs of every house in the city. It conducts and magnifies that power, but also absorbs it, helping the wielder maintain balance. By itself, it's merely a hunk of metal, albeit a very special one." The corner of his mouth twists as he looks at me. "It's pretty, but not that useful. Like you at the moment."

His words sting, but objecting would only draw his mockery. I've heard how he talks to Oskar.

"But when wielded by a person who possesses fire or ice or both at once," Raimo continues, "the cuff of Astia becomes the key to victory."

"So I'm a tool," I say in a dead voice. "Or maybe a weapon."

"That's the least interesting way to think about it," he replies. "It would be smarter to ponder this: you are a living, breathing, *thinking* Astia."

"Raimo!" a deep voice barks, causing me to jerk with surprise.

"Remember," Raimo whispers. "Tell no one. Gather your strength. If I'm right, a war is coming, but with true winter descending and no Valtia to push it back, you may have some time. Stay close to Oskar, who avoids trouble like it's his life's calling. Stay alive, please. Focus on healing." He snorts. "And on learning how to be useful. No one here has time to wait on you."

I curse myself for not demanding he answer my questions before now, even though I was too weak to protest. "Who are you, really? Why are you no longer a priest?" I lean forward and try to catch his sleeve, but he skitters out of my reach. "How is it that you know what I am when the elders didn't?" My left fist clenches when I hear Oskar's footsteps coming nearer. "Raimo, can't I stay here with you?"

He shivers, moving closer to the fire. "I've let you stay too long already, girl."

"Can't we meet again? There's so much I don't know!"

Raimo rubs his hand over his mostly bald head, looking regretful instead of mocking for once. "When the thaw comes."

"But—"

Oskar strides into the cavern. In one hand is a torch, and in the other he clutches a bundle of rags. His hair is pulled back from his face, but he looks more like a bear than ever, fur and all.

Raimo eyes the thick garment Oskar has wrapped over his shoulders and torso. "The weather must have taken a turn," he comments.

Oskar looks down at himself. "There was a frost last night." He moves closer to the fire and sees me lying on the other side of it. His gaze slides from my head to my feet, and his brows rise. For the first time since we met, I'm sitting up by myself.

I'm also wearing nothing but a blanket. His eyes meet mine. "You look better."

I clutch the thick woolen fabric a little higher on my chest. "Thank you. I feel better."

He holds up the bundle of rags. "I brought you some clothes. I think they'll fit." He looks away. "I'll be waiting outside."

He shoves the clothes into Raimo's arms and stalks out of the cavern. I watch him go with guilt sitting heavy in my gut. I remember how reluctant he was to take responsibility for me, how pained he sounded when Raimo demanded it. Raimo looks like he's trying not to laugh as he walks over and hands me the clothing. "Oskar is unwaveringly honorable. Usually it's irritating, but today we should count ourselves lucky."

"He doesn't want to take care of me."

Raimo shakes his head. "Not right now, no." He nudges the ball of garments in my lap with the toe of his grimy boot. "Get up and get dressed, girl. Your lazy days of convalescence are over."

He walks over to a flat rock near the fire, where he draws a deck of cards from beneath a stone ledge. As I clumsily unfold the clothes, struggling to manage with my still tightly bandaged right hand, he begins to deal out a game of solitaire.

I hold up the garments. Oskar has brought me a pair of thick, warm stockings, serviceable leather slippers, a shapeless gown made out of the same brown wool as his own tunic, and a kerchief for my hair. The clothing of a peasant. A sharp prickle of anxiety and shame makes me shiver.

It's not that I think I'm too good for these things. I'm grateful to have them. But I have barely the faintest idea of how to put them on. I've never actually dressed myself, and now I have only one good hand to help me accomplish the task. Yes, I have three fingers left on my right hand, but I can barely touch the pad of my thumb to my forefinger because they're so stiff and sensitive. My middle finger juts out, useless and crooked.

"The more you move and stretch them, the easier it will be," Raimo says quietly. "You'll probably never regain full use of them, but that's no excuse not to try."

I stare at Raimo's back. He has a card in his hand, but he's not playing. He's waiting, I realize, probably for me to ask for help or whine about my need for a maidservant. And right now, I want Mim more than ever, for so many reasons. But if I say that to Raimo, he'll only mock me. I press my lips together. *Pretty, but not that useful. Like you right now.* The words burn as I digest the undeniable truth of them, especially when I think of Oskar waiting outside, loathing the idea of taking me under his protection.

I'm not a jewel. Not a treasure. Not a wonder or a living miracle.

I'm a burden.

Determination forms like a fist behind my breast.

I will *not* be a burden.

With clenched teeth, I find the top of one of the stockings and shove my foot into it. It gets caught in the narrow tube of fabric. I let out a frustrated little grunt as I wrestle with it. Sweat beads across my brow. Pain gnaws at my right hand, chomping its way up my arm. But I don't give up.

I refuse to let a stocking defeat me.

"Is she ready yet?" Oskar calls from outside the cavern.

"Not quite," calls Raimo, who sounds like it's taking all his will to keep from cackling.

I redouble my efforts, squirming and twisting and groaning when my knee bashes into my cauterized knuckles. I'm nearly limp with exhaustion by the time I get the obnoxious garment pulled up to my thigh.

"Try pointing your toes and sliding them in rather than trying to jam your entire foot straight down into it," Raimo suggests, his voice trembling with mirth.

My nostrils flare. "It would have been easy enough for you to mention that several minutes ago."

"True." He resumes playing cards.

The second stocking goes on much more smoothly, thanks to his sage advice. And the dress is simple enough—I pull it over my head and thrust my left arm through a sleeve.

Raimo gives me a sidelong glance. "If I told you it was backward, would that upset you?"

"Not at all," I snarl. I yank my arm from the sleeve and turn the dress around. It's an odd style, with a high neck and a low back, but I won't complain—I'm lucky the thing doesn't have buttons, because then I'd be lost. It takes a minute or two to get my right arm through the sleeve because of the bandage on my hand and the odd, stiff position of my exposed fingers, and I sigh with relief when the dress unfurls and falls to my ankles. I slide my feet into the slippers and pick up the kerchief.

"Is she ready now?" calls Oskar, not bothering to conceal his irritation. "I have things to do today."

"Patience, patience," Raimo replies. "Greatness takes time."

My cheeks are burning as I stare at the kerchief. I have no idea how to put this thing on, but my hair is loose and tangled, so I need to do something. I fold the kerchief in half and plaster it over my head, then awkwardly tie the corners beneath my chin.

I step around the fire, to where Raimo is shuffling his cards, which are faded and worn—and completely blank. "Thank you for what you've done."

"I will find you in the spring," he says, not bothering to look up as he begins to deal them. "I wish it could be sooner, but I won't be available before then."

"Why?"

His eyes glint as he raises his head. "I hibernate. Keeps me young." He grins, showing me his yellowed teeth, his long, stringy beard bobbing beneath his chin. "I'll emerge when the ground thaws, and we'll have plenty to talk about. Until then, gather your strength, and for stars' sake, keep silent. If one person in these caverns knows your secrets, they all will."

I gape at him, but before I can ask if he's serious about hibernating—because it's impossible to tell with this mischievous old man—Oskar's voice echoes into the rocky chamber. "What in the stars above is taking so long?" he roars.

Raimo's bony shoulders shake as he starts to laugh, and I scoot out of his presence, rushing headlong into my new life—as an outlaw in the thieves' caverns.

# CHAPTER 10

I scramble toward Oskar, apologies on the tip of my tongue. But his tight jaw relaxes and his lips twitch as he sees me bustling out of Raimo's cave. When his gaze lingers on my hair, I pull the kerchief a little lower on my forehead. His brow furrows. "Your hand is giving you difficulty?" he asks, his voice a bit unsteady.

I shrug my right shoulder so the sleeve covers my crooked fingers. "Not much."

He begins to walk. "You'll stay with my family. My mother and my younger sister. I have to go hunting, so they'll look after you."

"I can help them . . . do whatever needs to be done." Though truly, I have no idea what would need doing. Does one sweep the floor of a cave? Is there cutlery to polish?

"How long have you lived in the caverns?"

"These? Only since the spring." He arches one dark slash of an eyebrow. "We thieves tend to move around a lot, and there are a lot of old mines and caves on the peninsula."

"This one hasn't been mined yet," I say, remembering how desperate the miners supposedly were to gain access—though now I wonder if they were half as desperate as the elders.

"It's one of the few that hasn't been," Oskar informs me. "Which means it's less prone to cave-ins. Our numbers have grown and safety is important."

"How many people live here?"

He gives me a sidelong glance and doesn't answer. I bite the inside of my cheek, but I can't stop myself from blundering forward. "Did you live in the city . . . before?"

"Did you?" he asks, acid in his tone.

For the first time in my life, I understand how threatening simple questions can be. It looks like we both fear the slippery slope of revealed secrets. If I don't want to give away any of mine, it looks like I'll have to curb my own curiosity. "I apologize for prying."

Oskar grunts and steps ahead of me as the tunnel grows narrow. "Watch out for puddles and loose rocks." Our only light is the torch in his hand, and it strikes me that he didn't have one when he made this journey with me on his back. He stumbled through the suffocating dark with a heavy burden pulling him down, just to get help for me. And now he's probably regretting it.

We make our way slowly. Something tells me Oskar is doing it for my benefit. I watch every step and yet still manage to stumble every few seconds. The tunnel seems to stretch forever, winding upward. My legs ache with fatigue. My breaths come harsh and fast; I'm not accustomed to walking so far, and especially not uphill. The three remaining fingers on my right hand are sensitive to any jarring motion, so I keep them tucked against my belly and use only my left hand to keep my balance.

Oskar looks over his shoulder when I stumble for the thousandth time. "Do you need me to carry you?"

"No," I snap, then soften my tone. "But if you could tell me how much farther, I'd be grateful."

His inscrutable gaze lingers on me. "The main cavern is just around that bend." He points the torch toward a distant crimp in the path. I wait to grimace until his back is turned again.

We eventually reach the turn and are greeted by the flicker of distant campfires. The tunnel widens, with a few openings on either side—smaller caverns where I can hear people talking and water splashing. The front cave comes into view a moment later. It's massive, at least as large as the domed chamber in the Temple on the Rock. Around its edges are . . . well, calling them cottages would be generous. At least forty small shelters line either side of the cavern, low walls of stacked stones from which jut rough frames of wood. Hanging from those are loose fabric, animal pelts, drapes made of dried and woven marsh grass, anything to give the residents a bit of privacy. None of the shelters have roofs, but they don't need them—the cavern provides one, though water drips from its black, spiky ceiling.

In the center of the broad, relatively flat expanse of this cavern is a crudely made hearth, and it's obvious that it's a community oven, as several women surround it, poking at dark-brown loaves of bread with sticks and wooden paddles. Children chase one another around the edge of it, their faces streaked with dirt, the knees of their trousers worn and holey. Men gather close to a large fire nearer to the front of the cavern, playing their games of cards. Some are working near their own shelters, oiling traps and untangling fishing lines. One man nearby is skinning a hare, peeling its fur from its flesh with brutal efficiency. I swallow hard and look away.

"And here's the main cavern," Oskar says in a low voice, leaning against a rocky ledge and sweeping his arm across the scene. "Otherwise known as the den of thieves. Don't they look vicious?"

Several of the cavern's inhabitants have noticed our entrance. One by one, they stop what they're doing to stare at me. "They don't exactly look friendly," I mutter, taking a step back.

Oskar's large hand closes over my shoulder. "They know you're under my protection," he says, waving at a stout, brown-bearded man standing near the big fire. The man raises his hand to acknowledge Oskar, then returns to tossing split logs onto the flames. "Newcomers make them wary. Mind your own business, and—"

"Oskar!" cries a piping voice. A young girl, perhaps ten

years of age, comes darting out of a shelter on our left. Two braids of dark hair on either side of her head flap as she runs. "Is this her?" she huffs as she stops in front of us.

"No, this is the other girl I rescued from a bear trap."

She slaps Oskar's fur-covered arm. "You are so grumpy when the cold comes." Her green eyes are full of energy as she turns to me. "Why is your dress on backward?" she asks, looking at my awkwardly high neckline. *Raimo strikes again.* "And what's wrong with your hair?"

My left hand rises to my kerchief. "I . . ."

"Her hand is injured, and she hasn't had the benefit of a mirror for several days," says Oskar, saving me from revealing my ignorance. "Or of female company. That's where you come in." He gestures at the girl. "This little bandit is Freya." He reaches out and tugs one of her braids. "My darling sister and a budding master thief."

"Thief?" The girl scowls. "What in stars are you going on about—"

"Of course you're not a thief," I say, glaring at her big brother, who merely looks back at me with challenge in his eyes. "It's nice to meet you, Freya. I'm Elli." I give her a curtsy, as I've seen Mim do so many times.

Freya snorts and imitates me, confirming that I've done something stupid. "All right, Elli, come on. My mother wants to meet you, and Oskar needs to go kill some furry woodland creatures."

Oskar touches her shoulder. "Freya, if the alarm is sounded—"

She lifts her chin. "I know what to do. I can take care of myself and her, too."

Oskar grins, his whole face brightening, and he tugs Freya into a quick, fierce hug. She disappears into the folds of his cloak and emerges with her hair mussed and a big smile on her face. "I'll be back in a few hours," he says.

Freya grabs for my right hand, but Oskar knocks her arm away just in time. "Remember what I told you about her hand!"

"Oh! Right," Freya says, then grabs my left and begins to pull me toward their shelter. I look over my shoulder for Oskar, but he's already striding toward the exit to the main cavern like he's glad to be rid of my company. I push down a strange twinge of disappointment and follow Freya, flashing a smile at anyone who'll meet my eyes. Most of them offer hard stares in return. I'm relieved when we duck into a shelter, which is sectioned into three small areas separated by walls made of animal fur. There's a wide space at the front containing a small loom, a grinding stone with a pestle lying on top of it, a fire pit, and a large pile of tools, many I don't know the names for. I've never seen such things outside the pages of the books used for my studies, and part of me wants to go over and pick each one up, just to see how they feel in my hands. The rest of me realizes that would only make me look more foolish than I already do.

The front chamber of this shelter is large enough to allow two tall men to lie head to head, and deep enough to allow one tall man—like Oskar—to lie straight. The fur walls, which are made from several different animal pelts stitched together with burlap string, are rich brown, glinting in the light of the small fire in the stone-bounded pit.

A woman about my height, her light-brown hair knotted into a bun on the back of her head, emerges from one of the smaller areas, moving aside a thick, furry pelt that's been nailed to the tall wooden frame. She looks like she's in her midthirties, her forehead creased and weather-worn. Her gray eyes focus in on my clearly ridiculous hair arrangement, and her lips press together. "You must be Elli."

"I am, and you . . . ?"

"Maarika." She's much paler than Oskar, who clearly spent the entire summer in the sun, and her appearance is neat, not a hair out of place, the opposite of Oskar's disheveled roughness. But they have one thing in common—they are both very difficult to read.

I curtsy again, because I have no idea what else to do, but Maarika only frowns at me. "Thank you for taking me in," I say. "I'd like to do anything I can to—"

"Can you grind some corn for me?" she asks. "I'm trying to make Oskar a new tunic to replace the one he shredded last week, and Freya's needed to fetch the water." She doesn't say it in an unfriendly or harsh way. It seems like she's simply informing me of the reality of their lives. "Well?" she asks when I hesitate. "Can you?"

I blink at her, stiffly moving the fingers of my right hand within the long sleeve of my dress and trying not to wince as the raw flesh rubs against my bandages. "Ah . . . yes. Of course."

She bobs her head. "Wonderful." She points to a pile of dried-out corncobs, their husks pulled back, sitting in a basket woven from green twigs. "Corn's there." She points to a wooden bowl sitting next to the grinding stone. "Put it there when you're done."

She disappears back into the small, torch-lit chamber at the back of the shelter. I slowly move toward the corncobs, my heart thumping. I've read about this vegetable, how it's planted and harvested, how it's an important crop for our people. But . . . the only time I've actually seen real corn is when it's been served to me on a plate, kernels roasted and plump and sweet. I know it can also be dried and ground into meal—and I also know that the pestle and grinding stone are used for that purpose. I smile. I can do this. It can't be that hard. I kneel, pick up a cob, and place it on the grinding stone. The moment I reach for the pestle, I hear a giggle from behind me.

"Who taught you to do it that way?" Freya kneels by my side. She picks up the cob and strips the kernels off with strong, confident strokes of her thumbs. The tiny golden nuggets fall with little plinks to the grinding stone. When she's finished, she piles kernels into the shallow depression, picks up the broad pestle, and crushes them with quick, decisive twists of her skinny wrist. She offers me the pestle. "Like that."

I blow out a breath through my pursed lips. "Of course. Like that." I accept the pestle. It's heavier than it looks, rough against my thin, untested skin.

She tilts her head and gazes up at me. "Your kerchief

really looks silly." Without asking permission, she unknots it, then folds it on a diagonal so it forms a triangle instead of a long rectangle as I had done. I feel like such a fool, but am grateful as she flattens it over my head and ties it at the nape of my neck, beneath my thick locks. Next, she tugs on my sleeve. Seeing what she intends, I pull my arms in, and she turns my dress around so that it's no longer backward.

"Thank you so much," I whisper.

"I'm sorry about your fingers," she says, looking down at my bandaged hand as it emerges from the sleeve. "Does it make you very sad?"

I bow my head so she doesn't see the tears starting in my eyes. Missing two fingers feels like a drop in the Motherlake compared to all the other things I've lost. "Not too sad," I say, trying to weave a bit of cheerfulness into my tone. "I'm glad to be alive."

"I'm glad you're alive too." Freya gets up and grabs a large wooden bucket from the corner. "We can always use an extra pair of hands, even if one of them has only three fingers." She ducks through the curtain of fur.

I stare after her, fighting the crazy urge to laugh and cry at the same time. A fortnight ago, I was the someday queen, and now I'm an eight-fingered girl with a back full of scars, whose only worth is in doing things I have no idea how to do. I used to be loved by an entire people, and now the only person in the entire world who cares about me is Mim, and I've lost her. She might even be punished because of me. At the very least, I've left her worried sick. I rub my hand over my chest, which feels like it's being squeezed in the grip of a giant. What I wouldn't give for her to appear and wrap her arms around me.

I swipe my sleeve over my eyes, and then my body buckles, unable to withstand the weight of my grief for another second. I wrap my arms around myself and lay my forehead on the cold grinding stone. I've lost everything.

*"How old was your Valtia when she died?" I'd been trying to gather the courage to ask her all night, and now we were waiting for my sedan chair to come and take me away from my Valtia until the planting ceremony, a whole winter away.*

*The Valtia put her hand on her stomach and took a step back, but when I rushed forward, apologies already falling from my lips, she put her hands up. "It's all right, Elli," she said, her voice thick with sorrow. "She was thirty-two, I think." Her smile was full of pain. "I wasn't ready to say good-bye."*

*She opened her arms to me, and I slid into her embrace, desperate to soothe the sadness that I had caused. "Why did you ask me that?" she whispered.*

*"I don't understand how someone so strong could fade so young." And I was terrified to think of when I would lose my own Valtia. She was fast approaching the end of her twenties.*

*"Our lives aren't ours, darling," she murmured. "We are only the caretakers of this magic. We don't use it to protect ourselves—we use it only to protect the Kupari. They call us queens, but what we really are is servants." There was no bitterness in her voice at all. But then again, she was only repeating*

what I'd been told at the beginning of my daily lessons for as long as I could remember.

"It's not fair," I mumbled into her shoulder. I could hear the footsteps of the acolytes coming down the hall. My time with her was ending. What if I never saw her again? My fingers curled into her sleeves.

She kissed my hair. "We were made for this. You and me. And that means we're strong enough to bear it." She gently pried my hands loose and clasped her fingers over mine. Her pale-blue eyes were fierce with determination. "You're strong enough to bear anything, Elli. That's why the stars chose you."

I raise my head. *Nothing has changed,* Raimo whispers in my memory. I might not be the Valtia, but if the old man is right, I was chosen all the same. I grit my teeth and reach for the pestle again. "Everything is different," I whisper. "But *nothing* has changed." And then I find it within myself to chuckle. "Except that now I really am a servant."

The fingers of my right hand are too clumsy and sensitive to grip the corn, so I hold each cob clamped between my ribs and my elbow as I use my left to strip the kernels, and then to grind them into meal. Maarika comes out after a while and tells me it's not fine enough, so I pour the bowl of crushed kernels back onto the grinding stone and return to work.

My left palm is blistered and the bandage on my right is dotted with blood by the time Oskar returns with a brace of pheasants. He glances down at me, hunched over the grinding stone. His eyes flick to my hands. And then he disappears into the back and has a murmured conversation with Maarika, so quiet I can't hear.

Freya returns and we have a quick meal, after which Oskar disappears to play cards. Freya takes me to a small side cavern and shows me where the relief chamber is, a deep hole one must carefully squat over as she does her business. When it's my turn, I spend several moments eyeing the pit, once again torn between a fit of giggles and a bout of tears. I wish I could ask Freya to hold my skirt, but she relieved herself without that kind of assistance a moment ago. It takes a few awkward minutes, but when I manage to do my business without falling in or ruining my dress and stockings, I count this as a true success.

The massive cavern is awash in noise and music and laughter throughout the evening, but I'm so tired I could sleep through anything. I lie on the pallet of fur that Freya sets out next to her own in the other small, curtained-off area at the rear of the shelter. "Why did Oskar tell you I was a thief?" Freya murmurs as she snuggles up under her blanket.

"Oh, he was making fun of me. I was told these caves were full of bandits."

She leans forward. "They are," she whispers. "But not all of us are criminals."

My heart kicks against my ribs. "Doesn't that scare you?"

Freya giggles. "Oh, no. I can defend myself, and even if I couldn't, no one would bother me. They won't bother you, either."

"Why?"

"Have you taken a good look at Oskar? Would *you* want to mess with anyone he cared about?"

"I see your point." And though he doesn't care much about me, Raimo said he was honorable, and knowing what little I do about Oskar, I believe it. With that reassurance, I sink into black, empty sleep without regard for anyone or anything around me.

I jerk awake to the noise of a groan. Tense and wary, I sit up as I hear it again—the sound of suffering. It beads my skin with cold sweat, awakening memories of the days I spent clinging to life and wishing for death. The cavern is mostly dark, and Freya is breathing deep and slow next to me, clearly asleep. But in a crack of open space between the pelt and the wooden frame, I see that the fire's still burning in the front chamber. A flicker of movement draws me to the space to peek out.

Oskar lies wrapped in fur next to the fire, so close to it that I'd think he'd be sweating. But instead, he's shivering violently. I push the pelt aside and crawl closer, wondering if he's hurt or sick. But then he rolls onto his back.

His breath puffs from his parted lips in a frigid white cloud. His eyeballs move rapidly beneath his closed eyelids, and he moans like he's having a nightmare. I scoot forward a few more inches and then freeze in place.

As Oskar lets out a pained sigh, ice crystals grow along his dark eyelashes, turning them white.

## CHAPTER 11

Freya stirs and mutters in her sleep, so I slip back to my pallet, my mind reeling with what I've just witnessed. While Oskar's dreams held him prisoner, a thin crust of frost covered his skin, spreading along his cheeks, turning his short, scraggly beard white like an old man's. His jaw flexed and his face twisted into a grimace, temporarily melting the ice, but a few minutes later, it had formed again.

It seemed painful. Exhausting.

Magical. There's nothing else it could be. And I remember what Kauko said about the terrible dreams: *It is a burden the most powerful wielders must bear.*

When I finally hear Oskar rise from his place by the fire, I close my eyes not a second too soon. He pulls back the pelt-curtain between us. "Elli?" he whispers.

I yawn and stretch like I'm just waking up. "Yes?"

"Can I talk to you?"

I get up off the pallet and follow him into the front chamber. Outside the fur walls, people are moving about, starting their day. "Is everything all right?" Fear makes my stomach churn. If he asks me to leave, I'll have nowhere to go.

"Everything's fine." He rubs at his face. The ice is gone, but he looks tired. "I just want to make sure you know enough about what's going on here to stay out of trouble."

"Trouble," I echo, remembering all Raimo's warnings, especially what he said about me being a weapon or an asset in the hands of any wielder. "Trouble is the last thing I want."

He nods. "I know you have contempt for magic. Many people in the city feel the same."

"It doesn't seem that way on the ceremony days."

"Maybe not for the magic itself, then . . ." Oskar shrugs. "But some are mistrustful of *people* who can do magic. I'm just saying I understand it if you feel the same. If you mention that around here, though, some will take offense."

"Are they so loyal to the Valtia and her priests?" The idea is terrifying—what happens if they find out about me? Will they give me up?

Oskar scuffs his boot along the rocky floor. "No," he mutters. "It's not that."

I meet his inscrutable gray eyes. "It's because some of the people here are magic wielders too." *Like you.*

He gives me a small smile, like he's happy I understand.

"Exactly. It's best not to talk about it, though. Not to call attention to it if you see it."

"I think I get what you mean." I clench my jaw to keep the questions from bursting forth.

He's picking up his hunting tools now, fixing some of them to the leather belt around his waist. "Nonmagical people get along fine here if they leave everyone else in peace. People aren't looking for a fight." His eyes narrow for a moment. "Well, most of them, at least."

I'm dying to ask why none of these wielders are at the temple where they should be, especially because it brings the guarantee of education and three meals a day, of safety and belonging, but I manage to hold back. "So nonmagical people like me should keep their mouths shut."

He pats my shoulder. "And like me. Just do as I do— you don't have to keep your mouth shut, but don't pry into people's business."

I stare at Oskar, turning his bold-faced lie over in my head. If I call him on it, he might toss me out of his home— especially because he didn't want me here to begin with. "Thanks for the advice."

He pulls his cloak over his shoulders. "I have to hunt."

I watch his boots shuffling toward the exit to the shelter. "I won't keep you."

He's quiet for a moment. But then—"Elli? My mother said you did an excellent job with the corn yesterday."

My head bobs up, but he's already gone. Even so, the strangest sense of accomplishment floods my chest. I'm not useless. I can grind corn, and put on stockings, and tie a kerchief, and relieve myself without an attendant holding my gown up for me. All things I'd never done before yesterday.

Over the next week, I learn to be useful in other ways. Maarika teaches me how to use the loom. She puts me to work using a thick copper needle to stitch a few pelts together. I chop herbs and pluck pheasants and patch holes in the elbows of Oskar's heavy winter tunic, eager to stay busy in the shelter and avoid the mistrustful stares and general notice of the other cave dwellers. What if the elders are searching for me, as Raimo feared? Would they ever think to look here?

Maarika peeks in on me often, her gray eyes somber and fathomless. She never smiles, but she doesn't scold, either. If I make a mistake, she merely shows me how to do it right, and she is careful with my damaged hand, patient when I can't quite manage something. I put all my gratitude into my work. Every night I fall onto my pallet exhausted and hurting but relieved; I wasn't a burden today. I was useful.

It is a livable life. I think of Mim every day, but the ache grows more bearable. The same is true of the realization that I will never be queen, that I will never feel the magic awaken inside of me—that I am already all I will ever be. Sometimes it even feels like I'm less, especially when my hand burns like it's been dipped in molten iron, when it's so sensitive to touch that the slightest brush against it forces me to stifle a scream. But I learn to endure that pain as well.

I am scarred, and I will never be what I was before, but I'm growing stronger.

Oskar seems to be doing the opposite, though. He comes in from days of hunting with his sled piled high with field-dressed game, enough to make the other men grumble with jealousy, but his lips are gray with cold and it takes an hour in front of the fire for him to stop shaking. He's grown his beard while many young men go clean-shaven. He eats his soup boiling and it's never hot enough for him. And the nights are the worst. He tosses and turns, his racked breaths huffing from him in a glitter of ice crystals. As the days pass, colder and colder, he grows silent and weary.

I lose count of how many times I almost cross the room to lay a hand on his shoulder, in the quiet hope that I could offer him some comfort. There is something about him that tugs at me. I find myself wanting to put my hands on either side of his face and tell him that I know what he is, ask him how I can help. But the only time he looks at me is in the morning as he leaves. He always turns back right before he steps out of the shelter.

"Elli? You did a good job with the patching." He raises his elbow and wobbles it in front of me, showing off my somewhat clumsy job. "Like new."

He says something like that every day, but his smiles are so rare that I want to collect them in a basin and hide them away. I'm sitting in front of the fire one morning after he leaves, eating a dry biscuit and trying to remember what his laugh sounded like, when Freya emerges from her mother's little chamber. "Get up, Elli. You're coming with me." She begins to fold pelts and place them in a basket.

"I have chores to do. I told Maarika I would—"

Maarika pokes her head out of her chamber. "It can wait. You've been huddling in this tiny space for days."

I scoot a little closer to the fire. "Haven't I been useful?"

The firm line of Maarika's mouth softens. "Very. But you're also acting as if you're hiding out, and that's making our neighbors nervous. Oskar's not here as often, so he doesn't see it."

Freya snorts. "And no one would dare approach him anyway, especially not now. But they're talking. I heard Aira telling Senja and her husband a story about you being the daughter of a city councilman, and that you ran away because you got yourself pregnant by a stable boy."

My mouth drops open.

"Senja's husband said it would be bad if a councilman came here, thinking we'd kidnapped his wayward daughter," Freya continues. "He doesn't want to give the constables one more excuse to attack us." She leans forward. "So was Aira right? Are you . . ."

She and Maarika glance down at my middle.

I put my hand over my flat belly. "Not even close."

"Ah. Well, Luukas will be pleased then. He thought that was an idiotic rumor," Maarika says. But before I can smile, she adds, "*He* thinks you're spying on us, trying to figure out which of us are wielders so you can take that information to the councilmen and priests, so that when they return to reclaim the caves and the copper hidden in these tunnel walls, they'll be able to kill us all. We've had spies try to infiltrate the camp before." The lines around her mouth grow deep. "And we've dealt with them before they had a chance to tell our secrets."

I draw my knees to my chest, imagining how the cave dwellers might "deal" with a spy.

Maarika leans on the wood frame. "Yesterday I heard Luukas in his shelter, telling Veikko—that's his oldest son, who happens to be a wielder—that they should tell Oskar to get rid of you or they'll make our whole family leave. Is Luukas right? You did show up only two days after Sig chased off the miners. Are you a spy?"

A hard chill rolls through me. "Definitely not," I say in a hollow voice.

Freya tugs my arm, trying to pull me to my feet. "But no one will know that if you don't get out there and act like a normal person."

I turn to Maarika, and my voice trembles as I say, "I never meant to put your family in any danger."

Maarika nods. "I know, Elli. But now you need to go out there and show *them* that you mean no harm—and that you have nothing to hide." She disappears into her chamber.

I meekly follow Freya through the main cavern as she barters bundles of Oskar's elk sticks and fur pelts for other basic necessities, like thread and cloth, a few loaves of bread, and a fat cube of lard. She introduces me to everyone as "the girl Oskar saved from a bear trap" or "the girl Oskar found mostly dead in the woods." None of the cave dwellers are openly hostile, but they're not a talkative, friendly bunch. I feel their wariness like a firm hand pushing me away. And I realize—all of *them* have something to hide. That's why they're so nervous.

I find myself wondering which are wielders—and which are criminals.

As we trade, I begin to notice signs of magic all around me. Small. Subtle. Unmistakable. We exchange a pelt for a stack of firewood with a black-bearded man named Ismael, who is coaxing a fire to full flame—even though he's using soggy leaves as kindling. Next Freya heads over to trade with a woman cooling a cup of boiling tea for her daughter with a swirl of her finger. It turns out to be Senja, the one whose husband, Ruuben, was worried I'd draw constables here in search of the councilman's pregnant runaway daughter. Senja licks tea from her finger as her gaze drops to my belly, and I smooth the loose fabric down so she can see there's no baby hiding in there.

"Lovely to meet you," she says brusquely, pushing her long blond hair over her shoulder and setting the cup in front of her daughter, who looks to be about six or seven years old. "Kukka, it's warm. Drink up."

Kukka, whose golden hair is curly and tangled, stares at the tea with a mischievous smile on her face. The tea in the cup freezes instantly.

My eyes go round and Senja groans. "Stop doing that, you little scamp!" She gives me a nervous look and blocks

Kukka from my view. "I'm sure you have work to do elsewhere."

"I would never tell," I say, though I'm still staring at the frozen lump of tea in Kukka's cup.

Senja's eyes narrow. "Well, I would hope not," she snaps. "Because anyone who tries to take my daughter from me will—"

"Thank you for the stockings, Senja. Enjoy the pelt!" Freya grabs my left hand and pulls me away from their shelter, telling Senja that Maarika will drop by later with some of the corn cakes Kukka loves so much. I trail Oskar's little sister through the cavern, my thoughts whirling. Senja's a wielder—and so is her daughter. Is magic passed from parent to child? I'd never considered that. Wielders don't have children; it has always been forbidden for priests, apprentices, or acolytes to marry, let alone breed. But then again, I'd always thought all magic wielders resided in the Temple on the Rock, devoted to the Valtia and a life in service to the Kupari, and apparently I was very wrong.

"Freya, is Maarika a wielder?"

She gives me a sharp look as we reach a shelter near the back of the cave. "No. Why would you think that?"

I blink at her. "No reason." *Except that I've spent at least an hour each night watching beads of sweat turn to frost across Oskar's forehead.* The suspicion on Freya's face is enough to shut me up, even though I'm wondering about their father, too. None of them ever mention him.

"Harri," Freya suddenly calls out, waving to a young man

with curly black hair who has a shelter full of fine weapons, several cloaks and pairs of gloves, and even a small pile of copper baubles like those worn by the wealthier women of the city. He trades us a new hunting knife for Oskar in exchange for a bundle of elk sticks, a beaver pelt, and the next turkey Oskar bags.

"Tell him it had better be fat," Harri says with a laugh, revealing deep dimples in his cheeks.

Freya puts her hands on her hips. "You know Oskar would never give you a skinny bird to pay for goods."

Harri puts his hands up. "I'd never challenge him on it. He's way too grouchy." He winks at me. "But maybe our new girl is putting him in a better mood?"

I wish that were true and am about to say so when Freya's mouth drops open. "Harri, you are the cheekiest boy in these caves." Her face is flushed. "Apologize."

My eyebrows shoot up. "For what?"

Harri laughs as he steps in front of me and bows low. "Dearest new girl—"

Freya pokes his arm. "Her name is Elli."

Harri's head hangs. "Dearest, dearest Elli, of the coppery hair and lovely blue eyes"—I take a quick step back, nervous that he's noticed my features, but he continues, his tone playful—"please forgive any thinly veiled insults, implications, innuendos, insinuations, intimations—" He looks up and grins, and I can't help but smile back. "Am I forgiven?"

When I nod, he straightens up. "And can I also assume that you and Oskar are not . . . erm . . . entangled?"

I gape at him, finally grasping why Freya was offended. "Yes. Please assume." Now *my* face is probably flushed.

Harri folds the beaver pelt over his arm. "Then I will definitely see you around."

Freya steers me toward the community hearth in the center of the cavern. "He's the biggest flirt in this camp. The biggest pickpocket, too. He'd never dare here, but he sneaks into the city—there are ways to do it—and he's always coming back with stuff." She holds up Oskar's new knife. "I doubt he came by this honestly."

Maarika is kneeling next to the hearth, kneading dough in a stone trough along with two other women. Her eyes meet mine as we approach, and I wish to the stars I could read minds. Freya waves the new knife at her, and the older woman smiles. "Looks nice and sharp," she calls out.

The other women look up, and their faces twist into identical looks of mistrust when their gazes land on me. The one on the left, a young woman about my age with thick black hair and light-green eyes, looks particularly sour. "That's Aira. She's Ismael's daughter," Freya whispers. "She's got a little thing for Oskar, and she hates that you're living in our shelter."

"Isn't she the one spreading the rumor that I'm pregnant by a stable boy?"

Freya chuckles. "It would be convenient for her if it were the truth." She waves at Aira and gives her a sugar-sweet smile.

"We've been wondering when you'd emerge from hiding," Aira says as we reach the trough. Her hands are crusted with sticky brown dough.

I glance around. Apart from the other woman, who's older than Maarika, with one eye that's cloudy and another bright blue, there's only one person at the hearth—a slender man no taller than I am, with a dented nose. He looks me over and grunts. "She emerges all right—whenever she wants to spy. Tell me, girl, when will the constables and priests be showing up?"

"Hopefully never," I reply. "But if they do come, it won't be on account of me." I hope that's true, and that for the sake of the people, they're looking for the real Valtia instead of wasting time trying to hunt me down.

"Luukas," says Maarika in a flat voice. "Elli was freshly injured when she came to us." She gestures at my right hand, my lurid pink scars and missing fingers. "If she is a spy, that's a fairly elaborate disguise."

Luukas chews on the inside of his cheek as he stares at my hand, and then his eyes rise to mine. "What happened to you, then?"

"I was a servant," I say, hoping he can't hear the tremble in my voice.

"In what household?" Aira asks.

I bow my head, my heart drumming a frantic beat against my breast. "I would . . . rather not say." I gesture at my back, praying to the stars that this is a believable story. "I was accused of stealing. I didn't do it. But my mistress didn't believe me. She whipped me and threw me out. And then I was banished from the city for stealing a meat pie. I was just so hungry." I glance up to find a bewildering array of reactions.

Maarika's brow is furrowed in what appears to be sympathy. The cloudy-eyed woman is on the verge of tears. Luukas's lips are pursed, like he's trying to find the lie. And black-haired Aira is scowling. "So you're a thief," she says. "And we're supposed to take your word that you were banished instead of fleeing from a worse punishment? How do we know for sure your mistress hasn't sent the constables after you?"

"Why wouldn't you believe her?" comes a rough voice from behind me. Oskar strides out of the back tunnel with a few other men. His long hair is wet; he must have just had a wash. His lips are gray with cold and his jaw is set like he's trying to keep his teeth from chattering. He wipes a wool cloth across his face and slings it over his shoulder as he and the others walk toward us. "How many here have similar stories? How many here have been banished? We have no choice but to trust one another."

"I'm sorry, Oskar," says Aira in a silky, careful voice. "I feel protective of the people in these caverns."

Oskar runs his tongue over his teeth as he gives her a hard look. "And you think I don't?"

She looks away. "I know you do."

"You trust her?" asks a boy about Oskar's age, jabbing his finger at me. He's lean, with a wary look in his gray eyes, and he's got a bundle of stained rags tucked beneath his arm. He leaves Oskar's side to stand by Luukas.

"Veikko," Oskar says to his lean friend, "when I found

her, she was as close to death as one can come." Oskar stands close enough for me to see the goose bumps on his throat. Cold rolls from him like waves on the Motherlake, but it doesn't make me shiver like a stiff wind from the outside might. Like I experienced when Raimo attempted to heal me, this cold is something I understand with my mind, though my body appears immune to it. What I am not immune to: the weary, miserable look on Oskar's face as he continues to speak to Veikko. "The lash marks on Elli's back were worse than any I've seen, save one."

Veikko, who I recall is Luukas's son—and a wielder—bites his lip and looks me up and down. "Aye. I remember," he mumbles. "And we've got bigger problems anyway."

Luukas slaps his son on the back. "Did you find out anything in the city?"

Aira sits back on her heels as she wipes the dough from her hands with a damp rag. "I thought the constables had plugged up the hole in the city wall. You found another way in?"

Veikko smiles, revealing a slight gap between his two front teeth that gives him a charmingly roguish air. "Made another one. It connects to an alley next to the Lantinen road. You have to crawl through a refuse pile, but it makes the opening hard to see." He gestures at his wet brown hair and waves the stained rags—which I assume are his dirty clothes—at Aira, who wrinkles her nose.

Luukas squeezes Veikko's shoulder. "And? Are we going to have a good winter—or a bad one?"

Veikko's smile disappears. "The whole town's talking about it," he says in a hollow voice. "How the ground is freezing and gardens are dead. And all the priests are saying is that the new Valtia has requested a postponement of the coronation so that she may mourn the death of the old Valtia."

My stomach drops.

Oskar frowns. "Has that ever happened before?"

The cloudy-eyed woman shakes her head. "But maybe the old Valtia's not really dead." Her doughy hands flutter over the trough. "I think the elders made up the whole Soturi invasion story to cover up a takeover. They've got the Valtia in chains somewhere. Doing bad things to her." Her voice rises. "Mark my words—it's the elders who're in charge now. They were just biding their time!"

The way everybody's avoiding looking at her, I'm thinking this isn't her first outburst. Maarika gently nudges the woman with her shoulder. "Josefina, hush. The Valtia's too powerful for that."

Josefina shakes her head, her grayish-yellow hair swinging around her face. "The Saadella's probably locked up too," she says in a choked voice. "The elders would do it. They would." She leans against Maarika like she's about to collapse, and Oskar's mother holds the older woman, though Maarika's forehead is sheened with sweat. I look closely at Josefina, wondering if she wields fire, especially when Aira winces and moves away, plucking at her tunic like she's trying to draw some cold air toward her.

"I was in the city when the Valtia's death was announced," I venture. "The elders went out in search of the new Saadella. They wouldn't do that if the old Valtia were still alive."

"That's true—they venture out every day, trying to find her," says Veikko. "They're offering a fortune if her family gives her up. They've doubled the reward." His eyes find Oskar's. "But then what's wrong with the new Valtia? The air is bitter with cold! Why isn't she giving us warmth?"

I look up at Oskar. "You feel it here in the outlands?"

He gives me a small smile. "Not nearly as much as in the city, I imagine. We have real winter out here, but she's kept the harshest cold away until this year."

Guilt rises unbidden inside me. Oskar needs that warmth. He's suffering without it. Aira stands up and approaches his other side. She rubs her hand down his arm. "Thank you," he murmurs.

I feel a twinge in my chest as I watch her fingers slide over his sleeve, wishing I could be offering him something too.

"What if . . . ," Aira begins. "What if the new Valtia died of grief? What if that's why there's no warmth?"

"That's another one of the rumors," says Veikko, moving a little closer to Aira, like he's hoping she'll touch him, too. I think she's a fire wielder, and she's giving off heat, though I can barely feel it. "The people are demanding to know why there's been no funeral for the old Valtia, and no coronation for the new one either. It's not good—especially because there have apparently been sightings of longships off the southeast coast."

Luukas goes pale. "From Vasterut?" He shakes his head. "We'd better hope the Motherlake freezes soon. Those Soturi bastards haven't given up. The Valtia may have destroyed part of their navy, but those weren't the only forces they've got."

"How do you know?" I ask. "How big is their empire, and what do they want?" These were all questions the priests dismissed, telling me I would know when I was ready, when I truly needed the information.

Luukas laughs. "What do they want? Copper. Grain. Meat. Slaves. Anything they can take. For the last fifteen years or so, they've been worrying our coastline, a few more raids every year, but nothing more than that. Until they took Vasterut, I would have said they were just a cluster of disorganized tribes, not an empire."

"But whatever they were before, now they have an eye for conquest," I say quietly. I remember when the news arrived at the temple, reaching me through Mim's clever ears and eyes—the Vasterutian envoy begged for the Valtia's help, but the elders turned him away without giving him an audience.

"Aye," says Veikko. "We should have known they'd come for us next."

"But the Valtia laid waste to their navy." I wiggle the sore fingers of my right hand within my sleeve, remembering the rolling waves and crashing thunder . . . and Mim, holding me through it all. "Surely that will make them think twice before trying again."

"Not if they realize we have no Valtia," says Oskar, staring into the hearth.

"With no Valtia, we might as well offer ourselves up as slaves right now," Josefina wails, running her hands, coated with sticky brown dough, through her hair. "The priests won't save us. They've only ever been out for themselves."

"And we have no army," adds Luukas. He shakes his head. "I never thought I'd say it, but I hope the elders in the temple have a plan."

"Oh, they do," Josefina whispers, her hair in matted clumps around her face. "They always do." She begins to sob, and Maarika puts her arm around the forlorn woman and helps her to her feet, then guides her toward a small shelter near the front of the cavern.

I swallow hard as I watch them go. Josefina's right about one thing—the elders are in charge now. But the Kupari need a Valtia. With everything inside me, I wish I was her. I was supposed to be. And if I had been, the people, even these strange cave dwellers, would be safer.

But I'm *nothing*.

I take a few steps toward the back tunnel, desperation filling my hollow chest. "I—I need to—" Thinking of an excuse is too much, so I wave my arm toward the tunnel and blunder forward, my vision blurred with tears. I have to find Raimo. I need him to tell me what I can do. If I'm supposed to make a difference, what is it? I exist for the people—that was etched onto my heart every day I was the Saadella. Raimo insisted that nothing has changed. So how can I stand by while everything crumbles?

Before I know it, I've run past the relief chamber, past the cavern that contains the freezing stream the dwellers use to wash their clothes and bodies, and turned the corner to reach the tunnel that leads to Raimo's lair. Without torches, the way is dense and inky black. My slippers slide on wet rocks, and my panting breaths are harsh in my ears.

"Elli!" Oskar's voice echoes down the tunnel. Orange firelight beats back the darkness. "What in stars are you doing?"

I lean against the rough, cool tunnel wall as he draws near, the flames from his torch making our shadows dance. "I need to find Raimo," I say, my voice cracking.

His brows draw together. "Are you ill?"

I shake my head. But then I remember that I'm not supposed to tell Oskar anything about myself, so I nod.

"Well, which is it?" He's shivering in the dank air of this tunnel.

"I—I—wanted to ask him . . . about my . . ." I hold up my right hand.

He lifts the torch and peers at my palm. "The blisters?"

I pull my hand back and gaze at the torn skin and toughening calluses. "No." The pain of them is satisfying. It means I've worked hard. "It's actually—" I gesture at my scarred knuckles and say the first thing that comes to me. "You'd think, once they'd been cut off, that they'd really be gone. That I wouldn't feel them anymore. But the opposite is true." My voice has become a strangled squeak. "They hurt me more now than they ever did when they were part of me."

I'm not just talking about my fingers, I realize. I'm talking about my life. Mim. Sofia. My future. My duty. All sheared away, all haunting me.

Oskar's eyes are dark as he moves closer. He offers his embrace hesitantly, like he thinks I might shy away. But I'm so wretched that I accept it, leaning my head on his chest and grimacing, my eyes squeezed shut, the pain of all my ghosts overwhelming me. He strokes my long hair and shushes me as if I were a child. "I didn't know you were in so much pain," he says quietly. "You seemed to be doing so well."

"I need Raimo." My hands ball in Oskar's tunic. I wish I could lay all of this across his broad shoulders, because I am so tired of carrying it alone. "Raimo sent me away too soon. He has answers that I need."

"You won't find him now, Elli. He disappears every winter, and has for as long as I've known him. If I thought it was possible to find him, I'd take you to him myself."

I believe Oskar would do it. I can tell by the sorrow in his voice. I press my forehead to his firm shoulder, inhaling the scent of wood smoke and sweat and something cold and astringent. "I don't know what to do," I whisper. "Everything fell apart, and I can't put it back together."

Oskar's heart kicks hard beneath my hand. I look up at him, but his face is tilted toward the tunnel's ceiling. "I know what that's like," he murmurs.

His arm falls away from me, and I step back. "And what did you do?" I ask.

"I went on," he says. "I kept living." He offers his free hand, and when I take it, he looks down at me. "I'm sorry it hurts."

*It will always hurt.* That's what his eyes say.

But what can I do? Fall apart? Scream and cry? No. I am meant for something. I'm not ready to stop believing that yet.

I swipe my sleeve across my eyes and let out a long breath. "I suppose I'll keep living, then," I say, the words echoing down the tunnel.

Oskar squeezes my fingers. With my hand in his, he leads me back to the main cavern.

# CHAPTER 12

As the days grow short and the darkness stretches long, I keep living. But Oskar seems to die a little every night. He stays up late and stares at the fire, but eventually he nods off and the ice begins his nightly torture. Though it's painful to witness, I can't leave him alone, even though he hasn't spoken to me since that day in the tunnel. I don't take it personally—he hasn't spoken to anyone else, either. It's as if his whole self is focused inward.

In the fortnight since Freya and Maarika put an end to my hiding, I've ventured out every day, eating lunch with the women around the community hearth, bringing Oskar tea as he plays cards by the big fire in the evenings. I meet people's eyes. I smile. Our conversations are about now— the best ways to oil boots to keep the damp from seeping in, how to angle a knife to more efficiently scrape fur from flesh, how much water to add to the cornmeal to keep us satisfied while stretching what we have left.

But there's a bigger *now* that won't leave our minds. Every day we talk about whether the Saadella has been found, why her family hasn't given her to the elders yet, how thick the ice on the Motherlake has become—and whether the Soturi would dare try to cross it on foot. I'm as hungry for answers as the rest, perhaps hungrier since I have so much to learn about this world and my place in it. But when the talk turns to the Valtia and why she's abandoned us, I make my excuses and leave in desperate search of something else to do, my stomach churning with a bitter brew of failure and shame.

One day Maarika sends me off to mind Kukka while Senja bakes. The little girl delights in her magic, luring icicles from cracks in the rocks and making them grow like fragile twigs right before my eyes. "Mommy taught me," she says, giggling, making me wonder what Kupari would be like if magic wielders lived like everyone else, had families like everyone else. If magic was taught as naturally as children learn to speak and behave—under the watchful eyes of their parents instead of in the temple, under the strict guidance of the priests. Would we be stronger as a people, or weaker? Would we have more magic among us, or less?

When Senja returns, I go back to the shelter and find Maarika building up the fire. "Oskar will be home soon," she murmurs.

I squat next to her and begin to pile flat stones at the edge of the pit—when he comes in gray and shivering, he'll be able to spread a cloak over them and have a warm place to sit. Maarika's gaze takes in my movements, and she presses her lips together. "I always wonder if today will be the day he doesn't make it home," she says.

The stark admission makes me fumble one of the rocks, and it topples off the edge of the pit and lands just a hairbreadth from my toes. Maarika lets out a quiet breath of laughter and helps me pick it up again. "I think it every day, but I rarely say it."

And now I'm thinking it, and I don't like the way it makes me feel at all. "Oskar seems very strong."

She shrugs. "I know. But people are lost in an instant in the outlands. It has always been that way." She sits back to let me continue my work, a haunted, faraway look in her eyes.

"You've lost someone." My voice is hushed—I'm afraid to scare away her words, because Maarika shares so few of them.

"My husband, many years ago." Her eyes flick to mine and then away. "A hunting accident. And before that, my brother and his entire family. They lived on the shore, in the house where I was born, where my parents died." She throws a bit of stray bark onto the flames. "We used to visit them often. My brother's daughter, little Ansa . . ." She smiles and leans over quickly, her rough fingers stroking at the ends of my hair before falling away. "She had hair like yours, and it gleamed in the sunlight. She and Oskar used to race each other up and down the dunes, and she would always beat him."

My brows rise as I start to chuckle. "Oskar's legs are very long—she must have been fast."

Maarika blinks several times and looks away. "Oh, yes. Very fast. She was a tiny fierce thing. Freya is a bit like her."

I place another stone on the rim of the pit, waiting.

"It was the Soturi," Maarika finally whispers. "They came up from the Motherlake one night. They stole everything of value and burned the place to the ground. One day my brother had the perfect life, a family, a beautiful daughter, and the next, all of them were gone. Ashes and cinders. It makes you wonder why we ever believe in tomorrow, why we assume we have the next minute, and the next, and the next."

"But you do," I say, gesturing at the fire, the rocks, the shelter. "And you believe Oskar does as well."

She gives me a flickering smile. "Oh, yes. I have hope." She touches a warming stone. "And I will protect it to my last breath, with whatever strength I have, however small it may be." Her eyes meet mine, and I read the message there. Oskar is her hope. Her family is her life.

She is trusting me—and warning me. Does she know that Oskar is a wielder—and does she suspect I know as well? I want so badly to ask her why he's hiding, why he suffers like he does, but I have too many secrets to keep myself.

"If I had a family of my own," I say slowly, "I would protect them, as you do."

Her gaze is unwavering. "But right now, we are your family."

"Then this is the family I will work to protect. Even if all I can do is heat stones by the fire."

Maarika squeezes my arm and then disappears back into her private area, and I stare at the place where she was, hoping I passed the test she just set before me.

The next afternoon I go down the trail into the dark rear caverns with Freya, where the underground stream sends icy water rushing through a wide trough before disappearing under the rock again. We peel off our stockings to wash. "Does Oskar seem all right to you?" I ask, haunted by my memories of his tortured sleep the night before.

Freya shrugs. "He's always grumpy in the winter, but it's definitely worse this year."

"It's more than grumpiness," I say, wincing as the soles of my feet touch the water. I only wash with my left hand, because my right is fearfully sensitive to cold now, something I discovered the hard way the first time I dipped it into the stream. It took hours for it to stop hurting, and the whole time, I thought of Oskar, how pained he looks when he comes in from the icy marshlands. "Do you think he might be sick?"

I'm so eager for her reply that I forget to be careful.

"Hey," she says when she spots the blood-flame mark on my calf. "What's that?"

I quickly yank my gown over it. "Just a scar," I say, my

voice loud and creaky. "Once when I was little, I got too curious around the fire and burned myself with a poker."

Freya cringes. "That must have hurt terribly," she says quietly. "Burns are the worst."

I thank the stars that she believes me. "Yes. I'll never do something that stupid again."

After we wash, me shivering from the frigid water and Freya oddly seeming to enjoy it, we return to the shelter and retrieve two baskets, then head out to gather twigs for kindling. I wrap my right hand in three layers of wool to try to protect it from the chill wind and sorely wish I owned a pair of gloves. As we exit the cave, we meet Aira and her father—Ismael, who has a bushy black beard, a scar that slices through one of his eyebrows, and, I recall, the ability to coax fire from damp leaves. Aira's carrying a saw, and Ismael's hauling a string of fish. Both are wearing light cloaks despite the bitter cold.

Veikko is with them, wrapped in a thick cloak of fur and wearing heavy gloves on his hands. "—got in through the front gate this time," he's telling them. "There's a shortage of vegetables in the city, so when I offered the constable a bag of potatoes, he let me right in!"

Ismael scowls. "Worse and worse," he says. "Soon the city dwellers will be coming out here and raiding *us*!"

Veikko looks down at the string of fish. "Most citizens have no idea how to fend for themselves. They're used to things being easy. Spoiled by the warmth and plenty. Now that it's gone, they're like orphaned baby birds." He raises his eyebrows. "They'd better hope a hungry weasel doesn't find the nest before their mother returns."

"If that weasel has longboats and broadswords," Aria scoffs, "it might not matter."

Freya and I meet them in the middle of the wide-open area in front of the cavern, surrounded by the high, steep stone walls of the hills that hide this cave entrance from view. Aira smiles at me. I believe she's noticed how Oskar doesn't treat me differently than he treats others, and she no longer considers me a threat to her romantic hopes. I smile back, despite the now-familiar ache in my chest every time I think of him. "If there are food shortages, is the temple sharing some of their surplus with the citizens?" I ask them. "They have food aplenty from their own gardens, and all the magic they need to keep things growing."

"The temple's not sharing a thing." Veikko frowns. "It's shut up tight now. Only the elders dare show their faces in town."

"Because the people are afraid of them." I remember how they made way as Aleksi and Leevi passed. I used to think it was awe and respect, but now I wonder if I was wrong, as I was about so many things.

"Aye," says Ismael, scratching at his beard. "No one dares approach them. But as people get hungrier, their desperation will outweigh their fear."

"It's already happening," says Veikko. "There was a riot in the market over food prices yesterday, made worse by a rumor that the priests have been hoarding copper in the temple that could be used for trade. A few people were shouting that they should raid the temple."

I shake my head. "The elders are worried about a copper shortage."

"But why would the priests care so much?" asks Aira. "Seems like the city council should be more worried."

"Because copper is—" Suddenly I realize I've stepped out onto some of the thinnest ice imaginable. Aira, Ismael, and Veikko are giving me equally curious looks. "I . . . was in a bakery fetching buns for my mistress's breakfast and over-heard one of the temple scullery maids saying that copper is the source of the Kupari magic."

"Heard Raimo say as much once," says Ismael, nearly making me sag in relief as the others turn their attention to him. But then he adds, "But how do you know the elders are worried about a shortage, Elli?"

My face burns with my fear of having revealed too much. "M-my master in town . . . he had recently done business with one of the elders and . . . he had dined in the temple. Apparently it came up. I overheard him telling my mistress that night."

"You overhear a great many interesting things," Aira says, her rosy lips curled with suspicion.

"It makes sense, though," says Veikko. "Those miners were desperate to gain access to our caves. And they'll be back."

Ismael looks slightly sick. "And they might bring priests, seeing as they have a stake in the copper too." He glances over my shoulder, into the main cave, where dozens of families are going about the business of daily life. "I suppose we might be thankful for a bit of the upheaval in the town. I hope it keeps all of them busy for some time to come."

"It may not be enough," says Veikko. "I overheard two of the constables near the gate, telling quite a story." He leans forward, clutching his fur cloak around him as an icy breeze gusts around us. "One claimed that a priest had sent him a message—asking him to be on the lookout for the Valtia."

A brutal chill runs hard down my back, but Aira lets out a peal of laughter. "What? As if she'd be roaming the streets?"

Veikko shrugs. "They said she'd gone mad with grief and run away. They think she might have escaped into the outlands."

I think I'm going to vomit all over the stones at my feet. "That's insane," I say loudly. "How could she even do that?" I clear my throat to chase away the quaver in my voice. "She'd be recognized immediately."

Ismael nods. "Maybe. Hard to see how she could hide herself, especially if she wasn't in her right mind. A bit scary to think about, if you ask me."

"Exactly," says Veikko.

Aira rolls her eyes. "You can't hide that much magic."

Oskar's face flashes in my mind. "I agree," I say quickly. "Especially if she's unbalanced. It sounds like that constable was playing a trick on his friend."

Freya laughs. "The stories coming out of that city are

crazier every week. Come on, Elli. We need to get going or we won't be back before dark."

I can't get away fast enough. I pull my cloak tight around me as we hike up the trail, as if it could protect me from my own fears. We walk all the way up the steep trail to the marshlands before turning west and journeying to a small copse of trees on a hill that overlooks the Motherlake. The whole time, I'm trying to convince myself that I was right, that the constable was playing a cruel joke. Surely the elders assume I'm dead. Surely they've let me go. Surely they've realized I'm not the real Valtia? But then I remember what Raimo said: *They never figured it out!* I swallow back dread as I gather dry twigs.

The sunlight is fading, and the frigid air bites at my cheeks. It might not have snowed yet, but winter has sunk its teeth deep. I've never felt cold like I have in the past few weeks. In the temple, it was always pleasantly warm or cool. But now I understand how lucky we all were—my fingers feel so stiff that I'm sure my blood is turning to ice, and the stumps of my pinkie and ring finger tingle sharply and painfully.

"So, what's your theory?" Freya asks after we pile our baskets full and begin the trek to the caverns.

"My theory?"

"About the old Valtia. Do you think she's dead?"

The pang of grief knifes through me. "Yes," I murmur. "I think she's dead."

"I'm not sure. If she is, then wouldn't the new Valtia

have shown herself to the people? Do you think she really went mad?"

There's that urge to vomit again. "Why do people out here care about that so much?" I blurt out. "Is it just the warmth? That's all the Valtia does for the outlands, right?"

Freya is silent, and when I look over at her, she's scowling. "We're Kupari too," she says, her voice shaking. "Just because we're out here doesn't mean we're not."

I blanch at having offended her, remembering Sofia's disagreement with the elders about entering the outlands to be seen by her subjects beyond the city walls. "Of course you're Kupari! I didn't mean to suggest—"

"But everyone in the city thinks we're criminals, right? That's what the miners called us that day they came to tell us to leave. Thieves. They painted us all with one brush." Her lips pull tight. "I'm glad Sig set them on fire!"

I stare at her with wide eyes. "And how did Sig set them on fire?"

She bites her lip, then grins with her secret knowledge. "He wields it."

"There are lots of wielders in the caverns." I thought I'd met all of them in the past few weeks—and none of them seem that powerful. "Which one is he?"

She shakes her head. "Sig hasn't been around since the fight with the miners. A bunch of the other wielders were angry after it happened—they thought it would draw the attention of the Valtia and her elders. So Sig and a bunch of his friends who are wielders left the caverns and haven't been back since. But believe me, no one wields fire like he does. He is *made* of fire."

The rumors Mim heard from Irina the scullery maid were right after all. There *was* a strong fire wielder among the cave dwellers. "If he has such an affinity for fire magic, why is he in the outlands instead of in the temple?"

"Why would he want to be in the temple?"

"To live a life of privilege and serve the Valtia and the Kupari people? Such a strong wielder would surely have been chosen as an apprentice, guaranteed to become a priest one day. Why would he want to live in a cave in the outlands instead?" This is something I've been dying to ask for weeks.

Freya's little face squinches up. "Because he didn't want to be gelded and shaved, to begin with?"

"G-gelded?" My stomach turns as I remember one of my lessons with Kauko, about how male horses often have this procedure to make them easier to control.

Freya leans forward, her braids swinging, and speaks in a low conspiratorial voice. "It's when they cut off a boy's—"

I wave my hand in the air. "It's all right. I understand." I think of the apprentices and younger priests, few of them as tall as a normal man, many of them with high, reedy voices. I think of all the little boys I've seen over the years, led into the temple after having been taken away from their families. And of Niklas, the boy who had been hit by a cart before Aleksi brought him in. Aleksi had said he was eager to get to the temple—but what if he'd been trying to get *away*? All the things I've seen over the years come back to me, painted with a much more sinister tint. For reasons

I don't fully understand, I think of Oskar and his freezing eyelashes. How was he not found by the priests?

I look into his sister's eyes. "The wielders in this camp weren't banished from the city, were they? They chose to live out here instead of serving in the temple. They're in hiding."

Freya's mouth twists as she chews that over. "Sometimes older kids will realize they can wield magic and escape before they're found. But sometimes their parents see what they can do and . . ." She rocks back as if she's caught herself on that slippery slope. "What do you think Oskar will bring us for dinner?" she asks, picking up her pace as we tread the well-concealed rocky trail that leads to the caverns.

But I can't hold back anymore. "Oskar's a wielder, isn't he?"

Freya stops, her skinny fingers tightly clutching the handle of her basket. "I don't know where you heard that, but it's a lie," she says fiercely.

"Freya," I say, trying to adopt the tone Mim always took when I was being stubborn about having my hair washed. "I saw him. Last night." *Every night.* "His face was covered with ice as he slept."

Her eyes shine with angry tears. "He doesn't want anyone to know. He made me promise not to tell." And now it probably feels to her as if she's betraying him.

"I won't tell anyone," I promise her. "I'm too grateful for everything you all have done for me. I'd never do anything to hurt him or your family. You know that."

She swipes the back of her hand across her cheek. "I wish he *would* tell people," she says, still sounding angry. Like the bear cub to her brother's full-grown grizzly. "I don't understand why he's hiding from it. Sig doesn't hide. He says we'd be just as powerful as the Valtia if we banded together."

This time I cannot hide my naked shock, at so many of her declarations. "We?"

Her cheeks glow with pink. "Oskar told me to keep quiet about it. But . . . I can wield a bit of fire myself." She bites her lip. "Nothing like Sig can, though."

"Sig thinks he can take on the Valtia?" My voice cracks as I say it. Here I'd thought I was foolish for believing the thieves' caverns were as dangerous as I'd heard—and now I realize they're more dangerous than I ever believed. "Surely he's joking?"

Freya may only have a decade or so of life experience, but she's clearly learned a lot. She peers at my face, then smiles and giggles. "I'm sure he was joking," she says, starting to skip as we descend below the earth. "Sig's funny like that." She gasps as we round the bend—there are several horses tethered to a post in the open area in front of the caverns.

"What is it?"

"Come on!" she says, grinning, tugging my sleeve.

My heart hammering, I walk with Freya into the front cave. There's a crowd of people milling around the center, where a young man is standing on the community hearth. He looks about Oskar's age, but they couldn't be more different. He's of medium height, perhaps two hands taller than me—and a hand shorter than Oskar. He's pale as a sequestered acolyte, like he never emerges into the sun. His cheekbones are so sharp they look like they could cut some-one. His close-cropped hair is white-blond spun with gold that glints in the light of the flames around him. Although most people are wearing cloaks or at least heavy, long-sleeved tunics, this man is shirtless, wearing only trousers belted at his lean hips and a pair of leather boots. His body is angular, chiseled muscles over long bones. His eyes are two black-brown points of darkness, the only thing about him that doesn't seem made of brightness. His arms are spread, and he's giving some sort of speech, his voice echoing so heavily that I can't yet make out the words.

"That's him!" Freya squeals. "Sig's come back!"

# CHAPTER 13

My stomach goes tight as we approach the crowd and I hear Sig say, "Now is the time to go on the offensive! This is an opportunity."

He doesn't sound like he's joking.

The people around him grumble. "Winter's on us," one man shouts. "We're better served by making sure our food stores last until spring!"

Sig smiles, and his dark eyes seem to glow. "But you could spend the rest of your winter in the temple," he says to the man, his voice smooth like melted copper. "I've spent the last few weeks exploring the city, listening to the rumors. I'm telling you, there's food aplenty in the Temple on the Rock."

"But what you're suggesting is suicide!" cries Josefina at

the back. "The Valtia would crush us—with the priests at her side."

Sig shakes his head, that confident grin still gleaming. "If there were a Valtia, perhaps. But where is she? Why hasn't she shown herself? Our winter warmth is nowhere to be found. The temple has been locked up tight since the day after the Valtia died, but the priests still come out every day to look for the Saadella. The elders are publicly saying the new Valtia is in mourning, but the streets are flowing with rumors that she's gone mad and run away."

"You're willing to bet your life that the priests are lying?" Senja asks.

I'm not imagining it—his eyes really are glowing. The dark pupils flicker with the flames inside. "I am," he says. "Who's with me?"

"There aren't enough of us," says Aira, standing right at the front. "The temple is full of *trained* wielders. We should gather more before we even consider entering the city as a group, let alone trying to take the temple."

My mouth drops open. Apart from the elders, there are thirty priests, thirty apprentices, and a legion of acolytes within the temple, all willing to defend it to the death. "You're woefully outnumbered," I blurt out.

I cringe as Sig's head snaps in my direction, looking for the person who made the comment. I don't breathe again until his gaze passes over me. "Maybe there are more of them than us, but the priests are lazy and soft," Sig says after a few tense seconds.

He raises his arms and twin balls of fire appear and hover over his palms. There's a murmur of admiration from the crowd. "They're too used to luxury to challenge people who have known true hardship." He brings his arms down and the flames shoot from his hands, right into the large fire where the men gather to play cards. It sends sparks flying into the air, and one little girl screams. I gape—I have never seen anyone but the Valtia conjure fire from nothing.

Another young man steps up onto the hearth, one I haven't seen before today. He's wearing a light summer tunic and has long, reddish-blond hair tied back in a messy tail. "I agree with Sig that this is the best time to take action," he says, and as soon as I hear his deep, buzzing voice, I recognize it from that first day outside the cave—he's the one Oskar called Jouni. He nervously rubs his palms on his trousers and grins when Sig nods with approval. "We haven't had the first snow yet, so I think we should—"

"The first snow is coming tonight," says a low, gruff voice behind us. Oskar's near our shelter with a full game bag. He's got his heavy fur cloak on, with the hood pulled over his hair. But I can see his eyes, granite and hard, as he comes toward the crowd and ends up next to me and Freya.

He pushes his hood back from his face and looks at the group around Sig and Jouni. "It's going to be several inches at least." His gaze finds Jouni's. "So what were you about to propose?"

Jouni looks crestfallen. "Never mind," he mumbles.

Sig, on the other hand, looks disgusted. His full lips

twist into a sneer. "Scared of a little snowstorm, Oskar?"

Oskar arches an eyebrow. "I'm more worried about the storm of stupidity that's brewing right in front of me."

There's an audible gasp within the knot of people around Sig, whose jaw clenches as he steps down from the hearth and begins to come through the crowd. I stagger back and bump into Oskar, who clamps his hand over my shoulder and moves me to one side, out of Sig's path. As Sig draws near, I catch his scent, smoke and a strange metallic tang, like the smells that come from a forge.

"Just because the miners haven't come out here yet doesn't mean they won't," he says. "They know these caverns are full of copper they could mine to trade for food with the south."

I glance over to see Ismael looking at me, perhaps wondering if I'm going to blurt what I know yet again. This time, I stay silent. I don't want to give Sig any more reason to attack the town or the temple—but it seems he already has all the reasons he needs.

"When things get desperate enough, the miners will return, with constables and maybe priests." Sig's voice is quiet even though he stands several feet away from Oskar, like he doesn't want to get too close. "It's only a matter of time."

I hold my breath, hoping Veikko won't tell him that the priests might also come to the outlands in search of the lost, mad Valtia, but Oskar speaks before he has a chance to.

"For the first time in years, I completely agree with

you." Oskar's large hands fall to his sides. "Which is why we should be guarding our home and not traipsing across the outlands with our heads stuffed full of impossible dreams."

"He's right, Sig," calls out Ruuben, putting his arm around Senja. "This place is safe for the winter. Let's forget about this for now."

Sig's nostrils flare. "Oskar," he says softly. "We shouldn't have to live like this." He lowers his voice even more. "We shouldn't have to hide. *Neither* of us should have to hide. This is our chance to change things." There's a fierce kind of softness in his eyes, a plea. *He cares what Oskar thinks.*

Oskar's stare is icy and hard, though. "I'm not hiding. I'm living."

"If you can call it that." Sig rolls his eyes, but they shine with barely suppressed emotion. "You are such a coward. You always have been."

Oskar's face is relaxed, his fingers loose. "Stay if you want peace. Otherwise, leave. No one here wants to help you start a war."

"War is what we were meant for, Oskar, and you know that." Sig turns slowly in place, his pale skin smooth in the chilly air of the cave. He looks at the crowd, faces full of wariness, pinched mouths, tense shoulders. For a moment, his eyes meet mine. His gaze is like a flame across my skin, trying to burn down to my marrow and see what's inside. He tilts his head. "You're new." He takes a step closer. "What's your name?"

The air around me suddenly grows warm, then hot, and

Freya grimaces and steps away, like she can't stand it. "Cut it out, Sig!" she whines.

Once again, I feel the heat like a thought, something without temperature. I know it's there, but it doesn't make me sweat. "I'm Elli."

His dark eyes slowly glide over my body and face. "Are you an ice wielder?"

What? Why would he ask me that? "I—"

"She's under my protection," says Oskar, stepping between us, menace radiating from him in palpable waves of cold.

Sig chuckles, but it's a bitter sound. "Oh, Oskar. No one told me you'd taken up with a girl."

My stomach does an odd swoop, and I edge to the side so I can look up at Oskar's face as he says, "Sig, leave. Now."

Sig takes a step back, wearing a sneer. "I can't wait for the day you lose that tightly wound temper. We'll have fun then, you and I."

"I said *leave*," Oskar growls.

Sig turns his attention back to me. "Nice to meet you, Elli. Try to stay warm." He smirks. "But I suppose you're quite fond of the cold, aren't you?" His eyes linger on mine for a moment, and then he strides out of the cavern and into the winter outside, as if it's a perfectly natural thing to walk around half-naked. As the lingering daylight reaches him, I see that his back is striped with silvery scars from the base of his neck all the way to his waist. *The lash marks on Elli's back were worse than any I've seen, save one,* Oskar had said.

At least eight young men and women, some in light tunics and some in heavy furs like Oskar, follow Sig out of the cavern. "We're at the dunes by the northwestern oak bluffs if anyone wants to get away from this coward's cave," Sig calls as he mounts one of the horses. He and the others canter away a moment later.

The temperature in the cavern drops back to its normal damp chilliness, and people talk nervously among themselves as they return to their dinner preparations. Jouni stares after Sig and the others like he's thinking of joining them, but then his shoulders slump and he heads over to the big fire with some of the other men, one of whom is clearly his father. The man, his skin weathered and spotted with age, hugs Jouni and asks him how the town was. Oskar trudges to the shelter, and Freya and I follow with our kindling, then grab pails and head out again to fetch water.

"*Are* you an ice wielder?" Freya whispers as we hike back down to the underground stream.

"Most definitely not. I'm the most unmagical person you'll ever meet." I try for a breezy tone, but my voice shakes a bit at the end.

"But Sig's heat didn't even affect you," says Freya, sounding awed. "I thought I was going to faint."

My heart races. I make a mental note to at least pretend to be affected by things like that in the future. Doing otherwise is going to lead to questions I shouldn't answer. "Oh, I suppose I'm just a summer girl," I say as we dip our buckets in the stream. "I don't mind the heat."

"That's like Oskar, though," says Freya. "He wishes it was summer all the time."

And he so obviously hates the winter—but I'm almost certain he's full of ice magic. That seems like such a contradiction, and it's yet another thing the priests never explained. I can't believe how many things I never thought to ask, how ignorant I truly was. Just as I'm about to ask Freya for the answers I want, though, a few others come in to fill their buckets, so I put the questions aside for later and we tromp back to the shelter. My hand is throbbing, the stumps of my missing fingers feel as if they're being stabbed by a hundred needles at once, and my muscles ache from a day of hard work. Like always, though, this kind of pain makes me smile. I've been in these caves for over a month now, and I haven't been useless. I've learned a lot.

When it comes to understanding what it means to be a "living, breathing, *thinking* Astia," though, I'm no closer than I was when I arrived. Those are all questions it seems much too dangerous to ask. All I know is that I can stand in the presence of a powerful fire-wielder and not break a sweat.

Maarika has prepared a dinner of cornbread and dried venison, and we eat in silence. Oskar looks grim and tired as he chews his food, and when he's finished, he disappears like he does every night to play cards with the men around the big campfire. He's still out there when Freya and I go to bed.

But as always, I'm awakened by the sound of his nightmares. I creep to the boundary between my chamber and his, and I watch him, locked in a desperate battle with the ice that seems determined to claim him. It spreads up his neck. It slithers into his hair. Tonight it makes his long body curl into a ball, like he's trying to hold on to any warmth he can find. His broad shoulders tremble. During the day he looks so fierce, so unaffected and unafraid, but when he turns his face toward me, I see the agony and fear etched within the strong line of his jaw and the wide sweep of his brow.

He lets out a choked, vulnerable moan, and that is beyond what I can stand.

I crawl toward him, my heart aching in the hollow casket of my chest. This feeling has been growing inside me every night as I've watched him suffer. Oskar could have left me in the woods to die. No one would have known that he'd passed me by, and no one would have blamed him. I was a nameless, discarded, injured girl. But he saved me. He did it for no reason except that I needed help. Not out of guilt, not because he liked me, not because I had something he wanted, not because I was special or magical.

He did it because he's good, and he values life. And every day that I've known him, he's taken care of me for the same reason. I'm desperate to give him something in return.

I stretch out my palm, and I lay it on Oskar's frozen cheek.

My mind explodes with visions of jagged ice, sharp enough to tear me apart.

# CHAPTER 14

This is no flurry of flakes but a raging blizzard. Avalanches rolling with killing speed into the rocky basin of my skull. Icicles sharp as knives, slicing and carving. I yank my hand away, breathing hard. I've seen the frozen Motherlake, the frost that coats the marsh grass, rivulets of ice along the cave walls. But never have I experienced anything like the frigid horror of the last few seconds.

Oskar's not shivering anymore. His long, dark lashes shadow the hollow above his cheekbones. His mouth is surprisingly soft when he's at rest, and I have the insane urge to skim my fingertip over the little bow on his upper lip. He exhales, and it's not foggy and frozen.

What just happened?

I lay my hand on his cheek again. The onslaught is less

jarring this time, but it's still powerful. And it's definitely coming from him. Are these his dreams? They're made of the rub and tear of ice on ice, thick slabs of it colliding and shearing off, shattering into countless deadly shards. They're blinding white and glittering and so cold it burns. But as I sit there, my palm to his skin, the brutal edge begins to dull. The hard ice pellets turn to heavy, wet snow. The ice sinks into the earth.

Because of *me*, I realize. I stare at the place where my skin touches Oskar's. And then I close my eyes as the icy magic crosses the barrier between us and fills my hollow chest.

Raimo compared me to the copper lightning rods that adorn most of the buildings in the city of Kupari. He said I could amplify magic, though I have no idea how I could do that, and he also said I could absorb it. That must be what I'm doing now. I smile as Oskar's cheek turns from frigid to cool under my touch.

He jerks away from me, and my eyes fly open. His are alight with fury as he scoots backward, pulling his cloak around him. "What in stars are you doing?" he whispers.

I look down at my palm, which is damp with the ice that melted off his skin. "I was . . ."

He rubs his hand over his face and pulls his fingers through his dark hair, which falls loose to his shoulders. "How long have you been there?"

I completely lost track of time while I was touching him. "Only a few minutes? Oskar—"

He pulls his knees to his chest, like he needs to put a wall between us. "Did you see . . ." He clenches his teeth. "Why did you come out here? Can't you respect a man's privacy?"

"I wanted to help," I say, edging a little closer.

His brows lower. "I don't need any help."

"It looked painful."

He grips the fabric over his shins and looks away. I can tell he's thinking about the ice, how it waits for him to slip into dreaming so it can carve the meat from his bones. But then his eyes narrow as his gaze abruptly returns to me. "Did you just do something to me?"

"Why, was something different?"

"Why are you answering my question with a question?"

*Because I have been holding them in for so long. Too long.* I wipe my palm on the sleeve of my gown. "I merely touched you. I wasn't trying to hurt you."

He glares at me. "It might have hurt *you.*"

If Raimo is right, it can't. But Raimo also told me to tell no one. "I didn't realize touching your face could harm me." I try to sound teasing, but my voice is too unsteady for that.

He grabs a tie from his satchel and pulls his hair back. "What possessed you to touch me at all?"

"I saw what was happening to you, and I wanted to make it better."

The corner of Oskar's mouth twitches, and he gives me a bemused look.

It makes me bold. "It's getting worse, isn't it? I can tell."

The look becomes a scowl. "It's none of your business."

"Tell me what you are."

He groans. "I'm nothing," he says, rising from the ground and holding his hands over the fire.

I get up too. "I don't have contempt for magic, Oskar. I might be nonmagical, but I don't have any prejudice against magic wielders. Surely you've seen that by now."

"I need to hit the trail. The snow will make it slow going, and I want to be back before the sun sets." He tries to step around me, but I don't get out of the way.

"None of the other wielders are suffering like you."

His mouth draws tight. "I'm not suffering."

"I would never hurt you, Oskar."

"I don't know you. And you don't know me."

"Why are you trying to hide what you are?" I blurt out.

His gray eyes turn hard. "Why are you so nosy?"

"Why are you so scared?"

"Why are you being such a pain in my arse?" he snaps.

As I gape at him, he lets out a harsh chuckle, takes me by the arms, and starts to move me aside. But anger flashes in my chest. I have no right to his secrets, but I'm driven by the memory of his agonized expression, of the ice freezing his skin, of how terrifying his dreams truly are. And if I'm right about what just happened, then I can help him. I grab at his hand, clamped around my upper arm. My fingernails dig in as I try to get free.

His skin flashes cold, and then his eyes fly wide. "No," he whispers, grabbing my sleeve and pulling my hand from his. "I'm so sorry. I didn't mean to do that. . . ." He flips my palm over.

He slides his finger over my skin, then gives me a searching look.

"What's wrong?" I ask.

"Tell me why Raimo didn't heal you with magic." His voice is low as he moves even closer, towering over me.

"I asked him not to—"

"You're lying." He grabs my left wrist and tugs my palm toward him, then touches the center with his fingertip. I understand that it's cold like I understand that grass is green, but I don't *feel* it. What I do feel: the danger. I rip my hand from his grasp and stagger back.

He tilts his head, staring at the spot he touched. I squinch up my face and rub at my palm. "Ow," I whimper.

"I didn't affect you at all," he says, reaching for my hand again.

I cradle it to my breast and retreat until my legs hit the stone wall that surrounds the shelter. "Of course you did." I moan, wishing I was a little better at pretending. "I—"

I stare at his broad chest as he gently takes my left hand in his considerably larger one and turns my palm upward again. The only things that mar my skin are my hard-earned calluses. The center of my palm is soft and smooth and warm as he traces it with a cool finger. "Tell me what *you* are," he whispers.

"Nothing." Tears sting my eyes. *You could be their most powerful asset—or their worst enemy,* Raimo whispers in my thoughts. Why did I risk revealing myself? So stupid. I clench my fist, as if hiding it will make him forget. "Oskar, I'm sorry for touching you, sorry for asking questions, sorry for everything, but I can't—"

He holds up his hands. "Stop." My mouth snaps shut. He smiles at my obedience. "Wait here."

He disappears into Maarika's little chamber, and I hear him murmuring to her. My heart seizes with fear—is he telling her there's something odd about me? Is he—

He emerges from her chamber with a pair of knee-high leather boots and a thick leather cloak lined with fur. "Get these on." He tosses a pair of leather gloves at me. "These, too."

Stars, he's going to turn me out in the snow. "I'm sorry," I say in a choked voice. "Please don't do this."

"Put them on, Elli." He sits down next to his own boots and jams his feet into them. "Move it," he says when I'm still standing there a few seconds later. "I wasn't kidding when I said I needed to get going."

I might be immune to ice magic, but dread is turning my insides cold. With shaking hands, I pull on the boots and clumsily lace them. I don the cloak and pull it around me. I slide on the gloves, which are also fur-lined. Once Oskar has completed his own preparations, I follow him as he strides through the front cavern, where it's still dark. Not many people are awake at this hour, though I see the glow of a few small fires in some of the shelters, and I hear the trill of little Kukka's laughter as Senja shushes her. My feet already feel like blocks of ice, even before we emerge from the cave and are greeted by a thick blanket of snow. "You were right," I mumble.

"I'm always right about snow," he says, and then tromps up the trail.

I work to keep up, grateful that he gave me these boots, because they keep the snow from soaking my woolen stockings. We hike along the narrow path that leads up to the marshlands. Where is he taking me? "Oskar, please. I'll work harder."

"Is that even possible?" He gives me an amused sidelong glance. "I've rarely seen anyone work harder than you do."

"I'll keep at it," I tell him. "If you let me stay, I'll—"

He stops walking. "Why wouldn't I let you stay?"

"Where are we going, then?"

"Hopefully to find a few snow hares. The tracks will be easy to see today."

My brow furrows. "Why are you bringing me with you?"

His gaze slides to my right hand, two fingers of my borrowed glove hanging loose. "Because if I'm going to do this, I don't want anyone else hearing or seeing anything."

I stare up at him with wide eyes. "I'd never tell anyone about you," I squeak.

Oskar begins to laugh, a beautiful, deep, *alive* sound I haven't heard for weeks. The knives at his belt clink together as he doubles over and puts his hands on his thighs.

"Your face," he says, his eyes tearing up. "I swear, you'd think I'd threatened to kill . . . you . . ." He stops laughing. "Wait. Is that what you think?"

I raise my eyebrows.

He stands up straight again. "You really believe I'd do that?"

My heart has slowed a bit, but the aftershocks of fear vibrate along my limbs. "Like you said, Oskar. I don't know you. You spoke more to me when you thought I was dying."

A strand of his dark hair has worked its way loose from the tie, and he sweeps it back from his face. "I spoke more before Raimo told me you hated magic, a lie he obviously concocted to hide the fact that there's something very strange about you."

I cross my arms over my middle and stare at his boots. His gloved finger nudges my chin up.

"When I was young, we lived in the city," he says, pulling his hood over his head and starting to walk again. "My father was a hunter."

I trip over my own feet and stumble as I start to follow. Oskar catches a handful of my cloak and pulls me upright. "Are you all right?"

"I'm just recovering from the shock. You actually told me something about yourself."

He rolls his eyes and hikes down a hill. "I didn't want to be a hunter. I wanted to stay inside all day, right in front of the fire, and carve little animals out of wood." He chuckles. "The cottage was full of them."

The sun is hovering above the trees to the east, making the rolling hills around us sparkle. It's a fluffy, dry snow, so I'm able to keep up with Oskar's long strides as he heads west, toward the dunes that mark the edge of the Mother-lake. I don't dare fall behind, because I'm clinging to every word he says.

"My father was a hard man. And he thought that I was soft. From the time I could walk, he took me with him in summer and fall, hiking these outlands in search of game, wolves and bears and beavers, pelts we could barter and meat that would keep us alive. When I was eight, he decided I would go with him every day, no matter the weather." Oskar pauses and turns his face to the east, closing his eyes as the sun offers a bit of warmth. "I hate the cold. I've always hated the cold."

"I don't understand." I look at the tiny smile on his face as the sunlight caresses his brow. "You're an ice wielder, aren't you?"

"You already know I am."

"How can the cold bother you, then? Why aren't you, I don't know, impervious to it?"

He looks pensive for a moment. "Do you know anything about the Valtia?"

I let out a dry croak of laughter. "A little." But I've learned more about magic in the last month than I did in twelve years in the temple.

Oskar nods. "So you know that she wields both ice and fire in perfect balance."

"Right." My voice sounds as hollow as I feel.

"And that she possesses extreme amounts of both." He beckons to me and begins to hike again. "But you also know by now that many people possess this kind of magic, just not as much, and not as balanced. They can't do anything like she does."

"Nothing like she does," I whisper, huddling within my cloak as we reach a copse of trees to the south of the rolling white dunes.

"Some people have a bit of ice, like Veikko and Senja and little Kukka, and others a touch of fire, like Aira and Ismael, and like Jouni, too. Most wielders tend toward one more than the other, but nearly everyone has some amount of both elements," Oskar continues. "Except for a few of us. We have only the tiniest spark of one element, and so much of the other that it nearly kills us." He guides me to a gnarled tree and sweeps his arm across a branch that's jutting out at the level of his hip. Then, without asking permission of any kind, he grasps my waist and lifts me onto the branch. I'm shocked by the feel of his hands on me, but he pulls away quickly. "You'll be more comfortable there, with your feet out of the snow."

"Thanks," I say, a bit breathlessly, surprised at how badly I wish he would touch me again. "So . . . you were telling me you have only ice magic."

"It feels like it's trying to tear me apart sometimes." He rubs his chest, and I have a flashing memory of ice blades jutting from Sofia's body, killing her from the inside out. "But worse than that, I have so little fire inside that I can't stay warm. And that's why I hate the cold."

I think of Sig, shirtless as he stalked out of the cavern

and into the chilly air. "Sig is the opposite of you, isn't he?"

Oskar grimaces. "I suppose you could say that."

"Why does he seem to hate you so much?"

He bows his head. "We used to be friends. He joined the camp about five years ago. He was alone, and my family took him in. He'd had a terrible time of it, but he healed up quickly. Raimo helped. It was good to have Sig around. We balance each other out." He curls his gloved fingers into fists. "But each time we were chased or burned out of our camps by the miners or the constables or the farmers, Sig grew angrier. He wanted to use his magic to fight back, despite the risk of revealing ourselves. And it wasn't hard for him to bring some of the others around to his way of thinking."

"But not you."

His eyes meet mine. "I don't want to fight. I only want to live."

"Don't you have to fight for some things?" I think back to that moment in the bronze cage, when I fought with everything inside me, just for the chance to take another breath.

Oskar takes a step away from me. "When I fight, people die." His eyes aren't inscrutable now. They're brimming with pain. I reach for his hand, but it disappears beneath his cloak and he closes his eyes. "There are bears in the forest. Grizzlies with heads the size of cauldrons. One pelt can buy enough food to feed a family for two months." His voice is flat as he spins out these words, like he's plodding through deep, deep snow. "My father was determined to find one. He set out traps, much the same as the one that took your fingers off. And one summer day, I went with him to check them. When we heard the snap of it, we ran. I was thinking I had so much energy, that I could run like this forever. I ran so fast that I passed my father, so fast that I didn't hear his shouts until it was too late."

He stares down at the snow. "The trap had snared a cub. It was squalling and screaming. I remember seeing its blood speckling the pine needles. It's the last thing I saw before the mother bear attacked." He pulls his cloak back and lifts his tunic for a moment, revealing the three slashing marks across his ribs, wide and pink. "My father hit her before she could kill me."

He raises his head. "That was the first time my magic came out. It was like"—he lets out a long breath—"an avalanche. And when it stopped, everything around me was quiet." Like his voice right now. "The bear was frozen solid. But so was my father."

Oh, stars. I hear Elder Kauko's voice in my head, telling me how the magic protects the wielder in a dangerous or stressful situation: *It usually bursts forth with such strength . . .* I imagine a dark-haired, granite-eyed little boy, staggering back in the wake of his own icy power. "What did you do?"

He holds up his hands. "I tried to wake him up. I wanted to drag him away—he was still in the bear's embrace. But when I yanked on his arm, it"—his face crumples—"shattered," he whispers.

I cover my mouth. *Everything fell apart, and I can't put it back together*, I'd said. *I know what that's like*, he'd replied. I grimace as I hold back tears.

"I ran for the town. I was bleeding so badly that I almost didn't make it. By the time the constables reached the scene, everything had melted. The cub, the bear, and my father were all lying limp on the ground. The constables couldn't figure out what had happened, and I lied. I was so scared." He shivers, and I push back the urge to hop off my branch and go to him. I can't siphon away this kind of cold. "But my mother . . . the day after my father's funeral, even though I was barely healed enough to travel, she packed up me and Freya, who was only a few months old at the time, and headed for the outlands."

"Maarika told me your father was killed in a hunting accident."

He winces. "And I suppose she was right."

"Does she know you're a wielder?"

Oskar slowly drags his finger along the rough surface of my branch. "I suspect she's always known. But she's never said a word about it, and I've never brought it up." His finger stops a few inches from my hip. "I think we both hate what I am."

The savage pain in his voice makes my throat tight. "But denying what you are is hurting you."

His fingers clutch the branch, and his tension vibrates through my body. "Embracing it would hurt everybody else."

*It won't hurt me.* The words are on the tip of my tongue,

fighting to break free. But fear of what that admission could bring holds them back. "Do you ever use it? Don't you need to?"

It seems like magic bleeds from him, whether he wants it to or not, and my suspicion is confirmed as he nods. "There is one good thing about it," he says, his voice taking on a playful tone, though I don't miss the current of sadness on which it floats. He looks out at the rolling dunes. "I'll show you right now if you want to see."

I nod eagerly, and he motions for me to stay where I am, then creeps toward the edge of the trees. At the base of a dune perhaps twenty feet from our spot are two white hares, hopping along, looking for a few tender shoots to nibble. Oskar squats next to a wide oak and stares at the two little animals. A sudden wind blows across the fluffy snow toward them.

Their heads jerk up, as if they smell a predator. But instead of scampering away, they both topple sideways into the snow. Oskar stands up and strides out of the trees, scoops up the two creatures, and carries them back to me. They hang stiff in his grasp, their bodies swinging as he holds them up.

"What did you do?" I ask, staring at the obviously dead animals.

Oskar looks down at his kills. "I froze their blood," he says simply.

I blink slowly, recalling what he said when I asked him if that bear trap had been his. *I never use that kind.* "Is *this* how you hunt?"

He shrugs. "It's quicker than traps. I think it's fairly painless for the animal." He lays the two hares on the snow at his feet. "And it allows me to get rid of some of the ice."

Which must be why he goes out every day, even now that the weather's turned cold, even though Maarika has more meat than she knows what to do with. "Do the others know?"

He stomps his feet, loosening some of the snow crusted on the toes of his boots. "Probably some of them suspect. But I hunt alone and field dress everything, so no one sees how I kill."

"Does Raimo know?"

"Yes, because when I was about thirteen and the nightmares were getting really bad, I was stupid enough to go to him and ask him if he could take the magic away. He set my pants on fire that day."

"What?"

"I withstand heat a lot better than cold," he says drily. "But I had to go back to my mother and explain my ruined trousers." He slaps his hand over his thigh. "Raimo wants to train me to control it. He says I'm something called a Suurin. An extreme. He thinks Sig is one too. Sig was only too willing to accept Raimo's training, and look what he's become."

The way Oskar says it, I know he doesn't think Sig's become anything good.

"How does Raimo know so much?"

"Maybe because he's as old as time?" he says lightly. "Honestly, I don't know. He's been part of the camp—sort of—since long before we joined, but no one can remember when he showed up. He heals injuries and some illnesses with his magic in return for food and goods. And he's never around during the winter." He slides his boot through the snow, wearing a path all the way to the dirt below. "So . . . did he happen to tell you what *you* are?"

I shake my head quickly, not able to meet his eyes. "He just said I'm completely empty of ice and fire, and therefore immune to the magic that comes from it. I'm a fluke." I'm guessing Oskar's been telling me all these things about himself in the hope that I'll do the same, but I *can't.* "Did he tell you what being a Suurin actually means?"

The corner of his mouth twitches as I abruptly swing the conversation back to him. "He wouldn't—unless I let him teach me."

That must be what Raimo was demanding in exchange for healing me. "Why won't you let him?"

"He'd make me use the magic, and I do that as rarely as I can. To hunt, yes, because I need it to feed my family. But if I go to Raimo . . ."

It would require him to embrace the deadly gift that killed his father. "What if he could teach you to control it?" And didn't Raimo say they couldn't wait much longer? What will happen to Oskar if he won't accept what he is?

"My magic can't be controlled, Elli. Trust me, I've tried. I'm not like other wielders." His tone reflects all his weary efforts. "I just want it to go away." He chews on his lip for a moment and then slowly lifts his gaze to mine. "And after what happened this morning, I was wondering if you could help me with that."

# CHAPTER 15

Though I've told Oskar virtually nothing about myself even after he laid himself bare, he asks me only one question. It's a simple request, and so hopeful that I can't tell him no, even though it makes me ache.

That night, after we stay out most of the day and he takes down eight hares with his ice magic, we return to the caverns. Oskar refuses to let me help skin them—he insists I stay by the fire and keep my hands, especially my right, warm. I would rather be useful, but I'm also relieved. My hand hasn't hurt this much since I was first injured, and I feel sick with the pain and my efforts to hide it. It's apparent that Oskar can see it, though, and Maarika as well. She brews me a tea that tastes strongly of tree bark, and I drink it with gratitude and try not to grimace.

Oskar gives me a veiled look as I disappear with Freya into our little bedchamber. She chatters at me for several minutes about how Harri was asking after me this afternoon, how she thinks he wants to "entangle" with me. I listen with half an ear, distracted by what I'm about to do. The moment Freya's voice trails off and her breathing evens out, I sit up and peer through the gap between the fur and the frame from which it's hanging. Oskar's waiting for me. My heart is beating so fast. I've spent a significant part of every night watching him out there, but as I crawl forward to join him, I know—this is different.

I'm not sure if I want it or not. I *do* want to touch him. I've wanted to touch him for a while now, and not only because I want to help him. As confusing as it is, when I think of putting my hands on him—and the few times he's touched me—my stomach drops in the same way it always did when I thought of those things with Mim. They are nothing alike—Mim was softness and comfort where Oskar is gruff and hard. And even now, after all these days and weeks, thinking of her still stirs that warmth and worry and want inside of me. But when I look at Oskar, I cannot deny the flutter, the silent longing inside. At the same time, I don't want to accidentally drain away all his magic, even though that's exactly what he's hoping will happen. I'm scared about what it would do to him.

Oskar has placed his own pallet right next to the fire, and he's laid out a second on his other side and put an extra fur blanket atop it. He swallows hard when I come through the curtain, looking more uncertain than I'd expected, given his delight when I agreed to do this. "Are you . . . ," he begins, then clears his throat. "Is this all right? Do you have enough room?"

My pallet is a good three feet away from his. "My arm's not that long."

His cheeks, the tan fading into winter pallor, take on a pink flush. "Oh. How do you think we should . . ." He gestures from my body to his.

I shouldn't be doing this. If Raimo knew, he'd be furious. But as I look at Oskar, inching my pallet a little closer—but not *too* close—to his, I can't refuse him. If this gives him any relief at all, I'm willing to try. If it seems to have any negative effect on him, though, I'm pulling away.

"I think we'll have to figure it out together," I say quietly.

I sink onto my pallet, the soft fur tickling the palm of my mangled hand. The pain from earlier in the evening has subsided now, but I still curl it against my chest to protect it. Oskar wraps his cloak around himself. We lie on our sides, facing each other.

The corner of his mouth quirks up. "I happened to overhear what Freya was saying to you about Harri. . . ."

My cheeks must be flaming. "I want absolutely nothing to do with him."

Oskar's quiet for a moment, just staring at me. "Good," he finally says, then reaches down and pulls the fur blanket up to my shoulders. "I'm grateful that you're willing to do this," he murmurs.

"No promises."

"Understood."

Tentatively, he slides his hand toward me, palm up, calloused and strong. It comes to a stop between us. Waiting. Once I do this, there's no hiding, no going back, no pretending there's not something odd about me. I look from Oskar's hand to his face. He's watching me, a frown tugging at his lips. His fingers curl like a snail pulling into its shell. "You don't have to, Elli. If you say no, it won't change anything at all. You'll still have a home here, for as long as you need it."

His hushed words fill the hollow space inside. My eyes sting with tears as I silently lay my palm over his.

It's the quietest of things, the most fragile of moments. I feel the coolness of his skin, but also the texture of it, hard and soft, rough and smooth, as his long fingers wrap over mine. As soon as our gazes meet, the cold magic swirls along my palm, around my wrist, winding its way up my arm until it trickles into my chest, glittering and frigid. Oskar's lips part. He looks stunned and stuck, like it feels too good to speak. The rush of magic intensifies, pouring into me so quickly that I swear I feel the tiny, cold kisses of snowflakes on my face.

"Oh," he whispers, his eyes fluttering shut. "Thank you."

I watch his face relaxing into the smallest of smiles as he falls into a peaceful sleep. He breathes evenly, a smooth rhythm from his powerful body, a much-needed truce after so much war inside him. My mind flickers with ice floes on the Motherlake, with icicles forming along branches and rocks, with snowflakes tumbling playfully through the air. The sight of his relief makes a tear slip from my eye, and I bow my head and kiss his knuckles, held tight in my grasp. I give in to it without guilt or shame. His skin tastes faintly of salt, maybe from my tears.

"Good night, Oskar." I close my eyes and welcome his frigid dreams into my hollow darkness.

Over the next fortnight, we develop a new routine. Every night, Oskar waits, and every night, I go to him. I siphon his icy dreams, and inside me they thaw. It doesn't hurt. The ice can't claim me. It can't even make me shiver.

But Oskar can, though I don't think he realizes it. Now that he sleeps easy, he rises early, refreshed and warm. He always tests his magic on the pail of water near the fire—after a night touching me, it's all he can do to make the surface freeze. And instead of being horrified that I've drained the powerful ice magic away, he's delighted. He brews me tea, as if he's worried his dreams will give me a chill. He never asks how I do it, or why I have this power. He always asks if perhaps I'm too tired, if I'd like to sleep with Freya in the other chamber. He seems embarrassed. I don't think he understands that it feels just as good to me. I had been scared I would hurt him somehow, but every day he looks better.

Maybe I'm keeping him safe from his nightmares and giving him rest, but he's giving me something too, more than the new pair of gloves that magically appeared beneath my cloak one afternoon, the one for the right hand crafted with only three fingers and extra padding over the knuckles where the ring finger and pinkie would have been. More even than the delicate carving of a dove that I found under my pillow the evening after that, its wooden wings spread in flight, the flex of its body ecstatic and free.

I'm not sure how to pin this feeling down. It's as elusive as the numbness that swirls inside my body. Every day, as the hours creep past, I find myself getting jittery, waiting for the sight of Oskar's tall figure striding into the cavern. And when he does, I can't stop the smile from spreading across my face—especially because his eyes search for me, and when they find me, he smiles right back. That in and of itself is magical and ignites a spark of pride inside me.

I gave Oskar back his smile.

One day, as I'm hanging our laundry up to dry by the fire, he emerges from the back cavern, clean-shaven. Some of the young men, including Harri, his curly hair damp from the stream, are joking with him. "Tell me, Oskar, was it difficult to kill the ferocious little beast that had made its home on your ugly face?"

Oskar runs his palm along his smooth cheek. Harri couldn't be more wrong—Oskar is far from ugly. He looks a few years younger without that beard, but his jawline is straight and strong. He laughs. "It was a close call," he says, then draws his hunting knife and waves it in the air. "But it was him or me." He looks over and sees me watching him, and I bite my lip and duck into the shelter again.

Even though we're locked in the hard grip of winter, even though it's so cold in the caverns that my bones ache endlessly, I've never been happier. Oskar had hoped I could take away his magic for good, but I'm ashamed to admit that I'm glad it grows inside him during the day and leaves him shivering on his pallet at night, waiting for my touch. That moment I slide my hand into his is the absolute best second of every day.

Each morning I wake a little closer to Oskar's side, until one morning, I wake up in his arms. I don't remember it happening, but my head is on his shoulder, and my forehead is pressed to the cool skin of his throat. Strands of my copper hair are sticking to his dark stubble. His fingers are woven into my thick locks. He's breathing deeply, still sleeping, sweet and quiet. But my heart is racing. Tentatively I slide my arm over his chest, feeling the contours of him, memorizing the feel of it. *This is what it's like to be in the arms of a lover,* my mind whispers.

This is a thing I never thought I'd experience, yet something I have imagined more than a few times. I know that Oskar and I are friends—that he appreciates what I do for him and cares for me because I do it—but for a moment I close my eyes and pretend. His other hand is on my waist, and one of my feet is tucked between his calves. I inhale his scent, wood smoke, sweat, and something crisp and fresh that I can only think of as the purest kind of ice. It fills me with the crazy desire to curl my fingers into the fabric of his tunic, to press my lips to his skin and taste him.

I can't help but think he would taste delicious.

I should move, but I can't quite summon the will. I want this to go on and on.

I should be cold, molded against the body of a powerful ice wielder, but heat is rushing through my veins. My body tightens, curving into him, edging closer. I'm not sure what I'm seeking, but I crave it like I've never craved anything before.

The slow swish of Oskar's breath falls silent. For the barest instant, his fingers tighten in my hair. And then he turns on his side, rising on his elbow. His hair hangs down, shadowing his features as his face hovers above mine. But I feel his eyes on me. Trembling, I reach up and touch the tiny bow in the center of his upper lip. His breath gusts warm over my fingertips as he begins to lower his head.

"Don't mind me," Freya says cheerfully as she pops out of her chamber. "Wouldn't want to interrupt." She strides out of the shelter, probably headed for the relief chamber.

Oskar sits up abruptly, tugging his cloak around his body as he peels himself from my side. He rises from the floor, scrubbing his hand over his face. "I, ah . . . I should . . . yes. I should." He walks out of the shelter, leaving me sitting on the floor, my hair a mess, my heart thumping in my once again hollow chest.

Freya returns a few minutes later and sits next to me by the smoldering fire. "You didn't think you were fooling me, sneaking out every night?"

I pull one of the fur blankets over my lap, twining my fingers in the soft pelt. "I guess I did."

Freya's dark-brown hair is loose and wavy, and she has her skinny legs pulled to her chest under her thick woolen nightgown. "You're not very stealthy."

"Are you angry?" I swallow hard and look over my shoulder at the curtain of pelts that covers Maarika's chamber.

"She knows, Elli." Freya tosses a stray bit of wood onto the fire. "But Oskar's been happier in the last few weeks than he's been in a long time. It's hard to be angry about that." She snorts. "I can think of a few people who might be, though."

"Oskar and I aren't . . ." I have no idea what we aren't. Or what we are. But I have the niggling fear that what happened between us just now might have complicated everything. And despite that, I want to relive it over and over. To understand. To savor.

Freya pokes my arm. "Oh, *sure* you aren't. I might be ten, but I'm not stupid."

I laugh. "Well, lucky for you. I'm sixteen, and right now I feel *really* stupid." I get to my feet and grab one of the empty pails. "I'm going to fetch some water."

Oskar's little sister gives me a saucy, raised-eyebrow look. "Make sure Aira's nowhere nearby when you do. She just might push you in."

# CHAPTER 16

Something tugs on my toe, and I jerk my foot away. Then it catches my ankle and pulls, and I emerge from sleep all at once. Oskar's shape fills the gap in the curtain. "Elli," he whispers.

"I'm coming." And full of relief—Oskar never came back to the shelter last night, and I was afraid he didn't want to sleep next to me anymore.

But when I clumsily crawl out of the little chamber, I notice Oskar's wearing his boots. "Where have you been?" I ask, trying to sound casual. "Is everything all right?"

He rubs the toe of his boot over a loose stone. "It's a thaw today. Unseasonably warm."

"How do you know?"

"I can feel it coming." He gives me a half smile. "I was

wondering if you wanted to go for a walk."

My eyebrows rise. I've gone hunting with him a few times in the past week, mostly on the wickedly cold days when I feel worried for him out in the snow, alone with no heat to guide him home. The pain that gnaws at my scarred knuckles for hours afterward is worth it—if I hold his hand, he weathers it better. But why would he need me on a warm day?

Why am I asking so many questions? The only one that matters is: do I want to go with him?

"Give me a moment." I cram my feet into my boots—I have my own pair now, which Oskar acquired from Jouni's father in exchange for a wolf pelt and several pounds of elk meat. I scurry to the relief chamber, do my business, then run down the trail to the rushing stream, where I splash my face. By the time I return, Oskar's ready to go. He wraps my cloak around my shoulders—another new possession, this one from Senja in exchange for four white hare pelts to make a wrap for Kukka. Oskar hands me a dry biscuit, which I eat as we hike out of the cave. On the way, he lights a torch in the cinders of the smoking central fire pit, and we march up the trail.

Oskar was right—even though it's still dark out, the air is beautifully cool instead of bitterly cold. "We'll have a good melt today," he says. "The last weeks have been awful. I'm wondering if the Valtia has finally decided to offer us some warmth."

I stop dead, grief weighing me down as the faces of Sofia and Mim roll to the front of my mind. It's followed closely by guilt—what right have I to be as happy as I've been without thinking of them, and of the people? All we've heard over the past weeks from the cave dwellers who sneak into the city is that Kupari is falling into chaos. Crime in the streets, constables accepting bribes, riots in the markets, farmers with sharpened scythes fighting off hungry citizens, and rage simmering in the hearts of the people. Toward the copper-hoarding priests. Toward the absent queen.

Could they have found her, the true Valtia? Could this be the solution to everything? "Amazing," I whisper. It is at once a pang of sadness and a burden lifted from my shoulders. "You're sure?"

"It's not a seasonal warmth," Oskar says. "This is the coldest month of the year. It has to be magic. The Valtia must be putting her grief aside, thank the stars."

"I would think you'd despise her. Didn't your mother flee from the city to prevent you from being taken to the temple?"

Oskar nods. "But I have no quarrel with the Valtia herself."

"The priests, though?"

Oskar kicks a stone that's sticking up out of the melting snow. "Well, let's just say I have no desire to be one of them. I've always wondered what it's like, locked away in that temple. I hear the Saadella never goes outside except for the planting and harvest ceremonies, and the Valtia emerges only slightly more often. How can that be good for a person?"

I pull my cloak tight around me. "Maybe, if she never knows what it's like, she doesn't know to miss it."

He grunts. "Like a wild beast living in captivity. I think, within its soul, the creature knows it's missing something."

The words strike me in the chest. I can't help but think of old Nectarhand, the fat, lazy grizzly who could barely walk, and I wonder what he might have been like if he had the entire north woods as his home. And then I think of how much I've changed in the last six weeks, and how for the twelve years before that, all my needs and whims were met without me ever having to ask. "But it's living in a gilded cage, most certainly," I murmur.

"A gilded cage is still a cage. I have to have the sun, and the trees and the grass. I want to come and go as I please."

I smile. "You don't sound like that little boy who wanted to stay inside by the fire all the time, carving wooden animals. Though you're still good at it." I've kept that little carved dove tucked away under my pillow, where I can look at it whenever I want.

He chuckles, his cheeks darkening. "Well, I didn't have much choice, once we left the city. But in the summer I rarely seek shelter. It feels so good to be out here in the heat." His smile is as bright as a sunrise. "It feels like summer to me today."

We reach the start of the marshlands, strands of stiff grass poking from the snow. The sun hasn't yet emerged, but it's beginning to spread pink, purple, and orange streaks across the sky. Oskar turns to the southeast and walks toward the light, shortening his long strides so that I can comfortably stay beside him.

"What are we hunting?" I finally ask. The caverns are

over a rise to our right and down a steep drop. One little boy tried to take that shortcut a few weeks ago and broke both his legs. We needed Raimo, but of course the old man couldn't be found. "We've never gone this way before."

Oskar purses his lips. "I wanted to show you something." He leads me around a bend and veers off the main trail, hiking the slope of the craggy hill that conceals our caverns from prying eyes. After several minutes, he points his torch at a jumble of boulders. "I thought maybe . . . you'd enjoy the sunrise."

My brow furrows as I look up at him. "You brought me out here to see the sun come up?"

Anxiety flashes in Oskar's eyes. "We don't have to. I just think it's rather pretty and—"

"No, it's lovely." It's also completely confusing.

He searches my face. "Yes?"

"Yes."

He grins and takes my hand, tugging me toward the boulders at a pace that requires me to jog just to keep up. When we reach them, it's apparent that *someone* has cleared all the snow off them. They're dry and smooth and waiting. Oskar plants his torch in a crack in the rock and boosts me up onto a squat boulder with a relatively flat top, then climbs up after me. We sit next to each other, our legs hanging down, facing the rising sun. I am a jangling mess of nerves and puzzlement as his hip nudges mine.

"I watch it from here, some mornings before I go hunting," he says. "This is the best spot."

I stare at the horizon as a line of orange seeps up from the ground and spreads itself thin over the land. At first it looks so fragile, so easy to smother or stamp out, but then a golden dome of sun rises up, relentless and unstoppable. *Like magic inside a new Valtia,* I think sadly. It's a sensation I'll never know. I didn't expect to feel this way, but as I think of another girl in the temple, wearing the cuff of Astia, wearing the crown, I can't help the ache. I'm glad. Relieved. But it also reminds me of everything I thought I was, and how it turned out to be a lie.

I push all of that away. It's over now, and the people have what they need, and everything will be all right now that the true Valtia has been found—I won't let it ruin this moment. "It's beautiful. I'm glad you brought me out here."

Oskar clears his throat. "I wanted to talk to you."

My nerves ball up in my stomach like a clenched fist. "All right."

"Yesterday morning, I . . ." He pauses and tucks a loose lock of hair behind his ear.

Stars, my face is so hot. "I know you were probably embarrassed when Freya saw us."

"No, I wasn't embarrassed." Oskar's eyes trace my cheek, and then he hesitantly follows the path with his fingers, which only makes my skin blaze hotter. He sighs as his fingertips linger. "Oh, this warmth," he says quietly. "I woke up to the feel of it pressed against me." His gaze drops to my lips, and my stomach does a wobbly little flip. "It was the best thing I've ever felt. Better than a thousand summer days."

I can barely breathe as his finger slides lower, along my neck. "For me, too," I whisper. Every part of me is tingling.

He leans down, touching my forehead with his. "I didn't know what to do with the want it awakened in me. And . . . I was afraid."

"I am too." I've never been this close to anyone, not even Mim. Oskar's lips are only a few inches away. "But I'm not scared of you."

The corner of his mouth curves up, and then he brushes his lips over mine. They're cool and soft and it's over way too soon. We stare at each other. "Can I do that again?" he whispers as his fingers slide into my hair.

I nod, my nose skimming against his as I eagerly offer him my lips. My body is tight and shaking as he leans in, pressing his mouth to mine, gentle but sure. And though he is made of ice, he sets me on fire with desire and uncertainty and fear. His arm wraps around my waist, and he draws me close as our lips touch and bump and nudge and slide. His thumb strokes along my jaw as his tongue caresses mine. Every place he touches tingles with his magic. I don't know if I'm doing it right—or if he is—but I know it feels good. I know I want more. *So much more.* My hand lifts to rest on his chest. His heart is beating as fast as mine, and I find it oddly reassuring.

Oskar kisses the corner of my mouth. "Stars, you are so beautiful, Elli."

My fingers skim over his rough cheek, his stubble pricking my skin. "So are you."

He laughs. "No one has *ever* said that to me."

"But you must know." I've seen Aira watching him from beneath her lashes. I've seen her gaze trail him as he strides out of the caverns—and she's not the only one. "Many girls probably wish they were in my position."

"Ah, well, they wouldn't if they actually kissed me. I might accidentally freeze our mouths together." He chuckles. "That actually happened to me the first time I kissed a girl."

My stomach drops, even though he's still smiling. "Because of your cold magic. I didn't realize it would affect—"

He rubs the back of his neck. "If I drop my guard, the ice rises up quickly." He grins. "But I don't have to worry about that with you."

My hand falls away from his chest as the hollow space in mine opens wide. "That's convenient." Suddenly my doubt bubbles up like Oskar's magic, powerful and unstoppable. Did he kiss me because of who I am—or what I do for him?

His smile falters. "I didn't mean . . ."

"It's all right." But my throat's gone tight, and my eyes are stinging. I blow a shaky, slow breath from between my lips, hating that this doubt could eat my happiness so quickly. "I—I just never expected to kiss someone," I babble. "I don't know what I'm doing."

Oskar gives me a strange look. "You *never* expected to kiss someone?"

I look away, panic wrenching itself loose inside me. Oskar's going to think I'm insane. I remember the moments when I wondered how it might feel to be in someone's arms, to know he wasn't there because I had commanded him to stay, but because he wanted it as much as I did. Now Oskar's right next to me, handsome and strong, actually asking if he can touch and kiss me . . . and all I can do is wonder if his affection is real, or whether he feels about me the way the people feel about the Valtia. Yes, they love her, but when her magic doesn't serve them, how long does the adoration last?

I lean over and kiss Oskar's rough cheek, which causes his brows to rise in pure puzzlement. "I'm sorry. I'm not good at this," I whisper, blinking idiotic tears away. What in *stars* is wrong with me? "And I've got chores to do." I scoot to the edge of the boulder and slide off.

Oskar's feet hit the ground at the same time as mine. "Wait—Elli! Didn't you want me to kiss you?" He sounds perplexed. And more than a little frustrated.

So am I. My mind is a mess of questions and fears and wants and wishes, and all I know is that I need to get away from him or I'm going to cry. I begin to walk, but I don't make it more than a few steps before Oskar's in front of me. "What did I do wrong?"

"Nothing," I say honestly as I try to step around him. "It just happened so fast. I'm . . . I'm not sure I'm ready. . . ." I grimace, bowing my head to make sure he doesn't see.

Oskar takes me by the shoulders. "If you're not ready, I can accept that. But I'm having trouble believing that's all that's going on." He pulls me closer, his gaze hard on mine. "Please. I've held myself back so many times. I've tried not to pry. But I can tell that there's a war going on behind those eyes, and I'm desperate to understand it."

"Oskar, if you'd never discovered what I can do, would we be standing here right now?"

He frowns. "How could I possibly know that?" He takes my face in his hands. "All I know is that a minute ago, I had you in my arms, and you kissed me back. It felt right." He hesitates. "Didn't it?"

It felt *so* right. But something inside me has gone all wrong. I want to tell him everything so he can help me figure it out, but Raimo's warnings keep my secrets locked tight inside. As long as they're there, I'll never know the truth of Oskar's feelings, because he'll never know what I really am. *I* barely know what I really am. I lay my palms on his chest. "This isn't fair to either of us right now. I—I think it would be better if we kept things as they were."

What am I saying?

Oh, stars, *why* am I saying this?

Oskar's gray eyes flicker with pain. "If that's what you want."

No. It's not. In fact, I want him to argue. I want him to challenge me. I want him to say again that we're right, that this is good, that he can't let me go because his heart won't allow it. I want him to *fight*.

But instead he lets me go and runs his hands over his hair. "I didn't mean to push you."

"I'll still siphon your magic," I say quickly, because he's backing away from me, not meeting my eyes. "You can still—we can still touch at night. You don't have to worry about that. Nothing has to change."

He looks up at the sky and lets out a strangled, hoarse laugh. "Right. What a relief. Nothing has changed." He pivots around. "I'd better hunt. The others are probably already in the forest." He stalks up the trail, back around the crest of the hill.

I follow, swiping my hands across my eyes, reeling in his wake. I feel hollower than ever. If my doubt hadn't grown like a poisonous mushroom inside me, maybe Oskar and I would still be on those rocks, his lips on mine, his hands on my body. Now he looks like he'll never touch me again. And maybe I should be glad, because I've shielded my heart and his from the danger of my secrets, but instead I want to curl up on the stiff grass and cry myself dry.

A high, quavering scream pierces the morning, followed by several others. Oskar's shoulders go stiff, and then he shoves off, sprinting full speed over the hill toward the noise. I follow after him, running as fast as I can, but by the time I reach the crest of the hill, he's headed straight for the edge of the drop-off.

"Oskar!" I shriek, but a burst of fire spirals up from the opening to the cavern, and he speeds up, his long legs destroying the distance.

He doesn't slow down as he reaches the drop-off—he leaps into open space and disappears from sight. It takes me another few seconds, filled with screams and shouts and smoke, to reach the edge.

What I see makes me choke with dread. Two women lie burned at the cavern entrance, their faces black, their hair and clothes singed away. Oskar, who somehow managed to make the twenty-foot drop without hurting himself, is standing with his arms spread in front of them, hatred flashing in his eyes.

Facing him are a dozen constables from the city, in matching brown caps and red cloaks, clubs at their belts. But they're hanging back. They're not in charge. Because standing in front of them are five priests—including Elder Leevi. He points a skeletal finger up at Oskar, who stands head and shoulders taller. "We have every right to search these caves," Leevi says, his thin, reedy voice at odds with his threatening posture.

"You have no right," Oskar roars. "We're not within the walls of your city, and you've attacked a cavern full of women and children!"

"These two," Leevi says as he wags his finger at the women lying burned on the ground, "were unauthorized magic wielders. They attacked us."

Oskar's face twists with rage. "Because you invaded their home!"

I drop to my knees, my fingers clutching the slippery hunks of grass at the edge of the drop-off. Either there is no Valtia and the elders worked together to create this heat themselves, or she's on the throne and sent them here. Either way, they picked the perfect strategy to make their travel easy and to draw the men away from the cavern, eager to hunt and fish on an unseasonably warm day. Anger knots inside me—and confusion pulls it tight as I spot Harri, his dark curls shining in the morning sunlight, standing among the constables. He's very still, like he hopes Oskar won't notice him.

"We'll clear out in the spring," Oskar says. "Tell the miners they're welcome to the copper in these caves once the thaw comes."

"That's quite a promise, coming from a pack of thieving murderers, but that's not why we're here today. We merely want to take a look at the young ladies," Leevi says with a smile, just as two more priests jog out of the cave, giving Oskar a wide berth.

"They're walled up in a small cavern at the back," one of them says. "At least one is a fire wielder."

Oskar pales, and I know he's thinking of Aira and Freya.

"We'll capture the unauthorized wielders and take them back to the temple after we find who we're looking for." Leevi turns to Harri. "Would you know her by sight?"

Harri's gaze darts to Oskar, whose eyes go wide with the realization that the black-haired pickpocket is working with the priests. "I would," Harri says.

Oskar stares at him. "What are you doing, Harri?"

Leevi pats Harri on the shoulder as he speaks to Oskar. "We don't have to do this with violence. We seek only girls with copper hair and ice-blue eyes."

"I assure you, the new Saadella is not here," snarls Oskar. "None of our little girls have hair that color." He nails Harri with his stony gaze. "And you know that."

Leevi steeples his fingers beneath his chin. His thick red eyebrows rise. "Ah, but we do not just seek the little Saadella. We are also searching for our new Valtia, a young woman sixteen years of age."

Oskar's brow furrows, and Leevi looks pleased. "You see," the elder says, "we're in a desperate situation. When the previous Valtia died so tragically while averting the Soturi invasion, the new Valtia went mad with grief. She ran away, and we're worried not only for her safety, but for anyone she comes into contact with. After searching every alley and cottage in the city for her, we suspected she'd fled to the outlands. So we combed all the homesteads on the peninsula for her and had begun to wonder if she'd managed to leave Kupari altogether—until this young man bravely came forward to let us know she was here. If you care about those women and children, you'll let us look at each of them, to see if our lost Valtia is among them, as we suspect she is. Copper hair and ice-blue eyes. She might have sought refuge here sometime in the past six weeks or so. Hmm?"

Leevi's words seem to hit Oskar like a blast of icy air. He blinks and steps back. And then his gaze darts up to mine, full of questions, before he tears it away. Harri doesn't miss it. He turns and sees me perched at the edge of the drop-off. *No,* I think. *Please don't.*

"There she is!" he shouts, his voice cracking, his finger jabbing at me.

Leevi's blue-eyed gaze streaks right up the rocks until it

lands on me. His mouth drops open. "It's her," he screeches.

I shoot to my feet, every shred of my body thrumming with fear.

My boot slips in the melting snow and my arms reel. All around me, I have the sense of fire, of freezing air, of violent wind. But it's the slippery grass that does it.

I fall to the sound of Oskar shouting my name.

# CHAPTER 17

I grab at the air, begging it to grasp my flapping hands and hold me high.

If I were the Valtia, I could use my magic to slow my fall. I could summon a hot wind to carry me. I could ask the ice to rise up and catch me.

But I'm the Astia. And that makes me helpless.

I land with a huff—but not on the ground. Oskar's arms close around me, and he falls to his knees still holding me tight. I gasp, knocked breathless by the impact as Oskar's forehead leans against my cheek. His body is between me and the priests, who are firing blasts of ice and fire at us with all the power they possess.

And Oskar is taking all of it. His face is a mask of agony as a blast of fire slams into his back. His chest shudders and he groans from between clenched teeth.

I don't feel the fire, but the sight of Oskar's pain causes molten rage to well up inside me and overflow. I look over his shoulder, right at Leevi, and see the tight, bitter determination on the elder's face as he and his priests close in, their palms outstretched, trying to destroy Oskar so they can get to me. *I will kill you for this*, I think as the elder sends a blast of ice at him.

My hands tangle in Oskar's hair as the ice collides with his broad back. "Give it to me," I whisper as he lets out a choked, shuddering whimper. I press my face to his neck. He shivers.

And then he gets to his feet. His eyes are still closed. It's like he's retreated inside himself just to survive—but his grip on my body is desperate and unrelenting as he pours excess ice magic through the places where our skin touches.

One of the priests reaches toward the large central fire in the cave, and the flames leap toward him like a trained animal. His eyes glow as he flings them at us.

My fingers curl tight against Oskar's scalp as I watch the inferno coming. My eyes narrow and my lips pull back from my gritted teeth. *No, you won't touch him.*

A wave of cold rolls across Oskar's skin. He pivots sharply, his eyes opening, his body pulsing with power. "Enough!" he roars, and, still holding me against him, flings his other arm outward. His fingers spread wide and then close into a fist.

My whole world spins as a strange pulling sensation fills my chest. Ice and snow swirl in the air, drawn from everywhere—the ground around us, the hill, the drop-off, the melting crystals on the grass. There is a deafening *boom*, and Oskar collapses. He lands on top of me as my back smashes into stones.

We're surrounded by silence. The priests have stopped their attack.

Oskar slowly raises his head from my chest. He's shaking, his breath fogging in front of his face. His lashes and hair are covered with rapidly melting ice crystals—but his forehead and cheeks are beaded with sweat. With a stab of horror, I remember Sofia dying in front of me, parts of her freezing while others burned.

"Elli?" he says, his voice laced with pain. "What—wh-what—"

I lay my palms on his frigid cheeks, trying to drain away the magic that's hurting him. "Are you all right?"

He blinks. "I d-don't know." His big body is on mine, his muscles are twitching.

"Oy!" shouts a voice I recognize as Jouni's. Boots slide in rocky terrain nearby. "What in the stars above?" His exclamation is followed by several others, full of puzzlement and fear.

Oskar rears back on his knees as if he's just remembered the threat, his arms rising to defend us. But then he goes stiff. Several of the cavern men have run down the trail, probably alarmed by the noise, and are pressed against the steep incline of the drop-off, staring in awe.

Before us is a scene of devastation, a moment literally frozen in time. Starting a few yards from where we sit and ending at the mouth of the cavern is an enormous, crystalline block of ice. It's the size of a large building, and within it are encased the constables, the priests, Harri the traitor, and Leevi. Many of them are suspended several feet above the ground, as if they were being thrown through the air when the ice hit. Their arms are spread wide as if to stop the onslaught. Their eyes are round with the horror of it but cloudy with their sudden deaths. Their mouths are gaping, held open by the unforgiving ice that has flowed down their throats, up their noses, into their ears. The sun shines down on all of it, adding a merry twinkle to the ghastly, transparent coffin.

Jouni whistles and yanks off his cap, running his hand through his messy reddish-blond hair. "Oskar. Did you . . . ?" He tears his gaze from the scene and turns to us. Then his jaw goes slack, like he's been hit over the head.

Oskar looks over his shoulder at me when he registers Jouni's shock. "Oh, stars, Elli, you—you're—"

That's when I realize I'm naked. I may be immune to magic, but my clothes aren't. All that remains of my gown and stockings are smears of ash. My boots are lumps of charcoal that crumble as I wiggle my toes. Oskar yanks off his fur cloak, which is blackened and full of large holes. He leans forward to spread it over me.

"Wait." Jouni grabs Oskar's wrist before he can cover my legs. "What's that?"

He points at my blood-flame mark, stark crimson on my pale, goose-bumped leg.

Oskar tears his arm away and covers me. "The priests and constables attacked the women," he says to Jouni. "Go make sure they're safe."

Jouni's eyes trace over my copper hair and focus on my ice-blue eyes. "Is that mark what I think it is? Did those priests come here looking for you? I've heard—"

"Jouni," Oskar snaps. "Now is not the time."

"But I heard rumors that the Valtia had gone mad and run away! Did Elli do that?" Jouni points to the mountain of ice before us. The others are edging around it, staring at the terrified faces of the men entombed there. "I've never seen ice magic like that before."

Oskar gives me a sidelong glance. "No. I did it."

Jouni laughs. "Sig told me you were a wielder, but this kind of thing would have required—"

"Stop arguing and go see if the others are all right!" Oskar's voice breaks as he sinks unsteadily to the ground, his teeth chattering. His back is covered in blistered patches I can see through the ragged, singed holes in his tunic. The ice inside him must have made him cold enough that his clothes endured the attack better than mine did, but he's still injured.

I sit up, clutching his burned cloak over my chest and curling my legs against my body. I want to touch him so badly that my fingers ache. But Jouni is still standing over us, his gaze on me. "Harri mentioned that the priests were offering a reward for anyone who helped find her. And then he brought them *here*."

"I'm not the Valtia," I say quietly. Oskar gives me a sharp, searching look. "I'm *not*."

Jouni stares at me for a moment longer before scratching a spot on his stubbly cheek and turning to the ice tomb in front of us. "Right." He walks toward the cavern entrance, his shoulders tense.

My hands are on Oskar's neck in the next moment, because I can't hold back anymore. He sighs and leans into my touch, but then abruptly wrenches himself away, ending up on his hands and knees. "I don't need your help," he growls, getting up clumsily, his muscular arms swinging at his sides.

"Oskar." His name is a plea on my lips. Does he blame me for this?

He stops with his back to me. "Now that he's gone, tell me the truth."

"I'm not the Valtia. I swear." I rise, pulling his cloak around my naked body. The rocks dig into the soles of my feet.

"I can't believe I've been so blind. Explain your eyes. Your hair. Your mark. Your ability to withstand magic. And then explain that." He points to the ice tomb.

"You did that," I murmur.

Oskar looks over his shoulder at me. "I might have ice magic inside me. A lot of it. I might even be a Suurin." His jaw clenches as he jabs his finger at the ice. "But I have never done *anything* like that."

"You know I don't have magic." But now I'm remembering what Raimo said, about how I could not only mute

259

and absorb magic—I could also magnify and project it, as the Valtia does when she wears the cuff of Astia. I blink at the frozen dead men within the ice, and the weight of their vacant stares nearly bows my back. Oskar didn't do this— not alone, at least. He worked the magic, but maybe I was the weapon, projecting it, turning it into a devastating force that destroyed anything in its way. If it's true, then together we've just killed twenty men. My stomach turns. This is exactly the reason Oskar didn't want the magic inside him. He never wanted to take another life.

Oskar's granite gaze is crushing me. "I only know what you've told me, Elli, and you've told me very little."

"Raimo told me not to," I say, my throat getting tight. "He said my life depended on it."

Oskar closes the distance between us and takes me by the shoulders. "You bear all the marks of the Valtia," he whispers. "And she has magic so balanced that it wouldn't be that difficult to hide it, not if she wanted to. She might even look immune to it, as you do, because she could coun- teract even the strongest magic with her own."

"Maybe, but Raimo still would have been able to heal me if I were the Valtia. Do you truly think I wouldn't have accepted that gift if I could have?"

"If you were desperate enough to hide, perhaps."

I nearly kick him in my frustration. "Explain how I siphon your power, then! Not even the Valtia can do that!"

"Then tell me what you are!"

I flinch as his grip tightens, knowing I can't escape

this truth anymore. "Raimo said I was the Astia."

His eyes narrow. "What? Like the cuff of—"

"Yes. It's why I can absorb your magic without being hurt by it—and why, together, we can . . ." My eyes stray to the ice tomb.

Oskar's looking at it too. "Did you know that would happen?"

"I had no idea. Oskar, please believe me," I squeak. "I was the Saadella, but when the Valtia died, the magic didn't come." I briefly tell him of my escape, and the whole time he watches me, dumbstruck.

"Why were they trying to kill you? Wait—are *they* the ones who whipped you?" Before I can stop him, he lifts his cloak from my shoulder and peers at my bare back, then curses. "Why?" he asks, that one word infused with cold rage.

"I let them whip me when I thought it would draw out the magic. And they thought that by killing me, they could awaken the magic in a new Valtia. They most likely still think that."

"Do they know you're this . . . Astia person?"

*Who isn't even supposed to exist.* I shake my head. "But Raimo did. I think he must have been a priest at some point. He told me I could do these things the night you brought me to him, but he never said how. Siphoning your magic—it just happens. And I don't know how I helped you project your magic just now, only that we were touching when it happened. But I do know that Raimo warned me to keep it secret.

He said any magic wielder would see me as an enemy—or a weapon, something to use to enhance their power."

Oskar's gaze drops to where his fingers are curled around my bare arms, which are tingling with the aftershocks of his magic, and he quickly lets me go. Maarika comes sprinting out of the cavern before either of us have a chance to speak again, her usually neat brown hair flying around her face. "Oskar!" she shrieks.

He whirls around to catch her in his arms, but staggers back as she collides with him. "You're hurt," she cries, clutching at his singed, holey tunic. "Oh, stars." Her voice is thick with tears.

"I'll be all right," he says softly.

Freya is standing several feet away, staring at the ice. "Oskar . . . ?"

Oskar pries his mother's hands from his arms. "I did it. Elli saw the whole thing." He turns back to look at me, his face smooth and expressionless. "Come into the cavern. We need to get you some clothes before you catch a chill."

Maarika looks me over, her brows rising. "What happened to her dress and boots?"

Oskar inclines his head toward the frozen priests. "They were burned off as the priests attacked. I used my magic to do what I could to protect her."

Maarika looks at me, and then up at her son. "Then I'm glad you froze them," she says, her jaw set. "They deserved that and more."

She holds her arm out, and my eyes sting as I step forward and it settles around my shoulders, pulling me close. Her other arm is around Oskar's waist. Then Freya appears on my other side, her skinny fingers burrowing into the holes in the cloak. I don't feel worthy of this, but there's no way I'll refuse it. Maarika was right—they are my family now, mine to love and protect. Their acceptance warms my body in a way fire magic never could.

We limp into the cavern, where we are confronted by heartbreak. Ruuben is holding one of the burned bodies in his arms, and I don't need to see it to know it must be Senja. He bends over her, his body convulsing with sobs, while Aira tries to comfort Kukka, who is screaming for her mother.

"Senja and Josefina tried to protect us," Maarika says, brusquely wiping tears from her cheeks. "Those priests showed no mercy."

Icy waves of air roll off Oskar as we walk by the scene. I suspect Harri's death is one that Oskar doesn't regret, and I feel the same. The pickpocket brought this fight to our threshold.

But so did I.

It hits me like a bolt of lightning, and unlike magic, I can't absorb it easily. Instead it sears itself along my bones, leaving nothing but scorched earth behind. If I had listened to the rumors, if I had paid attention instead of letting myself fall into this fantasy—of family, of belonging and normalcy, of Oskar, his needs, his body and his mouth, carved doves and warm gloves and granite eyes that always leave me guessing—I would have left days ago. Because I didn't, two women are dead, and those who love them grieve. A little girl has lost her mother. And Oskar . . . he has killed against his will, been drawn into a fight he didn't want, and now he's walking through the dim, chilly cavern, his back covered in blisters from both the heat and the cold.

As families are reunited, children clinging to their fathers' knees, women hugging their men, everyone cutting glances toward the ice tomb that blocks most of the cave entrance, Oskar, Freya, Maarika, and I make for our shelter. Jouni gives me a curious sidelong glance as he walks out of the cavern. Ismael and a few other fire wielders are already out there, palms out, their heat eating away at the frozen catastrophe so the bodies can be disposed of.

Perhaps we're all thinking the same thing: This is only the beginning. More will come. More weapons, more magic, more rage. There will be no winter respite now.

And it's my fault.

When we duck into the shelter, Freya immediately goes into her mother's room and comes out with Maarika's old boots—the ones that I used to wear before I had my own—some stockings, and a worn gown, plain and brown with holes at the elbows. While Maarika begins to cut off Oskar's tunic, parts of which are clinging to his damaged skin, I slip into one of the back chambers to change. With a lump in my throat, I slide the delicate carved dove from under my pillow and put it in my pocket.

By the time I emerge, Maarika has her boots on, and Freya is packing pelts into a sturdy basket for her to take. "There's a farmstead only a quarter mile south of here," Maarika says. "I can trade for the herbs I need to treat his burns."

"Is there no way to find Raimo?" I ask. "These wounds were caused by magic, and it seems like magic would be the best medicine. Doesn't anyone know where he's gone?"

Oskar is lying on his stomach on a bearskin pallet next to the fire. "We w-won't see him until the s-spring thaw." And that's two months away, at least.

Freya grimaces as she hears his shivery stammering. "I'll go get more fuel for the fire," she says, grabbing another basket and stomping out of the shelter.

Maarika's eyes meet mine. "Take care of him."

I don't look away. "You know I will."

She gives me a quick nod and leaves. I wait for Oskar to acknowledge me, but he doesn't. As my thoughts duel, I hike down to the stream to fetch a pail of water and carry it slowly back to the shelter, my fingers aching. I slip back inside to find my ice wielder where I left him, blistered and shivering. I set the pail next to the fire to warm the water inside, then sink to my knees next to Oskar. His forehead is pressed to the backs of his hands, the muscles of his back flexing as he tries to cope with the pain. "What would feel better, cold or hot?" I ask him, dunking a scrap of wool in the cool water.

"I don't know," he whispers. "Both. Neither." The tight, pained sound of his voice makes me ache.

"And this?" I lay my palm against an undamaged stretch of skin on his shoulder, and he tenses, perhaps feeling the ice magic leaving him.

"S-stop it," he says, his teeth chattering.

"You need it." And I need it just as badly.

His body shudders, sending vibrations up my arm. Suddenly the cold flowing into me recedes like a tide, and the chill returns to his skin, leaving me feeling hollow. The room spins, and I wobble unsteadily. "What are you doing?" I whisper.

"Get your hands off me."

I obey him, and as soon as my hands fall away, so does the dizziness. "What would you have me do, Oskar?"

He lets out a choked, humorless laugh. "Again, I don't know." He turns his head, and I lie on my side so we're face-to-face, like we've lain every night for the last two weeks. "But I understand now," he says quietly. "I didn't, this morning on the rocks."

Strands of his dark hair slide across his face, and I'm dying to smooth them back. "Why won't you let me touch you?"

"*Because* I understand." His eyes close, and mine burn. He leans his forehead against the back of his hands again, hiding his face. "Get s-some rest. You must be aching."

My fists clench. "You can't expect me to sit here and watch you hurting."

"You don't have to take c-care of me. You've done enough of that."

Pressing my lips together to keep from screaming, I look

up at the ceiling of the cave, stretching its rocky claws down toward us, hiding so many secrets in its dark shadows. I can't find a path back to the way we were a few days ago, before I woke up in his arms. My doubt about how he felt about me made me push him far away, and now he seems determined to stay there.

I stare at his long, shivering, sweating body. I've siphoned off so much cold in recent weeks, but the magic just grows to fill the space. My touch offers temporary relief, but not the permanent solution that Oskar craved. And now he's denying himself even that, out of . . . I have no idea. Honor. Pride. Sheer stubbornness.

Or maybe he does blame me. And maybe he should.

"When the priests and constables don't return to the city tonight," I tell him, "the others will know something has gone wrong."

Oskar doesn't speak, but his shoulders and arms look like chiseled granite.

"What will you do when the rest of them come here? Because believe me—their magic is powerful. I know you care about every person in these caves." I saw the look on his face as he stood between them and the priests.

"We'll leave," he says wearily. "Tomorrow morning. There's an abandoned mine about two miles to the northeast."

But the priests will chase. And they'll find. And they'll kill. The certainty swells inside me. "Then you'd better let me do what I can to help you rest and heal. You'll need your strength if you're going to protect them."

"If you think I'm going to let you touch me after everything that's happened—"

Maarika's footsteps scrape across the loose stones outside the shelter, and I scoot away from Oskar with ice encasing my heart. Part of me wants to force him to look at me, and part of me is glad that I can't see his eyes. It makes what I must do that much easier.

"How is he?" Maarika asks, setting her basket of herbs down. She's panting and windblown—something tells me she ran the whole way.

"Stubborn," I say, and she laughs. I smooth my palms against my cheeks as I rise to my feet. It's not easy, letting go, but the alternative would be much worse. "Did you get what you needed for his back?"

Maarika nods. "Now we just need Freya to show up with our kindling."

And that's my chance. "I can go find her."

"If you wish. She's probably picked up more than she can carry."

She takes off her cloak and offers it to me, but I push it away. "It's all right. I won't be gone long." I step back, my heart hammering. I want to thank her for her quiet kindness and patience. I want to beg Oskar to forgive me for bringing death and killing into his life again, but it's too late for all that. I allow myself one more look at him, remembering how only yesterday I was tucked against his body, happier than I've ever been. "Good-bye," I whisper.

My face crumples as I turn away and stride toward the

entrance to the cavern. Every step is an act of will. I ignore the fearful whispers as I walk by the row of shelters. None of that matters now, because this isn't my home anymore. These people will be safer because I'm not here.

I wrap my arms around myself and walk into the open air. My boots slosh in the water melted from the enormous block of ice. The fire wielders are still working on it, and they haven't yet freed a single body. Harri's foot is sticking out of the top, though, and one of the constables' hands is poking from the side, gray and still. The wielders give me uneasy looks as I shuffle past. Clearly everyone has heard, but they all look too scared to ask me—am I the mad Valtia?

They have no reason to fear me; they'll never see me again. I hike the narrow trail that winds upward toward the marshlands. Several cave dwellers pass me, leading saddled horses—the constables and priests must have left behind nearly two dozen well-fed mounts. I cross my arms over my chest and keep my eyes downcast, praying that Freya hasn't chosen these minutes to return. I don't think I could hide the pain of another good-bye. As I emerge from the cavern trail, a frigid wind tears the kerchief from my coppery locks, which twist in the gusts. I shiver—the winter is descending once more, and I have miles to go before I reach the city. But after weeks of getting accustomed to this kind of walking, I think I can probably reach the gates by nightfall.

Perhaps a quarter mile ahead of me is the long strip of woods where Oskar found me, though the actual spot must be miles to the north. I smile as I think of the first time I saw him, how scared I was of this bearlike boy, how quickly that fear turned to admiration and then slowly to affection. The wind gusts again, pushing me forward, and I turn away from the woods to take the path that connects to the road leading to the city. Freed from the snow by this morning's unnatural thaw, the dry marsh grass rustles and hisses. The tree branches of the forest scrape together. It almost sounds like they're screaming.

It almost sounds like they're screaming *my name*.

Behind me, there's a rumble of thunder. Another blast of breeze, but this one is warm. And the trees are still screaming through the roar of the wind. I look to my left and catch a flash of movement amid the tree trunks.

The thunder becomes the *clomp-clomp* of hooves. I gasp and whirl around. Two men on horseback are racing toward me. I stumble back as one of them raises a club—the kind carried by the constables. I turn to run, but my head explodes with agony and I fall. My vision blurs as I open my eyes to a cloaked figure striding toward me. He tosses his hood back to reveal white-blond hair and dark-brown eyes.

"Is this her, Jouni?" Sig asks, leaning over me. I try to scoot away from him, but my head throbs and it's all I can do not to retch. Something sticky and warm drips into my ear.

"That's her," Jouni says in his deep, buzzing voice.

Sig grins, and his eyes flicker with the flames of war. "Excellent."

# CHAPTER 18

I slap at Sig's face as he reaches for me, but Jouni dismounts his horse and coils a thick hemp rope around my body, pinning my arms to my sides. Sig swings himself into the saddle, and Jouni bundles me up to join him. I kick and claw, but I'm so dizzy that I can barely hold my head up.

"I'm sorry I had to hit you," Sig says, his breath hot against my ear as he anchors his arm around my waist. "I needed to catch you by surprise, seeing as I'm not eager to have my skin burned off." I feel a poke at my side and catch the flash of a blade in the sunlight. "But if I feel you trying, I'll be ready."

With that, he spurs the horse into motion, and it's all I can do not to vomit. My brain rattles in my skull and my stomach roils. Hooves pound the trail below me. Sig's arm is a bronze bar against my middle, and his chest is like a fur-nace against my back. Wind smacks at my face and tangles my hair. I don't know which direction they're taking me or how long we've been riding or what time it is, but I wish I could close my eyes and make it all stop.

Finally, I'm jerked from my stupor as Sig reins in his horse. Blinking in the midday sun, I catch glimpses of sandy dunes and blue sky as he pulls me from the saddle. My head lolls on his shoulder. He carries me along a short path between two dunes, to an open patch of sand. There's no snow here, and I wonder if the thaw caused that, or if Sig himself melted it all away. A large fire pit occupies the cen-ter of the space, and it's surrounded by sleeping pallets and cooking implements. A young woman, her long, brown hair knotted at the back of her head, is roasting what looks like a hare on a spit. She stares as Sig plops me down on a pallet. I turn my face to the wool blanket, fighting the nausea that bubbles inside me.

"Where are the others?" Jouni asks.

"I sent them into the city last night to fetch some sup-plies and information," says Sig, squatting next to me. "Yes-terday morning I got word that the priests opened up the temple, and I wanted to know what was happening." He pats my shoulder. "But maybe now we know. It didn't even occur to me when I saw you the first time. Elli, wasn't it?"

"I'm not the Valtia," I say with a moan.

"I told you she'd say that," says Jouni. "But I saw the mark myself. Take a look if you doubt me."

Sig chuckles. "I doubt everyone." His hand slides down my hip but pauses over my pocket, and his fingers dip inside. He comes up holding my carved wooden dove. His gaze traces its wings as my fingers flex with want—it's all I have left of Oskar. "Oh, my," he says in a low voice. "I haven't seen one of these in a long time."

His eyes meet mine, full of speculation and a darkness that I don't know how to translate. The bird looks so fragile, held between his pale fingers. I drink in the sight of it, expecting him to snap its wings off and toss it into the fire. Then, slowly, he slips it back into my pocket. I have no time to feel relief, though, because he pulls up the bottom of my gown. "Which leg?"

"Don't touch me," I whisper.

"Left," Jouni says.

Sig's warm fingers are on my thigh, and I clench my fists, wishing I could stop him as he slides my stocking down, past my knee, along my calf, and reveals the blood-flame mark. He whistles and pulls my skirt over my legs again. "How did you manage to hide yourself for so long?"

"Because I'm *not* the Valtia. I know I have all the marks, but I swear I'm not her."

Sig purses his lips. "Then how did you manage to encase so many men, a fair number of them magic wielders, in a giant block of ice?"

Jouni laughs. "And then she got Oskar of all people to take the blame."

Sig's head jerks up. "What?"

Jouni's smile evaporates. "Oskar. He was with her. Bragged that he—"

"Oskar would never brag, especially about something like that," Sig snaps. "You didn't mention he was there."

Jouni slides his cap off his disheveled reddish-blond hair. "I didn't think it was important. You told me he had ice magic, but I've never seen him do anything with it."

"That's not because he can't." Sig plops down in the sand next to my pallet, frowning. "He was protecting her, Jouni, either because of who she is—or who she's not. I need to know which it is, though." His eyes flare with light, and he shoves off the ground. His arms hanging loose at his sides, he takes a few steps back and throws off his cloak. Beneath it, he wears no tunic, only trousers and boots. He spreads his fingers, and twin spheres of flame burst from nothing and hover a few inches from his palms.

I wrench myself up to sitting, squeezing my eyes shut against the pain. My arms are still bound at my sides. "Just let me go," I plead.

"Free yourself, Valtia," he says. Then he hurls one of the spheres at me. It hits me in the chest, setting the hemp ropes aflame. They fall away from me as he hurls the second ball of fire right at my face. I feel the kiss of its warmth on my cheeks, a polite greeting, before the fire disappears. Sig's brow furrows and light flickers in his dark pupils.

Jouni curses and steps back, just like Freya did when Sig heated the air in the cavern. Sig himself is sweating now, cooking in the fire of his own making. A shining drop slides down his chiseled face as he watches me sitting before him, feeling nothing at all.

"Tuuli," he finally barks.

The brown-haired woman lays her spitted hare on a stack of flat stones. "You want ice?" When he nods, she grins. "As you wish."

She comes closer, regarding me with her dark-gray eyes. I smile wearily at her. I'm so tired of people shooting their ice and fire at me, and it's not like I can pretend anymore— it's impossible to fake serious burns and ugly frostbite, and I'm in too much real pain to put on an act. Tuuli's hands rise from her sides, her fingers shiny with grease. Her lips are pressed together and her arms shake with the force of her efforts to wield the magic inside her.

Perhaps she's trying to freeze my blood. The air around me cools, but I cannot help the thought—she is *nothing* compared to Oskar. Of course, the faintest reminder of him makes my throat tight. Will he be relieved when he discovers I'm gone?

Tuuli's chin trembles, and she shivers within the frost of her magic. Even Sig has goose bumps on his pale chest now. But me? The only thing that's left me cold is knowing that Oskar might be glad to be rid of me.

"You look chilled," I say to the magic wielders in front of me.

Tuuli lets out a frustrated breath, and her arms drop to her sides. She gives Sig a nervous look. "I—I could try to—"

"Don't bother," Sig says, staring at me.

Tuuli's shoulders sag as she returns to her cooking, but Sig looks more intrigued than disappointed. "Only someone with balanced magic could withstand fire and ice like that," he says, moving closer once more. "But why don't you strike at us?"

I'm saved from answering by the whinny of a few horses just beyond the dunes. Sig had said he was camping at the oak bluffs, a stretch of high cliffs over the Motherlake on the northwestern shore of the peninsula. The city must be only an hour's ride from here, northeast through the woods. If I can escape, perhaps steal a horse—

"Oy! Sig!" comes a gruff voice.

"Here," calls Sig.

A short, stocky man with a thick beard and coppery hair jogs between the dunes. "They've found the Saadella," he huffs, planting his palms on his thighs. "The herald announced it in the square this morning. Discovered her last night, apparently, as her parents tried to sneak her out of the city. And the temple just announced that the coronation of the Valtia will be at sunset. She's agreed to end her mourning and appear."

Sig's eyes narrow. "But . . . Usko, I thought you told me they were searching for the Valtia." He glances at me and then back to the new arrival.

Usko scratches at his beard and nods. "That's what I'd heard from a constable, but the priests' official stance has always been that she was in mourning."

Jouni scoffs. "Then why did seven of them—including

an elder—show up at the caverns this morning, looking for her?"

Usko pauses mid-scratch. "They did?" He looks me over. "Um . . . who are you?"

"Who do you think she is, idiot?" says Jouni, rolling his eyes.

Sig arches a golden eyebrow as he squats next to me. "So who are they crowning at sunset, Elli?"

My heart pounds against my breast. Could the elders have found the true Valtia, the one who always should have been there, the one whose place I stole? Is she the one in charge now, like Oskar and I suspected this morning? Do the priests want to kill me in order to silence me, or have they realized what I am and decided I'm their enemy? Would the true Valtia welcome me as her sister—or will Aleksi and the others poison her against me?

Anger at the elders burns inside me, and Sig must sense the heat, because his eyes snap to mine. He tilts his head, then offers me his hand. "Come with me."

When I hesitate, he wiggles his fingers, pure impatience. "I promise I won't hurt you. Not yet, at least."

Honestly, what choice do I have? I slide my palm over his, and his long fingers close around my hand. He grasps my elbow and helps me to my feet, then holds me as I sway.

"Tuuli, a cloth, please," he says. After she obeys, he presses it to the side of my head, and it comes away smeared with red. "This way," he murmurs, leading me away from his friends. None of them question it. In fact, as we walk between the dunes, they strike up a conversation about everything Usko and the others saw in the city.

Sig and I slowly hike to where the snow has been blown into stiff, icy peaks, lying over the sand like spiky armor. Sig kicks off a chunk, captures it within the cloth, and offers it to me, nodding at the bump on the side of my head. "I'm wondering if I've been a bit of an arse."

I laugh, then gasp as my head throbs. I press the cloth-wrapped ice to my temple. "A *bit* of an arse? You hit me in the head and tried to burn me to death."

He offers a sheepish smile. "Well, in my defense, I thought you were the Valtia and would defend yourself. I'm still thinking you might be her."

I sigh. "Sig, if I were the Valtia, you'd be a pile of bones and ash right now."

"If you're not the Valtia, then what are you?" He turns to me, taking my face in his hands. His scent is sharp and hot in my nose. My free hand rises to push him away, but his grasp is firm. "Don't lie. I know many ways to hurt a person that don't involve magic."

My mind whirls as I weigh the need to keep my secret with my need to convince Sig I'm not the Valtia. I focus on the feel of his palms on my cheeks, wondering why I don't sense the fiery maelstrom of his magic infusing my skin, gathering in my hollow chest. "I'm . . . something else. I'm not sure exactly." I decide on the truth—but only the half that will work in my favor. "Sometimes I . . . absorb magic."

His hands jerk away from me like he's been burned. "What?" He wipes his palms on his trousers.

It's hard to hide my smile. "I can't help it. I'm immune to fire and ice magic, and if I touch a wielder, sometimes I siphon it off."

He's looking at me like I'm poisonous. "Did Oskar know? Has he known this whole time?" Then he laughs, bitter and hard. "Oh, let me guess. Did he beg you to drain away all his magic? You must have been an answer to all his desperate prayers."

"You seem awfully interested in a man you think is a coward."

Sig kicks at the sand, the toe of his boot leaving a deep divot. "He's wasting his gift! And he won't lift a finger to fight for himself."

I pull the ice pack from my temple. "But he'll fight for others. I'd be dead if he hadn't fought for me." I toss the bloodstained cloth to the ground and thrust my hand into my pocket. My hand closes around the wooden dove. "You might know him, but you don't understand him."

Sig's face crumples and he turns away quickly, leaving me to stare at the silver lash marks on his back. "He's my brother," he says quietly. "Not by blood, but by magic and circumstance. He seems to have forgotten that, but I never will." He takes my elbow again and leads me forward until we reach the stony expanse of the bluffs. Beyond it stretches the frozen Motherlake, her winter ice glittering under the afternoon sun. "Did he tell you anything about me?"

"Oskar's not the most talkative person."

He lets out a short, amused breath. "True." There is the faintest spark of longing in his deep-brown eyes. I was so wrong. He doesn't hate Oskar. He misses him. Something we have in common.

"Would *you* like to tell me about yourself, Sig?"

He gives me a cautious look, then conceals it with a grin. "Why not? Perhaps that'll make things easier." His smile turns fierce. "And maybe we'll find we have a common enemy."

He holds his palm over a broad patch of crusty snow, and it melts away instantly. The melt-off boils, then turns to steam. Sig doesn't stop until the sand beneath is dry. He guides me to sit down, and I feel its vague warmth seep through my gown.

"When I was fourteen, I was an apprentice to my father—he was a locksmith. My mother died when I was a little boy."

His pale fingers trace the outline of a key in the sand. "The priests called my father to the temple one day, to install a new lock for one of their chambers. He invited me along. Said it was a great honor. He joked that maybe we'd see the Valtia. Or perhaps the Saadella. She would have been about eleven at that time." He leans in and whispers, "Which could make her about sixteen now."

My cheeks burn and he chuckles. "I thought so. You were the Saadella. Let me guess—did they torture you when you turned out to be a magical dud?"

I clench my teeth. "I thought you were going to tell me about *you*."

His mirth melts away. "Fine. I didn't want to go to the temple. I tried to get out of it. I was terrified."

"You knew you had magic."

He nods, still tracing that key in the sand. "But I'd managed to keep it hidden. A year before, my friend Armo accidentally froze water in a pump right outside the city council building. The priests came that night and took him, and I remember thinking it was as if he had died."

"Armo is an apprentice now," I say, deciding not to mention that he's the person who whipped me. "One day he'll be a priest."

"How nice." Sig lets a stream of white-gold sand spiral from his closed fist. "That was the last thing I wanted to be. And I figured, as long as I could conceal the magic, I could live just fine. I suppose it was arrogant to think that would work." He sighs. "It was one of the elders who escorted us into the temple. As my father worked, the elder asked me about my studies. I tried to be polite. He offered to show me some of the star texts, and I went with him."

"Do you know which elder?"

He shrugs. "Dark eyes. Dark shadow of hair on his shaved head. Round belly."

"Aleksi. Or . . . Kauko, maybe." Both are dark. "They're distinguishable only by their actions."

"Which one is crueler, then?" he whispers as he looks out on the Motherlake. He shudders, shaking off a cold memory. "When we entered the domed chamber, he asked me how I slept at night."

"And did you tell him about your fiery nightmares?" As powerful as Sig is, I can't imagine his dreams are peaceful.

Sig bows his head. "No. I don't like to talk about them. But I think the elder sensed my magic anyway. Because as I was peering at the star chart, he grabbed my arm. The sharpest pain flashed through me, hot and then cold." He grimaces. "And I couldn't help it."

"Your magic rose up," I say quietly. It protects its wielder—until it destroys him.

His face is still tense with the memory. "The star chart caught fire. The elder's robes burst into flames. The copper inlay below my feet melted. I couldn't control it at all. And then I passed out from the heat." He rubs his hands over his eyes. "When I woke up, I was in a cell in the catacombs, and my head had been shaved. One of the others told me we would be initiated in the morning."

My brow furrows. "And your father?"

"I imagine the elder told him about the fire magic and paid him off." And I can tell by the flames in Sig's eyes that he's never forgiven his father for it.

"What did you do?"

"I tried to escape. The first time, they caught me, and that dark elder personally oversaw my whipping."

"Didn't you . . . I don't know, melt the chains or something?"

"He used ice to counteract my magic," he says, an edge to

his voice. "He wields both, like all the elders do. And I think he wanted me to suffer. He wanted me to bleed. He . . . I actually think he . . . did something to my wounds. . . ." Sig squirms and swipes at his shoulder blades. "Stars, I don't know. I wasn't in my right mind. I have the strangest memories of that night."

Goose bumps ripple across my skin. I'm betting the dark elder was Aleksi. I wouldn't put any sort of cruelty past him. "But obviously you escaped."

Sig turns to me, heat rolling off him in deadly waves, sweat beading his brow. "I'm the son of a locksmith." He sweeps his hand over the key shape, turning the sand smooth. "When the elder was done with me, he put me in a cell. He was excited. He said he couldn't believe I'd gone so long without revealing myself. And he said that if I existed, there was another like me that they hadn't found yet."

"Oskar," I murmur. "He knew you were a Suurin."

Sig leans back, looking surprised. "Oskar actually told you what he was." His gaze darts to my pocket, where the dove hides. "I didn't know what the elder was talking about at the time. I just knew they had something terrible planned for me. But they didn't realize that I know how to open doors, no matter which side of them I'm on. The one gift my father left me with. As soon as the elder left to get the others, I escaped the cell. I found my way out to the temple dock and swam for my life. I sneaked out of the city and ended up finding the camp." He snorts. "Well. Oskar ended up finding *me*, if I'm honest."

I smile. "He found me, too."

Sig is quiet for a few moments. "Oskar told me I should never show the others how powerful I was, so that no one would ever be tempted to sell that information to the priests. He said I would be safer if the elders thought I was dead. And I tried. For *so* long." He stares at a patch of sand, and before my eyes, it melts into glass. "But now I'm done hiding."

I wonder if his hatred makes the fire burn hotter. "Now you want to take down the priests before the Valtia is in control again."

He lets out a humorless grunt of laughter. "I've wanted that for years. Give me one good reason why they should remain in power. Explain why they geld and shave and torture just to bend young wielders to their will. Explain why they keep the Saadella and the Valtia from mingling with the people. Explain why they use the Valtia until her body is destroyed, while they live long, long lives. And then," he says, his voice a flame unto itself, "tell me why magic wielders can't choose the lives they want. Tell me why we, of all people, are made into slaves."

I frown. "The apprentices and acolytes seem happy enough with their fates, and so do the priests."

Sig's fingers burrow into the sand. "Then explain why there are exactly thirty priests, all of them men, and exactly thirty apprentices to replace them—and yet there are a hundred or more acolytes at any one time, with more being brought to the temple every month. Have you ever seen an old acolyte?"

The winter wind buffets my back. "No, but they're cloistered after a certain age. They live in quarters within the catacombs."

"Mmm. Just a different kind of cave dweller, then." His eyes narrow. "And how many of them do you think there are now? Five hundred? A thousand? More than that? How do that many people live in complete isolation? How much food would be required to feed them all? Do you really believe that's what happens to them?"

A chill rattles in my chest, and it has nothing to do with the cold breeze. "What do you believe?"

He shakes his head. "I couldn't say, but I will tell you that I wandered that underground maze for hours, looking for a way out. I saw chamber after chamber filled with copper ore and bars, baubles and coins, but I never once came upon a single cloistered acolyte, let alone quarters meant to house hundreds of them."

I cross my arms over my chest and rub my hands up and down my sleeves. Sig starts to scoot closer, but I put my hands out to stop him. His eyebrow arches. "Just offering a bit of warmth."

I roll my eyes. "I'm fine."

"I'm trying to be nice. Don't flatter yourself."

"I wouldn't dream of it." I'm actually relieved to hear the disinterest in his voice. "And no matter your complaint against the priests, the Valtia is the one person who could change anything. She's the one—"

"Since when has any Valtia lifted a finger to help the acolytes—or any magic wielders?" Sig barks.

"Maybe she doesn't know what's happening!" I surely didn't.

"Or maybe she's a puppet." He stands up, dusting sand from his trousers. "If she's truly in charge, why aren't there female priests? Why would a woman with such power allow other women to be shaved and shut away?" He offers his hand.

I knock it aside and get up on my own. My head's still aching, but I'm so angry I barely notice it. "The Valtia is not a puppet," I snarl.

"So she's evil, then? That's the only other explanation I can think of. Either she's under the control of the elders, or she's as bad as they are."

My hands become fists. "How dare you." I'm trying to find my words within a forest of new doubts that have sprouted in my mind. "The Valtia is a queen willing to sacrifice everything for the good of her people. And if they've found her, you'd be wise to drop your plans to attack the temple."

Sig grins down at me, his short, pale-blond hair ruffled by the wind, the fire in his eyes once more. "Fair enough," he says, his voice shaking with a strange, manic energy. "If they've found her, I'll do exactly that." He offers his arm. "Elli, would you care to attend the royal coronation with me?"

If I go, I could see the Valtia for myself. Maybe I could find a way to talk to her. Raimo said she'd be powerful, but that the stars created me to keep the balance. She might have risen up to lead the Kupari, but perhaps she needs me.

What if I could save her from Sofia's fate? Will she listen to what I have to say?

Even if she won't, even if the elders drag me away and cut my throat, it will be worth it—they won't have any reason to send more priests to the caverns in search of the lost Valtia. Oskar will be safer, as will all the cavern dwellers. He'll have the peace he craves, and I want that as much as I want to help the true Valtia.

Either way, my journey ends where it began.

I take Sig's arm. "When do we leave?"

# CHAPTER 19

By the time Sig and I return to the camp, several more wielders have arrived on stolen horses. A tall, gaunt boy named Mikko, who has a beak of a nose and a long, dark plait down his back, has brought hunting gear and garb. He holds up a game bag and a bear trap, much like the one that took my fingers. "You said you needed another disguise," he says to Sig as I shudder.

And so we set forth, hunters returning to the city from a long day in the woods. Sig makes me ride with him, and I wrap my arms around his lean waist as he spurs his horse onward. He's wearing his cloak again, sparing me the uncomfortable intimacy of being pressed to his bare, scarred back.

We follow a trail through the skeletal woods. There's

no snow on the ground; it all melted off this morning as the priests came through, and so it's easy to believe spring is here, even though it's not due to arrive for weeks. I watch the ground for the little pool that marks the spot where Oskar found me, where he made the decision to save me. This close to Sig, it's hard not to wish for the cool blessing of Oskar's skin, the solid, reassuring feel of his body. For a moment this morning, I had that, and then I tossed it away.

Because I wanted his heart.

The forest floor becomes a brown blur as I will away my tears. I shouldn't mourn what I never had, and I must turn my thoughts to what lies ahead.

"When we get to the city, you'll keep your hood low," Sig says as we exit the woods and enter the marshlands that lead to the northern road. "If you call attention to yourself, I'll—"

"If I call attention to myself, the priests will take me into the catacombs and kill me. The threats aren't necessary."

"Sorry. Habit."

"Sig, I feel sorry for you."

"I bet you'll feel differently when I'm looking out over the Motherlake from the Valtia's balcony."

"What of the Kupari people? Do you think of them when you dream of destroying the order of things?"

His stomach muscles tighten. "I think of how many have been enslaved because of that order," he says in a sharp voice. "And I think of how the rest have exchanged freedom for comfort, how they delight in their year-round warmth and don't think of what it costs. So yes, I suppose I do."

The rage inside him heats his skin. It doesn't burn me, but his cloak is damp against my chest as our horse trots down the muddy road. The white winter sun is slowly descending in the west, but Sig is still squinting in its light. "You must hate the summer."

"You have no idea," he says quietly. "I can barely stand to be outside in the summer months. Did Oskar tell you how we're alike?" He reaches back and pats the lump in the pocket of my dress, the small, carved treasure in my pocket. "You must mean a lot to him if he gave you that. How much did he tell you about what he is?"

I put my hand over Sig's and move it off my thigh. "You already know he told me that he's a Suurin. Oskar isn't sure what it means, though."

"Because he doesn't *want* to know. When I realized Raimo understood, I made the old man teach me everything."

"Like what? Oskar doesn't believe his magic can be controlled."

Sig groans. "Because he spends all his time trying to cram it down instead of learning to use it! A wielder can't be truly good unless he has both power *and* control, and Oskar has one but not the other. He thinks he's a danger—and he's right."

"And you're not?"

"Of course I am—because I choose to be. There are so

many ways to wield, but most wielders can only do a little dull, diffuse magic. Like heating or cooling the air or water. If they practice, they can learn to focus that into blade magic—like channeling all the fire or ice you have into a smaller area."

Like when Sig melted a tiny patch of sand to glass. "You can actually wield ice or fire like a blade?"

Sig laughs. "If you work at it. But if you've only got a little magic, it's like fighting with a toothpick." He looks over his shoulder at me and winks. "I've got a broadsword at *my* disposal."

I look away. "How nice for you." We're moving slowly up the northern road toward the city. Only a few miles to go.

"Better than being unable to protect myself," Sig says, his voice hard.

"I think Oskar is perfectly capable of protecting himself."

"Oskar has never faced a skilled wielder."

Until this morning, when he faced seven of them. But I'm still wondering how much I had to do with that, so I don't remind Sig of it. "He doesn't want to hurt anyone," I murmur.

"Then he should learn how to control it! He probably doesn't even know the difference between manifesting and wielding. Only those with a lot of magic can manifest. None of the cave dwellers could do it—except for me and Raimo." Sig sticks out his palm, and the fire bursts forth, swirling orange and bright without fuel of any kind. Jouni, riding next to us, stares at it, then clenches his jaw and spurs his horse ahead of us. Sig chuckles. "Jouni can only wield—he needs an existing flame if he wants to throw actual fire. I think it makes him feel like less of a man."

Jouni looks back at the two of us, his face red. The temperature rises, and Sig blows out a shaky breath. "Sorry, Jouni. No offense," calls Sig, sweat dripping down the back of his neck. I could siphon that heat if he allowed it, but I know he never would. Jouni faces forward again and the heat lifts.

"You think Oskar can manifest ice? I've never seen him do that." I've only seen him freeze things. And when we killed the priests, he pulled the ice and snow and water from everywhere around us and used it to crush them.

Sig snorts. "Have you ever seen him when he's asleep? He manifests without even *trying*."

"You're right." I remember all the nights I've watched the ice forming from nothing, creeping along his skin and enclosing him. "I didn't know that's what was happening."

"Oskar and I are blessed and cursed. Each of us bears half the magic of the Valtia. We can do so much—but without any of the other element, we can't do some things other powerful wielders can do. We can't move objects easily, because you need both hot and cold magic for that." His muscles tense. "And we don't have the power to heal. If the Valtia is balance, we're the opposite."

"How does that much unbalanced magic not destroy you?" I ask. And then I think of Oskar, ice coating his skin, turning his lips gray. It *was* destroying him.

Sig is quiet for a few moments before saying, "Neither of us will live to be old men. Raimo told me that a long time ago, when I went to him for help. He said the Suurin are weapons. He trained me, and I've made the most of what I've learned. He said war is coming, and that's why we exist."

He told me a war was coming too. "Did you ask him how he knows?"

"When I did, he waved a torn parchment in front of my face and cackled about how everything was coming together. I think it was some kind of prophecy."

Realization jolts through me. "A prophecy . . . Raimo's had it this whole time." And he told me he'd been waiting. "Did he tell you more about what it predicted?"

Sig's fingers twine in the reins. "He didn't have to. I've always known who my enemy was. And if I'm a weapon, I'm also the wielder. No one else will ever control me."

He spurs the horse forward, and we pass Jouni, Usko, and Tuuli, each with hoods low and knives at their belts. Five others ride behind them, refugees who escaped the temple or the city so many years ago, all willing to follow Sig wherever he goes. The Kupari city lies up ahead. I can now see the high wooden arch of the eastern gate. Inside, our fate awaits us.

When we get to the gate, the same black-toothed, black-haired constable is on duty. There's a fear in his eyes that wasn't there the last time I saw him. I don't breathe until his gaze slides over me with only the barest interest. I wonder if

I look different after weeks of winter cave dwelling.

Sig tells him we're hunters bearing gifts for the new Valtia, eager to celebrate her coronation. As proof, Usko and Tuuli ride up, their horses laden with pelts. I try not to think of who they must have stolen from. Those hunters are probably lying burned or frozen deep in the north woods. It makes bile rise in my throat.

It's shockingly easy to gain entry to the city. The constable accepts a bribe—a glossy rabbit pelt—and waves us forward without questioning us. The muddy streets are teeming with people heading for the square. They huddle in cloaks and long coats, their boots sloshing through soft divots of earth, hoods and hats crammed over ears. Hands are red and chapped, unaccustomed to the brutal winter—this is the first time they've experienced the full weight of it. When they look up as we pass, I see a strange array of emotions—wariness and hunger, hope and fear. So different from before Sofia died, when their eyes held pride and confidence.

I see other signs of the hardship they've experienced since I was banished. Windows used to be open, but now all are shuttered or boarded up. The only exceptions are a few shops—but that's because they've been looted. Their doors hang open, gaping mouths leading to empty shells. People are turning on one another. Scared of one another. My heart aches for them. This is what happens when there is no Valtia. With everything inside me, I pray she's there now.

Sig, Usko, Tuuli, and the others tether their horses a few

blocks from the square, and Sig takes my wrist, his fingers firm over my sleeve. Ever since I told him that I siphon magic with a touch, he's avoided prolonged contact with my bare skin. I don't think he has anything to fear, sadly. After what happened with Oskar in our final moments together, I believe Sig would have to be willing to give his magic up for me to be able to take it. But I'm not going to tell him that.

His dark eyes find mine. "Ready, Elli? Can I trust you?"

"I just want to see her," I say. I truly can't say what will happen when I do.

He nods with a slow, playful curl of his lips. "So do I." He leads me into the crowd, weaving between carts and clumps of onlookers. I'm struck by how different they look from that last harvest day, how cowed and pinched.

When we enter the square, I peer at the platform, the place where I presided over so many harvest ceremonies with my Valtia. The steps that lead up to the grand platform are crowded with men, and they hold everyone's attention. Elder Aleksi is a few steps below the top, his thin lips arranged in a deep frown that creases his otherwise smooth face. He's holding a wool cushion, upon which rests the crown of the Valtia, its agate glinting with amethyst and carnelian perfection. The elder is utterly still, as if he's been frozen in place, but his eyes slide over the crowd in a way that makes me crave a hiding place. All the priests are clustered below him, their eyes downturned, their hands tucked into the folds of their robes. I count feverishly and realize they've already replaced the six Oskar and I killed this morning with apprentices. Armo is among them, looking wan and nervous. Sig goes still when he sees his former friend, his gaze calculating, but my attention is already on the eight people assembled on the steps below the priesthood.

They aren't temple dwellers.

They aren't even Kupari.

Five are men, three are women, and all of them look like warriors. Their cloaks are black and pinned at the shoulder, leaving their right hands free to reach for the iron broadswords fixed to their thick leather belts. Tucked beneath their muscular arms are metal helmets. A young woman and an older man stand one step above the others. Her light-brown hair is cut short and her body is lean and angular, but her eyes are wide-set and blue, her cheekbones high, her chin narrow, giving her a delicate sort of ferocity. The man next to her, with a grayish-blond beard and massive shoulders, might be her father—the set of their mouths is similar—but while the girl looks wary, he looks amused. Superior. Arrogant. I am drawn to her—and repelled by him.

And beyond any of that, I am horrified. Hissing whispers wind like snakes among us. *Soturi.* Here, in the city. They've sent a delegation, perhaps from Vasterut, and for some reason these raiders are being allowed to witness one of our most sacred, crucial ceremonies—the crowning of our new queen. Our city councilmen stand awkwardly behind them, casting nervous glances at the would-be invaders.

"The air reeks of desperation," Sig whispers in my ear. "Can't you smell it?"

I smell his sweat-and-iron scent, but little else. It doesn't speak to me of desperation, though. It's the scent of war. "What do you think they're doing here?" I incline my head toward the Soturi, some of whom are glaring at the people in the square, their palms lingering over the hilts of their swords.

"They're here for the same reason we are," he says, tugging me forward, pushing through the crowd until we're in the center of the square. "They sense weakness." His hatred vibrates up my arm as he watches the elder on the platform. I pull my hood lower as Aleksi's dark gaze sweeps over us, but Sig merely moves us a little closer.

The sound of a trumpet slices through the anxious muttering in the square, signaling the procession's departure from the Temple on the Rock. I look up at its greenish copper dome, which rises high above the buildings on either side of the northern road. She's coming. My heart pounds. Sig's fingers are firm and hot over my sleeve. The crowd lets out a cheer. Many shout their thanks to the stars. Their voices are cracking and desperate, a wail rather than a roar.

The little Saadella is carried into the square first, and I hear whispers of delight and relief from the people around us. *It's her. She's been found. Praise the stars.* As soon as I see her, there's a fierce, throbbing ache in my chest, and I have the strangest urge to shove my way over to her and take her in my arms. She can't be more than four or five, but she sits straight and stiff in her grand chair, borne high by her attendants, her tiny child's body clad in the same small, copper-and-red dress that I once wore. Her pale eyes are round and somber. She has a wide, smooth brow, and her little face is painted white, crimson lips and swirls of gleaming copper powder along her temples and eyelids. Her coils of coppery hair are pinned in place, and on her head rests the agate-studded circlet. I wonder if Mim stayed on as her handmaiden, coaching the little girl to remain absolutely still lest she crack her perfect exterior. I search for Mim in the entourage that follows the bearers into the square, hoping I don't burst into happy tears if I see her.

The Saadella's bearers carry her to the base of the steps. Today she will not be at the top with the Valtia, for this is the queen's day alone. The bearers set the little girl's paarit down, facing up the steps. I can see the top of her chair from where I stand, but she is hidden from me. I force down the desire to run forward, craving the sight of her. How fragile, how vulnerable she is, looking up at those Soturi envoys who stand not ten feet from her, their hands on their wicked broadswords. The girl-warrior stares at her with a startled sort of curiosity, but the others watch her with pure amusement in their eyes, and I know Sig is right. These barbarians are here to see for themselves whether we're strong enough to hold them back. And all around us, in the looted shops, the barren market, the muddy, rutted streets, and the hollow cheeks of our citizens, they have their answer.

My fist clenches and hope beats within my breast as I look toward the northern road, waiting for the new Valtia to appear. The acolytes and apprentices file into the square, taking up their places around the Saadella, facing north, their black-robed forms surrounding the platform. And then comes a new elder, one I remember as a priest—Eljas, the one who first whispered his doubt about me aloud in that chamber in the catacombs. As usual, Kauko must have stayed to preside over the temple, which makes Eljas the one in charge of the procession. His flat nose shines with perspiration and his blue eyes streak to the Soturi. From the platform, Aleksi's jowls quiver as he does the same.

They're *nervous*. My gut tightens as the trumpets herald the arrival of the queen. Her bearers come into view, turning as soon as they enter the square to mount the steps to the top of the platform. The priests and envoys have left a clear path. The Valtia's crown gleams in the dying light of the sun and with the flickering flames of the hundreds of torches that are being lit all around the square. The air fills with the scent of smoke. The people's cheers grow louder, more hopeful. They seem willing to forgive her for taking so long to accept the crown. The fires are reflected in Sig's eyes as he watches the whole spectacle.

The new Valtia sits ramrod straight, her pale fingers curled over the armrests of her grand chair, her high collar shielding her profile from the crowd. The skirt and sleeves of her dress shimmer as she's carried to the top of the platform, and her bearers turn her to face us.

299

My blood runs ice cold. Her white face is round and soft, and her crimson lips bear a familiar curve. The ceremonial makeup can't hide what lies beneath, not when I know the terrain of her face as well as my own. "No," I whisper as I stare at her hair. The coppery locks have been plaited and coiled atop her head, elegant and shining.

But her hair shouldn't be that color.

It should be brown.

"Mim?" I mouth, my throat so tight that I can't make a sound. The sight of her face fills my hollow chest with want and regret, and my entire body calls out for her. My vision blurs with tears. Her eyes stare into the distance, absent of all the fondness and life that was there less than two months ago when she gave me the chance to live. When I told her I loved her. When I walked away and left her behind. Now her face is smooth, empty of expression. She looks at no one. Sees no one. The horror is eating me alive.

What have they done to her? Panic and confusion jitter along my bones.

Aleksi holds up a hand, and the crowd goes silent. "Today we crown a new queen to lead our people." His mouth trembles for a moment like he's chewing over his next words. "As a gesture of goodwill and friendship, we welcome our friends from the north as witnesses. Chieftain Nisse"—he nods toward the broad-shouldered, blond-bearded warrior, who offers him a smirk in return—"and Chieftain Thyra"—he inclines his head toward the lean and stately young woman, who stands a little taller when her name is called—"and the other representatives of the Soturi people."

A long, low hiss comes from somewhere in the crowd, which otherwise remains silent, perhaps unbelieving, as I am, that we are formally recognizing our enemies on this sacred day. So many things about this are desperately wrong.

Perhaps sensing the tension in the crowd, Aleksi quickly turns to Mim, who sits unmoving in her chair. "We acknowledge you as the bearer of the magic that protects our people." His voice rises as he looks over his shoulder at the Soturi envoys. "We acknowledge you as the one who destroys our enemies and nurtures our land. We acknowledge you as our queen." He strides toward her, and Eljas steps forward to meet him in front of her paarit.

Mim stares straight ahead, like she's not even aware of their presence.

Eljas lifts the crown from the cushion in Aleksi's arms. "From this day until your final breath, you will lead us," he says in a high, brittle voice. "From this day until your final breath, you will protect and rule. From this day until your final breath, you are the Valtia!"

He places the crown upon her head and steps back, turning to the crowd with a wide smile. "We, the Kupari, can now celebrate our new queen!"

The crowd around us erupts, a wall of sound that can surely be heard for miles. Their relief is like a living thing. Sig whistles, and so do the magic wielders around me, but I can neither clap nor shout. All I can do is puzzle at the void in Mim's eyes, which used to glitter with energy and make my stomach swoop every time she looked at me.

Eljas leans forward and touches her elbow, and she rises abruptly from her grand chair. She stiffly raises her arms, revealing the cuff of Astia clamped over her right wrist. The torches around the square flare wildly, the flames lengthening and twisting in the air. The citizens scream with delight at her show of power. A few of them shake their fists at the Soturi, who frown as the fire stretches unnaturally long, rising like bars of gold, caging the barbarians in with us. The elders' gazes follow the arc of the flames as they dance and entwine above the square, creating a canopy of light.

Sig laughs, the sound molten and dangerous. "Stars, it's not coming from her," he says in an unsteady voice. "Can you feel it, Elli?"

All I feel is hatred for the elders. They've done something to Mim. They've hurt her. I know it. They're putting on a show to impress the Soturi, but at the expense of the woman who nurtured me since we were both children—a woman I loved with all my heart. Her gaze is vacant yet somehow full of pain as she stands there, arms raised. A *puppet*, Sig had said. He was so, so right.

Sig steps forward as the fire twists above us, swirling into beautiful designs, making the people shriek with joy and the Soturi gape with shock. Sweat beading on his brow, he drags me past a few cheering men and women, and I grab his hand to pry it from my arm. He's bringing us perilously close to the priests and elders, who may have other things on their mind at the moment, but who would be happy to recapture me if they realize I'm right in front of them. "Sig, wait."

His head swivels in my direction, his brown eyes glowing, his handsome face alight with glee. "She's an impostor," he says with an unhinged laugh.

My fingers curl over the back of his hand just as his other jerks upward, his palm outstretched. The fire above us suddenly spirals high, forming a solid pillar of flame that nearly kisses the sky. Eljas and Aleksi's eyes go wide as they lose control of it. Mim's empty stare glows orange as her head tilts upward, following its path.

There's a wrenching tug within my chest as Sig clenches his fist and drops it like a hammer.

The column of fire arches over the platform and slams down—right on top of Mim.

# CHAPTER 20

I'm nearly blinded as the inferno engulfs the platform. The square becomes a writhing mass of panic. We're shoved back and pushed to the ground. Sig is on top of me, his body drenched with sweat. I claw and kick, trying to rise, trying to see what's happening. We're going to be trampled.

Rough hands close around Sig's shoulders and yank him up. Jouni's hair is plastered to his cheeks, and his face is red. Sig leans against him, his eyes unfocused—just like Oskar's were after we encased our enemies in a block of ice. A sharp pain stabs through my stomach as I look up at the platform. The scream tears its way from my throat, joining with thousands of others. The Valtia's chair is a spiraling monster of flame and smoke as the elders on either side use their ice magic to suppress the fire. Aleksi looks untouched, but Eljas's face and hands are red and blistered. Jouni tugs me and Sig backward just as I move forward. "Mim," I cry in a choked voice.

"Come on, girl," Jouni snaps. "We have to get out of this square!"

"He killed Mim!" I shriek, trying to rip myself away. My Mim, who loved me, who gave me a life. Sig destroyed her. . . .

Jouni grabs the neck of my cloak and hauls me backward. "Shut up, you idiot! Do you want to be caught?"

Sig's magic wielders surround us, carrying us to the east, away from the holocaust on the platform. I catch glimpses and flashes, the blackened form on the throne, the crown lying discarded on the steps, the Saadella standing alone on her chair at the base of the platform, tears streaking through her white makeup, her pale-blue eyes wide with terror as she screams for her father. One of the acolytes grabs her and several others crowd around, shoving their way through panicked councilmen to get to the temple road.

The Soturi envoys are nowhere to be seen. They've probably fled, eager to report this catastrophe and marshal their invading force. I barely care. Right now my grief for Mim is too huge to allow fear for myself or our people a single thought. I struggle and cry as Jouni flings me over the back of a horse like a sack of grain. "The south road," Sig says in a ragged voice as he slumps against Tuuli. "I know how to get out."

Jouni mounts the horse, cramming his knees against my chest and thighs, pressing his hand against my back. I grab the edge of the saddle and try to kick at him, but when the horse begins to trot, it's all I can do to breathe. Mud from the road spatters my face, and I'm buffeted by shoulders and waving arms as the magic wielders kick their horses' flanks and flee the chaos. We're a river of bodies, horses, carts, screeching women, and crying children. In all the panic, no one gives me, a girl slung like cargo over the back of a horse, a second look.

"The Valtia's magic turned on her!" cries one man as he tries to push his way into a cottage, hopefully his own. "The stars have cursed us!"

The farther we ride, the more I hear this lament. *The stars have cursed us. The Valtia is destroyed. The Soturi will come now. We have no protection.*

Our path grows dark as Sig directs Tuuli down a series of alleys. Finally the road dead-ends at a crumbling, ancient gate, barred with green copper. A massive lock hangs from the latch. Sig slides clumsily from Tuuli's horse and pulls two metal picks from his pocket.

A moment later Usko and Mikko shove the gate open, its worn wood scraping against a stone lip and then swinging over rotten leaves. The wielders guide their horses through and then push the gate closed again. We're outside the city, within a dense copse of trees. "What in stars just happened, Sig?" Usko shouts. "You gave us no warning."

Sig runs his hand through his blond hair. "I didn't—I

wasn't—" His eyes narrow and he stares at me. "I only meant to wrest control from the elders. I could tell the girl on the throne wasn't wielding the magic, and I wanted everyone to know it. And then I felt this insane rush of power inside me."

The others flick the reins and set their horses into motion, moving us farther from the city wall. The wail of horns and cries of terror still rise into the sky, and the air above Kupari is smoky, lit by torches below. I can smell the panic of my people. The memory of the Saadella's face as she screamed for her father will not leave my mind. I want to jump from this horse, climb over the city wall, find her, and protect her from what's coming. But Jouni's grip on me is iron as he steers his mount along the trail.

Sig and Tuuli ride alongside us, but he's in front now. I watch Sig's booted feet nudge at the horse's flanks. "Elli had something to do with it," he tells the others. "She told me she absorbs magic, but she was lying—she does the opposite."

"What in stars are you talking about?" Usko asks.

"She was touching me," Sig says, his voice taking on that shaky, excited energy once again. "And when I took control of the fire, it was like I could do anything with it. Whatever I wanted."

Rage courses through me. "You killed an innocent girl!" I shout, my voice breaking with each of the horse's steps.

"Innocent?" Sig snaps. "Please. She was helping the elders deceive the people."

My body convulses with sorrow. "They hurt her! I *knew* her." The sobs choke me.

"What?" Shock turns Sig's voice hoarse.

"She was my handmaiden." My first love, my first protector, my truest friend. I can't stop thinking of her face, her smile, her bright eyes. The way she was before she gave up everything for me.

We ride in heavy silence until we reach a clearing, through which a little stream burbles, and by quiet consent, the wielders dismount and lead their horses to it. All we have is the moonlight, which paints its white glow along the bare branches of the trees above us. The air is warm, but I know that's from the fire wielders. Tuuli and Mikko, ice wielders both, are shivering, rubbing their arms. Jouni pulls me off his horse and holds me as I stumble. "What do you want me to do with her?"

Sig pushes his hood back. "Get her some water. Offer her food. Make her comfortable."

Jouni's mouth draws tight, but he guides me to sit down and then obeys. Sig squats in front of me. The moonlight glints off the blade of a knife that he's twirling between his fingers. "Now tell me everything you held back," he says quietly. "You say I killed that girl—but you know you had something to do with it."

I draw my knees to my chest and bow my head over them. "I had nothing to do with it." What a lie. But I can't face the truth, that I was the sword that cut Mim down. It's so cruel. She's the last person I'd ever want to hurt. Elder Leevi and his priests were different. They were trying to kill Oskar. And when Oskar struck, I felt fear, but not this terrible, piercing guilt. Now, though . . . Am I really cursed like this? To be a mindless tool in the hands of powerful wielders?

I think I'd rather die.

Sig nudges my chin up. "I felt it, Elli. You grabbed my hand right as I was reaching for the fire. And what I did . . ." He lets out a trembling chuckle. "I've never felt anything like that. With that kind of power, we could take the temple. We could rule it."

I shake my head. "I won't help you."

His long fingers close around my throat, and he pulls me toward him. His bottomless brown eyes meet mine. "I can feel it as soon as my skin touches yours," he whispers, his lips sliding along my cheek until his mouth is against my ear. "If I wanted to, I could set this entire forest aflame."

"I hate you," I say in a ragged voice. "And I'll die before I let you control me."

His eyes take on a golden, flickering glow. "You can't stop me," he says softly, his thumb stroking down the column of my throat. "Even now, with all that contempt, I could use you to rain fire on the outlands."

My eyes sting. "You won't let others control you, but you're willing to do it to me."

He grimaces, his glowing pupils shining with emotion. "Think of your handmaiden. If the temple dwellers hurt her and used her as you say, then don't you think they all deserve to die?"

Perhaps. But the memory of the acolytes' kindness in my worst moments can't be forgotten. The face of the Saadella won't leave my mind. The screams of the people won't fall silent. And knowing the Soturi now realize we're helpless makes the stakes impossibly high. I can't seek revenge without thinking about all of that. Would Sig listen if I told him? Would he care?

I look into his eyes, and all I see is fire. He wants blood and vengeance. He wants to take the temple for himself, not the people.

And I have to get away from him. "I'll think about it," I murmur. "Now let me go."

His warm hand falls away, and the cold air rushes in and caresses my throat. "We could be allies. We could do it together."

"I need to rest."

Sig's jaw flexes. "So do I. But tomorrow we're gathering more wielders, and we're going back. There will never be another chance like this one."

I curl onto my side, pulling the hood of my cloak to protect my cheek from the rotting leaves that will be my bed tonight. All I can think is how different Sig and Oskar are. Both so powerful, but one is ruled by hurt and hatred, while the other is ruled by a thirst for peace. For *life*. I squeeze my eyes shut and huddle within the furry folds of my stolen cloak as Sig and the others make camp, building a small fire and passing around the supplies they snatched from the hunters. They talk about what Sig did and speculate about whether touching me would work for all of them. Jouni wants to try, but Sig tells him he'll have to wait until tomorrow. When Jouni comes over to offer me a biscuit and a slice of meat, I pretend that I'm asleep until he goes away.

*You could be their most powerful asset—or their worst enemy.* That's what Raimo told me. But how can I be a feared enemy when I have no power of my own? When I don't have a say in how I'm used? Frustration grinds within me, becoming an endless ache of despair. Over and over I remember the horror in Mim's eyes as the fire descended. I swear, a moment before it hit, there was a spark of relief in her face, but it doesn't lessen the guilt at all. She defied the elders and helped me escape. Now I know why she never came to meet me that morning. I imagine her, chained in the catacombs, the lash of the whip against her soft skin. For weeks I've been nestled safe in a cave, growing stronger by the day, free to lose my foolish heart to someone else—because of her. And all this time, she's been suffering—because of me. My fists are so tight that I'm shaking. If I had known, if I could have taken her place, I would have.

And if I can be used to kill someone I love, I don't think I should exist.

Sig and the others go quiet after a while. The woods are silent but for the lonely hoot of an owl somewhere in the distance. The noise in my head is relentless, though. The Saadella's cries, the Kupari's despair. The air is frigid, making my toes numb and my right hand tremble with the stabbing pain the cold always brings. The temperature seems to drop with every minute that passes.

A quiet moan comes from across the clearing. I peek from my cloak. The still forms of the wielders are scattered near trees or by the fire. Usko is snoring now, as is Jouni. Mikko and Tuuli are wrapped around each other. And Sig . . . his white-blond hair makes him easy to spot. He's asleep far from the fire, shirtless on this winter night. His pale skin shines with sweat as smoke rises in lazy tendrils from the cloak on which he lies.

He's burning from the inside out. He's suffering like Oskar does, only from flames, not ice.

I could go to him and relieve his pain. I could take that inferno inside myself and tame it. He's asleep, unable to hold it back. I sit up. When he twists, caught in the fire, I see the silver scars on his back. The pain on his face almost draws me across the clearing.

But knowing his plans for tomorrow keeps me where I am.

I won't be used. I won't help him sow chaos and misery in the city. Carefully, I rise to my feet. My cloak makes almost no noise as I pull it from the damp earth. My fingers fist in the furry garment as I take a step backward. No one moves.

They probably assumed I wouldn't have the strength to run. Or maybe they know I have no place to go. But right now that doesn't matter, as long as I'm far from here. I take another step back. And then I turn around and tiptoe out of the clearing. I move slowly, terrified of waking the sleeping wielders. The farther I get, the colder the air, and I shiver as I pick my way along.

I hear the soft footfalls too late. Someone barrels into my back, and I fall forward as his hot hand slams over my mouth. "No you don't," comes the deep sound of Jouni's voice. "Sig said I should watch out for you." He chuckles. "Stars, I feel it. Exactly what Sig described." His palm flashes hot against my skin and flames shoot from between his fingers. "Who says I can't manifest fire?"

My fingernails tear at the soft ground as Jouni yanks me up. I slap and kick with everything inside me, my screams stifled by his merciless grip. From the warm bursts of air around me, I think Jouni's trying to subdue me with heat, but when he realizes it's not working, his arms clamp hard and hurtful around me. He wrenches my head back. "There's a stout length of rope back at camp, and it's got your name on it."

He starts to drag me backward, but then he staggers suddenly and drops me. I hit the ground face-first, and my hood flops over my head. I push it back to see a dark shape towering over Jouni's hunched form. I shove myself to my hands and knees just as the fire wielder lunges, wrapping his arms around his attacker's waist. But the man drives his elbow between Jouni's shoulder blades, dropping him to the ground. Jouni rolls over as the other man descends—and closes his large hand over Jouni's throat.

"Stop fighting me," Oskar whispers as he leans close to Jouni's face. "You have to stop, Jouni."

But Jouni doesn't. Pinned to the forest floor by Oskar's powerful grip, he kicks his legs up, thrashing wildly, trying in vain to shout for his friends. His palms sizzle as he clutches at Oskar's cloak, filling the air with the scent of burning fur.

Oskar shushes him, the sound full of desperation. "*Please* stop fighting," he begs as Jouni's eyes go wide. "I don't want to hurt you."

Jouni's fingers push through the holes he's burned in Oskar's sleeves. His knuckles are bloodless. The glow in his eyes slowly dims. His heels leave deep grooves in the dirt, and then his legs go limp. But his arms stay anchored to Oskar's until the ice wielder pulls away. I cover my mouth as Oskar rises to his feet, leaving Jouni on his back, his eyes wide and frosted over, his arms outstretched. The top half of his body is frozen solid. "I'm sorry, Jouni," Oskar mutters. He turns around, his jaw clenched.

"Oskar . . ."

He holds his hand out. I take it, and he pulls me to my feet. "Can you run?"

I nod. He tugs my hand and breaks into a jog, and I lift my skirt and follow, praying the struggle didn't wake the others. I'm shaking with what I just saw, with the knowledge that Oskar has killed again—and with the wretched understanding that he has done this terrible thing *for me*. My heart pounds in time with our footsteps. Finally we reach a wide trail leading south out of the woods, and I squeeze his hand. I'm stronger than I used to be, but I can't run forever. Oskar slows. "Freya saw you take the road leading to the city. And then she watched as Sig ran you down."

"How did you find me?" He found me. *He found me.*

"I went to Sig's camp, but it was deserted, so I followed the trail to the city. I had just reached the square when the fire . . ." He pauses when he feels the tension in my grip.

"Sig did it," I say in a choked voice. "But he was holding my hand. It was like this morning, with the ice. It was my fault, Oskar. And we killed someone I loved very much." I double over, curling around the pain of it.

Oskar touches my back. "Who?"

As best I can, I explain about Mim, who she was to me, how she saved me, and what I believe happened after. Part of me wonders how Oskar will react to my admission of love for my handmaiden, but he stays silent, his cool hand laid across my spine.

"This wasn't your fault, Elli," he says when I finish. "I saw you across the square after it happened. I heard the desperation in your screams and read the horror in your eyes—" He lets out a breath. "I suppose both of us are responsible for hurting those around us, but I also believe neither of us would if we could avoid it."

"Does that matter, if the result is the same?"

His hand falls away from my back. "I have to believe it does."

I straighten, drawn up by the pain in his words. I understand the necessity of that belief, especially for Oskar. There's no way I'm taking it from him. "Then it does," I say quietly.

He starts forward again, at a sure and steady pace. "To

be honest, even if it didn't, there was no way I was letting you go."

Up ahead the moon shines down on a wide expanse of marsh grass. We're almost out of the woods. "Why?"

He lets out a hard, hollow bark of laughter. "Why did you leave?"

"Why are you answering my question with a question?"

He smirks as I repeat his challenge from our last argument, then pulls the string from his messy hair and reties it so it isn't in his face. "You did it for us, didn't you? You left because you thought you could keep the priests away. You were going to give yourself up to them."

"It would have been selfish to stay."

He looks at me out of the corner of his eye. "It was selfish of you to leave."

"How can you say that?" I try to pull my hand from his, but his fingers are locked with mine.

He rounds on me, his dark shape blocking out the moonlight. "You let me believe you would come back, and then you walked away without a word."

"You were in so much pain, and that was because of me too!"

"Really? You forced the elders and constables to attack us? Amazing."

"You wouldn't have been hurt if you hadn't tried to protect me."

He makes a growly, frustrated noise and grasps my shoulders. "Do you have any idea how I would have felt if they'd hurt *you?*" He gives me a little shake. "I told you I under-stood why you pushed me away after we kissed. And what's so clear to me now is that you *don't* understand."

I look away from the intensity of his gaze, my hands braced against his chest to maintain the distance between us. "I don't want to fight." My voice is as shredded as my heart.

"Then we won't fight. But you're going to listen to me."

He releases my arms and starts to walk again but holds my left hand tightly. His cold magic pulses into me, and I close my eyes and feel snowflakes melting on my cheeks. "I'm listening," I murmur.

"Good." But then he's quiet for a long, long time, and I begin to wonder if he's lost his words. We're treading a path through the marsh grass, the frozen ground hard beneath our soles. To our right, the dunes glitter, and beyond them lies the Motherlake. The caverns are less than a mile away.

"You tie your boots wrong," Oskar finally says, his voice low but startling as he breaks our silence. "I always won-dered why. At first I thought maybe it was because of your fingers. Every time I saw you knotting the strings, I wanted to come over and tie them for you. I never did, though."

I glance down at the toes of my boots, poking from beneath my skirt with every step. "Why?"

The pale light from above caresses his stubbly cheeks. "You always looked so focused and determined, and once you'd finished, your smile was as bright as a star. I didn't want to take that from you."

"Well, now I feel foolish." I wonder if he hears the unsteadiness in each word.

He tugs my left hand, pulling me to his other side. His arm wraps around my waist, and he gently takes my mangled right hand in his.

He looks down at my open palm, stroking his thumb over the calluses on the fleshy pads beneath my remaining fingers. "In the first days you were with us, you had so many blisters, and I could tell they hurt."

I stop breathing as he lifts my hand and kisses the center of my palm.

"I know each one, Elli," he says softly. "This one's from grinding corn—" He traces the firm callus beneath my middle finger. "These came from the loom—" He kisses my three fingertips, and I feel every brush of his mouth low in my belly. It's the sweetest of tugs, almost lifting the weight of my sadness and grief. "This one from skinning pelts—" His lips skim over the flesh between my thumb and pointer finger. "Every time I saw a new one, I wanted to pull you aside and bandage you up."

"But you didn't." I wish I could stop shaking.

His eyes meet mine. "Because you were proud of them. I saw you looking at them with something like wonder on your face. I watched you run your own fingers over them, wincing and then grinning. And when I understood why, when I found out who you were and thought about what your life must have been like before, I was even more amazed."

Why does he have to say this now, when everything

is falling apart? I don't think I can stay with him. War is coming, the Kupari city is in chaos, and a few miles from here lies a group of magic wielders who know what I can do. They'll come after me. It won't take long.

As long as I'm alive, I can be used. A tool for killing and destruction.

I force my voice into lightness. "Had you been wondering why a maidservant from the city was so useless and coddled? Or did you think *that* was why they whipped me?"

He lets out a bemused laugh. "I suppose I brushed it off. We live differently out here. Or maybe I was too taken with you to question your magic."

"Magic," I scoff.

He smiles, one of those rare smiles that makes his eyes crinkle. "When I first found you, I wasn't affected by it, but every day, its hold on me grew stronger. And nowadays, your laugh makes me feel like I'm falling. When you look at me, I'm suddenly warm. The sight of you makes my heart speed. Do you really think the only magic in this world comes from fire and ice?"

He turns my hand over and kisses the shiny pink scars where my two fingers used to be, and that's all it takes to make my tears streak down my cheeks.

"Now tell me it wasn't selfish of you to leave," he says.

"I didn't want to be a duty or an obligation," I mumble.

"You're neither." He takes my face in his hands, cool palms against my hot cheeks. "Nor are you a convenience, a tool, a weapon, or, stars save me, a queen, though you have all the grace of one. Not to me. You're just Elli." He leans down and touches my forehead with his. "And you have to understand that is more than enough."

If he tries to protect me, he could be hurt. If I stay to protect him, I could be used against him by another wielder. Are the two of us together strong enough to hold off our enemies?

My head aches with these thoughts, when all I want to do is lose myself in Oskar. He swipes a stray tear away with his thumb. "Do you understand now?"

I close my eyes and nod, my hands rising to hold his against my cheeks.

He kisses my forehead. "Then tell me you feel the same, or I'm going to be pretty embarrassed."

The laughter bursts from me, sudden and real, and I open my eyes to see his devastating smile. I rise on my tiptoes, reaching for him. I want to absorb more than his ice magic. I want to freeze this moment in all its perfection, so I have it when I need it most. "You were wrong when you said you had no heat," I say with a husky laugh.

"I always feel warm when you touch me." He catches my hand and presses it to the side of his neck. "There's only one thing about it that feels bad." When he sees the question in my eyes, he continues. "I don't think there's any way it could possibly feel as good to you."

The look in his eyes melts everything inside me. "Wrong again," I whisper.

Our uneven breaths burst from us as we collide. His

dark, scraggly stubble scrapes my face as I fist my hand in the front of his cloak and pull him down, aching for more. I kiss him with everything inside me, all my gratitude, all my desire for him—my gentle, fierce Oskar. These frantic moments distract from the ache of Mim, but even more than that, they're light as air and hot as a spark in my palm. His cool skin renders mine taut and tingling. Even with his icy magic pouring into the hollow of my chest and filling my head with visions of the ice-covered Motherlake, I feel like I might catch fire at any second.

Wait. Icy magic. Pouring into me. *No.*

I push him away. Mim's love for me led to her doom, and now I'm placing Oskar at risk, too.

He draws his thumb along his bottom lip. "Is it Mim?" he asks quietly. "I know your grief is fresh."

"Yes. No. Actually, it's you," I stammer as his face twists with confusion. "You're giving me too much of your magic. It's not safe. You need it." When we first met, he could touch me without the ice flowing into me, but now . . .

He gives me a sheepish look. "When you're that close to me, I want to give you everything. I don't want to hold back."

I put my hand on my chest. "I feel it." And I recognize it for the gift it is. But I can't accept it.

Oskar sighs and turns his face to the east, where the sun is beginning to peek over the horizon. "We'd better get to the caverns. Everyone should be packed by now."

"Where are we going?"

"Someplace safe. Maybe the northwestern edge of the Loputon. There's a smaller cave system there that could shelter us until spring."

I bite my lip. This doesn't feel right. I don't have any intention of letting Sig use me to destroy the temple, but running away while the Kupari are suffering doesn't feel right either. Not with the threat of the Soturi looming, not with the chaos destroying the city.

Oskar sees my hesitation and frowns. "Where do you want to go, then?"

"I'm not sure yet. But Raimo said I was made to serve." For the last twelve years, I've thought about it every day, how my people need me, how it's my responsibility to protect and nurture them. "I can't run from that." Even though I have no idea what I'm supposed to do.

Oskar takes my hand. "Once Freya and my mother are safe, I'll go with you wherever you need to go. I'll face it with you." He puts my hand on his chest. "You can have my magic to wield as your own."

Hope rises inside me. "All right." But I hesitate again as he tries to pull me down the trail. "I don't think the cave dwellers are going to be happy to see me. I'm the reason . . ." A lump in my throat makes it hard to speak. "Senja," is all I can whisper.

"Like so many other things, that wasn't your fault. And I told them you aren't the Valtia. Once they thought about it, it seemed fairly obvious."

"Do they know what I am, though?"

He lets out a quiet huff of laughter. "That's a bit harder to explain. But here's what I did tell them." He waits for me to look up at him. "You're part of my family now. If they have a problem with you, they will have to deal with me." The corner of his mouth twitches. "And my mother. And Freya."

I shudder and giggle at the same time. "Oh, that must have cowed them."

Oskar grins. "They were terrified." He throws his arm around my shoulders. "Come on."

As the sun rises, we make our way down the trail and reach the open area outside the massive cavern entrance. It's a bustle of activity, with families loading horses with supplies. A few people give me startled or worried looks, but no one challenges my presence. The bodies of the elders and constables are gone, and the space is filled with bundles of furs, cooking pots, and tools, all laid out on blankets.

"Oskar!" shrieks Freya, scurrying out of the cave. "You found her." Her braids swing as she runs to us and throws her arms around me. "I was trying to warn you, but you didn't hear."

Oskar strokes her hair and then peels her off me. "Are we packed?"

She nods and points to a roan that's loaded with their belongings. "That's our horse."

"Go tell Mother we have to leave now."

"Already? She's cooking breakfast."

Oskar's eyes meet mine. "It needs to be now." He gives

her a little shove, and she takes off. "Don't think of running away again," he says to me as I entertain thoughts of doing exactly that. "I'd hate to have to tie you to our horse." His voice is teasing, but I detect the uncertainty, the worry.

I'm scared to leave him, and scared to be with him. I entwine my fingers with his. "I'm just scared."

He smooths a lock of hair away from my face. His smile is tender. He's opening his mouth to speak when the blast of fire hits him square in the chest, tearing him from my grip.

# CHAPTER 21

Oskar staggers back, agony etched across his face, as Sig and eight other wielders walk from the mouth of the narrow trail, their hands outstretched. With a hard flick of his wrist, Sig flings another ball of fire straight for my ice wielder, and Oskar barely manages to get his hands up in time to destroy it. He grimaces as the flames lick his skin, turning it red. Anxiety flashes in his eyes—at the moment he doesn't have enough magic to defend himself from all of them.

Most of the cave dwellers scatter, running for the cavern. Ismael, Aira, and Veikko stay, hovering near the cave entrance, looking back and forth between Oskar and the nine wielders here to bring him down. I am frozen with panic. I don't know how best to protect him.

Sig's hair is standing on end, and his dark eyes are wild as he glares at Oskar. "I should have known you would come for her as soon as I saw that ridiculous bird she carries in her pocket. But I'm afraid I'm going to need her back."

"Elli, get into the cavern," Oskar says quietly, his breaths uneven and pained, his eyes riveted to Sig's lean form. The other wielders fan out, surrounding us.

Ismael tries to push Aira behind him, but she insists on standing next to her father, her hands raised and her green eyes full of determination. She glances back at the smoldering central fire, probably wondering if it will be enough. "Sig, we've already dealt with an attack yesterday," she says in a loud voice. "Don't do this. What are we, if we're willing to turn on one another?"

Sig's fingers twitch. "My thoughts exactly, Aira. So why don't you ask Oskar what he did to Jouni?"

Aira gives Oskar a questioning look.

"Elli," Oskar repeats, more urgent this time.

I walk toward Oskar, reaching for his hand, knowing he needs me now more than ever. "I'm not leaving."

Sig's teeth clench and his hands rise. "Don't touch him."

"Elli!" shrieks Maarika from only a few feet to my left. Before I can stop her, she lunges in front of me, her arms spread to protect me.

Just as Sig hurls his fire.

Oskar shouts for his mother as the flames hit her skirt. Sig stumbles back, his eyes wide, but the others blast Oskar with their magic, pulling ice from puddles around them and fire from their torches, all of it aimed at my ice wielder. Maarika screams, and I stagger for her, planning to throw myself on top of her and smother the fire—it's made of magic, and it can't hurt me.

Before I can reach her, Oskar falls, his cloak billowing smoke, his arm outstretched, his fingers spread wide only inches from the flames. His eyes are filled with desperation and fear. I expect the ice and cold to flow from him, but instead, the fire peels itself off Maarika's burning skirt and jumps onto his palm. His fist closes around it, and he hurls it toward the magic wielders. Their eyes go round as it roars toward them, growing larger the farther it travels. Usko tackles Sig to move him out of the way while the others dive to the ground. It hits the steep rock wall of the drop-off and explodes into nothing.

Maarika falls backward and Aira catches her, patting frantically at her blackened gown. Her legs are pink with heat, but she's not burned. My heart thrumming, I turn back to the wielders. They're still on the ground. And their eyes are on Oskar, shock on their faces.

He's facedown. A choked sound comes from me as I sink down beside him. "Oskar. *Oskar.*" His skin is frigid. I try to draw the cold away, but it's like a solid block of ice beneath my palm. I can't siphon it off.

"He threw the fire," Sig says quietly, staring at Oskar's body.

"Because he didn't want to hurt Maarika," snarls Veikko, blade-sharp icicles growing along the rock wall beside him, manifesting his rage. If Oskar had used his ice, he could have frozen his own mother solid. Just like he did to his father.

"But I thought Oskar couldn't wield fire," I say in a ragged voice, trying to turn him over. Veikko rushes over to help, and we roll Oskar onto his back. He's stiff and cold and oh stars no . . .

"He can't wield fire," a creaky voice calls out. Raimo hobbles out of the back of the cavern, his white hair tufty around his head, a walking stick clutched in his knobby hand, a wooden box tucked under his scrawny arm. "And that's why he's dying."

Ismael, who's bent over Maarika and his daughter, so close that his bushy black beard is snagging on Aira's dark hair, straightens up. "Raimo," he says, surprised. "It's still winter."

Raimo jabs his walking stick at Sig. "Someone woke me up with a thaw."

"That wasn't me," Sig mumbles.

"It was priests and constables here to get *her*," says Aira, pointing at me.

Raimo's pale eyes meet mine. "Elli, what have you been up to?"

"Oskar needs help." Those are the only words that will come. My hand is on Oskar's cheek, but nothing's happening. I'm having trouble breathing as I stare at his unmoving chest.

Raimo's gaze flicks to Oskar, but then he turns to Sig. "Are you finished wreaking havoc?"

Sig gets to his feet and lifts his chin defiantly. "I came to get Elli. I'm going to the temple and taking her with me. There is no Valtia, and the city is in chaos. Our time is *now*. We're going to—"

"I'm not going anywhere, you arse!" I shout, my voice cracking. "You—you—" If I had magic, I would freeze Sig solid and then shatter him.

Raimo's hand closes over my wrist. "We *are* going to the temple," he says quietly. "You must. But first we're going to give our Ice Suurin back his spark, before his heart stops forever."

"His spark?"

He gives me an impatient look. "Oskar can't control fire. He was never meant to wield it, but he was powerful enough and desperate enough to call to it all the same. When he threw it, though, he sent his only spark of fire magic along with it."

I close my eyes, seeing that ball of fire grow as it raged toward the wielders, so big that all they could do was dodge. "And now he's freezing inside."

"Succinctly put." Raimo beckons to Veikko, Ismael, and some of the other men who are lingering nearby. "Carry him inside and lay him by the fire."

Five of them gather around Oskar's body. His head hangs as they lift him from the ground and lug him to the large fire in the center of the main cavern. Raimo points at the wielders who came with Sig. "You lot can stay outside. Come in and I'll destroy you." He mutters something like "obnoxious little scamps" under his breath, then points a shaking finger at Sig. "And you come with me. You owe Maarika an apology and Oskar his life."

Sig stays where he is. The temperature drops suddenly, and he shivers. Raimo stares at the fire wielder as cold bleeds from the old man's scrawny frame. "You can't do this without your fellow Suurin," he says in a low voice. "I told you that."

"Oskar's made it clear he has no interest in being my ally."

"That doesn't change a thing."

Sig blinks at him. And then he obeys Raimo, trailing us as we rush to Oskar's side. He's been laid on a bundle of furs. Veikko is piling flat stones nearby, and Aira and Ismael are heating them with their fire magic. Maarika is sitting by her son, arranging the hot stones around his shoulders, the only protection she can offer. Her hair hangs in sweaty tendrils around her face, half her dress is burned away, and her skin is streaked with ash, but she seems aware of nothing around her—except for Oskar, her hope, her life.

Freya is crouched by his head, stroking her brother's long, dark hair away from his face. Her green eyes narrow when she sees Sig. "I thought you cared about us," she hisses.

Sig stares at the ground. "I'm sorry, Maarika," he mutters. "I didn't intend to hurt you."

"Yes, you did," Maarika snaps. "But you were going to do it by hurting Elli. And my *son*." She raises her head, and her gaze is full of fury. "There was a time when I loved you like one of my own." Her lips clamp together, and she looks away.

Sig's eyes are glossy with tears. His jaw is clenched as he struggles to keep them inside.

"Peace, Maarika," Raimo says gently. "He's going to help fix Oskar."

I kneel at Oskar's side. His skin is a ghastly grayish blue. I lay my head on his chest. His heart thumps once, sluggishly, weakly, but it's the best sound I've ever heard.

Raimo sets down his wooden box with a clatter on the stone floor of the cavern. He looks so fragile, but his voice is full of authority as he says, "Take his hand, Elli."

Aira and Ismael give him puzzled looks as I slip my left hand into Oskar's right. His fingers are stiff and icy. I squeeze them.

"Now take Sig's hand."

"What?"

Raimo rolls his eyes. "Sig, get down here."

The fire wielder squats next to me. He gives me a veiled look as I reluctantly lay my mangled right hand over his palm. His gaze traces my scars as he carefully closes his fingers around mine.

"Elli, focus on letting Sig's magic flow through you. Magnify its strength and send it into Oskar."

"Wait," says Aira. "Magic flows *through* her?" She's looking at me with hard suspicion written all over her face.

Raimo waves his hand at her. "Priorities, girl. I'll explain all of it once Oskar's breathing again."

I close my eyes, waiting for the fiery magic to course up my arm. But I feel nothing. I open my eyes and look at Sig. "You have to give it to me."

Sig's mouth is tight. "There's a fight coming. I need it."

"Oskar will die if you don't."

He gazes steadily down at our joined hands. "And I might die if I do."

"Now who's the coward?"

A flash of heat blasts up my arm, but it zings back the way it came a second later. I sink my three fingernails into Sig's flesh as rage fills my empty spaces. When Oskar touches me now, his magic flows so freely, like he's offering himself. His feelings for me are the reason he was so weak when Sig attacked. His love for his mother is why he's dying right now. I can't let it happen. "Sig. Look at me."

Sig peeks at me from beneath golden lashes, every part of him trembling with tension.

"If you do this—if you save him—I'll go to the temple with you. I'll help you take down the priests."

Sig's brown eyes are fierce on mine. "Swear." I can smell his fear. He's spent his life surviving, doubting everyone, looking out for himself. He holds his magic so tight, afraid he'll be helpless without it.

*It's all he is*, I realize. Fire is all he is. Without it, Sig doesn't exist.

"You have my word, Sig." My voice is a caress. I smooth my fingertips over the divots left by my nails. "Now help me save Oskar. I know you don't want him to die."

Sig closes his eyes, and immediately I feel the warmth bleed from his palm and swirl along my bones. My mind becomes a sea of molten iron. Lightning. Sparks. Raging infernos. I gasp as the fire creeps its way through my body, lighting me up.

"Build on what he's offering and give it to Oskar, Elli," Raimo instructs.

"I don't know how," I murmur, caught in the dancing flames.

He pokes my shoulder. "One would think you're a use-less hunk of copper, girl. Don't you have a will? Use it!"

I bite my lip and focus, gathering the heat inside my hollow chest. I imagine kindling the fire, then scooping it up to my shoulder and letting it slide down my arm, straight into Oskar through our joined hands. But it merely sways and swirls inside me, flickering up before receding again.

"I think maybe you don't want him to live," Raimo taunts.

Sig's grip on my scarred right hand tightens, and he offers me more fire. It overflows my chest and courses down my left arm, my wrist, my fingers. But then it hits the icy wall of Oskar's skin and shrinks back. I push against it with all my might. Oskar is more than ice. He's more than magic. Without it, he's still a whole person, able to love and pro-tect and laugh and live. My hand shakes as I force the heat toward him, willing his heart to move warm blood through his chest, willing his body to accept what I'm offering, to reignite the spark he needs to survive. Slowly I melt the frozen barrier. And then, all of a sudden, it gives way, and the heat pulses into him.

He lets out a shaky sigh, his breath fogging from between his lips. I tear my hand from Sig's and throw myself on top of Oskar, pressing my cheek to his, offering him whatever warmth I have.

"My mother," he whispers.

"I'm right here," she says, her face creased with worry. "I'm all right. No burns."

"Elli?"

I lay my palms on his rough cheeks and press light kisses across his brow. "I'm here."

Sig gets to his feet, his boots scuffing against the loose stone. "But it's time to go."

Oskar's eyes pop open, dark as a thundercloud. He sits up with me still on his chest, so I end up in his lap. He coils his arm around my waist. The cold pulses from him, already stronger than it was. "She's not going anywhere with you."

Sig gives him a ghostly smile. "Oh, but she is. Just ask her."

Oskar's gaze snaps to mine. "I have to," I murmur.

Raimo uses his walking stick to pull himself to his feet. "Elli struck a deal with Sig," he says mildly. "But it barely matters. We're all going."

Aira, Ismael, and Veikko glance back and forth between me and Raimo with identical looks of confusion. "Us, too?" Veikko asks.

"Oh, yes," Raimo says. "It's time."

Oskar looks like he's been hit over the head. "What?"

Raimo sighs, so stooped that he's only a head taller than Oskar, who's sitting on the ground. "You've put this off for so long, Oskar, but you can't deny what you are anymore, or what you were meant to do."

"I'm not meant to do anything," Oskar says, moving me off his lap so he can get to his feet. "Except to care for my family."

"You're the Ice Suurin!" Raimo yells, his arms shaking as he holds on to the stick. "This war will find you whether you want it or not." He watches as Oskar pulls me to my feet and brings me close. "It already has, I'd say."

I touch Raimo's gnarled hand. "Tell us what you know. Please. You can't expect Oskar—or any of us, for that matter—to go into this blind. We're all here. We need to understand."

Raimo glances at his wooden box and rubs his palm over his bald head. "I suppose you *are* all here." He lets out a bemused cackle. "I've been waiting for this moment for so many years that it seems odd that it's actually happening."

"You were a priest," I prompt him. "And somehow you came into possession of the prophecy that's been missing from the temple for ages, didn't you? That's how you know all these things."

He grins, showing all his yellow teeth. "I stole it."

"But wasn't it kept in the temple?" Oskar asks.

"No. We were all living in the old fortress by the lake," Raimo says, picking up his box and hobbling over to the community hearth. He sinks onto the stone with the box in his lap. "The temple was still under construction at that time."

We all gape at him. "The Temple on the Rock is over three hundred years old," I stammer.

Raimo gives us all an amused look. "True. And so am I."

# CHAPTER 22

We settle ourselves around the old man, hungry for answers, stunned by the understanding that he's older than the temple itself. But somehow I can't bring myself to doubt it, and I can tell by looking at the others that they don't either. It makes a strange kind of sense.

Raimo's fingers slide over the carvings on the surface of the box. "Contrary to what many like to believe, the Kupari are not native to these lands. Our ancestors had only arrived here a few hundred years before I was born, fleeing the murderous warrior tribes of the far north."

Veikko's eyes go wide. "The Soturi?"

Raimo nods. "I suspect they are the very same, though they have only recently crossed the Motherlake in any number. Our ancestors made the great journey guided by the stars, believing they were safe on this peninsula surrounded by the vast waters. And so they were, for a long time. They discovered the copper that runs through the veins of this land, and here they settled."

"Did they know the magic came from the copper?" I ask.

He shakes his head. "That was a slow, mysterious process, so gradual that the link was not clear for centuries. Our people were fed by the magic in these lands, growing strong over generations as it seeped into our blood. And then, here and there, it began to manifest. Wielders were born." He looks over at me. "The first Valtia rose up, so powerful with ice and fire that she was named the queen. She ruled from that fortress on the northwestern shore. It's in ruins now. The platform in the square is made with some of the original stones. But it was within those walls that the first priests were initiated into her service."

His thumb toys with the clasp of the box. "Wielders walked free, but many of us were eager to learn and serve the magic—and the queen who seemed to have so much of it. But though any wielder can learn to control and refine the power he has"—Raimo's pale gaze flicks to Oskar, and he arches his eyebrow—"wielders have only as much magic as they're born with. Not everyone was satisfied with that, and some went in search of ways to increase the magic inside them."

"Like shutting themselves inside trunks of solid copper," I say with a shudder.

Raimo rolls his eyes. "Yes, and other, equally ill-advised methods. Some fasted, some had themselves whipped or put themselves through near hanging or drowning, and some decided to rid themselves of . . ." He clears his throat and makes a snipping motion with his fingers. The men around us quietly cringe, but Raimo cackles. "I always thought it was a stupid practice myself. And none of it worked, except to band together those who'd been through it in a warped kind of brotherhood." He opens the box. The only thing inside is a torn, creased sheet of parchment. "But some of us turned our eyes to the stars, just as our ancestors had, looking for wisdom, answers, portents of the future. After all, the stars were how we survived the scourge of our enemies and found a refuge where we could live in peace. We created the charts and argued over what they predicted." He chuckles, a phlegmy, weak sound. "Fun times."

Oskar sits down next to the fire. He's looking wan and weary, but still so much better than several minutes ago, when I thought I'd lost him. "Fun times . . . three hundred years ago." He eyes Raimo like he expects him to sprout wings or horns.

Raimo grunts. "The divine portents told of an object that would magnify the magic, and so we created the cuff of Astia for the Valtia as she grew into old age."

"She actually lived to be old?" I ask.

"Things were not always as they are now," Raimo says. "And we had no idea at the time that another would rise as soon as she died. We were all so new to the magic."

I look down at the parchment in the box. It's covered in the same runes the cuff of Astia bears across its thick, coppery surface. "But if the priests had found a way to create something that would magnify magic, and they wanted to increase their own power, then why didn't they make themselves cuffs too? We have more copper in this land than we know what to do with—well, we did, and especially back then—so why didn't every wielder have one?"

Raimo laughs again, his chest rattling enough to make me wince. "Again, you think the Astia is just an ordinary hunk of metal. No wonder you hold yourself in such low regard." He waves his hand as heat suffuses my cheeks. "Oh, it's a good question, Elli. And the answer is standing right in front of you."

His gaze finds Sig's. "The cuff of Astia was created using the blood of two Suurin, the only ones to exist before the two of you. They were the start of it all, so devoted to the Valtia that they were willing to die for her."

Sig grimaces in disgust. "*Die* for her? To create a piece of glorified jewelry? What a waste." He glances at Oskar, who's staring into the small fire at the center of the stone hearth.

Raimo shrugs. "The Suurin knew their fates. They chose to offer their magic to generations instead of forcing it to be bounded by their *brief* mortal life spans."

Sig too shifts his gaze to the flames, which flare as if they know their master.

"Their blood is in the red runes," I say, remembering the crimson shapes that glint on the cuff's copper surface.

"Blood is powerful," Raimo says. "Magical blood especially. And that discovery is how everything became so horribly twisted." He scratches his stringy beard. "One of the elders who created the cuff partook of the blood of the Suurin."

My stomach turns. "You said you found some of your colleagues to be a bit bloodthirsty. You meant exactly that."

Raimo nods. "As soon as he tasted it, he must have felt the power." He gives us a pained smile. "It took me a long time to figure out what he was doing, but by that time, he'd brought so many over to his way of thinking. Not everyone could have a cuff of Astia, but all could partake of blood, if they were willing—and if they had a source."

A tremor goes through Sig, and he takes a few steps back as if he's been shoved by some terrible realization.

"Then the old Valtia died and a new one rose up," Raimo continues. "That's when we understood that her magic was special. Like the magic of the Suurin, it was so vast that it outlived its vessel. The new Valtia had the same features as our dead queen, the hair, the eyes, the mark. She'd been a normal girl until the Valtia died, and then the magic roared inside of her." Raimo's dirty fingernails scrape at the carved runes on the box. "She was powerful. But she was just a girl. No match for a conniving old wielder who was willing to cut off his own balls and drink blood just for a chance to have more power. His was the insistent voice in her ear, guiding her every step of the way. She had to isolate herself from family and friends. She had to keep her body pure and untouched, for use as a magical vessel." Raimo's voice drips with contempt. "And then this blood-drinking elder and those aligned with him convinced her to change the laws. All magic wielders were to be brought to the temple. Like the Valtia, they were meant to serve the Kupari people. It was an easy enough thing for the citizens to believe. After all, suspicion and envy had begun to sprout up between those who could wield and those who couldn't. And the priests piled bronze coins into the hands of any parent who delivered a magical child to the steps of the new, grand Temple on the Rock, easing the path to oppression with promises of a life of discipline and service."

Sig sounds as unsteady as he looks when he asks, "But that's not what those children got, was it?"

"Oh, they did, in a manner of speaking," Raimo replies. His blue eyes flicker with rage. "The boys were gelded and the girls were shaved, to steal their identities and control them. They were all trained to trust in the elders. And they were all desperate for favor, because the priests picked their favorites to become apprentices. But the others, the ones whose magic was unbalanced, or who asked too many questions, or who seemed likely to challenge the elders' authority, or who had the great misfortune to be female in a temple filled with scared and selfish old men . . . They were broken. And their blood is what keeps the priests and elders powerful and young. Look at the elders, and then look at me. Who's prettier?" He gives us his hideous grin. "I found a way to prolong my life, but it has its price. Five months of every year, to be precise."

The ground beneath me spins, and I sit down heavily. "The priests drink the blood of the acolytes. The supposedly cloistered acolytes." I press my hands to my eyes, thinking of that lovely acolyte with the wide face, how she was going to be cloistered within days, how she's probably dead now.

Sig starts to pace, his fingers straying to his back, rubbing at the scars. His face is contorted with disgust. "I wasn't imagining it," he mutters, his voice tight, almost like he's about to cry. "It really happened." He grimaces and scrapes at his shoulder blades. The air gets hotter, and Maarika grabs Freya by the shoulders and leads her away. Aira and Ismael sink to the floor, wilting in the heat.

"Sig," Raimo says. "Calm yourself."

"He drank my blood!" Sig roars, his eyes orange with rage. "When I was chained and bleeding from the lash, that elder licked it straight from my skin!"

Oskar curses quietly. Waves of cold roll from him, counteracting the heat that's making sweat slide in shining drops down Sig's body.

"Now you understand the evil," Raimo says, staring at Oskar. "You see why you have to fight. Thousands of acolytes have been slaughtered, just to keep a few old men alive and in power long past their time."

"But what about you?" I ask. "If you knew this was happening, why didn't you try to stop it?"

The old man sags, his shoulders hunching. "With every drop of blood, they got stronger. The more powerful the wielder, the more powerful the blood, so no one was safe.

The priests began to turn on one another. It was impossible to tell who was an ally and who wanted to drink your blood with his dinner." Raimo cackles again, but it's pure bitterness. "And a few rose above the rest. They couldn't be stopped—because they were willing to do what no one else was." His eyes snap to mine. "Why do you think the Valtias rarely live past three decades, when the first Valtia ruled for nearly a century?"

The memory of Sofia's bandaged arms looms in my mind. "The elders drink from her." I want to scream with rage.

"Not constantly, but even a little of her blood is enough to give them the advantage. You see how they control things," Raimo says. "How they control *her*. How, as she comes into her own, as she starts to question what she's been taught, as she realizes she has it within her to be a true ruler, maybe to change things for the better, they weaken her enough to take her down."

I lower my hands to my sides, fighting the urge to sob. *Sofia.* She was meant to live a long, glorious life. All the Valtias were. "Why didn't you tell anyone?"

Raimo's bushy white eyebrows rise. "What makes you think I didn't? I tried to stir the few priests who had not corrupted themselves. I tried to build a coalition that could challenge the elders. But one by one, my allies were converted or killed. And the elders bribed the city council and the citizens until they were so soft and full and happy that they had no reason to question what was happening in the temple. I even went to the Valtia herself." He rubs at his nose. "She listened. She was horrified. I thought she would help me." He raises his head. "But then she sickened and died within the week, and the new Valtia trusted in the elders completely."

"You could have fought them," barks Sig. "You could have tried."

"Do you have any idea how strong they are?" Raimo scoffs. "It wasn't my power that had kept me alive to that point. I had to rely on my wits. So instead of committing noble, idiotic suicide by challenging them, I stole the knowledge they needed to take control forever, and I tucked it—and myself—away until the cosmos sent me the allies who could help me save Kupari." He lifts the parchment from the box. "After all, it was my fault this knowledge existed, seeing as I'm the one who made the prophecy in the first place."

"What did it say, exactly?" Oskar asks.

Raimo smiles, his entire face crinkling. "Ah, this is the interesting part. It depends on how you interpret it." He runs his narrow fingertips over the runes on the parchment. "The Kupari used to read the stars. We used to believe. *They* used to guide us—not the elders, and not a naive belief that the Valtia was in charge. Our faith in the stars is in our very language—what do you pray to? What do you say when you're surprised or frustrated? But which of you knows the first thing about them?"

Ismael combs his fingers through his beard. "My grandfather told me a few stories. About the celestial bear that moves the sun through the sky. About a great pack of wolves, commanded by the queen of the night and the king of the stars, that comes from on high to protect us from our enemies."

Just like the carvings in the temple. Except I was told they symbolized the magic of the Valtia.

Aira looks over at Ismael. "You never told me those stories."

Raimo nods. "And that's how we forgot who we were, generation by generation. That's how we came to worship our queen and our own power instead of the cosmos. But I knew how to read the stars. I put *all* my faith in them." He flips over the parchment, revealing a portion of a star chart, concentric circles dotted with the inhabitants of the sky and all sorts of scribbled calculations. His fingertips tremble as he slides them over the dots. "Karhu, the bear, the creature who lives a thousand lives, the one who brings wisdom and balance," he says, tapping one star before moving to another. "And Susi, the wolf, the implacable warrior. Together, they symbolize a mighty Valtia. They were aligned with the ringed planet, Mahtava—the portent of war. And right here"—he traces an invisible line to a cluster of dots—"is Vaaden, the steed. The myths say he aids the divine in their quests for magical artifacts. See how his spine creates this sharp angle with the alignment?"

He looks up at us, reads the blank looks on our faces, and rolls his eyes. "It told of a great power that would rise in a time of war," he says. "The vessel would come into existence when Karhu and Susi aligned. This alignment was so rare. My calculations weren't precise, but I knew it wouldn't happen again for nearly three centuries."

"And I happened to be born during that alignment," I say quietly.

"And so was *she*. The Valtia," says Raimo, looking down at the parchment again. "But that's what the elders didn't know. I had confided in a friend, my last supposed ally, but he told the elders of the prophecy, and they demanded to know what it foretold. I allowed them to read the part that I'd completed. When I saw the greed on their faces, I knew the time had come to take action. They wanted this power for themselves, not our people. That night, after staring through a lens of ice at the stars above, after completing the prophecy and realizing what it meant, I knew I couldn't stay." He runs his fingers down his beard. "My only goal became to survive long enough to see the prophecy come true, and to do my part to serve the will of the cosmos."

"So what do you know that the elders don't?" I ask.

"The elders thought this vessel would be a single person. And why wouldn't they? It could be read that way. But as I completed the chart, I saw *this*." He stabs his finger at a corner of the chart. "The planet Vieno in retrograde, right at the point of the alignment. Complicates everything. Always a sign of disunity. As soon as I saw that, I suspected it would be two—that the power and the balance would not inhabit the same vessel."

"How did you know about me and Sig, though?" Oskar asks. "What does that prophecy say about us?"

"Do you want me to explain how I read the stars, or just to tell you what they said?"

"What they said," Sig and Oskar say in unison.

Raimo lets out a huff of laughter. "The second part of the prophecy foretold the Suurin, who would rise only when nothing else could save us. But it also says they will stand with the Astia." He rubs his thumb along a different part of the chart. "A triple conjunction of planets—Jatti, Vieno, and Kaunotar. They work together. Each one is needed for victory."

Oskar glances at me. "But how do we know the prophecy isn't just about the cuff, the magical artifact? Maybe we're supposed to use that. Not Elli."

The old man pulls his patched cloak closer around his bony shoulders, even though he's sitting not six feet from a fire. "The signs were different from the ones that portended the cuff. Yes, the presence of Vaaden indicates an artifact, but the aspect indicates opposition. Stress. Something *pushing back.* This on top of the indication that the mighty power would be split into two components, the power and the balance. This time, the stars foretold an Astia with a *will.*" He raises his head, and his pale eyes lock with mine.

A will. Frustration courses through me. Does will matter when it's overwhelmed by the power of the wielders who use me?

Raimo gives me a sly look and drops the parchment back into his box. "So, here we are. The Suurin were born, just as the stars foretold, and now they've become men. The Astia has risen. I'd say all of this proves that I'm brilliant."

Oskar crosses his arms over his chest. "Aren't you forgetting something? This extraordinarily powerful Valtia who, unlike past Valtias, doesn't have balance because Elli got all of it?"

Raimo sighs. "Only the stars know where she is, but at least the elders don't have her. I'm actually shocked that she hasn't revealed herself yet. If she wasn't raised in the temple, she wouldn't necessarily know what was happening to her. But we know she's alive, because the Saadella hasn't come into the power yet." His brow furrows. "Correct? I feel like I've missed some important events."

"No, the Saadella has no power," I say quietly. "But the elders have her. She's just a little girl." One I want to gather in my arms. One I want to protect. The urge is powerful and instinctual, its own kind of magic.

"They found her?" Raimo curses. "That's not good."

Oskar lowers his dark, slashing brows. "Apart from the obvious, why?"

Raimo's eyes glitter with ice. "Because if the Saadella dies, the magical line dies. Only the death of a Valtia can create a Saadella, and once she is made, there is no chance of making another until the next Valtia dies. Why do you think the priests are so frantic to find the new Saadella every time a Valtia perishes?" He jabs his finger at me. "Why do you think they lock her away in the temple and attend to her every need? Yes, they want to control her, to make sure she has no will or thoughts of her own. But also—her death means losing the magic, and that magic is what's keeping them in power."

"Then the girl should be in no danger," says Sig. "Wouldn't they protect her at all costs?"

Raimo mutters something under his breath and shakes his head. "Everything is different now." His creaky voice is made of urgency. "The last of our copper is being mined, and who knows what will happen to the magic when it's gone? The fire and ice could fade away—or they could turn on the very ones who bled the land of their source. The elders know this, and I don't doubt they've been planning for it."

My hands ball in my skirt. "They'll want to ensure that when the time comes, they have all the power."

Raimo nods. "We are truly standing on the precipice of disaster."

Oskar stands up, looming over the three of us. "I've heard enough. I'm ready to fight."

Sig grins. "It's about time. This is going to be fun."

Oskar smiles, walking toward him until they're only a few feet apart. "I knew you'd say that."

His fist arcs forward and catches Sig in the jaw, sending the Fire Suurin to the ground, his head lolling and his eyes unfocused. Oskar leans over Sig, his knuckles bleeding, menace oozing from every inch of him.

"Understand, though," he says quietly. "Throw as much fire at me as you want. I don't care. But if you ever harm someone I love again, you and I will be enemies forever. And I promise—you will die with ice in your veins."

# CHAPTER 23

Oskar stares down at Sig for a few long moments, then offers his hand. The entire cave goes still. No one breathes. The wielders look poised to defend themselves if Sig retaliates, their hands hovering flexed at their sides. Sig blinks a few times and moves his jaw from side to side, blood trickling from the corner of his mouth. His dark eyes focus on Oskar's face, and he lets out a pained chuckle. "Fair enough." He accepts Oskar's help in getting to his feet, and all of us let out a sigh of relief.

Oskar turns to Raimo. "What's our plan?"

Raimo smirks. "We take back the Temple on the Rock and separate the elders from the source of their power— blood and copper. We save the Saadella and liberate the acolytes. But I'd feel more reassured if you'd been preparing for this for the past few years."

Oskar's nostrils flare as he draws in a breath. "Perhaps I would have, if you'd actually told me *anything*."

"Amazing. I agree with Oskar," says Sig, his voice molten, blood smeared on his chin and the back of his hand. "All these years, you kept this from us."

"And what would you have done, eh?" Raimo lurches to his feet and pokes Sig's sweaty chest. "Hot-tempered idiot. You'd have blundered straight into the elders' clutches, and they would have drained you dry. You might be powerful, but you were both boys, and without the Astia, you're not strong enough to face Tahvo and the others."

My brow furrows. "Tahvo? There's no elder by that name."

Raimo rubs his grizzled cheek. "Crown. That's what it means. Ironic, no? It's possible he's taken another name over the years."

A jowly, thin-lipped face floats dark in my mind. "Aleksi. He's the worst of them. He was always trying to tell the Valtia what to do. He seemed eager for my death." I glance at Sig. "Would he have tried to drink my blood too?"

Raimo's fingers twist in his long, stringy beard. "The blood of the Astia. Now there's an interesting thought. He didn't know what you are, so he might not have. But if he had . . . ? Hmm. I don't know what would happen." For a moment he looks like he'd like to find out. Would it steal the elder's powers, or would it make him stronger, magnifying his own magic to untold levels?

The idea of Aleksi's thin lips covered in my blood makes me shudder.

Oskar reaches for my hand, but I pull it away before his fingers close over mine. I won't let him touch me now. He frowns as his arm falls to his side. "Do you really think Elder Aleksi is the same person?"

Raimo shrugs. "Dark? Round-bellied?"

"That describes the elder who . . ." Sig looks away, rubbing at his back again.

I grimace as I remember Aleksi's hard smile while I suffered. "Is he really hundreds of years old?"

"If you have relatively balanced fire and ice," says Raimo, "along with knowledge of how they work, you can find a way."

I don't miss the hollow looks Sig and Oskar exchange. They are the opposite of balance, uniquely powerful—and vulnerable. "Are all the elders that old and strong?" Sig asks.

"The one with copper hair was easy enough to kill," Oskar says.

"That was Leevi," I say. "I remember when he became an elder. He was the newest of the three."

"Probably the weakest, too." Raimo plants his walking stick in a crack in the stone and leans on it. He's always been scrawny, but he looks shakier than he did when I first knew him. Leevi and the other priests caused the thaw that awakened him two months too soon—but just in time to help us. I only hope he's strong enough to do it.

"The priests are a deceptive, dangerous group," he says.

"Not one of them trusts the others. And I haven't been in the temple in centuries, so I don't know the players. But I have no doubt that Tahvo is still there. By the time I fled, he was by far the most skilled and powerful of them. He was probably waiting for the ascension of this foretold Valtia—if he had her blood, he might be able to equal her in power. That's why he'd be willing to kill the Saadella. He wouldn't think he needs her, and he wouldn't want anyone to rise to challenge him. With the cuff of Astia, he could rule Kupari."

"For all we know, the cuff of Astia is a melted mess of copper right now," I say. Sig and I tell Raimo what happened in the city, how he brought the fire down on poor Mim, who was wearing the crown and the cuff as the flames devoured her.

Raimo shakes his head. "The cuff is like you, Elli. Immune to magic. It can't be destroyed that way. And like you, it can magnify the magic of any wielder who's touching it. Tahvo might use this crisis as an excuse to claim it—and the throne."

"Unless the Soturi strike first," says Sig. "The barbarian envoys were right there at the coronation. The elders were putting on quite a show for them."

"And you revealed the lie." In the most fiery, awful way. My voice breaks as I remember that I'll never see Mim's beautiful, kind face again.

"You helped," Sig says drily.

I bow my head. He's right. And despite the fact that I channeled all that power, I feel more powerless than ever.

Oskar shifts so his big body is between me and Sig. "You used her."

"And something tells me you did too," Sig says with a laugh. "How else did you have the control to bring down enough ice to encase twenty men? You might have endless ice magic inside you, Oskar, but you've never learned to wield it. You never even wanted it."

"But I have it, and I'll wield it now," Oskar says quietly.

"Only because you're besotted with *her*."

The temperature in the chamber drops so suddenly that Raimo shudders. "Does it matter why I'm doing it?" Oskar snaps. "You've wanted me to fight alongside you for years, and here I am."

Heat rises to meet the cold. "Here you are." Sig reaches around Oskar and grabs my arm. "And here's the reason we'll win. Did you feel the power of touching her, brother? We can bring down the temple with the elders inside. *This* is the war we're meant to fight, with her beside us."

"No!" I shout, ripping my sleeve from Sig's sweaty grasp before Oskar has a chance to. "We're going there to destroy the elders and take back the temple. But I won't help with anything else. The acolytes and apprentices are innocent. The Saadella is a *child*. And the Kupari people need protection, especially now! Destroying the temple will destroy them—their hope, their will—and with the Soturi at our borders, I won't let it happen." My mouth snaps shut, but my voice is still echoing throughout the cavern. Every cave dweller's eyes are on me.

"Spoken like a queen," Raimo says with amusement. "You hear that, everyone?" He points to me. "If you can wield, come with us. It's time to reclaim the Temple on the Rock."

We set out perhaps an hour later, and by that time my fear and hope are twined so tightly inside me that I'm barely aware of what's going on around me. Small things filter in, though. Oskar's loud fight with Freya about whether she can come, and the blast of heat she sends at him as she tries to convince him she can help. Sig's laughter as he watches, and the way he makes the air around her so hot that her skin turns pink and she starts to cry. Oskar's grateful look as the two of them walk out of the cavern and leave her behind, safe in her mother's arms. Maarika's inscrutable gray eyes, following her son's tall form as he strides into the winter sunlight. "He's still got burns all over his back," she says to me. "He almost died an hour ago."

"I'll do my best to protect him." I kiss her forehead and turn away, already wondering if I can keep that promise. What if I have to choose between protecting him and protecting the Saadella?

We have twenty wielders in all. Two Suurin. One tottering, centuries-old man. Sig's eight wielders, including Usko, Mikko, and Tuuli, lean and wary as they glare at me and Oskar. And nine cavern dwellers—Veikko, Ismael, Aira, and six others—each of them somber and pale as they hug their families and clear bundles of clothes and food off the horses. We're not moving camp today.

Instead, we're going to war. Us against thirty priests and three powerful elders. Thirty apprentices and at least a hundred acolytes who could fight for either side. We might have a better chance now than ever before, but our odds still don't seem good.

Oskar, his hair tied back, the circles under his eyes telling me of all he's been through in the last day, joins me as I stroke the neck of the roan mare. "What will happen if we succeed?" he asks.

"Isn't that a question for Raimo?" I murmur.

He brushes a coppery lock of hair from my brow. "I don't think so."

I look into his eyes. "I'm a weapon in this war. I'm not fooling myself that I'm anything more than that."

His lips curve into a half smile. "I think you *are* fooling yourself."

"You said it—I'm no queen."

His gaze on my face feels like a caress. "I said you weren't a queen to me. I don't get to say what you are to others."

I turn away from him, fiddling with the horse's reins as it nickers softly. "It's pointless to think about now."

Oskar sighs. "Will you ride with me?"

"No. You need your strength."

"I have plenty, Elli. More than I want sometimes."

My fingers stray along the horse's silky, warm neck. "Can you do this, Oskar? You never wanted to be a part of this. You've never fought—"

His cool hand closes over my shoulder. "Stop," he says

quietly. "Raimo says this is what I was made for."

"But Sig told me all these things he could do, manifesting versus wielding, blade magic—do you know *any* of that?"

"If I told you I'll learn quickly, would that help?"

"No," I say in a choked voice.

His thumb strokes my shoulder blade. "Then I don't know what to say, except I'm sorry. I've been denying my magic for so long, but I can't walk away from it or this battle any more than you can now."

"But you want to."

"No."

"Because of me?"

He gives me a squeeze, and I sway, wanting to feel his fingertips slide along my neck, to lean back and feel his arms around me, to tilt my head up and let his scratchy stubble abrade my cheek.

"I think I was supposed to save you," he says. "How could that have happened by accident? It seems like the stars fated us to meet. Even then, I was yours—your sword, your shield—as much as you've been mine. As for how I feel about you—" He places a cool kiss on the top of my head. "That feels . . . separate. I want to tuck it away and keep it for myself. It's not the reason I won't walk away. Now that I know what's happening in the temple with those acolytes, I can't. I want you to stop feeling guilty, Elli. I need to help them."

I laugh, but it's strangled by my tears. "Because no one

else is there to do it," I whisper, echoing his words from weeks ago—the reason he said he saved me. I want to tuck *him* away until everything is safe. "You know why I can't ride with you. I'm scared to touch your skin now." Though I want to. Stars, I want to.

His hand slides off my shoulder. "Fair enough. You won't ride with me. But do you even know how to ride a horse?" he asks, his voice teasing.

I press my lips together. Honestly, I have no idea. "If I told you I'll learn quickly, would that help?"

He lets out a bark of laughter as I mimic his words. "Knowing you, I don't doubt that you would. But it would be a tragedy if you broke your neck before we even reached the city gates."

"Elli will ride with me," calls Raimo. "Oskar, your weight alone is enough to break that poor mare's back." And then comes that cackle, and this time, it makes me smile. I step around Oskar, but as I do, I close my fingers over his sleeve. His powerful muscles tense at my touch. It's difficult to let go.

Raimo's in the saddle of a black gelding that's impatiently stamping its front hooves. Ismael comes over and offers me his knee. I take his calloused hand, which pulses with warmth, and let him boost me up behind the old man, whose musty smell wrinkles my nose.

"Elli," Raimo whispers, "what did you do to Oskar?"

I glance over to see Oskar standing next to the roan, looking at me in a way I feel low in my belly like a long, slow pull. "You told me to stick close to him."

"I never told you to take the boy's heart—or to offer him yours."

"It just happened," I mumble. It happened so deeply and thoroughly that I'm having trouble thinking around my worry for him, even though he told me not to.

"You'll regret this love," Raimo warns, kicking lightly at the horse's flank. "Best to smother it now, while it's still kindling. Trust me on that."

My hands tighten around his scrawny waist as the horse trots toward the trail to the marshlands. "Will you tell me why?"

He shakes his head, his tufts of white hair waving in the cold wind that gusts down the narrow path. Behind us come the clomps and clacks of hooves as the others follow. "Sometimes knowing the future is a curse."

It feels like I've been kicked in the gut. I focus on breathing, on the trail ahead of us, winding through tufts of pale-brown marsh grass, once again frozen stiff and rustling by the merciless cold. Oskar must be chilled. He's bundled in his furs, but I know how winter makes him ache.

I push the thought of him away, at least for now. I have to keep my mind on what we must do—and how we must do it. "How are we going to take the temple?"

"Let the Suurin use you to project their power. Together, with you to amplify their magic, they are as strong as a Valtia wearing the cuff of Astia."

That's what Sig said as well. "But they barely speak to each other." I look over my shoulder to see them riding side by side, Sig with a light cloak thrown over his bare shoulders, his white-gold hair shining under the sun, and Oskar, dark, grim, and drawn-looking, his broad shoulders hunched against the chill. Neither of them acknowledges the other.

"They'll work together when the time comes. Deep inside, they recognize that they need each other, and they know they share the same fate. Their bond isn't an easy one to break, no matter how badly both might wish for it sometimes."

It seems like a flimsy foundation on which to build a war. "How can the two of them work together that well, though? The Valtia is one person who controls both extremes."

"The Astia is no different."

My eyebrows shoot up. It sounds like what Oskar said, about letting me wield his magic as my own, about being my sword instead of me being his. And it makes no sense. "I couldn't be more different! The Valtia wields her magic with absolute control, and me—" My frustration is choking me. "Other people wield me."

"Only because you allow it, stupid girl. You and Oskar make the same mistake, thinking you can't control things when you actually can."

I grit my teeth. "When Oskar or Sig want to withhold their magic, they can. Both of them have done it to me. And when they decide to offer it, they do. But I can't withhold anything. When Sig touched me in that square, he took the power from me, even though I never would have hurt Mim."

"You forced that warmth into Oskar."

"Yes, when he was mostly dead and unable to resist."

Raimo's scrawny frame jounces in the saddle as we gallop along. His words come between ragged breaths. "As long as you think like that, you'll be as brainless and helpless as the actual cuff of Astia. Use your will, Elli, for surely you have one. How else did you survive the torture that nearly killed you? How else did you make it to the woods? How else are you right here, after weeks of winter spent living in a cave, for stars' sake, looking stronger and healthier than I ever expected? No will, my arse," he scoffs. "Remember who you are. Realize what you are. Do both those things, or you'll either be completely useless—or too dangerous to help anyone."

My thoughts churn. We're only an hour from the city, and I have no time to learn how to do the things Raimo says are within my power. But that doesn't change anything. The Kupari—*all* the Kupari, not just the citizens of the town, but all the wielders who've escaped to the outlands, the acolytes doomed to die in the catacombs, the little Saadella at the mercy of the elders—need to feel safe.

But is that what we're doing? Or are we destroying the last shred of safety they have? "Raimo, I think we should try to talk to the elders. If they were desperate enough to try to pass off Mim as the Valtia, they must fear the Soturi. They were trying to put on a show of strength. Maybe—"

"And, what, are you thinking they'll agree to stop living off the blood of young wielders, grow weak and old, and die? You think they'll step down and allow a Valtia to truly rule the land, and that they'll change the laws and let all wielders walk free—wielders who'll have children who will grow in strength and magic, enough to challenge the priesthood—just because we ask them nicely? Oh, yes, let's give that a try."

My cheeks burn as we ride along the wide road that leads to the northeast. Up ahead, dark smoke still hangs over the distant city. Within that haze, the massive, pale-green dome of the Temple on the Rock looms high and ominous. "The Soturi will come," I say. "It's only a matter of time."

"Then perhaps the Kupari need wiser rulers than a group of blood-drinking sorcerers who are more interested in maintaining their positions than protecting their own people—and letting the people protect themselves."

Sig and Oskar bring their horses alongside ours. The fire wielder has a wide grin on his face. "Can you see it? Can you feel it?" He lets out a shaky chuckle. "Chaos," he mouths.

I glance at Oskar, who nods toward the city gate. "It's open," he says. "No one's guarding it."

I squint into the distance and realize he's right. Every minute brings us closer, and now I can see straight up the eastern road that leads to the square. "What's happened?" It can't be the Soturi—we'd surely have seen them on the march.

"We killed the Valtia, Elli," calls Sig, every word dripping with triumph. "We've turned the world upside down."

My heart seizes up like a fist as we reach the threshold of our great Kupari city. Yesterday it looked bad, but today it looks ravaged. The streets are empty, save for debris that litters the streets, the guts of ransacked, looted homes. A few scared faces peer at us from alleys or open doorways, but no one questions why twenty horses just cantered through the city gates. No one tries to stop us. We pass block after block, and signs of mayhem are everywhere. Carts left at the side of the road, their wooden wheels broken. A smear of blood on the stones of the council building. And then—

"I hear them," Sig says, kicking his horse into a gallop.

Raimo curses and does the same, and Oskar and the other wielders follow close behind. I hold on tight to the skinny old man in front of me, both of us puffing with the exertion of trying to stay in the saddle. We're nearly to the square, and already I can see the crowds, arms waving and hands fisted, all pressing up the northern road that leads to the temple. "It looks like we're not the only ones who decided to storm the temple," Oskar calls.

We ride to the outskirts of the main square, which is full of enraged citizens bearing whatever weapons they've been able to find—mostly the tools of their trade, scythes, bows, hammers. The Kupari have never had an army. We've never needed it, never wanted it—all because the elders didn't want anyone challenging their rule, so they convinced us that the Valtia would take care of us forever.

And now, without her, we're helpless.

"Oy!" Oskar shouts as he reins in his mount near the back of the crowd. "What's happening?"

A stout man with curly blond hair and a wind-chapped

face gives us a puzzled look. "Where've you been in the last day? The priests have locked themselves and our new Valtia inside the temple, and we want to see her! The barbarians are coming one way or the other—overland or by the lake, and we want to know what she'll do about it!"

"Let us through," Sig shouts.

The red-cheeked man looks at him like he's crazy. "You think I can magically move thousands of people out of your way?"

Sig's eyes glow and he lifts his hand, tongues of flame dripping from his fingertips. "No, but I can." A ball of flame bursts forth from his palm, and he hurls it over the heads of the mob.

Oskar lets out a frustrated sound and swipes his arm through the air, his movements in synchrony with Raimo's. Extinguished by their magic, the fireball disappears just before it lands in the middle of the crowd. "You arse," Oskar hisses. "You could have killed dozens."

Sig's grin is pure war. "That's what I came here to do, brother." His pale arms are tense as he spurs his horse forward. But the crowd merely shouts and heaves, too packed in and confused to move aside. My stomach clenches—if they panic, we'll have a stampede, and innocent people will die.

Raimo pulls his walking stick from the back of the horse and pokes the stout man, who is gaping up at Sig in silent terror. "You're going to help us. Because I have the true Valtia right here. She'll get the priests to open up."

The man tears his eyes from Sig. "What?"

"What are you doing?" I whisper.

"You won't recognize her without her ceremonial makeup, but look closely," says Raimo, amusement in his voice. "Coppery hair, pale-blue eyes." He elbows me in the belly. "Show them the mark."

A few other people have turned toward us, and the noise of the crowd has quieted a bit. My lips barely move as I speak right into Raimo's whiskery ear. "You know as well as I do that I'm not—"

"Ah, she's a modest thing. Didn't want be seen without her makeup and fancy dress," Raimo shouts to the crowd.

More people are peering at us. I have to look away from Oskar when I see the raw worry in his eyes.

"Do you want to get through this mob without hurting them, or do you want Sig to burn the whole city down?" Raimo whispers. "Show them the mark, and I'll take care of the rest."

My hands shake as I pull my skirt up and clamp my three fingers over it as I slide my stocking down my left leg. It's an odd, intimate thing to do in front of a crowd of gawkers, and my heart slams against my breast as my blood-flame mark is revealed. The gasp rolls through the entire square, followed by a flurry of anxious muttering.

"Was that other Valtia an impostor?"

"We thought her magic turned on her—but was it all fake?"

"Who is this girl? Could she really be the lost—"

"Let us through!" Sig shouts again. "I got your Valtia right here! Let us through!"

Oskar edges his mount close, like he's prepared to kill anyone who makes a grab for me. But already the crowd is stepping aside, offering us a path. Waves of bitter cold flow from my ice wielder as we move forward.

"Keep it up and you'll kill your horse," Raimo says to Oskar as we weave our way among the scythe-wielding citizens, all the way to the north end of the square. Atop the Valtia's platform, the burned remains of her ceremonial paarit remain, copper solidified in oozy dribbles along its sides, riveting it to the stones beneath it. I stare at it to avoid the eyes of the citizens, who are looking at me as if I'm their salvation. It kills me to offer them a second false Valtia in as many days, especially when I hear the jubilant whispers. "It really *is* her! She's come back! Stars save us, she's returned."

They chatter about how they recognize me, even though some of them probably kicked mud in my face when I was banished from the city. They wonder aloud where I've been, whether I really did go mad as the rumors said. They talk about me as if I can't hear them, and I'm happy to pretend that's true.

Sig is on my right, Oskar on my left. Both of them have set jaws and fierce looks, and the oddest thing is happening around me—the air swirls with wisps of cold and hot, sliding across my face and gusting my hair. "On my signal," Raimo says quietly.

"On your signal, what?" I whisper.

"I'm not talking to you," he mutters.

As I look between the two buildings that bound the northern road, I can see our path to the ceremonial gates. The constables and the councilmen mill about several yards away, their brown cloaks pulled tight around them as they argue in urgent tones. They've always depended on the elders to tell them how the Valtia wants the city to be run, and in exchange for their cooperation, they've grown rich and fat—and indecisive.

The head of the council, a man named Topias who I've watched on several harvest days, passing his requests for favors from the Valtia to the elders while they all dined on venison and grilled trout, notices our arrival and stalks forward. "What's this I hear about the Valtia?" he says in a rumbling voice, his thick brown beard brushing his heavy copper councilman's medallion as he speaks. "We know citizens want action, but we're trying to negotiate with the elders—"

"You don't have to, since I have the true Valtia right here," Raimo replies, slapping at my calf until I hold it out and show the councilman my mark.

"If you're really the queen," says Topias, removing his embroidered velvet cap and smoothing his hand over the few wiry strands of hair on the top of his head, "you'll have to prove it." He gives me a cautious look.

I sit straighter in the saddle behind Raimo, even though my fear is making it hard to breathe. His cold hand closes over mine, and I feel the pulse of his power magnified by my own. "Very well," I say in a high, quavering voice.

"Gates," Raimo breathes.

I lift my left hand and point at the gates.

They glow and crackle. I can feel Raimo tugging more power from within me, and I don't fight it. The councilmen dive away from the solid copper slabs as they undulate with heat. And then a sudden burst of ferocious, icy air whooshes forward. The gates explode inward.

The crowd cheers. "She's returned! We're saved!" the councilmen shout.

"Nice work, Valtia," Raimo says, looking over his shoulder at me.

He turns to the front in time to be hit in the face with a blast of ice. As councilmen scatter in panic, Raimo collapses against me, giving me a view of the white plaza through the shattered gates.

It's filled with at least a hundred black-robed acolytes, hands outstretched, ready to defend the temple to their last breath.

# CHAPTER 24

I catch a glimpse of the priests and apprentices pouring from the temple entrance before Sig yanks me from the saddle. I grab for Raimo—the old man is so fragile that the fall could kill him—but he's already disappeared over the other side of our horse.

"Oskar has him," Sig says, then holds my hand tightly and sends a horrific blast of flame straight through the gates. The screams of the acolytes jitter down my spine as Sig drags me to the side, behind a marble pillar on one side of the destroyed gateway. A terrible, gut-wrenching noise behind me signals that at least one of our horses has been hit by ice or fire. The wielders who came with us are on either side of the gates, their backs against the low stone walls. Aira's pale-green eyes are alight with fear. Veikko's hands are shaking. Oskar presses in next to me a moment later, panting, Raimo in his arms. "Elli," he says, but I'm already reaching for the old man. I grab his limp hands to siphon the excess cold.

Raimo's pale eyes flutter open. "You'll have to get through them. Or convince them to join us."

The acolytes are battling for the very men who plan to drink their blood. It's so twisted, but as the blasts of fire and ice come shooting out from the white plaza, I'm not sure how to make them listen to us.

"We have to show them the Valtia's power," Oskar says, looking down at me. "If we want to get through without killing, you have to make them believe."

"I'm all right with killing a few," snarls Sig, but I jerk my hand away as he reaches for it, unwilling to let him use me until I have a chance to figure this out.

"You'd rather eliminate our one advantage?" he asks. "That's what happens if we're separated. Raimo said we were supposed to fight together!"

I peer around the pillar and watch a small acolyte stumble over his own too-long robe at the bottom of the steps. And when he throws back his hood, I see that it's Niklas, the little boy Aleksi brought to the temple all those weeks ago. "Maybe this isn't the war Raimo prophesied. I'm not sure fighting is what we're supposed to do right now."

Sig lets out a sound of pure frustration. "Go on, then. Just remember—you might be immune to magic, but that doesn't mean they can't hurt you."

Oskar touches my sleeve. "He's right."

I let out a long, slow breath. "It's worth the risk. If we shock them, maybe they'll stop long enough to hear us out. And if they won't, I trust you to get to me in time."

"Oskar, use the fountains. Can you?" Raimo asks.

Oskar, strands of his dark hair skimming along his cheeks, looks toward the two massive fountains in the plaza, each burbling with water year-round because the temple is heated with magic. The twin statues of the Valtia tower above them. "I can try," he says quietly, tossing me an anxious glance. "My control—"

"I'll help you," says Raimo wearily. "You have the power, but I have the technique."

Oskar nods, but he looks worried, and I can't blame him—Raimo's breaths are shallow and unsteady, and he can barely hold his head up. "We can do this, but then you're staying back," Oskar says to him. "If you go in there, you'll die."

Raimo seems too weak to argue.

"I'll cap it off," says Sig, as if he already senses what they're going to do. "They need to see both ice and fire together."

"And I'll look the part," I mumble.

"Move your hands," says Oskar, "so they think it's coming from you."

"Sig could sense that the magic wasn't coming from Mim. Will they—"

"We don't want to give them time to," says Raimo. "Make this quick."

Sig gives me a little push, and I step from behind the pillar. The acolytes grit their teeth and the air warps around me. Sig curses, and I walk forward quickly to draw the heat away from him. The acolytes' eyes go wide as I stride into the white plaza, my arms rising from my sides, my coppery hair flying about my face. The water in the fountains glitters with ice that suddenly spirals into the air. It's as if the frozen column is drawing the liquid straight up from the Motherlake, growing thicker and whiter as it builds on itself, forming an arch over the marble slabs of this plaza, higher than the towering statues, nearly as high as the dome of the temple. The acolytes around me and the priests and apprentices on the steps stare as the ice shifts and shimmers, creating an intricate lattice over my head.

And then it shatters and melts, raining down—but turning to steam before a drop touches the ground. The acolytes lower their hands and look at me, shock etched on every face.

"I've come back to claim my throne," I say, praying to the stars that only I can hear the unsteadiness of my words. "The elders and priests have lost their way, but I can set things right."

One of the acolytes steps forward, and the spots on her face stir my memories. "Valtia," Meri says in a broken voice. "Is it you?"

I smile at her. "It's me, Meri." She was a ray of kindness in a storm of cruelty. I hold out my hand to her.

She pushes her black hood back and walks toward me,

her face alight with joy. But her smile becomes a scream as her robe bursts into flame. The acolytes around her stagger back as she shrieks in pain, the flames devouring her, smoke billowing into the air. I look across the plaza, toward the steps leading up to the temple, and spot Armo the former apprentice, his face twisted and his hands clawed as he burns Meri down. My eyes narrow as rage pulses through me—she was his *friend*.

"The girl's a fraud!" he yells. "She has no magic. Destroy her!"

Oskar shouts my name as the acolytes lunge for me, hot and cold hands tearing at my clothes. No sooner has someone grabbed my hair than all of them are thrown away from me with a fierce gust of icy wind. It thunders through the plaza, knocking everyone but me back. I look over my shoulder to see the wielders, with Oskar and Sig at the front, pour through the gates. Raimo is nowhere in sight, and I can only hope he's safe.

The magic erupts around me. But none of it touches me. It's almost as if time has stopped. Sound is muted. Priests and apprentices storm down the vast temple steps and into the plaza, flanking the group of terrified acolytes to take on the rebel wielders. As Oskar runs for me, ice arches from the fountain and crashes down as a wall between us. It melts a moment later, long enough for me to see a flash of Sig's white-gold hair and pale skin, but then it re-forms as spikes, which fly into the air—and come straight for me.

Knives of ice, wielded by blood-fueled priests. My death

looks like glittering diamonds in the sunlight. Oskar and Sig are under siege—they can't stop it. But right before the frozen blades hit home, they veer off track, flying silent and sharp around me, close enough for me to feel their cool kiss. Acolytes scream as their bodies are stabbed straight through, and they fall, writhing, to the marble slabs.

*Nothing* magical can harm me. I look behind me, and there's a crowd of black robes between me and my Suurin, who are fighting for their lives against a horde of priests and apprentices. If they can't reach me, I can't magnify their power. But even without me, the small group of rebels is holding their own, pushing the enemy back. Oskar and Sig are shoulder to shoulder now, protecting each other and wielding as one force, though the fire strikes with precision and the ice is wielded like a blunt instrument.

And I'm standing in the middle of the plaza. Forgotten. Unchallenged. I look up the long flight of steps leading to the domed chamber. Inside is the child Saadella—and the elders. The fury twists inside me. I walk forward, only dimly aware of the Valtia statues in the fountains cracking, of marble exploding outward as blasts of fire and ice tear them apart. The shards pock the marble slabs at my feet, but not a single bit strikes me. But when a wall of flame crackles and blasts against my back, the ashy cinders of my burning dress fill the air. With a pang of sorrow, I know my carved dove is aflame, but I let the fiery garment fall from my shoulders. My boots become charcoal as the marble at my feet becomes hot as a roasting pan.

Naked, barefoot, I move forward. The instinct is so deep. Suddenly I understand why Sofia was so kind, so loving to me. I may not have inherited the magic, but I inherited this. With every shred of my being, I love that little Saadella, as much as I love myself. I don't know her name, but I don't need to. She's my sister, my daughter, my heart. I will never allow the elders to harm her or have her.

There is blood all around, suffering all around, death all around. I can't look. I don't want to know who we've lost. My eyes burn as I think how all of it could have been prevented. I mount the steps, leaving gray footprints on the pristine white marble and gleaming copper inlay. My hair is ruffled by wind that others will feel as a gale. None of it can slow me down. I hear my name and look behind me. Oskar and the others are advancing—they've reached the destroyed fountains now. My dark-haired Ice Suurin looks strong and fearless as he and Sig coordinate their movements, manipulating the temperature to lift a hunk of marble statue in the air. The giant slab of stone falters, and Sig yells at Oskar to focus the cold above the rock and keep it there. Together, they clumsily hurl it at the priests, who barely deflect it.

The elders inside must be aware of what's happening, but they haven't come out. They're depending on their acolytes and priests to die for them, while they hide in the temple with the Saadella.

What if they're hurting her?

What if they're escaping?

I stride quickly up the steps until I reach the semicircular plateau of stone that marks the entrance to the temple. Pillars of marble rise mighty and strong every twenty feet or so, holding up the massive copper dome above us. The battle has progressed to the base of the steps, and when I glance beyond them, I see people flooding into the plaza. Nonmagical people, wielding their scythes and spades. Sig and Oskar are surrounded by black-robed wielders, deflecting spikes of ice and magically hurled chunks of broken marble. A small crowd of acolytes have their hands up in surrender, but bodies of wielders litter the wide expanse, crushed and stabbed, burned and frozen. Magic can kill in so many different ways. The elders must know all of them.

But none of them will work on me, and perhaps that's the reason I'm here. As Oskar and Sig begin to climb the steps, I walk into the domed chamber, my only thought the helpless little girl held prisoner here.

"Is your nakedness meant to distract us?" says the hard voice I fear the most. "I hate to disappoint you." Aleksi strides out of the Valtia's wing, his dark eyes full of hatred.

On his wrist is the cuff of Astia.

I look down at my own soft, naked body. It looks so ordinary. I raise my head. "My clothes aren't fireproof, unfortunately."

For a moment, uneasiness flickers across his expression, but when his fingers stroke across the copper cuff, he grows bold again. "Where have you been all these weeks? Gathering a tiny army to challenge us? I should freeze you right here and let your body decorate our chamber." He raises his arm to strike.

I don't flinch. "Where is the Saadella?"

His thin lips tighten. "Lahja is safe from your influence."

"Lahja." Her name is like a drop of sweetness on my tongue. "I need to see her."

He grimaces. "Do you have any idea what you've done?"

"Do you?" I stand my ground as he stalks forward. Any minute Oskar and Sig will stride into the temple, and we'll put an end to this madness together. "I sensed you were evil. I just never knew how much."

His jowls quiver. "We've guarded and protected the Kupari our entire lives. We sacrificed in a way you could never understand. We've done everything we could for the people. And you—not only did you find a way to deny the magic that should have been yours, you've raised a rebellion right when we need unity!"

"Unity." My fists clench. "Did the acolytes feel that unity as you bled them to death? How many have you tasted, Aleksi? How many have you killed?"

He pales a shade. "This is a ludicrous accusation."

"Then where are the cloistered acolytes?"

A drop of sweat slips from the top of his bald head and slides down his cheek. "I don't owe you any answers. You've destroyed this great people, Elli. Your rebels were responsible for the fire yesterday, weren't they?"

"Why Mim?" I ask, sorrow tightening my throat.

"The Soturi announced that they were coming to meet

with our queen, and we needed someone to play the part," he says simply. "And she had no magic of her own. No will, either. We knew she wouldn't cause trouble."

"Because you tortured her!" I shriek, my fury hot as iron.

Aleksi sneers. "Like you, she was worth nothing! But you are even worse. You felt entitled to what you never deserved. Instead of obedience and submission, you—"

"Obedience and submission? The Valtia is supposed to be the queen!"

"You are far from a queen." His thin lips curl in contempt. "Your rebels will bring the Soturi to our borders. Their chieftains are probably galloping straight to Vasterut to gather their forces. When they return, our downfall rests on your shoulders!"

His fingers flex, and fire bursts around me, a swirling, dancing, roaring wall of flame. The warmth licks at me like a tender caress, and despite my instincts to cower, I walk forward.

The flames part like a curtain to allow me through. Aleksi's eyes go wide. He raises his arm, and the cold descends, but it can't even raise goose bumps along my skin. "You were prepared to kill me. You whipped me, you nearly drowned me, and then you were going to discard me. Had you planned to drink my blood, too?"

He edges toward the entrance to the catacombs, tossing nervous glances at the Saadella's wing as he does. He touches the cuff of Astia and tries another blast of flame, but it dies quickly. "You found your magic," he says.

I smile as I hear Oskar's voice just outside the temple, shouting to Sig about where to strike next. "I guess you could say I did." I take a few steps backward. I want Oskar and Sig to reach me quickly.

"They're coming!" screams Armo, staggering into the chamber with burned hands and patches of frostbite across his bald head. "We can't hold them back!" He stumbles and falls, then scoots along the floor until he's over the seal of the Saadella. "Elder, pl—"

Fire rolls between two pillars and unfurls across his back. The plea becomes a scream as Sig stalks into the domed chamber, glaring at his old friend with flames in his eyes. Aleksi snarls and shoves his arm out—but the attack isn't made of ice. He sends pure heat at Sig, who has no cold to counter it. I start for the Fire Suurin, desperate to protect him, but Aleksi lunges forward and grabs me. I slam my elbow into his soft belly and he huffs, his chubby fingers twisting in my hair. Sig falls to his knees, his skin red, his eyes squeezed shut. Aleksi wrenches me against him as he sends another blast of fire toward Sig.

It hits a wall of icy air. Oskar strides into the temple, thunder in his gaze as he takes in my naked form, legs drawn up to my chest, fighting to free my hair from Aleksi's merciless grasp without touching his bare skin—I don't want him to have my power, or even know of it. Unfortunately, that means I can't free myself just yet.

Oskar hooks his hand under Sig's arm and lifts the fire wielder to his feet. Sig draws in deep breaths of the cool air in Oskar's wake as sweat streams down his bare torso. His cloak clings to his damp back and shoulders, and he leans against the Ice Suurin to stay upright.

Oskar's jaw is tight as he stares at Aleksi. "You're making your final mistake, Elder," he says quietly.

"The only mistakes are yours!" shouts Aleksi. "Listen to the destruction in the white plaza. So many young wielders! Our future!"

"*Your* future!" Oskar roars. His voice rings with disgust—he's killed over and over, and he looks sick with the knowledge. "How many futures have you stolen to ensure your own?"

Aleksi drags me backward. "I have lived to serve the magic of the Kupari," he snaps. "Everything I've done has been for that reason." As we near the entrance to the catacombs, I get desperate, and my fingernails claw at his skin. He lets out a surprised grunt and grabs my right hand, grinding the stumps of my lost fingers between his own and making me shriek with pain. He looks down at the cuff clamped over his thick wrist, and then down at me. The swell beneath his chin trembles as one of his hands disappears into his baggy sleeve. "Why didn't we think of this?" His eyes are shining, and panic fills my hollow chest. "Why didn't we guess?"

Oskar and Sig both step forward at the same time, but the sharp prick of a blade at my neck stops them dead. "Come any closer, and her blood will paint these hallowed grounds."

I stare at Oskar. *Freeze his blood. You can do it.* But worry clouds his features. He's probably scared he won't be fast enough, that Aleksi will feel the ice magic and kill me. And for all I know, Aleksi is powerful enough to counteract it, especially since he's wearing the cuff.

"There are so many things you don't know," I tell the elder, hoping to distract him long enough for the Suurin to strike. "The elders have been half-blind all these years. And how many has it been, Tahvo?" As soon as I say that old, evil name, the elder edges the blade up under my throat. The stinging line of pain feels like heat and cold at the same time.

"I know exactly who told you that name," he says, his voice ragged. "And it explains so much. But it's you who are half-blind."

Oskar and Sig strike at the same time, their teeth gritted as they send dual blasts of magic at us. Aleksi's broad hand clamps itself over my neck, and I feel the pull of his magic as he tries to use me to retaliate. Every muscle in my body turns to stone—the horror of being used to hurt Oskar and Sig is more than I can bear. As fire and ice burst around me, I fold in on myself, becoming as small as I can, shielding that bottomless well inside me that wielders use to amplify their own magic. I won't give it to Aleksi. He'll have to kill me first.

As if he hears my thoughts, the blade of the knife lifts, and I glance up to see it arcing down toward me. I throw myself back to avoid the slice of it just as Aleksi staggers under the heat of Sig's fire. Scrambling out of the elder's reach, I make it halfway between the wielders when Oskar's fingers rake the air. Aleksi lets out a choked cough. He pounds at his chest and drops his knife.

Oskar runs toward me, Sig right behind him. My ice wielder reaches down to take my hand, but then he's lifted off his feet and hurled against the stone wall opposite the Saadella's wing. The force of it is so intense that I feel the impact shudder through the floor. I scream and launch myself toward Oskar, but Aleksi's hand catches my ankle, and I tumble forward, losing my air as I hit the marble. Oskar falls at the same time, sliding to the side, his eyes closed and his arms limp, his big body shivering and shaking. My eyes meet Sig's. That strike didn't come from Aleksi.

"Help me, sire!" Aleksi calls out as a dark-robed figure moves in my periphery. "Elli—she's an—"

"There's no time!" says a familiar voice. "Hold them back!"

Sig wheels around as Elder Kauko jogs out of the wing, a struggling little girl in his arms. Her coppery hair is in tangled ringlets around her face, and her round cheeks are streaked with tears.

*The Saadella. Lahja.* My entire being vibrates with her need and terror.

"That's him!" comes Sig's broken shout as fire shoots from Aleksi's hands, arcing through the air toward the Fire Suurin. I jump between the flames and Sig, letting them caress my bare back.

Sig staggers under the heat that manages to reach him, pointing frantically at Kauko. "That's him, Elli! He's the one!" he yells as the elder disappears into the catacombs with the Saadella. But then Sig's gaze streaks from that dark passage, his eyes glowing. His voice becomes a guttural growl. "Don't you dare."

Aleksi screams, high and tortured. The knife he'd been about to plunge into my back falls from his blistering fingers. His skin sizzles and weeps as his robes catch fire, as the copper beneath his feet melts and bubbles. He crumples, and even then, Sig doesn't let up. He seems determined to reduce Aleksi to ash.

I run for Oskar, laying my palms across his frigid cheek and feeling an avalanche inside my hollow chest. I pull the magic with all my might, wrenching it from his veins and bones and mind, and Oskar moans. But no sooner have his eyelids started to flutter than Sig is yanking me away. "We have to go after him," he says, his voice flat with fury. "Oskar will live, and I need your help."

To kill Kauko. Who has the Saadella. And who downed the Ice Suurin with one skillful strike. All these years, Kauko's been the physician to the Valtias. He bled Sofia, and now I know why. "You're right—he's the one," I murmur. "He's been the one all along." All that friendly patience, all that mercy, hiding so much evil.

Aleksi called him "sire," as if he's the father of all of them.

I force myself to turn away from Oskar and let Sig pull

me to my feet. He rips his cloak from his shoulders and wraps it around me. "I can't do this without you," he says, his eyes glowing yet still full of pleading. "He's getting away."

The damp cloak ripples around my body as I turn toward the catacombs, where Kauko has descended into the earth, taking the future of our magic with him. "Let's go."

# CHAPTER 25

"A few of the priests and apprentices are still fighting," Sig says as he pulls me past Aleksi's burned body, his palm sweaty in mine. "A whole group of them escaped into the town as well, more interested in fleeing than fighting. Seeing them run sapped the will of many of the remaining fighters. And the townspeople are on our side. It's a mess, but we're winning."

"Is it still winning, with so many wielders dead?" I whisper.

Sig clenches his jaw and keeps moving.

I dig in my heels as copper glints from Aleksi's ruined form. "Wait." I squat by the elder's corpse and pull the cuff from his red-and-black wrist, wrinkling my nose at the smell of roasted flesh. The cuff of Astia glints as I cradle it in my hands. The magic bleeds from it, dripping from my fingers in invisible drops. "I think we're going to need this."

I clamp the cuff over Sig's pale, lean forearm. His eyes flash with flames. "Oh," he breathes, his chest heaving, his fingers flexing. The wave of heat rolls from him, warping the air. He looks down at our joined hands, and then at the cuff. "I feel like I can do anything."

"You can't, though." Oskar walks unsteadily toward us, his left arm folded against his chest, his teeth chattering. "If that elder sends fire at you, Elli won't be able to keep all of it off you. He's too powerful."

"But you're hurt," I say.

"Just my arm. I think it's broken."

"Are you strong enough?"

"I can keep the heat off Sig." His eyes meet Sig's. "You'll have to do the rest."

Including protecting Oskar from cold and ice. Sig gives him a curt nod. Together, we reach the stone steps that lead into darkness. Sig creates a ball of fire to float above our heads and light our path. He goes first, then me, then Oskar, whose steps are not nearly as steady as I want them to be. "Oskar—"

"I'm fine," he whispers. "Stop worrying."

Raimo's words slide through my head. *You'll regret this love.* I grasp the edges of my borrowed cloak and stare at Sig's back.

Sig tenses as we reach the base of the steps, his head swiveling back and forth as the maze stretches before us. His ball of fire disappears, plunging us into darkness. And then he takes my hand. "To the left," he murmurs—at the same time Oskar says the same thing.

They feel the magic. Which means Kauko will feel us coming. Sig's palm is hot on mine as he pulls me forward, but I stretch my deformed right hand back, my fingertips skimming the fur of Oskar's cloak.

His cool hand gently closes over mine. I tense, expecting the icy flow of his magic inside me, but nothing comes. He's holding it back, keeping it for when he needs it. But the feel of his palm against mine is a tiny island of safety. I close my eyes as goose bumps ride along my skin.

When I open them, I realize we're not in total darkness. There's a guttering light at the end of this long, dripping tunnel. And I know exactly where it leads.

"He might be luring us," warns Oskar.

"Or trying to escape," I say. "This is the path that leads to the temple dock. There's a boat."

"He has no idea how powerful we are." Sig's grip on my hand is so tight that it hurts.

A tiny, high-pitched sob echoes down the tunnel, followed by a metallic clatter. "Lahja," I whisper, as if she could hear my voice, as if I could reach her. "We have to get her out safe."

"We will," murmurs Oskar, squeezing my fingers.

Sig tugs us down the tunnel, his hatred throwing off heat so extreme that the air is filling with vapor. "Elder," he calls out in a jittery, excited voice. "We'd like a word."

He tows me around the corner, then pulls up short, cursing. The chamber is lit with several torches. Elder Eljas lies on the table that occupies one side of the chamber, his flat-nosed face turned toward us. It's blistered and blackened from the fire yesterday. His wrists are red and swollen and crusted from his efforts to free himself from the shackles that hold him prisoner. His eyes harbor his silent scream, but already they're going dim. His body is trembling and pale, and it's clear he doesn't have enough strength to free himself with magic. One of his sleeves is pushed up to his shoulder. Blood flows steadily from several deep gashes along the inside of his forearm, which is positioned over a hole cut in the table's surface. The thick splatter of droplets echoes as it collects in a copper pitcher sitting beneath the hole.

Next to the stool is an overturned cup, a trickle of blood on its rim. Elder Kauko has probably just gorged himself, stealing Eljas's magic to grow his own power. And at the back of the chamber is the entrance to the wide stone corridor that leads to the dock. A ball of fire floating within the passage reveals the silhouette of the elder, dragging a little girl toward the rusted metal door at the end of the tunnel. On the other side lies the pier—and the boat.

"Stop!" shouts Sig, but Kauko spins, wickedly fast, and sends a wall of ice at us. I feel Sig's magic reverberate through me as he sends an inferno out to meet it. The tunnel fills with steam that becomes ice crystals that fall to the stones at our feet.

Kauko grabs Lahja by the hair and pulls her in front of

Sarah Fine

him as she shrieks. "Strike at me again and she'll die."

I squeeze Sig's hand and he stops. We're about twenty feet from the elder. The docks are a few dozen yards behind him. "Let her go, Elder Kauko. I know there's a spark of kindness and mercy in you." I can't believe he's the one. I wish it weren't true.

A sad, sympathetic smile curves his thick lips. "I was always fond of you, Elli. You understood how badly we needed the magic."

"For the people, though. Not for the elders and priests."

"It's the same thing. We are the magic that defines the Kupari. They're nothing without us. But I'm sorry you were caught up in it. We all thought you were the Valtia. It was a terrible mistake."

I nod at the gasping, struggling child clamped to Kauko's fleshy middle. "You don't want to hurt her."

"And if you don't either, you'll let us go," he replies. "Haven't you all killed enough today?" He drags Lahja back a few steps. "I'm trying to protect her!" His gaze is dark and desperate on mine, begging me to understand.

Sig lurches forward, his entire body vibrating with readiness. "Do you remember me, Elder?"

Kauko's eyebrow arches. "Should I?"

"I've got a back full of lash marks that says yes," Sig hisses. Heat rolls off him like nothing I've ever felt, making the dripping water along the cavern walls boil and evaporate.

Lahja starts to cry as her skin turns pink.

"Stop it!" I cry, tugging at Sig's hand. He's crushing my fingers.

Oskar counteracts the heat, cooling the air. "Sig," he says softly, a warning. "The girl . . ."

Kauko's eyes narrow as he regards Sig. "You're the one who escaped. And I know what you are. I tasted it." His fingers curl over Lahja's chest and his eyes drift to me, full of accusation. "Elli, do you have any idea how dangerous and unbalanced he is? He'll kill us all. He was never meant to walk free. What have you done?"

There are so many things I could say to that, but none of them seem important as I stare at the tiny figure huddled against the elder's round belly. Her red dress is damp at the hem, and her slippers are sodden. Her rosebud lips are trembling with terror. "I've come to take the Saadella," I say. "She belongs with me."

"She belongs with the *Valtia*," Kauko snarls, his lips peeling back to reveal the blood on his teeth.

"And you plan to use the girl to lure her in," Oskar says, his voice a blade.

Kauko looks Oskar up and down. "Ice wielder." He blinks as the temperature in the tunnel drops suddenly. There's a glimmer of surprise in his gaze, but I swear, I see hunger as well.

"Kauko," I bark, drawing his attention back to me. "We'll let you live if you release her."

Blazing heat courses up my arm, but Sig stays quiet.

Kauko backs up a few more steps. Lahja whimpers. "I

don't know how you convinced all these wielders to follow you, but you're an impostor," he says. "You only want her to make a false claim on the throne. You shouldn't even be involved in this!"

Sig takes another sudden step forward. It feels like my arm is caught in the jaws of a bear, tugging relentlessly at the power I harbor in my hollow chest. "She's far from an impostor, *Tahvo*," he says.

Kauko's eyes widen, but then he controls his surprise. "I haven't heard that name in a long time." His smile becomes a grimace of anger. "Raimo took something that belongs to the priesthood. I'd like it back."

Power pulses from Sig, and it smells of hatred and a deep, bitter need for vengeance. His pale body glows in the darkness of the tunnel, like he's lit from within. "Oh, I'll give it back," he says in that familiar, shaky voice.

"Sig," I say, trying to rip my hand from his as I feel his magic drawing from the well inside me.

"Sig," shouts Oskar as we both feel the heat. But as he reaches for Sig, the fire wielder twists and sends a blast of devastating flame right at Oskar, who's thrown against the tunnel wall, stunned and smoking.

Sig drags me out of Oskar's reach, and it's as if he's scraping his fingers along the inside of my ribs, scooping up the power and preparing to hurl it at the elder. Only a few minutes ago, I was able to prevent Aleksi from using me as his weapon, but Sig's hatred and determination are pure. His magic is sharp and cutting, hungry as a wolf—and has no balance to temper it. I pull back with all my might, but I can't stop him.

Kauko's mouth drops open as Sig stalks forward with me jerking at his hand, trying to wrench myself away. Lahja shrieks when she sees the fire in Sig's eyes. She falls to her knees, finally free, as Kauko grits his bloody teeth and raises his hands to defend himself.

It won't matter. Sig is a volcano. He's a raging fire. It's all he is.

And Lahja is helpless as he descends. Her heart pounds in my ears. Her fear crystallizes like a diamond in the center of my chest.

I will not play a part in her death.

I have a will. And I'm not Sig's weapon to wield.

I stop resisting his pull. With a desperate lunge, I round on him. My left hand remains clamped in his right, but I wrap the three fingers of my right hand over the cuff of Astia on his left arm. We become a circle of flesh and bone.

Right as the magic erupts.

Sig arches as his own fiery power loops through me—and back into him. My mind fills with roaring light. The world goes silent and golden, and the pain singes along every inch of me. The magic moves like lightning, circling through the Fire Suurin and back into me, over and over, heightening, winding tight, until finally it explodes. I'm thrown backward as Sig is torn from my grasp. My back slams into cold rock.

I'm blind. The only thing I can see is white.

"Lahja!" I shriek, clawing at the air as pebbles pelt my belly and face. Is she hurt? Did we kill her?

A muscular arm loops around my waist. I clutch at fur-covered shoulders and feel the vibrations of a broad chest pressed to mine—he's shouting. "Ever," comes his distant voice.

"Lahja!" I scream as I'm lifted from the ground. I can't tell which way is up, which way is out. All I know is that the world is collapsing. I blink frantically.

"Ever!" It's Oskar. I'm in his arms, and the sky is raining rock.

"No, we have to get her!" My vision is coming back, blurry and indistinct. His broad form wavers in front of me, like we're underwater. I kick and struggle. "Lahja!"

Oskar's face appears right in front of mine. His gray eyes are fierce. His lips move, exaggerating each movement. "I. Have. Her." His hand clutches mine in an unforgiving grasp. My ears fill with the sound of crumbling, cracking rocks.

He lets me go for the briefest moment—and then presses a squirming form against my body. My arms coil around her as she cries. Tears stream from my eyes as I lean my cheek against her curls, which are coated with gritty stone dust. "Oh, my darling," I hear myself say. "I have you. I have you."

Oskar grips my hand again. "I need you," he says from between clenched teeth. "Please, Elli, work with me. I can't do it without your help."

I hold Lahja in my arms and let Oskar haul me along a brutally cold path. He's pulling on me as hard as Sig did, but instead of resisting, I offer him all I have, letting it flow from me and into him. We're surrounded by blackness as his magic pours from him, pushing along in front of us. There's ice beneath my bare feet. "Oskar?"

"It's caving in. I'm using the ice to hold it up so we can get through."

Together we stagger toward a flickering light, Lahja holding tight, her arms around my neck, her legs clamped around my waist. Behind us, there's the dull roar of rocks falling, and I turn to look behind me, but Oskar yanks me forward. I nearly fall as we start to run.

We dive into the torch-lit chamber just as the tunnel to the docks caves in completely.

Oskar falls to his knees and braces his palm against the stones, his broken arm tucked to his body. Panting, he looks at the wall of crumbled stone behind him. Sweat beads his brow and his teeth are chattering. His eyes meet mine. "We should get up to the surface. I don't know how stable these catacombs are."

I stroke Lahja's hair, my body made of instinct. She's shivering, her face pressed against my neck. "Kauko let her go," I murmur.

Oskar shakes his head and slowly gets to his feet. "Elli—"

"I had to do it, Oskar." Though I'm not entirely sure what I did. "I couldn't let Sig hurt her. Vengeance was more important to him than her life."

Oskar's granite eyes are shadowed with an emotion I don't understand. "It happened so fast. The two of you became a blinding light, but then you exploded apart." He inclines his head toward Lahja. "She was thrown free, but Kauko—"

"Is he dead?"

Oskar stares at the caved-in tunnel. "I don't know. When Lahja landed, I grabbed her, and then I grabbed you." He turns to me and runs a gentle hand down Lahja's back. "The tunnel was collapsing, and it was all I could do to get the two of you out."

Dread burbles in my stomach. "I didn't mean to hurt Sig."

"You made a choice," Oskar says softly, putting his arm around me and guiding us out of the chamber. "And so did I." He lets me go and plucks a torch from a sconce, then holds it in front of him as he leads us up the tunnel.

I made a choice. And because of that choice, Sig is probably dead. It feels wrong. Not because I didn't make the right decision, but because I shouldn't have had to choose in the first place. If my will had been strong enough, couldn't I have stopped his magic, tugged it right out of his grasp? I swear, if the stars give me more days than this, I will learn how to control this gift better.

But right now I have something else to attend to. I press my face into Lahja's hair, which smells of warm honey and cold rock. She whimpers and hugs me tighter. "You're safe," I whisper to her. "And I'm going to take care of you."

We reach the steps leading up to the domed chamber. Oskar walks in front of us. I sense his icy power pulsing from him. We don't know what's waiting for us at the top.

I touch his back. "Thank you," I whisper. In case I don't have another chance to say it.

He looks over his shoulder at me. "I'm yours to wield."

We reach the top of the stairs. Oskar stands in front of me. "Raimo," he says.

"Do you have her?" comes the creaky reply.

Oskar steps aside and guides me into the chamber with the Saadella still clutched against my body.

We're surrounded. The chamber is packed with people. Raimo, leaning on his walking stick, his pale eyes glittering. Usko, half his coppery beard singed away. Veikko, his fingers gray with frostbite. Tuuli, her brown hair loose around her face, still shivering but otherwise unhurt. Aira, her neck and hands burned and blistered. No stout, black-bearded Ismael. No beaky-nosed Mikko. But there are at least twenty constables, clubs at their belts. Countless citizens, still bearing scythes and hammers and tongs, their faces smudged with ash. A few dozen acolytes, their robes torn, some of them bleeding, some of them burned, some of them shuddering with chills. And the councilmen, all staring at me—my nakedness covered only by Sig's cloak and the child huddled against my chest.

Topias, the head councilman, removes his embroidered cap and steps forward, his head bowed. "My Valtia," he says quietly. He kneels in front of me. "We acknowledge you as our queen."

My heart thumps hard in my hollow chest as every person in the domed chamber falls to their knees and bows, their foreheads touching marble.

# CHAPTER 26

I walk into her chamber with my offering behind my back. I'm running late because I've spent half the day in meetings with Topias and the other councilmen. Lahja's already dressed in the new scarlet-and-copper gown made just for her, those bouncing ringlets tamed into coiled braids at the back of her head. She's lying on her belly on a soft rug in front of the fire, her stockinged feet kicking in the air as she stares down at a picture book. Her handmaiden, who also happens to be her older sister, Janeka, a girl of about twelve with a quiet demeanor and long black hair, sits nearby, knitting her a new cap. I chose her myself. I wanted Lahja to have a familiar face within these walls. I want her to know she is safe.

Janeka's eyes go round when she sees me standing at the

edge of the rug, and she makes a startled squeak. Lahja's head jerks up, and she spins around, looking frightened.

"It's just me," I say quietly, dropping to my knees. "I brought you something." I bring out my gift, a doll given to me by Sofia, one I found tucked away in my belongings, the ones Mim packed before I escaped and she was taken into the catacombs. I hold it out to Lahja. She's such an exquisite creature, wide, smooth brow, big blue eyes, rosebud lips. But her serious, wary expression tells me of everything she's been through. There was no Valtia to enfold her when she was brought to the temple. A few of the maids told me she hasn't said a word since she arrived, but Janeka has told me she used to be a chatterbox.

"Do you like it, darling?" I ask as the little girl inches forward, her eyes on the doll, which is painted like I will be soon. My coronation is today, and all my fears sit heavy inside me, enough to bring me to the ground. I stroke my fingers over Lahja's little hand as she touches the doll's face, but I keep my right hand tucked beneath the porcelain figure, afraid my missing fingers will scare her. She rubs her thumb over the soft, silky fabric of the doll's dress, and a tiny, fragile smile pulls at her lips. She nods, and my chest squeezes tight.

"Good," I whisper. "Later, we'll play with her. It's almost time for me to get ready. I just wanted to see you before I got dressed."

Before I look like Mim did, in the last minutes of her life. Lahja's eyes meet mine. She leans forward and kisses my cheek. Slowly she puts her arms around my neck, and I enfold her, silently promising to do right by her. She's not mine. I'm not hers. The true Valtia should be here, not me. But until she is, I'm going to stand between Lahja and any danger that comes.

I kiss her good-bye and stride into the hall. I won't let them carry me in a sedan chair, seeing as I'm perfectly capable of walking. I enter the domed chamber. It's been cleaned and repaired in the last two weeks. A few of our acolytes are placing candles around the edges of the chamber in preparation for the procession. One of them is Kaisa, the girl with blue eyes and a mole on her cheek. Her head is covered in short blond fuzz. It seems ridiculous for the acolytes to be bald unless they really want to be, and I told them so. She waves at me as I make my way toward the Valtia's wing, and I wave back.

If she knows I'm not the true Valtia, she's not saying. No one is. Their need to believe is so strong and desperate that it silences all doubt.

*Never doubt,* whispers Sofia. I will never stop missing her.

My stomach tightens as I enter the ceremonial dressing chamber. It's just me today—I won't let Lahja be painted up for this occasion. She's so young, and I'm afraid she'll associate it with what she went through, watching Mim burn before her eyes. Today she'll ride with me, on my paarit, and she'll be comfortable. I'll make sure of it. We need her smile today.

I glance out the window at the Motherlake. Her winter

armor is cracking, but it hasn't yet thawed. I never thought I'd fear the spring, but now the thought of it fills me with dread.

Raimo hobbles in from the balcony, wearing a new black robe belted with hemp rope. He's taken charge of the fifty or so acolytes and apprentices who lived through the battle and didn't decide to flee the city, as all the surviving priests did. We believe at least a dozen escaped with their apprentices, and there's been no sign of them. One more worry to add to my list—which makes me all the more grateful for the frail old man in front of me . . . and afraid that his early emergence from his self-imposed hibernation will take a lasting toll. His walking stick clacks against the stone floor, and his stringy beard swishes back and forth as he comes forward.

"The council granted me access to the archives," I tell him.

"And?"

"The news isn't good. There were three girls born during the alignment, including me. And the other two are dead. Their deaths were recorded in the registers." One of the names gave me such a pang—it was Ansa, Maarika's beloved niece, who died when her family's homestead was attacked by the Soturi.

Raimo sighs. "And that means our Valtia's birth was probably not recorded. Either her family was living outside the walls or they were homeless beggars, too poor to pay the birth tax."

"What do we do now?"

His eyebrows twitch. "We keep looking. She can't hide forever."

"And do you have news?" I ask. "I'd especially appreciate the hopeful, non-dire kind."

He shakes his head. "I checked with the relay riders. The constables at the border have seen no sign of the Soturi yet. I'm wondering if the barbarians are waiting for the Motherlake to thaw. They could attack simultaneously by land and water if so."

I let out a shaky breath. It's only a matter of time until the Soturi come for us, and I'm determined to stop them—with the help of my people. "All right."

He clears his throat. "They finished clearing out the tunnel connecting the dock to the catacombs this morning."

A sharp pang stabs through me. "And?"

The knobby lump in his throat bobs as he swallows. "Sig and Kauko were nowhere to be found."

I close my eyes. "The boat?"

"Gone."

"Sig," I whisper. I hurt him. Burned him. And then left him at the mercy of the man who'd whipped him and drunk his blood. "Do you think he survived?"

Raimo gives me a pained look, his face becoming a maze of wrinkles. "Kauko, as he's called now, has always been a talented healer."

I lay my hand over my stomach, feeling sick. I made a choice, and I didn't choose the Fire Suurin. And now . . . "What will he do to Sig?"

"It's hard to say, Elli. But it won't be good."

"We have to find him."

He nods. "Oskar said the same."

Our eyes meet. "You talked to him?" My heart kicks against my breast.

Raimo smiles, but it's tinged with unease. "He's been quite successful. He knows all the camps that harbor wielders throughout the peninsula. It will take some time to earn their trust, but he's working on it."

"Who's with him?" Who protects his back? Who kindles the fire when he shivers at night?

"Usko, Veikko, Aira, Tuuli, and a few others from the caverns. You shouldn't worry about him, Elli." Raimo's tone is full of bleak warning.

I turn away from him. I don't want him to see my face. It would feel too much like opening my chest and letting him look at my heart. My hand slips into my pocket and clutches the wooden dove I always carry with me—a new one that he made just after Raimo healed his broken arm . . . and right before he left for the outlands.

Raimo lets out an exasperated sigh. "You're wasting your energy. Oskar is big and strong and well able to protect himself, even without magic. He's known in the outlands—and respected by wielders and nonwielders alike. Truly, you couldn't have a better recruiter for the magical branch of this army you're raising."

"How many do we have so far?"

"Oskar didn't say. But he seems determined to dredge

up anyone who can do so much as light a candle or freeze a puddle, so long as they do it with magic and are willing to train and work together."

"It's not enough, Raimo."

He grips his walking stick a little tighter. "We won't be relying on wielders alone. You're doing good work, Elli." He cackles. "I daresay those councilmen were shocked when you walked into that first meeting."

I smile in spite of myself. Their wide eyes and slack jaws were comical. But their fear of my power made them listen. The Kupari have grown dependent on magic, and Sig was right—they exchanged freedom and responsibility for security. The first thing I told them was that we would have no magical warmth this winter, but the temple food stores would be distributed to the people. I explained that we needed to focus our attention on the Soturi and face them as a people. Not everyone is pleased. I'm sure I have enemies. I've more or less told them that the temple will provide—but now it's time for *everyone* to stand up. Now we need every arm and every mind. We have magic, but it's not all we are. It can't be, because the copper that created us has been pulled from the earth, drained like the acolytes' blood. Once it's gone, our power might leave us too.

Many have stepped forward to offer themselves. "We have five hundred men in our nonmagical forces so far, and the smiths believe they can forge weapons for up to a thousand before the thaw. We have another three hundred women and men who have volunteered as archers. A few of the hunters are working as bowyers, and Topias thinks we'll have enough for every recruit. But—"

"Will our soldiers even know what to do with them?" Raimo asks, completing my thought. In comparison with the Soturi horde, our forces are paltry and ill-prepared. Yes, Sofia decimated the Soturi navy, but as one of the cave dwellers pointed out, that was only part of their might. We're so vulnerable, but we have one thing they don't. When the time comes, I'll face the enemy at the front with our army, alongside Oskar and his wielders.

I'll be his shield. He'll be my sword.

But we needed Sig, the Fire Suurin. We needed the cuff of Astia. We need a Valtia. We need a well-trained army. The odds rise high, looming over me like a mighty wave about to break.

I lift my head and straighten my shoulders. "Thank you, Raimo."

His gnarled fingers close over my upper arm. "I'll be on the platform at the coronation. It's going to be fine. No one will know. And you won't be alone."

His shuffling footsteps signal his exit. "Then why do I feel that way?" I whisper. I walk over to the copper mirror and sink into the chair. I stare at my reflection, then close my eyes. *You were born for this*, Mim whispers as a lump forms in my throat. I can almost feel her soft hands on my shoulders.

"I'm sorry, Mim," I whisper. "I'll never forgive myself for leaving you behind."

When I open my eyes, I swear I see her shadow in the mirror, brown curls, soft smile. *I'm proud to serve you. Elli, you will always be my queen.*

"You're in my heart," I say in a choked voice. "And you'll always be safe there."

"What's that?" Helka asks as she bustles into the room, her grayish-blond hair braided and coiled at the base of her neck.

"Nothing." I smooth my hands over my face and blink away unshed tears. "I'm ready."

She begins to brush and braid my hair, and I sit up straight and still. I've come to believe that the ceremonial makeup was just another way for the elders to silence the Valtia, to imprison her in a mask of beauty, but the changes I plan must come little by little. Today I will wear it, because the Kupari are just learning how to stand on their feet and test their own power, and they need a symbol to give them confidence until they have enough of their own.

For as long as they need me, that's what I'll be.

The coronation was a success. The people cheered. The constables were able to recruit several dozen young men and women for our new army. The sight of me in full regalia inspired their patriotism, and I'm glad—we all have a part to play in our own salvation. Lahja smiled and waved, lifting spirits high. When Raimo made the torches flare and twist, she pressed her head against my chest but didn't scream.

My limbs are leaden as I step from the tub and let Helka

dry me off. She's done this dance so many times, which is why I asked her to return to the temple as my handmaiden. She brushes my hair and plaits it loosely. I can tell by the solid slowness of her movements that she's thinking of Sofia, all the days they shared together—so many but not nearly enough. Her dimpled chin trembles as she lowers my gown over my head, and I sigh as it slips over my body and falls to my ankles, soft and comforting. "Is Lahja awake? I promised to play with her."

Helka lets out a sniffly chuckle. "When I went down to make sure her dress was properly packed away, Janeka told me she was already sleeping. Today tired her out."

I swallow back my disappointment. The warm weight of her body soothes me, gives me purpose . . . and beats back the loneliness, for a few moments at least. "I see."

She strokes my arm. "My Valtia—Sofia—she loved you like you love that little girl. You were Lahja's age when you came here. Sofia hated not seeing you. But she made sure we gave her reports of your activities every single day."

My face crumples with the grief of lost years. The elders kept us apart. Another part of their scheme to break the Valtia's will, to bend her to their desires, all under the guise of keeping her strong and pure in her magic. And because she had dedicated her life to being all the Kupari needed, she complied. But it hurt both of us, and I won't let that happen with Lahja. "Things are different now. I'll see her tomorrow."

Helka smiles. "I'm glad, my Valtia," she says hoarsely.

She smooths back a tendril of blond-gray hair from her wrinkled forehead. "Do you need anything else?"

I shake my head. "Thank you," I murmur. "Have a good night."

The emptiness in my chest yawns wide and numb as I pull open the doors to my balcony and step into the night air. We have a month of winter left at the most. The icy wind swirls about me, sending shivers from the top of my head to the soles of my bare feet. The moon hangs high in the darkness, shining down on the fissured white face of the Motherlake. The stars twinkle, mysterious and silent, carving out our future in the ebony expanse.

My fingers curl over the marble railing, and I close my eyes, letting the icy breeze skim over my face, pretending it's Oskar's magic instead. It slips along my neck and under the edge of my gown, giving me goose bumps. "I miss you," I breathe.

I'm queen now. I can't be loved by one. And especially not the Ice Suurin. Raimo's warning is never that far from my thoughts. But neither is Oskar himself.

"I miss you, too," the cool wind whispers.

I whirl, my heart lurching into my throat. Oskar stands at the far side of the balcony. He steps from the shadows, his thick cloak hanging from his shoulders, his footfalls silent despite his size. His hair is loose around his shoulders, and he hasn't shaved in at least a week. He smells like earth and horse and smoke, the knees of his trousers are smudged with grime, and his boots are crusted with mud.

He's never looked better.

"I thought you were in the outlands."

He runs his hand over a smear of dirt on his cloak. I don't miss his shiver as the wind tosses our hair. "I was. And tomorrow we're riding to the western shore where it meets the Loputon. There have been reports of fires in the sky."

I frown. "More wielders?" Someone powerful enough to send fire above the high hills on the coast. "Do you think it could be her?" Oskar's not just looking for recruits—he's looking for our Valtia. We might be taking steps to save ourselves, but we need her more than ever.

He shrugs. "No way of knowing until we get there. We can always hope."

"Be careful," I blurt out. "It could be the escaped priests. Or—Kauko probably has Sig, and—"

"Raimo told me." His eyes glint with the ice inside. "I have no intention of letting the blood drinker have another Suurin. But I won't abandon Sig either. If he's there, I'm going to get him back." He looks so fierce that it's easy to believe.

I reach up and run the backs of my fingers along his rough, chilled cheek. "Why did you come?"

He arches his eyebrow. "Do you really need to ask?"

I grin. "How did you get in here?"

"During your coronation. It wasn't difficult. We need to talk to Raimo about guards for your wing and Lahja's." His eyes linger on mine. He's worried but trying not to say it.

My mouth twitches as I fight a smile. "So you've been

shivering out here on my balcony the whole time my hand-maiden undressed and bathed me?"

He clears his throat. "Well. As eager as I was to see you, I thought it best not to poke my head in while you were . . ."

"It's nothing you haven't seen before." Along with nearly everyone in the temple. What I wouldn't give for a fireproof gown.

He rubs his hand over his scruffy face. "Would you forgive me if I told you the memory of it kept me warm while I waited?"

There it is, that tug low in my belly. It only gets worse as his gaze slides from my bare feet up to my face, not missing so much as an inch in between. "I would."

He reaches for my right hand, the scarred one that is now tingling painfully from the cold, and draws me toward him, kissing each knuckle. "And I wasn't just spending my time lost in thoughts of you." The corner of his mouth quirks up. "I was practicing."

He turns my palm upward. As we stare at it, crystals of ice burst from nothing and cluster in the air. They dance and swirl as they spiral downward, collecting on my hand and entwining until they form an eight-pointed star. One of the points is rounded and another juts out long and sharp, but neither flaw decreases my awe of it—and him.

"My control is getting better," he says quietly, picking up the star and examining it. He holds it close and blows frosty air from between his lips, and the star disintegrates into a glitter of ice dust. "Sometimes small magic is the most difficult."

I lay my palm on his cheek. "Does it feel all right?"

He bows his head. "I'm ashamed that I avoided it for so long."

But he had every reason to be scared, and I understand it completely. "You should be proud of what you're doing now." I smile up at him. "I have something to show you, too."

His eyebrow arches. "By all means."

I focus on our connection, my skin against his, and imagine reaching through it, plunging my hand into the endless sea of ice inside him. Shivering, I stretch out my other arm, palm up. My eyes squeeze shut and sweat beads at my temple, but when I hear Oskar gasp, I know I've done it. I open my eyes to see the lump of melting snow on my palm, and my jittery laugh fogs the night. "Raimo has been letting me practice on him."

Oskar rubs his chest. "I could feel you . . . inside."

"Did it hurt?"

He shakes his head. "Not at all. I told you I was yours to wield."

And that's probably why I was able to do it. Raimo says it will take more work to pull magic from a wielder who's resisting me, but even this has nearly exhausted me. I lean into Oskar, and my thumb strokes along the dark scruff on his jaw. "How are Maarika and Freya?"

He smiles. "They're well, but Freya still hasn't forgiven

me for not letting her join the army. I told her I was just following your orders. You *are* the queen, after all." His amusement slips away as he gazes down at me. "You looked lovely in the square, so regal." His fingertips slide down my cheek, and his icy magic tingles along my skin, swirling inside my chest. "But you look a thousand times more beautiful now."

"Because I'm just Elli," I murmur.

He slides his arm around my back. "And you understand that is more than enough."

"I do." About this, there's no doubt, but somehow it only makes this time more fragile, a treasure I'm not supposed to have.

His lips are cool and mine are hot. I gasp as he cups the back of my head and pulls me in. It's the delicious rub of ice and fire, hard and soft. His scruff scrapes my face, and I lunge onto my tiptoes. I want to look in the mirror tomorrow and see my own swollen lips, the raw pinkness of my cheeks and chin. I want to know this was real, more than the memory of his hard-muscled body against mine, more than the recollection of his handsome face, more than the echo of his voice in my head.

His magic fills my hollow chest, roaring and fierce, pure, icy power. But his hands are almost warm as they caress my flushed skin. His silky hair tickles my cheeks and brow as he draws back, kissing the corner of my mouth. "Stars, if we don't stop, I won't be able to leave," he says between breaths. His forehead touches mine, and we close our eyes, holding on with all our strength.

"It doesn't matter if we stop," I say, my throat tight. "I already can't let you go."

He kisses me again, this time slow and deep, his fingers sliding under the neck of my gown to stroke my bare shoulder. This is so unfair. Every single thing about it feels right and perfect and good. I want it to last forever.

But we're fated by stars, our lives mapped and foretold. I can't forget that, and I know Oskar hasn't either when he pulls away once again to kiss my forehead, his lips against my brow as he says, "I know it would be a terrible scandal if I were found here with you, but what I wouldn't give to sleep by your side again."

A tear slides from the corner of my eye, and he swipes it away with his thumb. "I miss those nights so much it hurts."

His smile is sad. "Perhaps someday, when this is over."

My stomach feels as hollow as my chest. "Perhaps someday." Right now it feels better to pretend.

I turn toward the Motherlake, and Oskar wraps his arms around me, drawing me into the shelter of his cloak. I lean my head back against his chest and look up at the moon, treasuring this collection of minutes, savoring each as if it's the last. Because it might be.

Our future rushes toward us like a storm on the Motherlake, and our enemies are powerful.

Kauko is out there, perhaps leading two dozen rogue priests and apprentices. He has the cuff of Astia. He also has the Fire Suurin—along with hundreds of years of blood-fueled cunning.

And the Soturi, hungry for our wealth, eager to domi-nate, they're out there too.

But so is *she*. I'm only a shadow compared to her. When we find her, I'll be her Astia. Together, we'll be perfect bal-ance and infinite power.

Together, we'll save the Kupari.

# ACKNOWLEDGMENTS

So much gratitude goes to the team at Simon & Schuster for taking my story and turning it into a beautiful book. To Ruta Rimas, my editor—thank you for your careful eye, endless enthusiasm, tireless advocacy, and the occasional clever and clarifying stick-figure drawing. Thanks also to Justin Chanda and Eunice Kim for support at every level, to Debra Sfetsios-Conover for designing yet another powerful cover for me. And thank you to Leo Hartas for creating the stunning map of Kupari.

As always, I am grateful to my agent, Kathleen Ortiz, for being a true partner in this business. Thanks also to the rest of the New Leaf team, including Danielle Barthelle, Joanna Volpe, Jaida Temperly, Jess Dallow, and Dave Caccavo, for amazing auxiliary support.

I owe many hugs to Virginia Boecker and Lydia Kang for

reading early versions of this manuscript and giving me the encouragement I needed to keep working on it.

Thanks to the CCBS team—it is a pleasure and a privilege to work with all of you. Special gratitude goes to Catherine Allen, who supplies coffee and wisdom and laughter, and to Paul and Liz, for being Paul and Liz.

My family has been a source of unending support, and without them, it would have been so much more difficult to face the various storms of the past year. Mom and Dad, Cathryn and Robin, Alma and Asher, you each inspire me in different ways. I love you.

And to my readers, thank you for making this work so worthwhile. It's a privilege to share my stories with you.